THE
SLASHED
CANVAS

THE SLASHED CANVAS

DEB SANJOY DUTTA

PARTRIDGE
A Penguin Random House Company

ISBN: Hardcover   978-1-4828-6890-6
               Softcover   978-1-4828-6891-3
               eBook   978-1-4828-6889-0

To order additional copies of this book, contact
Partridge India
000 800 10062 62
orders.india@partridgepublishing.com

www.partridgepublishing.com/india

DISCLAIMER

THIS NOVEL IS a work of fiction and any resemblance to any person living or dead is purely coincidental. The author does not intend to hurt the sentiments of any individual, community, sect or religion. The author also does not promote or subscribe to smoking, consumption of alcohol or any other intoxicants.

CONTENTS

Dedicated to the women of the world.
Also dedicated to a woman whose memories
inspired to pen this novel, and to my wife.

THE END

'I WALKED INTO THE bedroom, opened the cupboard and pulled out the drawer. I gripped the revolver I had stolen from Rohit. He got it from the Army when he took the premature retirement. I felt the hard metal on the skin of my palm. It was a Taurus 85 .38 caliber five-shot revolver. I clicked open the magazine, took out the five live cartridges from the steel box in which they were kept, loaded the magazine, and then clicked it back. I looked at Anjali. She was deep asleep as I walked out of the bedroom.

Sitting on the chair for the last time, I looked at Time, still laughing at me. I closed my eyes and pressed the barrel on my temple. I could see them all looking at me: Esha, Anjali, Aitreyi, Jayant, Roy, Tirtha, Mankar, Pandey. Everybody I ever knew, even Lipika and Anwesha. Their eyes expressed sympathy, pity. I could take no more. I pulled the trigger lightly. Nobody believed me anymore. My world seemed only to be mine.

And I pulled the trigger harder.'

The burst of the revolver tore through the silent darkness of the night. Surprised, few crows cawed out harshly. The head lay in a pool of blood amidst a dismantled wristwatch. Darkness, silence, still.

CHAPTER 1

1 976. THE INTERNAL emergency declared in 1975 by Mrs Indira Gandhi was still on. Everything seemed to be falling into the right place, at least, which is what I thought at seventeen. That is what I saw around. The jigsaw puzzle that was India was slowly taking shape. Government employees had to reach office five minutes before ten o'clock. Trains left at the scheduled time. Precisely for once, the Indian system was working. For once I thought we could build a great nation. That is what I felt, the adolescent me.

Those were the times; I plunged into a world of insecurity to accomplish my goal. I walked out on my parents, from the home that I belonged, to become an artist.

My aspirations did not match my parent's projections for my life. I ran away from the premier defence institute National Defence Academy. I aspired to be an artist and not a defence officer. It so often happens and I was not much perturbed by this miss matching; but I was disturbed by my parent's changed outlook towards me thereon. I was put under strict and controlled regimen. Father was not on talking terms while mother aggressively tried to debrief me. Nothing to do with art. Even small pencil sketches that I did on the sly were immediately destroyed on detection. The more she became stern, the more I experimented with art. After two weeks of torn sketches and no outings, I decided to stay awake in the night and create behind my closed doors. I thought that if

1

my creation was more of a constructive piece with physical existence rather than just paper and paint, which was so easy to destroy, it would have more chance of survival.

That night, I experimented with clothes hanger, pieces of bangle, a key chain, pieces of tin plates, broken glasses, and other brick-a-brack. As the crows started cawing at dawn, never tiring of the same routine, my four feet creation stood complete. 'Junk art', it was. In the morning, I hanged it from the ceiling above our dining table before my parents started their day. It survived till 9 a.m. when Mamoni, my mother, entered the dining room to lay the breakfast. She took no time to climb onto the table, reached out for it and got it down with one jerk. I stood watching her breaking it into pieces in rage. In the next five minutes the creation was no more. How strong was her urge to separate me from art? I felt frustrated again, like in the Academy, where the mechanical routine left my brain blank whenever I sat with a piece of paper to draw. And then I decided I had to leave the Academy. And now I decided that I had to leave once again, my home.

It intrigues me. Mamoni was a fine amateur pencil sketcher in her pre-marital days. I treasured a sketch of a temple by her, a beautiful landscape rendered by pencil. But a career in art? It just did not fit in my parent's mindset. After all, Nikhil Biswas, the last of the Bengal school of art, lived just opposite us. My mother was an ardent fan of his. Father appreciated his paintings too. But the poverty, the uncertainty of the future, the poor family life, subconsciously built in them the fear for the world of art.

I did not leave home immediately. Lipika persuaded me to stay on. I was in love with her, could not refuse, and also took a chance on her expectations that things will improve soon. Improve it did. I was given limited liberties, though not in art, but otherwise. Education came to a halt on leaving the Academy and the ensuing turmoil. I was allowed to go out for restricted period to enquire about colleges to pursue graduation. Though I felt it was irrelevant to be a graduate, I took the opportunity to meet Lipika. For the first two days we sat under a tree in the sprawling green lawns of Victoria Memorial.

Victoria Memorial, the last bastion of colonial splendor, still well maintained. Built with the Taj as inspiration, it felt short of the Taj's grandeur. But the beautifully sculpted marble and bronze statues all around, made up for the shortcomings. A life-size Queen Victoria on a raised platform with stairs in front of the monument, and that of other Viceroys of the colonial period spread across the beautifully landscaped garden, were masterpieces. No wonder it became the Eros' garden for the lovebirds of Calcutta, it was not yet Kolkata. In the roundabout just outside the main entrance to the garden, was the statue of Lord Curzon, now replaced with that of Sri Aurobindo. But do razing down past and replacing with the new, really change history? The Communist Government of West Bengal thought so. All the beautifully sculpted bronze statues of the colonial period were pulled down one by one and replaced with national heroes. I feel there is nothing wrong in Nationalism. But razing history has nothing to do with Nationalism. More so when we are talking about pieces of beautiful sculptures. Communism though dead in its original dictate, is a closed system; and human mind cannot flourish in a closed system. Forget experimenting.

One look at the art of erstwhile Communist countries says it all. They are simply State sponsored propaganda material.

Lipika appreciated my point in being an artist and I accepted her view about the necessity of graduating in a system that is India. She bunked her college and took me around colleges that she knew.

Calcutta, though my city of birth, I knew very little about. Spending major period in hostels outside Bengal, I was unfamiliar with the topography. Soon I enrolled at the Umesh Chandra College of Commerce for reasons beyond my own comprehension. But I cared little as I wanted to be an artist and everybody thought I must be a graduate at least. So be it, was the attitude. And once again I was beating the beaten track. Lipika walked me to it. Or actually she let me walk away from her, little realizing what the future had to unfold. Our love or less of it had nothing to do with our separation that was to come.

Enrolling in a college got me a pat from Bose Kaku, a friend of my father and a closer confidante of my mother. It also got a smile to still not conversing father's face and a gleam in my mother's eyes. I felt confused.

The pats, the smiles, and the gleams were not quite encouraging for me. Inside me throbbed the urge to draw, to paint, to create in terms of visual language, to be an artist.

College had commenced. Everything, though calm, was not well, particularly with my inner self. I started attending the classes, and Lipika also stopped bunking hers. We would meet once in three to four days after our classes for a short while — under the trees, in the lawns of the Victoria Memorial. But it was not as before; I could no more sit by her side or rest in her lap and talk just pleasant nothings. I was disturbed within and it showed. On each meeting she would bear patiently with my anguish, outrage, and breakdowns. She would console me and hope for a better tomorrow. What else could she do? She did her best.

It was the fourth day at the college. Eleven of us from the college had already bonded into a group. Chandan was also with us. He was an old classmate from my early schooling days in Calcutta. During those days in school, which I left in class seven to join the Military School, we surely were not friends. In fact, I and my group of friends found him to be snobbish. He used to come to the school by car—none of our fathers owned one—with a big Alsatian dog looking out from the window of the backseat. A luxury for us in those days, used to eat delicious tiffin, we had sandwiches at best. He never talked to us and we too never tried to break the ice. After the military school upbringing, now I feel it was all a middle class prejudice of the period. Middle class families then were not the people who were successful as today, and an undefined barrier was there in accepting someone from a well-to-do family as a friend. It was a common psyche to label well-to-do people as either Gods or Devils, either white or black. Middle class of the time attributed their unambitious, low productivity, and even a lower capacity of dreaming to fate. They were the sub-humans, they could not change their lives, and they were destined to suffer, at least, that is what they thought.

But for now, Chandan was a good friend of mine. The old school background worked for us in this new environment. The barriers of the past just disappeared. Human relationships are not evolved or limited by human beings and their characters. The relationships develop through circumstances and situations the two humans are living in.

We, the group of eleven, often bunked classes and spent the morning hours at College Square—a park in front of our college with a lake in the middle—often eve-teasing girls from other colleges. At eight thirty, we entered the Coffee House from the backdoor, which opened its gates to public at nine in the morning. Without fail we occupied a rather large marble-top round table in a corner and discussed sex to Shakespeare over cups of 'infusion' in the ratio of two to one. For the unordained, 'infusion' was black coffee, the cheapest item on the menu and the ratio meant that each cup was shared by two. Naturally, pocket money was a constraint. Among us there were a few adventurous types who would visit all girls' tables and have a jovial time. It was rather a matter of pride if one could get treated to an omelet or a cutlet through such visitations. Chandan was the most outgoing and adventurous among us.

In the orthodox context of middle class Indians of the time, the Coffee House provided a natural platform to youth of both sexes for exploring each other for the first time outside the confines of home. It was interesting to watch the myriad reactions at these cross-sexual face offs. Today I am amazed at some of my own reactions of yore. Comparatively, I was reserved and not really interested in interacting with girls. I was deeply in love with Lipika, and objectives of life along with her were very clear. At least it seemed so to me till then.

It was the fourth day at the college and we were at our table in Coffee House as usual. A group of girls had entered and occupied a table very close to ours, right behind my back.

It was only on adventurous Chandan's ideation of invading the table that I looked over my shoulder. She was there. Looking straight into me. For a fraction of a second I was dazed by the look. For the first time I felt being penetrated. I felt being naked. Turning back, I joined the conversation at our table.

A hot debate was on about the possibilities of the Naxalite movement of early seventies. We all had spent our early teens with graffiti like 'Decade of Seventies—The decade of Liberation', 'Long live Mao-tse-Tung', and not Mao-tze-Dong as it was spelt later. Well, Beijing also was Peking then. The university students dropped out in hordes and joined the movement—the Naxal movement. The call by Charu Mazumdar, Kanu Sanyal, was irresistible for the youth of Bengal. Everything collapsed in Bengal, particularly the education system. There were these brilliant students engaging themselves in face-to-face encounters with the police machinery armed with sophisticated weapons: on the streets, over the rooftops, in the city, in the suburbs. Bengal was on fire and the impression was still raw in us. Most of our age group in the late teens were sympathetic to communists or were treading the path somewhere in between socialism and communism. But surely we all were idealists.

Rahul ordered another round of 'infusion' as we debated on. Was Charu Mazumder slowly poisoned by the government machinery? How could a mole be planted in such a dedicated movement? Otherwise, how could police one fine afternoon trace Charu Mazumdar to a flat in Entally and arrest him. Rap-a-tap they picked up few more senior leaders from their hideouts simultaneously all across Bengal.

It was sort of strange. The debates, in which I vociferously took part in, had turned cold for me now. As if it was on a table far from me. A few mumbles came every now and then. I could recognize the voices but could not relate to the words. I was thinking of the girl at the table behind me. The first glance was so sudden I could not even visualize her features. I looked over my shoulder again. And there she was staring at me: the same penetrating look, high cheekbones, a bit elongated jaw line, a pug nose, wheatish complexion. Extremely beautiful, she was not. But surely she was mysterious. It must have been long since last I had expressed my view in the debate, for Chandan patted me to get back.

'What's wrong?'

'Er, nothing. I was just wandering. Wandering if mysteries could be sensed?'

'Bondhu, at times you really go vague. Anyway you all continue while I explore the possibility of arranging a treat for us from the next table. Haven't seen them before. Anybody for company?' Chandan moved towards the table behind me, and Anshu followed.

Graham Sutherland once said, 'To explain why I feel compelled to paint a given object is as impossible as explaining why I am attracted to certain people. One reason (for painting) is because of the way light transforms objects, there are shadows which create a mysterious atmosphere, changing before your very eyes.' Nothing much did change that moment but there was a mystery. Was it because of the stillness of the light that poured in through the Victorian windows of the Coffee House onto her?

Only five minutes had passed since Chandan had left our table. He came back with a scoop. All the girls were shifting to our table. We accommodated their chairs around us as the waiters and other guests kept watching. She sat next to me. Consciously I was not looking at her. And it seemed she knew it. She sat so close to me that it was really a farce that I pretended not to notice her. Anyway I tried my best to put on the act; got up and said that I was going to get a pack of cigarettes, taking a chance that when I return the sitting arrangement may change. I was feeling uneasy. Before I could move out she took control of the situation, pulled my shirt from the back. 'I'll pay for the cigarettes and Anshu will get them.' Somehow all my past techniques to firewall advances were failing. Or was it that I wanted them to fail? I accepted the happenings because I wanted to. I wanted to be closer to this mystery girl. I took my seat. We looked at each other and she smiled. I had no other option but to smile back, though quite hesitatingly.

Cutlets and more coffee followed. Discussion continued on lighter aspects of life. A lot of glances from her and I stole a few too. She talked a lot, more than other girls. By twelve thirty I knew she was Esha and a lot other things about her. Or maybe I knew what she exactly wanted me to know. I had to meet Lipika at the gate of St. Paul's Cathedral at one. Esha requested me to stay back. I refused.

I was late. It had never happened before – It was always me who waits for Lipika to arrive. The dry leaves of Mahogany rattled under my footfalls as I increased my pace on seeing Lipika. I could see her smile from afar. The innocence in her smile made me feel guilty and wanted to cry out loud, 'Lipika, I am getting interested in a girl named Esha.' But I could not. On coming near, I reached out and she did too. Locking our palms I felt relieved. No, nothing could happen to our relationship. I reaffirmed myself.

We walked down the pavement hand in hand, sharing our day's experience. She told the truth and I lied. When we reached the lawns of Victoria Memorial, I did not know what caused her anxiety.

'Are you listening to me?'

'Surely,' I replied.

'But you are not replying to my questions.'

How could I? I could have if only I knew what the questions were. It was all of Esha that blanketed my mind.

'I was lost.'

'But where?' she asked.

'Let's sit under this tree. It is quite shady even at this time of noon.'

We sat down and I held her palm tightly in mine. I did not want to lose her. I loved her but for reasons unknown I felt otherwise. I wanted to reach out and embrace her but was not possible. I lay in her lap and looked up to her.

'Feeling disturbed?' she asked.

I broke down into tears. 'I know it is tough the way you are living. But one day you will surely make it to the top.'

At that moment I did not know whether I was reaching for the top or not. But surely I yearned for a fulfillment that was Lipika. It is strange. If I really pined for Lipika, why was I developing an interest in Esha? Like at times one cannot explain or find logic to one's own behaviour, I too, was ignorant. I loved Lipika. Esha attracted me. I tried to reason out that it was only inquisitiveness.

Next day seemed to be similar when it started with the roll call at the college. Well, all days were apparently the same. Our group of eleven slowly walked out of the class after the roll call, and then proceeded to College Square, and

then to Coffee House. Esha was there, too. She walked down
to our table and acquired a seat next to me.

'You bunk classes?'

'We do it nearly every day, but what about you?' I asked.

'I didn't have the first two classes. So I came to meet you.'

I felt more comfortable sitting next to her than yesterday.
'Adda' continued. Both of us, knowingly or unknowingly,
were supporting each other's views. I do not know if out
of conviction or conscious about the bonding that was
developing. Or was it being developed?

Durga Puja, the most revered festival of the year for
Bengalis was coming close. Being an experience of a year-
time, we, college friends, were planning early. I had my
programme fixed. On Shaptami evening I would spend
time with Lipika going around the decorated pandals. We
decided to go out only on one day, as I was not very sure
about the amount of freedom that will be allowed to me
by my parents. I thought I could bargain a day's freedom
in exchange of staying home for the other five days of the
Puja.

'What are you all doing during the Pujas?' Esha asked.

'A ten-day trip with my parents to Puri and other spots
of Orissa,' replied Ranjan.

'I'm not going anywhere,' said Chandan, 'And am open
to any programme that may be chalked out.'

'Why not we meet one day and spend time together,'
Sonali suggested.

'How about Shaptami?' Esha asked.

I felt miserable. I wanted to be with her outside this
Coffee House atmosphere, but Shaptami was out of question.
It was blocked for Lipika.

But a consensus was arrived on for Shaptami. Finally it was Chandan, Ayan, Suneet, Esha, Sonali and I. We all agreed. We were to meet at Chouringhee Cabin, a small eating joint on the Chouringhee Road, at four in the evening. This joint and the one next to it, Anadi Cabin, were small but very famous for their Mughlai Parantha. Well, the dish was simple: thin bread rolled out, inlaid with egg batter and mutton mince, and deep-fried. Anadi Cabin claimed it was their invention but actually, nobody knew about its origin. Whenever it might be, it had nothing to do with the Mughal era as its name suggested. Just as a misnomer like the French toast in India, which the French could not have imagined in their wildest dreams.

My outing with Lipika was also slated for the same day. We had decided to meet at T-junction of Watgunge Road at five the very same evening. We were not to meet in between and I had even cut down on the Coffee House adda to gain that little freedom on the Shaptami with Lipika.

But now I had two programmes on the same day. It was not about wriggling out of one to join the other. It was Lipika or Esha. It was the uncertain world of Esha pitted against the foreseeable world of Lipika. I stopped thinking and waited for the day.

I won my parent's nod to go out on Shaptami. At three in the afternoon, I started dressing. It was autumn, the advent of winter. Earlier it used to be very pleasant, but for the past few years the weather was changing and it was quite hot out on the streets. The cotton ball rolling clouds that once used to spread over the sky during this time of the year are now a rare scene. The clear sky with the sun still at a high angle and no breeze, it could well be termed late summer. Humidity in the city being in the Tropical region and for its proximity to the sea added the woes of heavy sweating. I put on a cotton full-sleeved shirt and a pair of jeans. I had shaved, applied cologne, brushed my hair, looked at the mirror, and yes I was ready.

On reaching Chowringhee Cabin I found only Chandan present. Sonali came next. She was a close friend of Esha and was already dating Chandan. Suneet and Ayan followed next. But it was a long wait for five of us before Esha arrived dressed in a georgette sari, lipstick, and light makeup. I looked at my watch. Lipika was waiting at the Watgunge Road junction. For once I felt like excusing myself and leave. But I did not. Each of us had a Mughlai Parantha at the Cabin. We had no fixed programme as such. As always, Esha took the initiative and said, 'Let's go to the Victoria Memorial,' and all agreed.

We took a bus down joking and laughing our hearts out. I felt like any other college student and Esha seemed only a girl among a group of friends. We reached Victoria Memorial. Maybe otherwise, too, I would have been here with Lipika after visiting two or three pandals. We walked down the pebbled lanes, Chandan and Sonali paired out and moved ahead. Suneet and Ayan said they would get some peanuts from the vendor at the gate, leaving Esha and me together. It was evening and the sun had gone down the horizon. We kept following Chandan and Sonali, but at a distance.

We crossed the tree where Lipika and I often sat. Lipika looked up at me and said, 'Everything will be Ok' I rushed to her, got her onto her feet holding her hands. She was looking beautiful. She never used any makeup. Her innocence glowed on her face. I embraced her tightly and kissed her on her forehead. I will never let her go from my life. But I did.

It so happens and intriguingly so often. We act, react; take decisions at times really against our true longings. Esha and I walked on silently. I waited for her to speak.

'Have you ever fallen in love?' she questioned uprooting a dry blade of grass from the ground.

I was taken unaware. 'Aha! Yes.' I tried to manage my expression to look bold and believable. At the back of my mind I tried to work out a background story to my answer; a background story, without Lipika.

'With whom?' She seemed to be cool and casual. She did not even look at me as we walked side by side. All this made me more uneasy.

'With you,' I replied, and was astonished at the pace I got myself together and lied. It had taken me three long letters from Dehradun to express my love to Lipika. And here I reacted promptly. With Lipika it was through conviction; here, at random.

At five feet five inches she was taller than average Bengali girls. She turned to me with a raised glance.

'Do you really mean it?'

'Surely.' I fumbled being not so sure. I tried to make up and reached for her palm. I was not very sure if I could make it. But she made it easy for me. She opened out her palm and clasped onto mine. For a moment I felt I did not want to lose her. For a moment I felt I loved her. But I felt similar about Lipika as well.

'Do you know . . .' I thought I will speak out the truth.

'I do not want to know about your past,' she cut me short, 'because then you will want to know about my past.

And I am really not interested in the past. I live for the day and at times I do look forward to the future.'

There was something very uncommon about her. She was eloquent, decisive, and at times downright drastic. I even believed she lied at times and all this made her the mystery girl whom I wanted to unravel. Though I had no proof about her lying, I could feel it. I had a strong feeling that often she took cover under the pretence of being rich, flamboyant and extravagant. But then she did have a lot of money compared to us. She did bear a lot of our expenses spending on our group's snacks and cigarettes, and of course 'infusion'. The more I thought about her I would come round the same bend to find myself at the day one of our meeting. With all my efforts to demystify her, I only made her more mysterious.

'Chandan was telling that you wanted to be an artist. Is it so?'

'Yes, that's my ambition. And it was for this reason that I left National Defence Academy.'

'Then why are you studying commerce?'

'I really don't know.'

'So you do things for which you have no reason. Isn't that strange?'

'Could be. But are you sure that you always have reasons for whatever you do?'

'Surely, I always have reasons for my actions.'

'Ah, I had put it the wrong way. It is easy to justify one's actions. Actually, I wanted to ask that do you always act, as you want to. You never did anything which you did not want to or you were not interested in doing.' Her confidence suddenly gave way to doubt. She looked up at the sky. I too looked up. Through the narrow slit between the rows of trees, there was this slice of the sky. It was already dark; only a few stars bejewelled the sky to break the monotony.

'You are right. Many a times I did what I never wanted to do,' she said very slowly. It seemed she felt exhausted by some thoughts. Turned towards me and said, 'Why do we often have to act as we never want to?'

Her voice was mellow. The arrogance, the firmness was lost. I knew that for the first time I had infiltrated into her.

'Circumstances.' I philosophized.

'You are right. A human is not complete by oneself. Circumstance has so much power. It shapes the final being.'

'I wouldn't say I disagree, but would like to differ by a degree. We have the capability to overcome circumstances. We can ignore it. It is the self that matters,' I said contradicting my own statement earlier.

She looked at me sarcastically, 'Then why are you studying commerce and not fine arts?'

I had no answer. She was right, or was it that I did not have the right explanation. 'Could be that I leave commerce halfway as I did National Defence Academy.' I tried to support my conviction. 'It is a clash between the being and the circumstance around. The stronger one wins. And I feel human beings are stronger than circumstances created by human beings.'

'I'm sorry to say, you are still naive. You are still ignorant about what circumstances can be: circumstances are not always created by humans, and I know that they are all imposing. Give a thought to it.'

I really thought for a few seconds. I was studying commerce because circumstances led me to. But I was arguing otherwise. She proved to be a good conversationalist.

'You said you love me.' She changed tracks into the lawn. 'Yes and on your part?'

'No. I wouldn't use the word love.' She was again her firm self. 'I think that would be a very wrong interpretation. I would rather generalize it as liking. Yes, I surely love to share your company, stay close to you, and a lot such things. But to say I love you would be wrong. Because I do not know much about you and same is the case with you. I still do not know what your term of reference for love is. Is it only an attraction, a flash of emotion or just lust? How could you love me without knowing my total self? You have knowledge about my existence in space - the physical existence. You are totally ignorant about the fourth dimension - time. The physicality is not the human being. The totality is our physical existence in real time. Rather plainly, I would put it that human beings are a product of the physical self and circumstances.'

There was logic in what she said. Love was the most used word in such circumstances, but the wrong one. It was the sense of inquisitiveness that drew me towards her. And now with her palm in mine, shoulders brushing, walking close, I could also feel the element that was hidden under my conscious self - passion. Or was it, as she said, lust?

'You just cannot isolate human beings from their circumstantial existence and place them in a void, and yet term them as human beings. They just cease to exist.'

'Maybe you are right. But how do I explain my strong urge to stay with you, to caress you, to hug you, and maybe even kiss you? Not just for once, but again and again.'

She looked at me. We were in near total darkness as if in a timeless capsule. I reached out for her and hugged her close. I could feel her soft breasts crushing on my chest. Her thighs were tight against mine. She clasped my back looking straight into me. We slowly let our lips touch. We kissed. We kissed wildly. Kiss had never been as fiery. She worked wonders with her tongue. Penetrated me, excited me, and invited me into hers. I never knew that even a kiss could be so stimulating, passionate, and erotic. It was the first real kiss of my life.

'Ahem! Ahem!' Suneet and Ayan sounded their presence from the lane. We broke off. I looked back and waved at them; moved onto the pebbled lane and took long strides to keep our distance from them.

'It did explain your question. Didn't it?' Esha questioned.

'I did not get you.'

'It's sex, which explains your urges. I too was drawn towards you from day one because of it. I wouldn't hide. I had a crush on you and still have. But that does not make up love. Yes, an element of love is surely there but not in totality. And because we are from conservative backgrounds we immediately idolize such crushes as love and conclude it in future marriage.'

I agreed in silence. Yes there was a crush for her behind my conscious self. And the kiss had now opened the floodgates of passion. Again, there was this element of mystery. Her behaviour, her boldness, her maturity of thought put together with the lies, somehow did not fit the being that she projected to be. It didn't even fit that she was just another middle class Bengali girl trying to project being from the upper strata of the society. No it couldn't have been just that.

'Now, here we are, two human beings having crush for each other and we react. Isn't that beautiful?' I questioned.

'Of course, it is beautiful. I will cherish the moment all through my life. But it is the circumstance, the Time, which allowed us to react the way we did. It could have been otherwise too.'

'But the situations are created by us.'

'Time. It is the overpowering Time that creates situations. Human beings just react to situations.'

'Isn't our reaction at this time enough to love each other?'

'No. It is just good enough for the relationship that we have now. We are not our total selves at this point of time, now. I would rather like to have it that way.'

'But why?'

'For the fear of losing you.'

I brought her closer by her shoulder. I tried to imbibe in her the feeling I was not here to get lost. But I had instilled the same confidence in Lipika too, and I let her go.

On reaching home within the time permitted, I found out there was a phone call for me. Mamoni said it was a girl who enquired about my whereabouts, but hung up when she enquired about her. I asked the time. 'Around seven thirty.' Mamoni replied. I knew it was Lipika. Waiting all along. It had never happened before. I rarely was late and not turning up was unthinkable. I felt sad. For I knew I had walked out on her, never to meet again. For her, it would still be a few more days of expectations, presumptions, anxiety, and finally the void. A relationship developing over the childhood suddenly did not exist.

Esha's statement came to my mind. 'Time. It is the all-overpowering Time that creates situation. Human beings only react to it.'

Taking an overview of the end of my relationship with Lipika, I wandered if one should disbelieve human characters and start believing in the power of Time. I'm not sure. The search that started through the probe into the mystery that was Esha, had only led me to greater mysteries: the mysteries of life.

It was a Thursday. After seeing off Esha at the College Square bus stand, I took a bus to Esplanade. I realized I had to make a living to be able to live the way I wanted to. Oberoi Grand, the star among the five star hotels then. It stood with palatial grandeur. I walked into the reception. I had no idea about the world of employment.

'Whom can I talk to about employment?' I asked at the reception.

'Mr Tug, Personnel Manager,' the front desk assistant replied indifferently. 'Second office down the right corridor.'

I followed the instruction. There was this brass plaque with 'Mr J. N. Tug' inscribed on the heavy wooden door. I knocked on it.

'Come in.'

'Good afternoon, sir.'

'Yes, what can I do for you?' He was a short, dark complexioned man wearing a dark grey suit with a bifocal on his nose.

Before I took the seat, I spelt out the need.

'I need a job, sir.'

Those were the days of high unemployment. It was a government concern and in many competitive exams it was the subject on which essay was asked to be written. Mr Tug was caught off guard. Here was this young guy, should be attending college, barges in, and asks for a job. It was something that did not happen every other day.

As I took my seat, he pulled himself together and with the cool that senior executives cultivate, replied, 'But we have no vacancy.'

I knew it before. 'But sir, I need a job to continue my studies. Any type of job will do.' I told selective truth about my background and added a few sentimental twists with some lies. He thought for a while and I felt my story was working.

'But your qualification is only Higher Secondary pass. You can't get anything good, that is to your liking.' I heaved a sigh of relief. So surely there was something.

'We recently had advertised for Trainee Waiters. We have already shortlisted and called them for interview. They will be put through training for three months at a stipend of Rupees three hundred and fifty plus one free meal. On being regularized they will get a salary of six hundred and fifty rupees and other benefits as per company rules. But the timings are rigorous. It is from eight in the morning to seven in the evening with one-hour lunch break. With your morning college I doubt you can make it. Anyway, drop in next Wednesday. Let me see what I can do for you.'

'Thank you, sir.' I shook hands and left confidently to welcome my approaching freedom.

Next day, I and Esha broke away early from the Coffee House milieu. Under the shades of a Gulmohar tree with the fallen fiery Gulmohar petals as carpet, we sat face to face. I explained my situation at home and the developments the day before.

'I'm going to move out of the house.'

'Think again and again. You are not acquainted with the harsh realities of life. Will you really be able to pursue art, college, and the job? Again there is the question of a shelter. I think you are taking too big a risk at too early an age.'

'But I just can't live in that house. I can't gradually suffocate myself to death. It is true I would be living comfortably there, but without being myself I would be as good as dead.'

Esha looked up at the Memorial in front. In fact, now I know she was looking far beyond. I plucked a blade of grass, split it and chewed the end. It was sweet and had a mild fragrance.

'Ok.' she came out of the stupor, 'Don't worry, and take the risk. I have an uncle who stays in Bangkok and loves me a lot. He keeps sending a lot of gifts. I will ask him to send a few dollars as well from next time. Don't worry about the details, but whenever you are in need of money do let me know. Where do you think you will stay?'

'I will put up with a friend of mine. With Gule and his family. He runs a small lathe machine shop floor. Of course this will be till I get the job and then I will shift to some working men's hostel.'

As the days passed I grew more restless. Suddenly the sexual passion over Esha took a backseat and we would meet only to discuss the future course of action. I had no fixed date for moving out and my parents never got inkling. My restlessness, they believed, was more to do with me going loony. I even overheard them talking with neighbours about psychiatrist and psychotherapy.

It was a beautiful Monday afternoon; diffused sunlight poured onto the city through intermittent white clouds. Pleasant breeze wafted down the lanes. I packed my belongings in a suitcase. Walked up to Mamoni and said, 'I am leaving.'

She did not react. She was calm. 'Let your father come from office.'

'No. I am leaving now. You inform him when he comes.'

And it was all over. I left my home.

Coming down on the street, I felt free. I took a deep breath of fresh freedom, took the bus to Howrah and landed at Gule's home.

It was a three-room dingy house in somewhat a ghetto. The open space outside the house had asbestos corrugated sheet on bamboo poles to create a shade and was being used as a kitchen. Though we were friends for some time now, I had never visited his home. He was the only earning member among us friends of the Howrah circle. But on reaching his house for the first time, I realized the harsh realities behind him. They were four brothers and four sisters, only one of the brothers being elder to Gule. There was his retired father with no pension and mother. And Gule had his hands full. I was amazed. He was doing a terrific job for his age. He used to drink a lot at the evening 'addas' and at times when I tried to cut short a few drinks, he would plainly say, 'I need to sleep peacefully tonight to work tomorrow.'

I could not then relate heavy drinking with sound peaceful sleep. Now I did. His elder brother was a front rank action cadre of the Naxal movement. During the fourth month of emergency, he was picked up by the police and has been languishing in the Dum Dum Central Jail since then.

I had asked Gule, 'Aren't you trying to get him out?'

'There he gets free meal yaar, here it is already too short.' I was shocked at the plain talk. But now all these statements were falling into place.

I knocked at the tin door. All the children poured out. His mother emerged and started questioning me after my introduction.

'So you are a friend of Gule.'

Realizing it would be long before I will be allowed inside; I dropped the suitcase by my side. 'Yes.' I replied, 'And I would like to stay with you all for some days.'

'You are going to stay with us?' she was shocked.

'Yes. As I told you, only for a few days, till I get a job.'

'Have you been already selected?'

'Not exactly, but soon I will get one.'

'It is always like that. Jobs, so near yet so far. They just don't materialize these days. Surely your wait will be long. But don't you have a home?'

I found it difficult to summarize the whole fact. So, told that Gule knew all about it. One of the sisters clinging to mother's sari asked to confirm, 'Ma is he going to stay with us?'

'I don't know. Your Dada knows about it.' She was a bit jittery.

'But then, where will he sleep? And will meals be halved because of him?'

Another brother seemingly elder declared, 'I'm not parting even a little from my meal.'

I was dumbstruck, ashamed, wanted to run away. I could never stay here eating into their existence. Gule arrived, 'So, Sid you have arrived bag and baggage.'

'Yes as I had told you, I need a shelter for a few days.'

He patted my back and smiled, 'Why for a few days? I'm honoured to offer my bed to one of the great artists of the future. Stay as long as you want.'

Turning towards his siblings he scowled, 'What are you monkeys doing here? Bunk before I thrash you all.'

I stood dazed as I watched all of them rush into their dingy rooms just like a pack of rats. His mother also left.

'Try to be home as little as possible.' Gule told me, 'And when you must, just keep your eyes and ears shut. They are just a nasty lot. I can't do away with them, as they are my family. But I am really fed up.'

'You shall sleep with me. In my room it will be only you and me.'

'Where will they adjust in?' I questioned, being well aware that there were only two other rooms.

'Stop worrying about them. They have been packing themselves well in the other two rooms till date. Let's drop your baggage and head for the 'adda'. I will not go to the shop floor today. After all, it's a day to celebrate.'

I moved into the house, into Gule's room, and placed the suitcase in one corner. There was a dim bulb, a small old table fan, a bed with a soiled sheet and a stained pillow, a wooden table, and a small window. It was quite dark at this hour of the afternoon even with the bulb on.

There were so many times I could have walked out or should have walked out. But my determination that was there in me to be free did not allow me, even at the cost of being utterly selfish, I stayed on.

The whole group had not assembled. It was early. Bhai, Kishore all greeted me, as I was not a regular. Gule told them that from then on I would be a regular but no daily contribution was to be taken from me. This contribution was collected every evening to buy country liquor. I had also contributed in many earlier occasions when I visited them. There was no fixed amount. The amount was voluntary but the contribution a must. The consumption of the liquor was also open-ended. Anybody could consume what he wished till stock lasted. The system sounds crazy particularly in the context of consumption of liquor, but it worked. A real communist welfare commune, at the most odd of all places.

Shyamal came at seven in the evening. 'Hi, so you are finally on your own?'

'Not yet. Putting up with Gule.'

'Does that really make any difference? I mean, you are your own boss now. You can think as you desire, you can aim as you desire, and you can achieve that you desire.'

And I felt great.

After three glasses of sixty, that's what the country liquor was called as it had sixty per cent water and forty per cent alcohol, I felt my ambition was a step closer to realization. I would be a recognized artist soon. Idealist as I was, I was envisioning the future in an ideal circumstance, which never happens.

I got up in the morning with a bad hangover and a severe headache. I had downed quite a few glasses of sixty to prove the freedom to myself. Gule was already getting ready. It was six thirty in the morning. I jumped out of the bed, brushed, dressed, and got ready for breakfast. Gule squeezed a fifty rupee note into my palm. 'You will need it. Whenever you are 'phut' let me know.'

'But . . .'

'Put the note in your pocket fast.' He did not let me finish. 'They are terrible.'

I knew even if they were terrible they were rightly so. I had no right to carve out of their rights. But I needed the money.

Breakfast was served. Two chapattis each for Gule and me, along with a cup of tea each. I noticed the portion of chapati became smaller with age - the youngest one got half a chapati, and a cup of tea.

I took the double decker bus to my college. Sitting on the upper deck I looked out of the window. The Howrah Bridge was approaching and the Hooghly River quietly flowed. The city was waking up to another day's cruel realities. There were only a few people yet on the roads. The bus moved on. A beggar with a bandaged hand, red and black paint applied on it, moved with long strides down the footpath below. He seemed to be perfectly fit. He had to reach his spot before the crowd poured onto the street,—another day of sordid acting as a leper, on some footpath.

Esha came a little late to the Coffee House. I had been waiting eagerly to break the news of me leaving home. Unlike other days she was gorgeously dressed in a chiffon sari and looked beautiful in the makeup she applied. She smiled. By now all our friends knew that Esha and I, as everybody generalizes, were in love. Esha knew and also had made me realize that it was only an open-ended relationship.

She smiled at all of us as she walked down to the table and took a chair next to me. She had a wonderful perfume on.

'Siddhartha has made it. He has left home yesterday,' Suneet declared.

During those days, particularly in our age group, rising against the establishment, established norms were heroic. I could feel Esha was not as ecstatic as others for my act of defiance. She made up with a smile and asked, 'Where are you staying?'

'With Gule.'

'Do you have money on you?'

'Yes, though borrowed. By the way, are you going out for some occasion or function?'

'No. No.' She burst out laughing, 'It must be my dress. Do you recall I had told you about my uncle who lived in Bangkok? He came to our house last night. He had to take the morning flight to Delhi. So my mother and I had gone to the airport to see him off. Mother dropped me at the college on her way back to her duty.'

We left Coffee House a little earlier than other days. We walked down the College Street.

'What are you planning now?' she asked.

I was clear about my preferences, at least it seemed so.

'First, find a job; next, find a hostel, continue studies, and start painting.'

'Tomorrow you have the interview at The Grand.' Esha reminded.

'Yes. But today I will enjoy my freedom. Suddenly time is in plenty. I will need a lot of it when I start painting.'

'So how about spending the day with me.' she proposed.

'You know I would love to.'

'So let us plan it this way. First, we will have lunch together, then we will see a movie, spend the evening at Victoria Memorial and leave for tomorrow.'

It sounded great.

'Where do we have lunch? Nizam is good and cheap. I can have the beef curry and paranthas for one rupee twenty five paisa and if you don't want beef curry you can try the mutton rezala, a little costlier though.'

'No. Today, we will have lunch at Mirana.' It was a restaurant that I had not visited but knew it was at the middle rung and surely too costly for our pockets. Moreover, there were the film tickets as well.

'But that will be a costly affair.'

'Do not worry; I will bear the costs today. Today I have a little more in my kitty. My uncle gave me five hundred bucks as gift.'

Five hundred was surely a big amount in the late seventies. I was planning to live a month off the three hundred and fifty rupees of stipend that I might get if I was selected at The Grand. So, five hundred was surely big bucks.

We walked past Hind Cinema, down Lenin Sarani, Grant Street and reached Esplanade. It was twelve thirty in the afternoon. We entered Mirana. At the entrance, a board displayed that there was music and crooning in the evening; but for now it was almost vacant. Only a couple at a table, and a man on the other, and a few waiters made the ground floor. She led me up the wooden stairs to the first floor. There were wooden partitioned cabins with heavy curtains on both flanks. The open space was well laid out with arranged tables and chairs. I had seen such cabins in many Calcutta restaurants. They were generally used by families, where the open space was male dominated. Well this floor was totally vacant.

A waiter came running up and held aside the heavy curtains to one of the cabins. We entered and the curtains were dropped as we settled down. The cabin was quite small with a rectangular table, four sitter and soft sunlight entering from the opaque windowpanes. I could now hear a conversation, which came as muffled whispers, probably from a cabin next to ours.

'The place is packed up in the evenings. Lunchtime is more easygoing, not having to queue up at the entrance for a table to clear. You can spend hours on your lunch but for dinner, you have to rush through.' Esha said.

'Have you been here before?' I asked.

'Many times,' she replied, 'I love a few dishes of theirs. So whenever its lunch and I'm out, I just drop in here. My mother also likes the joint.'

Was I wrong somewhere? Was she actually no mystery at all? Only a rich girl with lot of freedom and a habit of telling occasional lies. Well that could describe her as well. I just let the thought take a back seat. The waiter knocked before raising the curtain and served two glasses of water. I lit a cigarette.

'Why did you sit on the other side? Come and sit by my side as we always do.'

I changed my seat. Again there was a knock and the waiter arrived with the menu card.

'What would you like to have?' she asked while going through the menu card.

'Anything that you think is good.'

I brushed through my card. I liked good food and I liked to read a menu card in detail, trying to understand the ingredients and flavours behind a particular item. It was a multi-cuisine restaurant. There were the snacks, Chinese and the Mughlai, followed by the beverage section. Suddenly 'Mutton Afghani' caught my eye. I had never tasted it before. Suddenly, the images of Afghanistan floated before me: high mountains, deep gorges, horses cantering, macho tribesmen in their loose flowing robes, moonlit nights, camp fires, a whole sheep being roasted. The images were from a film that I had seen in my schooldays. That was not the Afghanistan that went through Talibanisation and later de-Talibanisation by the United States of America. The 'Mutton Afghani' I thought could be a piece from that whole roasted lamb.

'How would this taste?' I asked pointing to my choice.

'Ah! That is one of my favorites. We will take paranthas with it.'

I glanced through the rates. A quick estimate and our meal would cost about fifty bucks. A big amount for me. I had only sixty bucks including Gule's loan. But then the lunch was on her. I did not have to worry. I looked through the curtain, called the waiter, and she ordered.

'And serve it after half an hour.' she added.

With the waiter gone, curtains drawn, I turned towards Esha. Her pallu had dropped from her shoulders. She wore a low neckline blouse flaunting her deep cleavage. Blood seemed to be rushing to my brain. I felt short of oxygen and was breathing hard. She caught me by my hair and pressed my face hard into her bosom. Feeling the soft breasts all over my face, I took out my tongue and licked onto the exposed skin. Moved my hands onto her breasts over the blouse and lightly fondled them, fearing to hurt her. It was much later and through Esha only, I learned that girls can take much more on the delicate bosoms than I had thought.

I raised my face to breathe. Breathlessness and heavy palpitation was killing me. Before I could fill in my lungs she had her mouth planted on mine. I could feel myself harden in the trousers and to hide the shame of an erection, I withdrew.

We looked at each other and once again locked ourselves into a wild kiss. With each encounter my lust for her increased. Now I wanted to bare her, see her; make body contact with her in totality. It was not possible in this restaurant cabin.

It is not that the girls of Bengali middle class society are pure souls till marriage. It is but natural for an adolescent to develop sexual inquisitiveness, which further develops into urges. But the pressures of societal upbringing of the day stopped them from being adventurous, self-searching, and are best kept repressed till the society offers the window of opportunities on a platter after marriage.

Esha stood out. She was bold, daring, and the mystery thickened. Was it her self-searching that made her bold? Was it the power of money backing her that made her bold? Or was it yet something else?

Esha was to meet me in front of the Grand Hotel at ten in the morning. I had the interview at eleven. I was on time. I had faced many interviews, first being during the entrance to the military school, there was no pressure on my mind. My attitude towards interviews had always been a round of interaction rather than being a platform for achievement. I was equally casual that morning as I sauntered on the pavement.

Esha arrived, we talked a little about last evening's film and I left her outside for my interview. I walked through the large hotel gate and knocked at Mr Tug's door.

'Yes, come in.'

'Good morning, sir.'

'Oh, you. Have a seat. I think I have some good news for you,' he said while adjusting his bifocal spectacles. I knew I had made it as I sank into the plush armchair.

'I have talked to the GM. With your background and leanings, he is a bit skeptical about your continuing in the field.' Now this did not sound like good news.

'So he has asked me not make you sign the contract which makes it mandatory to work with us for minimum three years after your training. Moreover, as you attend a morning college, you can join in at ten thirty instead of eight in the morning.'

Now that's what you call good news. This was better than what I was expecting. 'Thank you very much, sir.' I was highly obliged.

'Your training starts from next Monday. You drop in your application with the CV anytime before that and I will have it processed. As a trainee, you will be offered a stipend of Rupees three hundred and fifty, and the lunch.'

I thanked him again and walked out, head held high. It was my first job. I was going to earn all by myself. It took only ten minutes from living on borrowings to my own earnings. I was exasperated. Three hundred and fifty was more than enough for me.

As I came out of the hotel, Esha was watching a display on a shop window. I walked down to her with a beaming smile and she knew it all.

'From when are you joining?'

'Monday.'

'Let's celebrate.' She took my hand, 'The Mirana way.'

Again the blood rushed to my brain. I could feel the movement under my zip. It was just yesterday and needed no recapitulation. The experience was there with me on my flesh and feelings.

The same waiter, the same cabin, the same food, and the request for half an hour gap before service. I was bolder. She did not have to drop the pallu make-believing it to be accidental. I removed it for her. Her bosoms were heaving to give dynamism to the shadow between her cleavage. I placed my right palm on her breast and slowly moved down the cleavage into her blouse beyond her bra. She came closer and we locked into a violent kiss. Tongues moving in and out; wet with saliva all around our mouth. She took my hand and placed it on her thigh. I clasped onto the soft flesh. She clawed my back and I was hard under my zip. Suddenly I felt something touch my hard on. It was her palm. I let loose all inhibitions—inhibitions of sharing my private parts with someone of opposite sex.

She opened the zip and slid her hand in. I raised her sari from below and ventured into her panty. She moved her torso making her vagina more easily accessible. I brushed over her pubic hair and slid down. There she was, wet, hot. I liked the feeling of my fingers being drenched with her secretion. I kept playing with her crotch at times putting a finger into her. I could feel she liked the penetrations. But what's next? It was climactic without any possibility of the climax. Fucking was out of my mind. I could not think that far as yet. Otherwise, too, a restaurant cabin was no place to fuck. Well it was not a place to sexually explore each other, either.

'Masturbate me,' she whispered. A bolt struck me. I knew about masturbation as I often did myself, but to masturbate a girl?

'How?' I asked.

She looked at me and smiled. I felt a little ashamed of myself. I had read in the books but doing it practically was different. And I had this feeling that I would hurt the inside of her vagina. It was so soft to touch. She left my cock, pulled up her sari a little more and asked me to tickle at the top of her vagina. I tickled it as she put her middle finger deep into herself. It was minutes of fucking by the finger and she came. She groaned and locked me into a kiss, tight enough to hurt my tongue. She was over. I felt like an idiot sitting with my erection out of the zip, all wet and messy.

She put her sari back into position and started masturbating me. After I ejaculated she asked 'Do you hate me now?'

'Why should I? In fact I loved it.'

'No, I mean my exploring sex even before marriage.'

'But that is what our relationship is all about. And as soon as I earn a good living we will get married.' It was difficult for me to think beyond societal ethics. I could not accept the act in its own time and space context. I had to accept it in relation to consummation through marriage. I was programmed thus.

'Why talk of marriage?' she retorted. 'Do you mean to say that if we don't get married, I'm a bad girl in relation to today's happening?'

I did not have an answer, as I had not meant thus. It was just that I was unable to get out of my mindset and social upbringing. Truly, why should her being depend on a future uncertain occasion? I knew I was changing, and Esha was the one to open my eyes onto new horizons.

'Not at all. I will never again say that I love you. But surely I like you. And now I like you even more.'

'Well that's because I release your sexual urge. It has nothing to do with mind. It is purely a physical want. At least the part of extra liking that you have developed for me.' she dissected me in cold blood.

I knew myself as one entity, and here she was slowly disintegrating me. I was of mind; I was of body; the psyche and the physique; I surely was two different entities, and everybody is. No human can claim a sole entity with a perfectly synchronized psyche and physique. At times they do act singularly, but they act otherwise too.

Self-realization is an evolving process of studying one's own self in the context of external developments. And Esha unknowingly led me to it. I did not realize then. I was living to know why I was, though it was unconsciously. It was the beginning of the journey into me, into human beings, into life, and existence itself.

CHAPTER 2

FOR YEARS, BUBLU feigned sleeping with closed eyes and a baited breath. Bublu's father, SK, as his friends called him, had not returned home. It was late in the night and Bublu's mother, Sandhya, stood by the window peeping out of the curtain. Last night also he had come late. Bublu had got up to a shrieking Mamoni and bad-mouthing Bapi, his father. He kept quiet and tried to hold his breath to avoid parents from knowing that he was awake. There was a fierce quarrel on between the two but before Bublu could figure out the reason, he had fallen asleep.

Tonight seemed to be similar. He could feel the tension in the air as Mamoni walked up and down the room and again waited by the window.

'Bublu, are you awake?' Mamoni asked.

Bublu rolled over and closed his eyes tighter. There was a knock on the main entrance. Sandhya walked out of the room to open the door. Bublu could hear voices, which grew louder as his parents approached the bedroom.

'Next time, I am not going to open the door at this hour of the night,' Sandhya shouted. 'You better spend the night there itself.'

'What do you mean? Why won't you open the door?' SK asked.

'I know where you were. Go and spend the night with her.'

37

'Don't cook up stories. You know very well that I was playing cards with my friends.'

'I know everything. Playing cards till so late in the night?'

'I told you before also; leave me alone on Saturday and Sunday evenings. Previously, I used to go to the Race club. You asked me to stop and I have agreed. Now, don't get after my card games.'

'Card games?' Sandhya was bitchily sarcastic. 'I know what games you play. I don't know what you found in that bitch.'

'Sandhya! You are getting out of limits. Just shut up and serve me dinner.'

'Dinner? Couldn't you have asked her for it? She would have been very happy to make you sit on her lap and feed you.'

Bublu was feeling suffocated. He could not understand the conversation in totality. Who was this lady Mamoni was talking about? Why was Mamoni being so rude to Bapi for coming late? Before he could think more there was this noise of a tight slap. Bublu unconsciously shrieked in fear.

'Bublu has got up.' Sandhya screamed.

'Next time watch out your words or else...'

'Yes, let Bublu get up. Let him see his father's romantic gallivanting.'

'Will you shut up.'

'No, I won't.'

And it was a repeat of last night's scene. Bublu watched in the semi-darkness through little slits between otherwise tightly closed eyelids. SK caught hold of Sandhya's long hair and slapped once again. Sandhya picked up the hairbrush and smashed it onto SK's head. She tore off his shirt as he tried to get a hold on her. It was wrestling, wriggling, slaps, kicks, loud abuses, torn dresses, exposed private parts fading into a long darkness of nothingness. Bublu fell asleep.

Bublu got up next morning at SK's pat. 'Get up. It is already six in the morning.' SK said, 'You are growing up. Now you should get up all by yourself. Do you see anyone waking me up?'

Bublu idolized his father. Every child does. But for Bublu, it was in overdose. Particularly because of this highly polished image that SK maintained. Being in the British Navy earlier, his way of speaking, his gait, his dress sense, made him stand out among the middle class crowd. Bublu had met many of his classmates' fathers at school, but Bapi, to him was class apart.

Today too was like any other day. Only that Bublu noticed a red patch on Bapi's forehead and remembered the nightmare. Sandhya was already in the kitchen preparing breakfast. He noticed both Bapi and Mamoni doing their morning chores but was not talking to each other. He often tried to understand the cause of the fights, which often broke out on Saturday and Sunday nights after a lull of few weeks. Otherwise, everything seemed normal. SK took them out for films or dining out, or at times, to visit relatives. Sometimes he would take only Bublu for a children's film in which Sandhya showed no interest. Sometimes he was left back home with the maid in attendance as SK and Sandhya went out. It was a happy childhood for Bublu except for those occasional, but very violent nights. And at times they were so violent that on the very next day Sandhya would call her brothers from Chaibasa to settle the matter. And it was always settled amicably with SK giving a patient hearing to his in-laws. But the peace never lasted long.

SK always took the family on tour to hill stations, beaches, and historical places during Bublu's summer vacations. It was during one such tour to Darjeeling and Shilong that SK's family met a family group travelling in the same compartment. They were a family of three brothers, two wives, and their children. The eldest among the brothers, Hiren, was a bachelor. Both the families developed an intimate vibe and spent the vacation together. It was fun. Bublu recalled for long, how Bapi and the uncles once stopped the vehicle they were travelling in beside a cornfield and stole so many corns, which later were roasted for evening tea once back in the hotel. The relationship with the whole family did not last long after the vacation as the family was staying in the suburban town called Duttapukur, quite far away. Only Hiren stayed alone in Calcutta. He was a clerk with the government of West Bengal at the Writers Building. He used to visit his parental home in the weekends to nurture relationships. Once in a month he visited the SKs after office hours. SK, Sandhya, and Hiren often sat in the evenings over cups of tea or coffee and shared talks on common interest like Rabindra Sangeet, theatre and films, as Bublu sat alone in the other room completing his homework. Bublu did not hate Bose Kaku, as he used to call Hiren, but was not too fond of him either. Hiren was dark, on the fatter side with a receding hairline. He wore dhoti and kurta, or a long shirt instead. According to Bublu, he was shabby and was in no class with his Bapi. Though not conscious about it, this class difference of a marine engineer and a clerk was quite apparent to Bublu, which reflected in his indifferent behaviour towards Bose Kaku.

Soon after Bublu was promoted to class one, there was turmoil in East Pakistan from where SK hailed. His mother, elder brother, and elder sister with their family, still resided in Khulna of East Pakistan. Muslims were attacking Hindu households. There were cases of atrocities, rape, and land grabbing. The homogenous fabric of the social structure was breaking. The whole family barring elder brother of SK shifted to Calcutta and put up with SK. The elder brother stayed back to take care of their immovable assets, which translated into cultivable land, a few orchards, and a sprawling old mansion. The elder brother of SK had seven children, and there was his wife, SK's elder sister with her husband, and two grown-up daughters, and of course, his mother. It became a house full to its brim. It was fun for Bublu. With so many people around, there was always hullahbullah all over the house. And the tension between his parents decreased. In fact, it seemed to have disappeared totally.

He did not realize that it was another developing tension, which was engulfing the earlier one. With only SK earning, it was slowly telling on the home front economics. The outings became less, Bublu did not get Bournvita in his morning milk, and a silent demarcation of territorial divide was taking place. The master bedroom was the domain of SK and his family. Now, this served as the study room for Bublu as well. Bublu's study room was occupied by SK's elder sister and family, while the living room was taken over by SK's elder brother's family and mother. Often there were skirmishes in the kitchen and slowly it started spilling over to the open spaces and rooms. Nobody asked Bublu not to visit other rooms but he no more entered the other rooms. Bublu's space was shrinking. But he never minded it though. The children had the open courtyard to play and mingle in the evening before they retired to their rooms. As the quarrels increased, the reasons for the same became pettier. Bublu could feel the cousins slowly distancing themselves. All the families started taking their meals to their own room. SK returned late from office to avoid the showdowns and complaints from Sandhya. Hiren had also stopped visiting. When Sandhya learnt about SK's promotion to Chief Engineer, she felt happy. But as soon as she realized that SK would now once again have to sail out on ship for fifteen days at a stretch and stay in city for three days, all hell broke loose.

'I am not going to face these problems of your relatives' everyday, all by myself,' Sandhya protested. 'Even with you around there is so much trouble, imagine the situation without you at home. I cannot stay like this.'

Next evening there was a meeting of all the family members. Bublu did not know what transpired till he saw the families leaving within next few days. They had found separate accommodation and moved out. Grandmother stayed back. Calm returned. Bublu got back his study room, though now he had to share it with his grandmother.

With all the cousins gone, grandmother showered a lot of love on Bublu. In fact at times she became the shield to Sandhya's ire on Bublu. He now had a savior in his grandmother. The more he became intimate with grandmother, the more he started adoring her. She was very fair, with a dense, boy cut, white hair. She always wore an off-white sari without a blouse, and had a cotton cloth pouch in her left hand. She always kept her left palm inside it unless using the same for some work. Much later Bublu learnt it contained a basil wood bead garland, which she kept turning between her forefinger and thumb, bead by bead, mentally chanting some God's name. Her mornings started with offering of Ganga water to the Basil plant that she had planted in a pot in the open courtyard. Basil plant is attributed to be holy in Hindu scriptures. Thereafter, she would help Bublu get ready for school; walk down about half an hour to the Ganges embankment; take a holy dip in the river; offer prayers at the temples nearby and return home. Bublu would accompany his grandmother for the holy dip on Sundays and holidays. He liked this new routine. He never took the dip as he did not know swimming and was afraid of the flowing river. He would stand on the stairs of the embankment and watch a group of children who dived into the gushing waters to come out with coins from the bed of the river. Many people throw these coins into the Ganges believing it to be a pious deed. On taking the dip in the Ganges, grandmother would fill her brass pot with the holy Ganges water, put a little of it on Bublu's head symbolizing the holy dip, and take him to the temples to offer prayer.

One of the temple's priests had brass moulds of holy symbols, like two feet supposed to represent God Narayan's feet, the sign of Om, Lotus, etc. He would put sandalwood paste 'tilak' on Bublu's forehead with these brass moulds. The priest also had a small mirror. After applying the tilak, he would let Bublu look into it. Bublu, for some unknown reason, liked the 'two feet' one and always insisted for it. Mamoni did not like this 'tilak' ritual and washed away the marks as soon as he reached back home. But she never objected to it because of grandmother. With grandmother around, Bublu found that there were changes in many facets of their life. Mamoni did not beat him like before for petty mistakes. The quarrel between parents had stopped. Bapi returned home in time even on Saturdays and Sundays when not out on sail. Though Sandhya cooked well, grandmother's arrival added a few traditional dishes into the daily menu. Particularly, Bublu liked the preparation of banana flower that grandmother used to cook all by herself.

SK was very fond of pets. Once he had brought home a pup. But Sandhya was against the idea. 'Who is going to take care of the dog? And it will be a mess with his falling hair all over the house.'

She soon got rid of the pup by gifting him to a neighbour the very next day. But now with grandmother around, it seemed SK too, was taking chances. One evening he returned from office with a white hen. Sandhya as usual, declared that she had nothing to do with her but finally agreed on grandmother's pursuance and SK's assurance that he will take all the necessary care. And he did. First, he built a wooden roost with wire mesh window for the hen all by himself on the very next Sunday. He had two trunks full of various tools. They contained tools for carpentry, mechanical works, welding, electrical repairs, etc. He not only enjoyed repairing, fixing household objects, but also actually had made a wooden chair, a swing, a divan, and now the hen's roost. SK had told Sandhya that the hen would lay eggs, but it did not for quite some time and Sandhya would often tease SK for the same. Over a month the hen became very friendly with everybody and even Sandhya liked her as she found her apprehensions coming wrong. The hen was very fast in learning. She did not excrete anywhere but near the drain in the courtyard. She did not go into the rooms. She was somewhat like a pedigreed pup. SK generally let loose the hen in the morning and gave her feed whenever he was in town. Otherwise, it was Bublu's duty.

One fine morning SK dashed into the bedroom, 'Look, the hen has laid an egg.' And he held an egg in his hand. Suddenly there was joy among all in the household. Everybody rushed outside into the courtyard to have a look at the hen. And there she was proudly moving around occasionally nibbling her feed kept in an earthen pot. It was after SK came back from the next sailing trip that he broke the story. The egg that brought joy to the whole family was not laid by the hen. SK had taken the egg from the kitchen cupboard. He had a good hearty laugh and so did Sandhya, Bublu, and grandmother.

It was about a month later, when SK was out sailing; Bublu went and opened the roost door to set the hen free in the morning. She walked out, fluttered her wings to get rid of the sleepy lethargy, and moved around in brisk steps with chest held high. Bublu noticed that she was charged up more than normal. She walked up to Bublu and again moved away to go around in circles. As if she was trying to tell something. Bublu turned to the roost to drop the door and lo, there was this egg—a big, white, egg. He picked it up and ran to Sandhya in the kitchen

'Mamoni the hen has laid an egg.'

Sandhya's immediate reaction was to open the cupboard, take out the basket of eggs and count them. No, none were missing.

'Mamoni I am telling you the truth. I got it from the roost.'

So at last the hen started laying eggs. She laid one every week but mysteriously, whenever any guest came to stay overnight, that week she would lay two eggs, as if one in honour of the guest. Her eggs were specially served to Bublu alone for breakfast. It continued for long till one unfortunate night Sandhya forgot to down the shutter of the roost. In the morning as Bublu walked into the courtyard to release the hen, to his utter shock he found blood, torn bits of flesh, feathers all around. Frightened, he ran to Sandhya. 'Something has eaten up our hen.' Sandhya too was shocked and ran out into the courtyard. She stood stunned as grandmother too walked out from her room.

Few days back Sandhya had noticed a cat jumping into the compound in the night and making rounds. She knew the culprit. But now she could do nothing. All had ended last night. On returning from his sailing assignment, SK did not show his pain and instead consoled the family on the hen's loss. To everybody's surprise the very next day he came home from office with two cute small white rabbits.

Sandhya always had logic against having pets. 'Don't you know they breed very fast.' she said, 'Soon there will be a dozen of them. How will we take care of them?'

And SK had his, 'Both are male. So there is no question of breeding.'

Sandhya couldn't argue further and the rabbits stayed. The hen's roost now became the home for the cuddly white pom-poms. Bublu found new playmates. He often would sit in the courtyard with one of them in the lap and caress him. They loved it too, and sat quietly closing the eyes and enjoying the adulation. But they were not as polished as the hen and would excrete all over the courtyard. This was irritating for Sandhya, as she otherwise kept the house spic and span. Now she had to clean the courtyard every alternate hour. She complained to SK.

The backyard was a stretch of two feet broad barren earth spreading fifteen feet, between the house and the boundary wall. SK found a solution. He released the rabbits in this stretch in the morning and blocked the entrance with a wire mesh. Soon, this wire mesh was replaced by a proper gate crafted by SK. The rabbits stayed and played in the alley all day long, and in the evening they were put to bed in the wooden house. Every morning when SK went to the market to purchase the day's fresh vegetables, he would collect cauliflower leaves in one bag for the rabbits. This was their staple diet. Bublu loved standing at the short entrance gate to the alley and call out, 'Choo ... choo ... choo.' The rabbits knew that their food was ready. They would rush to the gate and nibble at the cauliflower leaves from Bublu's hand. Both were voracious eaters. The backyard had a tall papaya tree planted by SK, which never bore papayas, and a lemon tree. One fine morning as Bublu went to feed the rabbits, he found the papaya tree missing. For a moment he stood astonished as he realized the tree lying flat on the ground. The rabbits had nibbled into its soft trunk to bring it down. First, the leaves were relished by them. Then they started eating into the trunk. They ate the inner core creating a tunnel through the outer bark. It took them only four days to complete the tunneling. They also invented a new game. One would chase the other through this papaya bark tunnel. They ate, played, and grew bigger. So was Bublu, growing up.

One morning when SK had gone to the market, Bublu walked to the backyard to see the rabbits. He was shocked to find that the rabbits had shrunk in size. There were the two playing along but they had become much smaller.

He ran to Sandhya, 'Mamoni the rabbits have become small.'

Sandhya thought it to be a prank, 'Go and get ready for school. I am busy and have no time for your silly things.'

'Why don't you believe me? Both the rabbits have become very small.'

On not being able to convince Sandhya, he cajoled grandmother to have a look at his discovery. He pulled her to the backyard for a greater shock. There were no rabbits at all.

'Now you know grandma, I was telling the truth.' Bublu said, 'I saw them growing small and now they have vanished.'

Grandmother, though did not believe Bublu's version, could not figure out the disappearance act as well. She went to Sandhya, 'Sandhya, the rabbits are not there.'

'What do you mean, Ma? SK put them in the backyard just an hour back.'

Sandhya could not understand what was going wrong. Bublu playing prank was still ok, but now Ma as well?

'Sandhya, I'm not blind. There are no rabbits in the backyard.' Grandmother felt a bit irritated on not being taken seriously. Sandhya had no other option but to go to the backyard to clarify the fact. As all three approached the backyard, still more surprise awaited them. There were three rabbits playing around and all were small. For Bublu, it was magic in real life.

He looked up at Mamoni, 'It's magic. I told you they were becoming smaller. Then they vanished and now they have come back with one more. It is real magic.'

Bublu was very excited; but Sandhya immediately analyzed the reality. She took a few cauliflower leaves and entered the backyard as Bublu and grandmother followed. At the end of the stretch there were big holes in the ground. Sandhya held the leaves at the opening of the burrows and called out 'Choo, choo, choo . . .' Both the big rabbits slowly emerged from the burrows to nibble at the leaves.

'Ma, this is what I was afraid of.' Sandhya told grandmother, 'SK said both were males, but it turns out that one is a female. They have given birth to these three. Let SK come from the market.'

When SK returned from the market, he vehemently denied any knowledge of one being a female, but smiled within, as he knew the fact from day one. As time passed, the rabbit family grew larger. By the time Bublu was in class three, their number had swelled to eleven. SK installed a barbed wire fence on the boundary wall to keep the errant cats away and allowed the rabbits to live in the self-made burrows in the backyard.

It was during this period that grandmother fell ill and took to bed. Bublu's Sunday sojourn to the Ganges embankment stopped. He saw doctors frequenting their home as grandmother became quieter by the day. Her health was deteriorating fast. She spent most of the time lying in the bed in the living room across the open courtyard. Often, relatives, even those whom Bublu never knew existed, paid visits. One Sunday late afternoon, SK and Sandhya had retired to the bed after lunch for an afternoon siesta. Grandmother too, was sleeping. Bublu got an idea as he was playing in the living room. SK was a chain smoker and always smoked imported foreign cigarettes. Rothmans, Triple Five, or Dunhill. The cigarettes came in bundles of twenty, packed in a tin. Bublu always wanted to taste a cigarette; but knew it was a taboo. Now he found the opportunity. He tiptoed into the bedroom and took out one from SK's tin. There was the lighter lying beside, but he decided not to take it in case Bapi got up and wanted a smoke. Bublu took the matchbox from the kitchen cupboard, and slowly crept under grandmother's bed. He took the cigarette in between his lips like SK did, stroked a match, and lit the cigarette. A burst of cough followed and he sat with the cigarette in hand, trying to understand the pleasure beyond coughs.

Sandhya woke up at the noise of Bublu's cough. Following the direction of the sound, she entered the living room. There was smoke trickling out from underneath the bed. She stooped down and raised the bed sheet to look under.

'What are you doing there?' she asked Bublu. In the dark under the bed, she saw a light. 'What are you doing with fire? Come out.'

Bublu crawled out with the cigarette in hand.

'Are you smoking?' Sandhya came into a fit of rage. She pulled up Bublu onto his feet and started thrashing. Slaps rained like a hailstorm. Grandmother watched silently from the bed. Like other occasions, she could not save Bublu from Sandhya's wrath. She was too weak. Sandhya dragged Bublu to the bedroom.

'Look, what your son is up to.' and held out the burnt cigarette.

Two common questions that Bublu always faced from relatives were, 'Who loved you more, Bapi or Mamoni?' and 'Who beat you more, Bapi or Mamoni?' Bublu always replied that both loved equally but while Mamoni thrashed by hand and cane, Bapi only used to hit softly with a rolled newspaper. SK never manhandled Bublu. He had a different approach in imbibing discipline.

He took the cigarette and looked at Bublu. 'Have you done the right thing?'

'No.' Bublu replied looking at the ground.

'I am keeping the cigarette.' SK got out of bed and placed it on a small showpiece in the wall cupboard with glass shutters. 'Whenever you look at it, remember your sin and never repeat it.'

Bublu was happy with Bapi letting him go with little, in fact, no punishment for such a major mischief. It was only the next morning that he realized the true depth of the punishment. As he woke up in the bed, the cigarette was just staring at him. A cold chill ran down his spine. The feeling of guilt made him feel sick. He jumped out of the bed and ran into the bathroom. With the passing days it became a silent torture for Bublu. He would avoid looking at the cigarette when he used to rise in the morning or while crossing the cupboard, but just the knowledge that it was there was unbearable. It was a year after that Bublu could get rid of this guilt.

When he had entered class four, SK and family shifted their residence to a new locality. On the day of shifting, everybody was busy packing. Bublu too was helping, but his mind hovered around the cigarette. He could not let this torture be carried to their new house. At the first opportunity he took out the cigarette from the cupboard without his parents' knowledge and threw it away on the road. At last the big burden of guilt was removed. Bublu felt free. He breathed deeply like he had not done for a long time.

Meanwhile, before SK and family shifted to their new address, grandmother had died. Hiren had again started visiting. SK had again started coming late in the weekends. The fights between SK and Sandhya reappeared in Bublu's life, but this time, recurring more often. But Bublu now had a separate room. His study room was now also his bedroom, and hence did not have to face the quarrels and fights in graphic details like before. He noticed that Bapi was taking him out more than before to wrestling shows, circus, films, etc. and Mamoni was spending more time with neighbours and friends. On returning home with Bapi, Mamoni now secretly started enquiring about where they had gone. Many a times she would mention about an aunty, if she was around or had they visited her house. Bublu never met her and was quite confused about the existence of this mysterious aunty, but he could feel his bonding with Bapi growing stronger. He could also feel his parent's bonding growing weaker.

SK was always game for any new developments. Like he was one of the very firsts to acquire a scooter when it was first launched. It was a Lambretta. He even introduced his family to Chinese cuisine at Waldorf, the only Chinese restaurant in Calcutta on Park Street. Sandhya even learnt from SK to cook Chowmein at home, a rare feat in the late sixties. So when the Russian Circus came to Calcutta to perform for the first time, it was obvious that SK would not miss it. One evening, SK returned early from office and asked Sandhya to get Bublu dressed up.

'Where will you take him,' asked Sandhya.

'To the circus,' SK replied.

'I don't understand what you find so interesting. You have been to so many circuses,' Sandhya did not know about the Russian troop, and SK too did not clarify.

'Bublu likes them,' SK justified, 'that's why I take him.'

Bublu knew Bapi would get through all the blockades of Mamoni once he had decided, so he was sure they were going. He got dressed, and soon father and son were on their way to the circus. They took a tram. Bublu did not have much idea about the roads except for the ones that his school bus took to and from the school. The conductor pulled a string to ring a bell in the driver's cabin once. It was the signal to stop the tram. Twice meant the tram could start. 'Entally,' the conductor called out declaring the stop. SK caught hold of Bublu's hand and alighted from the tram. They walked down to a big building on the main road and entered the main entrance, which was open. The area was not well-lit but Bublu saw a staircase going up.

'Bapi aren't we going to the circus?' Bublu asked as they climbed the stairs.

'Yes, we will,' SK replied, 'First meet an aunty. She will also come with us.'

It was brighter on the first floor. It seemed the ground floor got a stepchild treatment. SK knocked the door with the large iron ring attached on the door. These were meant for such knocking or for locking by putting a padlock through the two rings that were fixed on the two sections of the door. Bublu looked around. The place had an old world charm. There was a small chandelier hanging from the ceiling just in front of the door. It was not lighted and was dust-laden. Light came from the two beautiful glass shades on lamp holders fitted on both the sides of the door. SK knocked once again. This time the door opened and a lady in sari asked them to come in. The door opened into a long verandah. SK guided Bublu to the first room on the left and asked him to sit on the sofa. The room was very big. It had a very high ceiling with a large chandelier at the centre lighting the room. There were carved wooden sofas with velvet-covered cushions on them. The walls were adorned by big, framed, black-and-white photographs. Bublu could understand they were scenes from Bengali films but did not find the relevance of putting them up on the wall, till he noticed that one particular lady was common in all the frames.

'That must be the aunty Bapi wants me to meet,' Bublu thought. But is she then a film heroine? And how does Bapi know her? As he was trying to put together the jigsaw puzzle, the lady in the frames walked in. She was older than what she looked in the pictures. 'She is not as beautiful as Mamoni but is good looking.' Bublu thought.

'Shu, I hope we are not late already? I will take just five minutes to finish my make-up,' she turned to Bublu. 'What a lovely child.' She came rushing to Bublu, held her close and planted a kiss on his cheek, 'What's your name?'

'Siddhartha Sircar,' Bublu replied.

'That's a lovely name. As lovely as you are.' Bublu felt shy.

'But your Bapi has always been referring to you as Bublu, so I will also call you Bublu. Is that fine with you?' Bublu felt elated. For the first time somebody was asking for his opinion. Everybody reacted with him the way they liked. They always reinforced the idea through their behaviour that he was too small and his opinion did not matter. And here was a lady who was asking if it was Ok if she called him Bublu. It was not that there was any other option but the feel good factor made Bublu speak out, 'Yes aunty, you can call me Bublu.'

He got up and bent down to touch her feet. She caressed him by brushing her hands through his hairs and walked out in a hurry. 'You sit here. I am just coming,' SK told Bublu and followed her.

Sitting all alone, looking around the room, a feeling of out of context was just setting in as the aunty in the frames walked in with a plate of sweets and a few books. 'Your Bapi had told me you love sweets. So enjoy them and go through these books as I get ready,' she said, 'I promise we will not be late for the show.'

She caressed his cheeks and walked out. Bublu did like sweets. Particularly 'rosogolla', a typical Bengal preparation of cottage cheese balls boiled in sugar syrup. Apart from other sweets, there were four rosogollas. He finished all four and started flipping through the books she had given. They were all children's pictorial books. He was expecting to be introduced to some child in the house. But that was not happening. Whenever he had visited any family with his parents there was always at least one child in the house. Maybe he or she was elder or younger to him. But always there was a child with whom he used to spend the time as his parents engaged themselves with the elders. But here he was all alone flipping through the books. On finishing seeing the pictures of the first book, he looked around. There was a big wall clock on one of the walls. It was six ten. He had no idea what time the show was. But the big silent room made him uneasy and he picked up the second book. Bapi and the aunty walked in. 'Let's go,' she said.

She looked so different. It was not that Bublu had no idea of make-up. He had seen Mamoni on so many occasions sitting in front of the dressing table and applying make-up. But this aunty had worked miracles. She looked like the one she was in the photographs on the wall. She looked much younger. They walked down the stairs, took a taxi and went to the circus.

Bublu had been to many circus before. The Bharat circus, the Ajanta circus, and the Apollo circus. Circus always weaved a magical atmosphere all around. Lines of parked cars, the huge canopy rising into the sky, mesmerizing lighting, large hoardings depicting scenes from the circus, exiting and entering of the crowd, hustle bustle, a beautiful chaos. It was all there at the Russian circus but on a much larger scale. In addition, there were moving beam of lights being thrown up into the sky, which Bublu saw for the first time. The circus was on a grand scale. The performances were breathtaking. For the first time Bublu saw a seal performing. The lion show did not have the iron railings as in Indian circus, but had a net dropped from top making it more hair-raising. All the girl performers were very beautiful. Bublu had only one disappointment. There was only one joker. That too he was tall. Indian circus always had four to five midget jokers. At the end of the show, SK dropped the aunty before returning home. It was nine thirty in the night.

After dinner, Sandhya walked into Bublu's room. 'Did only you and Bapi go to the circus?' she asked.

'No, there was an aunty with us. She was good to me and gave me a lot of sweets when we visited her home.' Bublu replied.

'Bapi took you to her house?' Bublu could feel Mamoni's temper rising.

'Yes, a good aunty,' he replied.

'Good aunty. My foot,' Sandhya dashed out of the room. Bublu could not understand the reason for her rage. The door of his parent's bedroom banged shut. He could hear Mamoni shouting though not clear enough to comprehend about what. The quarrel started. Bublu went to his room, pulled the wrapper over his head and went to sleep.

CHAPTER 3

I T WAS NOT the first time. Engulfed in the darkness of a tunnel, peeping out of the train window, and watching the circular beam of light from the entry, then slowly exit at the other end. It was not the first time but more exciting, because this was not a journey for a hill station summer vacation with parents as in the past, but a long stay in the Doon valley. I was joining the military school in Dehradun and was going to stay away from my parents and I was happy. It sounds queer, but that was it. No more of those extra arithmetic sums over and above the homework. No more of essay writing on anything and everything that Bapi could think of. No more of lots of things. Freedom at last. And the exit of the tunnel seemed to be the entrance to this new freedom. I felt like a little bird taking its first flight out of the nest. A little bit of fear, churned in a lot of ecstasy.

I will stay for the next five years in this valley in between the Shivalik Mountains and the magnanimous Himalayan range, completing my schooling. Thimayya Road, a short road winding up and down, led us in. Lined by Deodar trees on both sides, a culvert midway over a dry brook generously spattered with small and big pebbles. It was like the illustrations from the childhood Radiant Reader's pages unfolding in reality. The landscaping was typical of the bygone British era: gigantic old trees, verdant lawns, decorative beds of seasonal flowers, and roads lined by slanted red bricks. Long single storey Tudor style buildings with slanted roofs, huge ventilators, and tall continuous line of glass paned doors and windows.

Other newcomers along with their parents had also assembled in front of the office building. Registration was an efficient and short procedure. Colonel Jojhar came out of his office and greeted everybody, 'Welcome to RIMC.'

Well, that was the abbreviation for my new school, Rashtriya Indian Military College. At that point it had not struck me that the name was an odd combination of Hindi and English. Later I learnt about the reason for the anomaly. The institute was inaugurated by the then Prince of Wales in 1922 and was named Prince of Wales Royal Indian Military College, which practically came to be known as Royal Indian Military College with the abbreviated form of RIMC. The cadets of the institution were known as Rimcollians. After independence in 1947, though the 'Royal' seemed to be out of context yet the glory of the Rimcollians in the battlefields had to be treasured. A compromise was achieved by replacing Royal with Rashtriya, which meant National. RIMC remained RIMC and so did the Rimcollians. I think it is one of the best marriages between languages. The communication was complete and the purpose achieved.

The lunch at the 'T' Mess, thus called for its T shape, was grand. Rows of long tables with white linen, bordered by wooden chairs and benches, laid out with white crockery and sparkling cutlery. I kept looking at the walls decorated with swords and muskets, interspersed with stuffed real heads of deer, antelopes, and one that of a huge bison. There were huge, awe inspiring fireplaces in dark teakwood with numerous silver trophies on the wooden sill above it. We all sat down, as waiters in white, served us. The butler, as if hinting at the delicious food served in the mess, was big and fat; but he looked smart in his outfit with the bow tie and waistcoat. He moved around the tables overseeing the lunch proceedings and giving instructions to the waiters. It was Indian lunch served in courses ending with fruits.

After lunch, parents had to leave. In the lawns in front of the mess, all the parents were giving their last piece of advice to their wards. Mamoni, sitting under a large tree, pulled me close and kissed me on my cheek. With all the people around I felt shy and pulled myself out of her embrace to see tears in her eyes. It took me thirteen years to feel the pain in those droplets. Thirteen years later when she died and I could not attend the funeral. But that time, I felt like a man in withdrawing from that spontaneous show of affection, thinking I would be a sissy otherwise.

The cadets, as the students were called, had designated sections namely: Pratap, Shivaji, Ranjit, and Chandragupta. Each dormitory had kit rooms for changing, cupboard section, and the rows of common toilets and bathrooms. There was a huge coal boiler in each section, which was fired in the winters to provide hot water. Later during my stay, they were replaced by electric geysers but the huge black iron structure remained till I left the college in 1975. The dormitories were lined with iron beds with springs, and laid with red blankets, white sheets, and feather pillows. Being from the civilian background, the immaculate symmetry and order impressed me. And it was this symmetry and order that I would be shunning later. It is strange that this place of order sowed the seeds of chaos in me and initiated my quest for asymmetry through art and life.

I used to draw and paint from early childhood. So it was natural that I chose Art as my hobby club when it came to selecting one among a plethora of options like gardening to photography to music to crafts to clay modeling and what not.

But my liking for art was a joke among the three Bengalis who became my friends—Jayant, Tirtha, and Roy. They were all from Calcutta, but six months senior to me. Jayant was designated to be my cadet guardian with the job of initiating me into the system that RIMC was. It was on day three, a Sunday, standing in the midst of one of the many football fields with Jayant, and I was enjoying the panoramic view of the Himalayas. The passing clouds created changing patterns of light and shade on the mountains. I was moved and told Jayant, 'I will like to paint this scene.'

'I will shove the brush up your ass if you don't mug the name of the appointment holders by tomorrow. Remember if I get screwed, I will fuck you dry.' was his response.

I was already getting used to this new lingo. I knew it was not to be taken literally. There was so much I was unaware of. Every moment was so clockwork systematic that the day ended even before one could feel the day passing. A six-month senior was to be addressed as 'Sir', physical ragging was common under the garb of punishment, even manhandling by seniors was something one could not report about to the authorities. It was an unwritten law. I could feel military discipline slowly seeping into my veins. It was fun, it was tiring, it was exciting, and at times it was demoralizing too. The bugle every morning brought in new hope, fresh energy, and maybe the day will be better—less of punishment, a little less tiring—but the day went on as usual.

The ragging for freshers was usually programmed after lunch during the rest period or after dinner. They were summoned by the most senior batches that are on the second semester of class eleven. The modes ranged from being asked to perform extreme physical feats or being fooled into utter embarrassment, to extremely comic situations. One of the common one among non-physical was loudly reading out the explicit sex scenes from Harold Robbins' novels or other pondies. Being introduced to such writing at the age of eleven to twelve, many of the freshers ended up giggling, and that was their damnation. You were expected to read out objectively and any involvement mentally, shifted gears of ragging to physical level. There were many of these physical engagements termed as punishments, haunching, legs up hands down, front roll, back roll on gravels, heat treatment, and one was pushed to the extremes till one broke down physically, drenched in sweat, hidden tear in eyes, and a hope for a better tomorrow.

During one such session after certain physical punishments as we stood in attention pose, our Section Commander growled at me, 'Sid, you better pull up your socks.'

I bent down to obey and found both the pairs in order and a big blow on my back.

'What the fuck are you trying to prove?' It was a new phrase that I learnt the hard way. Every day brought in something new. Truly it was a whole new learning process—a process of imbibing discipline. The very same discipline that later helped me to revolt against the system of life. How contradictory things get at times.

The nineteen cadets that we joined in August of 1970 were all from different States with different socio-cultural backgrounds. The only commonality was that we were all aged between eleven to twelve years. We were learning fast. Thinking back, I feel astonished at the rate we grew tough physically and mentally within the first three months. We could do three hundred sit-ups at a stretch, could handle several punches into our stomach, and could roll across fields. We also learnt about lesbians, homosexuals, intercourse, and masturbation. We were already masturbating during bath behind closed doors, in the bed under sheets.

Another thing I learnt was that everybody had a girlfriend back home. Some were bolder to declare that they had more than one. Well I had none. In truth maybe nobody had one. But I had to be in the league and I declared that my girlfriend's name was Lipika.

Lipika, one who would emerge into a fact of my life in years to come; a fact, a part of life, which is hard to forget. First love.

Lipika Ray or Shona, as was her pet name at home, was the second daughter of Shefali Ray, a nurse at the Calcutta Port Trust Hospital. My mother, Mamoni, being asthmatic, was often admitted in the hospital and soon befriended this short, umber lady in white. Staying close by, Mamoni often paid visit to her home, with me in tow. In class three, with no friends, strict routines, I used to look forward to these visits. I found two new friends in Shona and Kekadi, the two daughters of Shefali Mashi. While our mothers gossiped over a cup of tea, I, Shona, and her elder sister, Kekadi, played in their large cemented courtyard. 'Catch n Catch', 'Police n Thief', and 'Crocodile in the water' were the common games. At times I accompanied the two sisters to the nearby park and joined a larger group of children for games.

Shona was elder to me and was studying in class five then. But the age difference hardly mattered in the growing up days and we continued having fun while graduating from one class to another. I was never the first boy of the class but did not do badly in studies either. I ranked within the first eight and I was happy about it. But my parents were not, and they tried harder every year. Bapi sat for longer hours with me on my homework and Mamoni always placed the clock on my study table and kept increasing the study hours.

When in class four, we shifted to a new rented flat which was a little far from Shefali Mashi's house. The frequency of our visit to their house reduced. It was now fortnightly or at times even once in a month. The games also gradually changed with growing age. Now, we three, sat over some board or card games. I still loved this break as they provided me an escape from the ever-extending hours of studies. In class seven, I appeared in the All India Competitive Exam for entrance to the military school RIMC. I awaited results. Shona had graduated to class nine. It was by mid July that we were informed about my selection to the premier institute. We were soon to report for the August Seventy semester. It was fourth of August, Mamoni asked me to personally go over to Shefali Mashi's house and bid them farewell. She was not coming as she had met her two days back at the hospital during her routine checkup.

Evening was gradually descending as I walked into their house. Shefali Mashi greeted and congratulated me for the achievement. So did Shona. Kekadi had gone out. Shefali Mashi excused herself for the evening puja. Shona and I sat for a long time in stupid silence. It was strange. We talked so much every time we met and here we just sat dumb. I had nothing to say but she should have. It was always her who anchored the time pass conversations. It was more than fifteen minutes when Shefali Mashi walked in with the 'prasad'.

'When are you all leaving?' she asked.

'On the night of sixth August, by Doon Express,' I replied. 'We are supposed to report on the eighth and the semester starts from the tenth.'

I got up to touch her feet and leave. I looked at Shona. She was looking out of the window into the dark night.

'I am leaving.' I tried to get her attention. She looked at me. I had never seen so much pathos in her eyes before or maybe I had imagined it. I too suddenly felt the pain of leaving a close childhood friend. She followed me to the gate as I walked out.

'Will you forget me?' she asked as I stepped out of their door. 'Will you write letters, be in touch?'

It was difficult to board onto the unknown future leaving behind a true friendship that developed over the years. And now she was making it more difficult. I assured that I would be the first to write giving her my detailed address.

So in RIMC, when the subject of girlfriend arose, it was but natural that I took her name as my girlfriend, as she was the only girl I knew and she was a friend too.

The RIMC days introduced me to the colourful world of Bollywood films. They were earlier banned at home. The only films I had seen earlier were based on biographies, children's films, and a lot of films on Second World War. The Bollywood films opened a world of vibrant fantasy, which I was unaware of. Romance, songs, cliff-top fights, the archetype villain, and above all, the Super Star of the era, Rajesh Khanna. It was 'Aan Milo Sajna', my third film while at RIMC on a Sunday leave. Once every month, on Sundays, we were allowed to go on leave to the Dehradun town with four rupees in cash as pocket money. We spent on the bike hired from Garhi Cantonment behind our school, the cinema and a lunch of Chhole Bhature. In fact, we always shared one plate amongst two and ate more tomato ketchup from the bottle on the table to fill our stomach. Generally, the bottle used to be empty when we left. The restaurant guys were getting smarter and soon we found a small bowl of sauce was placed on our table as soon as we occupied one, and the bottle was removed.

The heroine was in the midst of lush green valley with a broken down jeep. This man in all white, who was mounted on a white horse, enters the screen. The audience stood up en masse and started howling and whistling as I sat trying to understand the reaction. Mankar, my fellow cadet, caught hold of me by the shoulders and jerked me onto my feet.

'That's Rajesh Khanna yaar.' He was pretty excited.

'So?' I was still unaware of his aura.

'Arre! He is the great Rajesh Khanna. He is the hero.' He burst into a whistle.

I looked at the screen. So this was him. I had heard about him from my friends who were initiated to Bollywood films at home. I liked the man. Graceful, stylized, and smart. Yes, style was something that he gave to the youth of those days. Many of his mannerisms percolated from the screens to the streets of India. And like everybody else, he grew on me. He was the 'Guru' to the youth of the seventies. The 'oohs' and 'aahs' about their girlfriends from fellow cadets and this new world of Bollywood opened yet another undiscovered feeling in me: Romance.

The silence on the parting day from Shona, the blank distant looks of hers seemed to be falling into place. Or at least it seemed so to me. Human chemistry works wonders on human minds. The friend metamorphosed into a lover. Shona, the pet name, gave way to Lipika. Yes, I discovered I was in love with her as I picked up a pink pebble from the walkway in front of Pratap Section dormitory to add to my growing collection of rocks and minerals. The feeling of love made me a different person. Not altogether, but surely partially. I felt grown up. I became romantic. The beauty of the mountains yonder became more beautiful. The first raindrops and the earthy fragrance now conversed with me. The never-ending variety of patterns in floating clouds now projected recognizable images to me. Everything around communicated with me in a language unknown till yesterday. Ah! That realization of first love. I wanted to cry out to the world, 'I love L i i p i i k a a a'.

But all this without even knowing about Lipika's thoughts. Presuming she too felt the same. From the silence, the look and the last spoken sentences. 'Will you forget me?' 'Will you write letters, be in touch?' A storm started brewing in me. I had to communicate with her. I had to tell her about my newfound feeling of first love. I had to tell her that I loved her. And the stinker; to find out if she too loved me. As nights rolled on, I rolled over and over again pondering the pros and cons of communicating. I feared I might lose a good friend if she thought otherwise. I also feared being exposed to her parents and the matter intimated to Mamoni and Bapi.

It was a Sunday afternoon in early October. I mustered enough courage to pen down the facts and post it to Lipika with a thumping heart. During lunch, the incoming letters were distributed to the cadets and with each passing day no reply coming from her, the days started to grow even longer and the nights unbearable. At times I burst into sweat at the thought of losing her as a friend or what if her parents had read the letter. Nine days later, a pink envelope passing through a few hands from the end of the table came to me during lunch. I knew it was from Lipika. My parents always wrote on the inland letters and never sent letters in an envelope. So it couldn't be them. My heart started pounding, I was losing breath and it showed on my face. Jayant, sitting next to me, whispered, 'Her letter?' I nodded yes.

Reaching the dormitory after lunch, I rushed to the lavatory, closed the door, pulled down the seat cover of the toilet, and sat on it. On slowly tearing the envelope, a birthday greeting card peeped out, and in its fold, there was a letter written on an exercise notebook paper.

'Dear Siddhartha . . .' she had written in quite certain terms that she was elder to me, she was supposed to be my 'Didi' and I should not have written a letter like this. I was shell-shocked. I read the letter four times trying to grasp the contents. Was it all a one-sided affair? Did she really feel elder to me? How could I wrongly read those last parting moments? Was it over enthusiasm of discovering first love? I sat confused.

I looked at the greeting card, turning it over and over again. And suddenly as I opened the door, incoming light did the trick. On the backside of the card there was something written as if with the blunt backside of a pen.

Only an impression remained. I walked out of the lavatory into the daylight, tilted the card, and the world erupted into twinkling stars in many hues. 'Siddhartha, I love you.'

It took me seconds to figure out the fact. The letter must have been seen by Kekadi, and she forced Lipika to write the letter against her will. She only got a chance to scratch the sweet message before sealing the envelope under supervision. I thanked my stars that Shefali Mashi or her father had not seen the letter. If they would have, it would not be a letter in the negative only, but some nasty reactions from Mamoni and Bapi. I immediately wanted to rush a letter to her but realized that would invite more trouble. I rested the thought and carried on happily with the routine, waiting for something to happen. Three days later, there was another envelope for me at lunch. And this time, it was a letter enveloped in love. I read it again and again. I read it in the bathroom, during breaks between classes, in the playground, in bed. I always kept the letter with me. The letter had her friend's address, whose parents never opened their daughter's letters. So began the years of love affair that majorly found expression in these letters.

During vacations, I visited her, now without Mamoni. We rarely spoke. It was only in the presence of Shefali Mashi and Kekadi I told the RIMC tales, and she asked a few questions. Otherwise between two of us, it was just silence; silence that expressed more than words could ever have; silence that made our bonds even stronger; silence that nurtured our passions within. Passions that found expression in our letters. We touched, kissed, and caressed each other all through these letters. And we communicated in silence when we met in person during vacations. Silence, the divine silence of love.

Love opened up yet other avenues for me. I started studying the experimentations in the field of art and working on cubism and other modern schools. My art hobby class became the arena for me to express my pent up emotions. I took the challenge of oil painting and painted vigorously. While some made sense, others were wild experimentation with colours and textures. However worthless they might have been, they were passionate expressions of my inner self, my love. And they helped me develop certain techniques of art, giving me freedom from the bondage of realism. I did not like to paint the sceneries, still life, and figures in realistic way anymore. Though childlike, I kept experimenting with form, colour, and medium. It was great to have Mr Verma as our art teacher. He silently watched and supported the chaos in my art.

By class nine, myself, Mehta, Mankar from my class, and Patnaik, Gazmere six months junior to us, had developed a bond with a notorious twist. We often hanged out together on holidays when I was not with Jayant, Tirtha, and Roy. We had already started smoking, hiding in remote corners of the campus or when in town on leave. We planned guava raids at night in the faraway orchards with the consent of our seniors; smashed the windowpanes of teachers' residences who, our seniors thought, were acting too tough in class. And with the development of a technique of entering locked rooms through windows by removing a glass pane, our team was often assigned tasks of the evil order by our seniors. We planned and took up individual challenges all by ourselves as well, for the sheer excitement of the adventure. In fact, it was mostly the military training that was being imparted to us that we used to carry out these adventures. We felt like carrying out the covert operations in a war scenario. We got caught by the authorities many a time, ending up with rigorous official punishments. But we never felt guilty.

Gazmere and I were sort of the team leaders planning the operations. The two of us had even started drinking rum in small measures whenever we could. One of our successful heists was the raid of our bakery, where we got in through the large ventilators above the roof. We used bed sheets knotted together to scale the walls to get on top of the roof. We looted four tins of biscuits and twelve loaves of breads. It was a night-long operation, and we used the abandoned iron boiler to store our loot. Next night, the spoils were distributed among all the cadets. No one talked when our Commandant and the Adjutant called the college for investigations and we never got caught. On another occasion, we broke into the room in the education block were the question papers for the on-going Higher Secondary exams of our seniors were sealed. We managed to get a copy of the Hindi paper. But it did not work to our seniors' benefit as on discovering the leak next morning, the exam was cancelled.

Major Mangy was our Adjutant. A 'cut surd' that is a Sikh who had cut off his hairs. He was handsome, smart, and a highly eligible bachelor. He often reminded me of Marcello Mastrionni, the Italian actor whom I had seen in a few Hollywood films. There was an aura about him, and so were wild rumors floating around. He was projected as a womanizer in whispers that went around our dormitories. Many claimed they saw different girls being pillion-ridded to his residence at night. We believed he had wild parties late in the nights. Enough material for planning our next covert action—investigate the truth by breaking into his house. A rough plan was chalked out. The date was finalized as Guru Nanak's birthday. On every religious occasion, the whole college attended the function irrespective of the religion one belonged to. Particularly, the ones at the Gurudwara were looked forward to by all cadets as the 'Karha Prasad' served was very tasty and we were allowed as many helpings as we wanted. The whole college, the teachers, and officers will all be at the Gurdwara for one full hour. And hence the day fitted into our scheme of things. Enough time to raid the house, investigate, and collect evidence for seniors and return.

Four of us were from Pratap Section and Gazmere from Chandragupta. Mankar reported sick and stayed back in the dormitory. Patnaik had got his knee bruised the earlier day and took permission to go to the hospital. Mehta had taken leave and was supposed to leave for town. I decided I would go to the Gurdwara, and on the way manage to fall out. Gazmere had said he would manage himself to get away. Always there was a fall-in in front of the Section and dressed in OG, each section marched to the Gurdwara, the venue of the celebration. As we reached the Gurdwara and were dispersed, I slid into a tall hedge without anyone noticing. It helped to be in OG as the colours of hedge became a good camouflage. Slowly, the whole college walked into the Gurdwara. It was time for me to move out and take a long route avoiding the main roads to reach Major Mangy's residence.

The college wore a deserted look. The plan was to reach the hot spot individually without being noticed by anybody.

We were to meet at the back of the house. Each residence had a huge lawn in front and back, and the boundaries were marked out by tall, thick hedges. So once we were inside the boundary and if no one was there at home, chances were we will not be noticed from outside. When I reached the meeting place, all had arrived except Patnaik. We did a recce of the house to identify our entrance. The main door had a big padlock, another door next to it was high-risk zone as it was in the front of the bungalow and anybody entering the premises will immediately notice. We finalised to use the kitchen door, which was on the left flank of the building. I took a small screwdriver and started scraping the putty off the glass pane. Patnaik joined as I worked on the pane. It used to take about five minutes to remove the putty, loosen the four nails that further held the glass, and get the pane off. I put my hand through and reached for the latch at the bottom of the door from inside. All the buildings were built in the same pattern, so we knew exactly how to go about. Generally, the doors were locked from inside by two latches: one at the bottom, and one at the top of the door. So two panes were removed, one to reach the top latch, and the other for the bottom. But this time we were lucky. As I pulled open the bottom latch the door opened. The top latch was not bolted.

We entered quietly and bolted the door again from inside. Chances were anybody casually passing will not notice the single removed glass pane and will not come to know about our actions inside the house. Among us, only Mehta had a wristwatch. We saw the time. There was only half an hour for the total operation. Mehta opened the refrigerator that stood in one corner. We found some cakes and pastries and finished them. Then we moved into the bedroom. It was a well laid out room tastefully furnished. There was a glass bowl filled with loose coins on the bedside table. Patnaik went for it and pocketed the bowl clean. But I was looking around for the adult stuff that we thought must be present if the rumours were true. There was nothing that we found. I moved into the adjoining room. It was laid out with plush sofas and in the corner there were two wardrobes. Both were locked with small padlocks, the type most of us used on our cupboards. I knew the trick to open these locks with the same screwdriver. Generally the percentage of failure was very low. I put the screwdriver into the lock, a little twist, and it gave way. The cupboard was a Pandora's box. It had a movie projector, two cans of sixteen-millimetre films, which we presumed to be blue films; a bundle of Playboy magazines, many English novels of which many seemed to be pondies by their title, and two small boxes of condoms. We were all delighted. Our mission was successful. Patnaik had already collected his booty, the coins. Mehta picked up two Parker pens that were lying on the sofa side table. I flipped through a few Playboys before stuffing them inside my shirt. Gazmere and Mankar also picked up the rest of the Playboys and a few pondies.

Our operation was over. We were so confident of not getting caught that we decided to play some pranks. Mehta pulled out the roll of the sixteen-mm film and unrolled it all over the bed. Patnaik and Mankar took out the condoms, blew them into balloons and scattered them all over. We moved out, bolted the door as before, fixed the glass pane back with the four nails that was in place, cleaned the floor of the putty waste, and left. We moved out individually to avoid being noticed being in a group.

The college still wore a deserted look. There was still time before everybody would return from the Gurdwara. On safely returning to the dormitory, I sat down on my bed to go through the Playboys. It was my first initiation to the women's body in the nude. I had seen a few painted nudes in some painting books but they were tame to what I was leafing through. We did read pondies but the visual exploration of the women's body in nude got me highly excited. I placed the Playboys under my mattress and headed for the lavatory. When I came back after masturbation, Mehta, Patnaik, and Mankar were there. Other cadets were trickling in as well. There was still some time for lunch. Four of us collected all the Playboys and went to our Section Commander's room. We handed over the magazines and books. He immediately called all his classmates to his room to listen to our scoop. Two days passed without any sign of trouble. We were becoming confident about our success. During the third day lunch, after the operation, an orderly came to our table and informed our Section Commander that Adjutant had called Patnaik to his office after lunch. I still thought it was for something else until after lunch, Patnaik told me that Major Mangy's orderly had spotted him on the day while he was moving out of the hot spot, though a little away from the bungalow. I broke the news to Mehta and Mankar. Four of us got together in the Kit Room to discuss the pros and cons.

'Walking by the house does not prove that you had broken in.' Mankar told Patnaik.

'Yes, just deny any knowledge of the break in.' I reaffirmed him.

'Just don't break down.' Mehta tried to add some confidence. Patnaik left for Adjutant's office. Fear had set in all of us but we had not panicked yet. I was a little apprehensive, as I knew that Patnaik was the weakest link in our team. We did not have to wait long. As the bell rang for hobby clubs, Patnaik walked into the dormitory and said the Adjutant wanted all five of us in his office. We knew he had spilled the beans and we were caught. Panic struck.

On the way to the office, we decided that we will return the coins, the pens, and accept eating the cakes and pastries from the fridge, but not to mention anything about the Playboys and the pondies as those were not with us anymore.

As we entered his office, Major Mangy stood up from his chair and growled, 'What all have you stolen from my house?'

As decided, Patnaik owned up about the coins and Mehta about the pens.

'Come out with the facts.' Major Mangy said in a low and cold voice.

'I have not taken up the matter officially. I am giving you an hour to get all the stuff to my house. And by saying all the stuff, I mean all. You buggers know better. It's three twenty now, by four thirty I want five of you at my house with all, I repeat, all the things. Or else you will face severe consequences. Disperse.'

We saluted and left. When we reached back, the seniors at the dormitory were already aware that we were caught.

'Just don't take our names that we are aware and just deny stealing the magazines and the books,' our Section Commander told us.

At four thirty, when we returned to Major Mangy's residence with the pens and the coins only, our fate was sealed.

'That's all!' Major Mangy exclaimed.

We kept quiet.

'You are awarded the highest punishment. You will be caned bareback in front of the whole college. Disperse.'

Next day, it was officially notified that all five of us will be caned bareback. The reason was breaking into Major Mangy's house and stealing things. The whole college was ordered to fall in at the Drill Square after lunch on the day. Our Cadet Captain read out the order in the mess during lunch. I wanted the whole affair to finish off fast. All the cadets were querying about the incident. The teachers and officers looked at us in contempt. Only the seniors were sympathetic and we knew why. I did not take lunch.

It was two-thirty. The whole college had fallen in at the Drill Square. The Cadet Captain got the college to attention and reported to the Adjutant. A JCO was holding a plate on which the cane rested. Major Mangy handed over the order to the Cadet Captain. A full drill followed. He read aloud the order. Our Section Commanders made us fall out and marched us to the Cadet Captain, who in turn marched us to Major Mangy. He did not speak to us. The JCO ordered us to take off our shirts and vests, bend down, and touch the toes. Our backs lay bare facing the sky awaiting the pain. First it was Patnaik. With the very first cane, he cried out loudly and by the third he was sitting on the ground crying. I imagined the pain. Major Mangy was not just caning. He was lashing out his fierce anger. Anger on losing his well-kept secret; anger on his private sensual world being exposed. Next was my turn. I could not cry. I could not lose my image of being tough in front of the whole college, particularly my juniors. I imagined Lipika's face and closed my eyes. Zap. Zap. Zap.

And then it was Mehta, Mankar, and Gazmere. It was over. But the Playboys made rounds of the senior dormitories till the end of the term.

Class nine semester was an eventful one. The seeds of want for chaos were being sowed within. Bollywood films continued in large doses and they made their dent too. The heroes starting from nothing and becoming great successes, the self-made man, finally winning his heartthrob, what an inspiration. It was one such stay in the hospital during a November evening that Pandey, my classmate, visited me. I expressed that life at the campus was boring and we got to do something about it. He seemed to agree and soon we decided that we ought to leave campus and venture out on our own, make a livelihood, and become successful.

It did not take much time to conceive the plan to run away. The very same night during the study hours, Pandey would excuse himself and come to the dormitory. We, cadets, were not allowed to keep cash but we all had a little hidden in our cupboards. To venture out, we needed cash and together we had three rupees, which we thought were not enough. One by one we broke open six cupboards. We collected twelve rupees and a Click III instamatic camera from Ashwin's cupboard. There was a greatcoat hanging in the Kit room, and we took that as well. The greatcoat was of great value to us. Though it was supposed to be returned to the college authority on passing out, most students sold it to the orderlies. It fetched a good ninety rupees. So with the greatcoat with us, we were ninety rupees richer. We packed a little of the necessities like toothbrush, toothpaste, comb, etc., a few dresses into my dressing gown, and left in the darkness of the night. We knew the alarm would be sounded when Pandey will be missing from the dinner table. As for me, it would be till next morning when bed tea will be served in the hospital.

We decided not to go to the station, as that would be the first spot college authorities would raid. We walked down the Rajpur road. We were quite tensed till we crossed the city limits and reached the highway. We kept signaling the passing by trucks for a lift but with little success. It was late into the night that one truck stopped and asked us to hop in.

'Where do you both want to go?' the driver asked.

'We are going home.' I replied.

'But why at this time of the night and where is your home?'

Too many questions at a time, to be handled right. But I just managed, 'In our hostel seniors beat us up badly. So we are running away in the night, or otherwise they will not allow us to go home.'

I must have sounded pretty convincing. He spoke to his helper in Punjabi which we did not understand but could feel his sympathy for us.

'Hop in. Where will you go?' he asked again in Hindi.

'Drop us at the nearest Railway Station on your way and we will manage.'

'There is Muzzaffarnagar coming up and it has a station. I will drop you there.'

We thanked and kept quiet.

We disembarked from the truck onto this ghost of a town, Muzzaffarnagar. Well, on a dark cold winter morning, when the dawn breaks late, any such town would be thus. There were a few cart pullers gearing up for the day's routine. We asked them the way to the station. It was nearby. The yellow board at the station mentioned the train timings. There were only two main cities where the trains headed for. One for Delhi, and the other for Shimla. Pandey suggested that we head for Shimla. His logic, there would be apple orchards and we could find work there. I argued for Delhi. My logic, being a big city there would be many shops and finding a job would be easier. Childish visions influenced by some of the most popular Bollywood films; surely not the right recipe to make it big in life.

We finalized Delhi and bought two tickets. The first morning light was breaking in. The city was waking up to a new day. Our train was to pass the station much later in the morning. We walked down the nearly empty lanes. A few people sat in a corner around a bon fire to escape the winter chill. We were hungry. We asked them if we could find some eatery. They pointed to a shanty down the lane but it had not opened. We walked to it and sat on the wooden bench kept outside.

It must have been another hour later; two men came wrapped in blankets and took seat beside us.

'When will this shop open?' I asked.

'Just anytime now,' One of the strangers replied.

Pandey had taken out the camera and was fiddling with it.

'From where are you?' the man next to Pandey questioned.

'We are going to Delhi.' he replied.

'Show the camera.' the man took the camera from Pandey and started exploring its functions. I explained him the details.

'We need some cash.' I wanted to sell it off, 'Do you want to buy it?'

'How much will you sell it for?'

I found him taking interest. I knew a brand new Click III camera cost sixty bucks.

'Thirty rupees,' I offered. The shop owner had arrived and started the regular chores to get the shop going.

'I can buy it for ten rupees,' the stranger took out a ten-rupee note from his pocket.

I took the camera from his hand, 'Not less than twenty.'

He took out another five-rupee note and the camera was sold for fifteen rupees. Till last night it belonged to Ashwin. Just by the break of the dawn it will now take pictures for this unknown stranger in this faraway small town of Muzzaffarnagar. The shop was not an eatery. It was only a tea stall. We had a cup of tea and five big, locally-made biscuits, and headed for the station.

It was a local train halting at all stations. We reached Delhi only by afternoon. We walked out of the crowded platforms of Old Delhi Station into the pleasant winter sunlight. It was pandemonium outside. Coolies, cycle rickshaws, autos, people all in a hurry added to the confusion. I had been to Delhi with my parents in childhood but the memory had faded. This was my first real time encounter with the city of Delhi and I did not like it. It resembled the Burra Bazaar area of Calcutta: crowded and disarrayed.

It was much later when I came to Delhi for my UPSC exams that I actually discovered true Delhi, the New Delhi and the cosmopolitan, modern Delhi. Near the station gate, there was a makeshift cart selling hot, fresh, Chhole Bhature. Three Bhatures and Chhole for a rupee. At Moti Mahal, we got two for ninety paise, and even the size of the Bhaturas were smaller. For the first time, we had a plate each. We kept walking through stream of unknown faces, melting into the strangers with no one asking about our identity. We felt reassured. The area seemed to be a busy market place with shops flanking both sides of the street. I thought we were at the right place to start searching for a job. As we passed a cinema hall with big posters depicting sensually dressed women, a man with a dagger in hand and a big 'A' at the right hand corner in a circle, both of us communicated, as if through telepathy. We looked at each other and we knew we wanted to see the film.

'We will start looking for the job after the film.' Pandey said and I agreed. But we were disappointed. Being an adult film, tickets were denied to us. Not to give up and with the craving for a film, we enquired from the counter and landed at the next cinema hall. 'Samadhi' was being screened. We bought two tickets and moved in.

As the film unfolded, I slowly withdrew into myself. The sounds faded away, the scenes just moved meaninglessly and faded away too. I could see Mamoni, Bapi and my little sister Shampa, our home in Calcutta. I felt a lump in my throat. The busy street that we came through suddenly became deserted. It was dark and cold all around. The shops lay unmanned and the showcases empty. At the end of the road, a faint light of a candle from a shop across the road beckoned me. I ran frantically towards it, banged into a streetlight pole, and fell down. Blood was oozing out of my forehead as I lay on the pavement and looked up. With a fluid motion, the pole swayed down and wrapped around my body, and jettisoned me into dark unknown space. I shrieked. The lights came on. It was interval. I was sweating as I looked at Pandey. We both felt homesick.

We decided that we were going back home after the film. With the tension gone, we enjoyed the second half of the film.

At the station, we found out that Lucknow Mail was departing at eight thirty. We came out on the road and had Chhole Bhature from the same stall and cold drinks from a nearby paan shop for dinner. I bought a packet of cigarettes and a match. I lit a cigarette. We had spent quite a substantial portion of our cash. There were twelve rupees left. We shared six each and decided to keep it for emergency and travel home 'WT', that is, 'without ticket'.

WT travelling was nothing new to us. I was introduced to it at the end of my very first semester when we were travelling back home for vacations. All the cadets travelling East were taking the Doon Express. A whole compartment was booked under military quota. As soon as we were dropped at the Dehradun Railway Station I saw all queue up in front of a counter barring five cadets. I was also asked to stand in the queue by one of my seniors. They were returning their train tickets and taking a refund. Jayant, who was among those who were not in the queue, explained the system to me. Being a military compartment, no ticket examiner came to the compartment. So there was no need for the ticket. This money from refund was used by all as pocket money during the vacation.

'But how will we get out at Howrah station?' I questioned.

'You don't worry about that. You will come to know.' Jayant replied.

'And why are you not returning your ticket?' I asked Jayant.

'I have a railway pass.' I knew his father was working for Indian Railways. We got ninety-three rupees and some paisa as refund. It was a great feeling to think that I will be rich during the vacation. The train started at 9:10 in the evening and travelling the whole of next day, it reached Howrah at ten in the morning the day after. On reaching our destination, all the cadets handed over thirty paisa to the five who had not refunded their tickets. I realized that all these five had Railway passes. They went out of the gate and came back with platform tickets for the rest of us. We walked out as if we had come to receive these five friends with railway passes.

We reached Lucknow next morning. We spotted an opening in the barricade beside the station, which was being used by many passengers to get out instead of the main exit. I understood that they were all WT travelers. We took the same route to get out of the station.

Pandey was from Pratapgarh, which was not far away from Lucknow. I suggested that we sell off the greatcoat and buy tickets for the rest of our journey home. Pandey disagreed and would not part with the greatcoat. A quarrel ensued and we parted our ways.

From the Enquiry Office, I learnt of the next train to Howrah. It was already on the platform. I boarded a general compartment and stood near the gate. Without ticket, I did not have the courage to occupy a seat. Slowly it got crowded before it started and I sat on the floor with many other passengers near the door. It was after a long spell with only the sound of the moving train on the tracks that the man sitting next to me asked, 'Are you WT?' I was taken a little aback, and did not know what to reply. But soon, I felt the man to be harmless and replied in the affirmative.

'Where are you heading to?'

'Howrah.' I replied.

'Don't travel by this train,' he suggested. 'There are many ticket examiners on board. Get down at Rae Bairelly and take the Punjab Mail from there. It will be safer.'

I followed his advice and reached Howrah safely the next morning. As the train slowed down in the yard, I alighted and got out through an iron gate. Once outside the railway compound, I felt safe. I took a taxi to home and when I arrived, I lied about being beaten up by seniors. Mamoni sympathized with me but Bapi packed me back to the college three days on.

Thus, that ended the scripting of a Bollywood blockbuster.

CHAPTER 4

14ᵀᴴ August, 1947. SK sat down in front of his radio in his Sinthee flat listening to Jawaharlal Nehru.

'Long years ago, we made a tryst with destiny, and now the time comes when we shall redeem our pledge, not wholly or in full measure, but very substantially. At the stroke of the midnight hour, when the world sleeps, India will awake to life and freedom. A moment comes, which comes but rarely in history, when we step out from the old to the new, when an age ends, and when the soul of a nation, long suppressed, finds utterance. It is fitting that at this solemn moment we take the pledge of dedication to the service of India and her people and to the still larger cause of humanity . . .'

SK was a young marine engineer in the British Navy. He had the option to continue in the re-christened Indian Navy of independent India. But he wanted to step out of the old routine. Running away from home at sixteen and joining the British Navy as a crew, and riding the high seas through the World War II in a minesweeper while pursuing certification in Marine Engineering, had him tired.

Getting in touch with family after four years at sea made him home sick. His father had died when he was a child and he had only faint memories of him. But the joint family in Khulna that he belonged to had many loving members. There were uncles, aunts, his elder brother and sister, six cousins, and his mother to pamper him. He actually never missed his father. He was a happy child. But after completing Matriculation, an inner urge to explore the unknown had him run away. He continued for four years in the British Navy while graduating to be a Marine Engineer.

But now, the time had come to be with the family, to rekindle the old loving relationships that he had left behind. He joined the Calcutta Port Commissioners. He could not go back to Khulna as India had been partitioned, and now Khulna was in East Pakistan. Moreover, he had to sail in and out of Calcutta Port. He rented a flat in Sinthee and planned to get mother and all the members of the family who wanted to come over to India. Thus, he could have a slice of the past around him. It was the reason he had rented a three-room big flat.

India had become independent from the British Raj, but two hundred years of cultural domination had left its mark. The leaders wore 'khadi' but most were Anglicized in their behavior and thinking. Same was the case with most city dwellers. The club culture, the live shows, the live band at the bars, and restaurants in Calcutta, all remained.

SK was a chain smoker, an occasional drinker at social dos and at the club, which he became member of on joining Calcutta Port Commissioners. He would swear by British etiquette, but he had not forgotten his roots. He would still bend down and touch the feet of elders as a mark of respect and he would never smoke in front of elders. Soon his flat was chock-a-block with his mother, elder sister and her husband, with two daughters and three cousins coming down from Khulna. He often had to sail out but now not into the high seas, but down the river Hooghly till the Sand head where the river met the sea. Whenever he was in town, he would catch up with the latest Hollywood film, and spend time in the club playing cards. If there was a weekend thrown in during his stay, he would visit the RCTC race course to bet a few bucks on racing horses.

One evening, as SK sat on the high bar stool enjoying his drink, Chakraborty, a colleague, walked in. There was a gorgeous lady by his side and they walked in straight to the bar counter.

'Hi, SK, this is Jyotsna,' Chakraborty introduced the lady. 'You must have seen her. She is a heroine of Bengali films . . .' he muttered out a few names of Bengali films which were all Greek to SK. He never watched Bengali films, but thinking that expressing ignorance would be discourteous to the gracious lady.

'Of course I have seen her. She was gorgeous in the film I saw.' He lied.

Jyotsna held out her hand and instead of shaking it, SK planted a small kiss on it.

'You are very handsome,' Jyotsna told SK.

'Oh, thank you. But would think twice before I would propose you for a date,' SK flirted. 'To say you are beautiful would be far from the mark. By the way what would you prefer?'

'A Tom Collins,' she replied.

'I would take my usual. A large whiskey on the rocks,' Chakraborty added and lit his thick cigar. Ordering the drinks and a plate of snacks, SK led Chakraborty and Jyotsna to a table.

The bar hall was big. But it had a stuffy atmosphere with everybody around smoking. Some were smoking cigarettes; some cigars, while some were enjoying pipes. It smelled strange with a concoction of perfumes, tobacco smoke, and different kinds of liquors. A Bing Cosby number was playing on the radiogram. There were four aged men at a table in one of the corners. They talked in low voice, and at intervals burst out into loud laughter. Must be sharing some dirty jokes. There was a fat middle-aged man with a fat cigar in his mouth on another table. He showed no interest in his even fatter wife on the table. He was drooling over the lady in sleeveless blouse and sari on the next table. Three young officers sat on the bar counter on high stools and were engrossed in their own world. But now with Jyotsna in the room, glances from all corners started being fleeted towards her.

'I was not wrong to say that you were more than just being beautiful,' SK said to Jyotsna. 'Do you feel the glances all around?'

Jyotsna was enjoying the attention she had generated. 'But it would have been same for you if it would have been in a women's joint.' She returned the compliment.

'Can I ask you for a dance?' SK asked.

'But I don't know how to do dance,' She said.

'Don't worry. Come with me, I will teach you a few steps.' SK held out his hand for her. 'Chakraborty we will be back from the Ball Room in a little while.'

Chakraborty had nothing to say but accept with a nod. SK and Jyotsna walked out to the Ball Room hand in hand.

The Ball Room was a large hall with a very high ceiling and chandeliers hanging from it. There was a live band playing soft English numbers. Many couples were dancing on the floor while some stood on the sides watching. SK led Jyotsna onto the floor. He held her right hand with his left, and slid his right arm around her waist.

'You also put your arm on my shoulder,' he guided her. The locking of arms got them close. He directed her a few steps and she tried to follow. Soon they were in smooth motion with some right steps, some wrong, and with a little improvisation. They held each other closer and tighter. SK could feel her bosoms on his chest and she could feel his thighs rubbing against her pelvis. Jyotsna put both her arms around SK's neck and he got him tighter onto his body by wrapping his arms around her waist. They danced along exploring each other's body till the band paused for the next number. SK kneeled down on one of his knees and took her hand and planted a kiss as a mark of thanks. They walked out of the floor with arms around each other's waist. A bond was in the making. A bond of love laced with physical attraction.

Soon, SK and Jyotsna became the talk of the club. They would bolt in like a gush of fresh air into otherwise staid atmosphere. They were like wanton lust surging through the arteries of otherwise an impotent dangling penis. And who would not love it? Most of the people soon became acquaintances. Some close enough to share a drink and some just 'Hi' types. SK and Jyotsna would drive in her car, have a few drinks, dance to several numbers, walk in the lawn under moonlight, and at times, fleet footedly move into the shade of a tree and lock themselves into a long deep kiss.

He took her to the club, the RCTC Race Course, the Hollywood movies, and to fine restaurants. She took him to the sets of her shooting, for long drives down winding roads into the suburbs, to her house, into her bedroom. Jyotsna lived in a palatial house. She only had her mother, and a maidservant staying with her. She had lost her father long back. The first time SK visited her house, he was introduced to her mother. She was in the late fifties and seemed to be a reclusive lady and did not talk much. She left soon after the introduction, to disappear into one of the many big rooms, never to reappear. In fact SK had met her only that one time till he saw her again being carried away for cremation on death after three years.

As Jyotsna's mother left, she threw herself on SK and looked up for a kiss. With no one around and the privacy of the room adding to the romantic ambience, he pulled her up onto himself and kissed like he had never kissed before. Jyotsna suddenly broke off.

'Come with me,' she said.

He followed her as she led him into her bedroom. This too was a large room with an intricately carved wooden four-poster bed at one corner. There was a large dressing table with a big life-sized mirror flanked by equally big movable side panel mirrors. There was a rocking chair and a set of sofa. There were a few wooden wardrobes on one wall. Jyotsna opened one of the wardrobes and took out a bottle of whiskey.

'You keep whiskey at home?' SK asked.

'I have to. In the film industry, most people drink. Nobody asks for tea after sundown,' she explained. She walked out as SK rested on the sofa and looked around. She came back with two glasses, a bottle of soda, an ice bucket filled with ice, and a jug of water on a large silver tray.

'Should I pour the drinks?' she asked as she kept the tray on the centre table.

'Let me have the pleasure,' SK took the bottle and unscrewed it.

SK had learnt the art of lovemaking from the Hollywood films. He loved the foreplay as much as the fuck. He believed as much in the journey as in the goal. He always fantasized foreplay while masturbating. Now, he was living his fantasy. Jyotsna lay naked on the ruffled satin bed sheet with eyes closed. The conservative backdrop of the Bengali society made the women of the era a passive partner in sex. Many even were ignorant about orgasm and thought that providing pleasure to the partner was a woman's ultimate goal of sex. Some were slightly forward thinking, knew about orgasm, and faked it if the partner ejaculated early; but could never demand one's own orgasm. But Jyotsna, being from the more free-thinking, and to some extent promiscuous film fraternity of the days, when women were not held in high esteem for being associated with films, was conscious of her own sexuality. She had flirted quite a few times earlier and even slept with a producer to land a coveted role in a film. That was before SK breezed into her life.

The two drinks were working in her brain. She undressed SK behind her closed eyes. He had a good, fair body with slight hint of muscles in the right places. A tight tummy, a rarity among the people she mingled with. She opened her eyes as SK pulled out his brief, letting loose the imprisoned rebellious dick. It was not fair-skinned, as SK otherwise was. It was very dark brown, which she had never expected on a fair complexioned man. She closed her eyes again. In her mind, she had distaste for the look of a naked man below the waist. It looked so ghastly and odd. She felt a hardened cock broke the symmetry of a well-shaped man; it was like a bulging belly, like hair out of nostrils, like overgrown dirty nails. It was nasty. But it was there where the pleasure dwelt.

Jyotsna felt a light kiss on her cheek, and again one a little below, one on the nape. She lay thinking next will be on the lips. But SK moved down. He did not touch her and kept his hands and body consciously away from her. Next one on the neck, but this was not a kiss. Jyotsna felt SK's tip of the tongue give a succinct lick. The lick moved down, exploring her heaving breasts. It moved around like a nimble-footed nomad lost in the maze of sand dunes. The more he explored, the more he got lost and his pace increased. He crossed over one dune to face the highs of another. He did not even realize he was going in circles around the same dunes. Jyotsna wanted to reach out and pull SK onto her. But she resisted herself and clutched the bed sheet instead. She had never felt anything like this. She could feel herself wet, very wet down under. The lick reached the nipple and transformed into a swirl around it and a very soft suck.The nomad suddenly found his way. He moved down the dune onto the subtly undulated planes of the midriff, the belly, the pelvis. A hint of touch on the tip of the cunt and Jyotsna could not hold herself. She clasped the bed sheet tighter than before and pulled her legs up. SK's strong hands held her legs by the knees and straightened them out once again. She knew there was more to come. The journey continued down the inner thighs, behind the knees, slowly onto the feet. He took her toe into his mouth and sucked it hard.

Jyotsna gasped for air and wanted SK to penetrate immediately, but suddenly, there was nothing happening. There was no sound, no touch. Time stopped. There was no SK. As she prepared to open her eyes, she felt SK's strong hands holding her legs and parting them. His face banged into her pelvis and his tongue penetrating her vagina. She never expected it and did not get the time to stop him. It was all messy down there; and now his saliva adding onto the mess. He sucked, licked, tickled, and ate into her. She reached out with both hands and held him by his hair and pressed him further down into herself. She cried out, 'Do it, do it,' as she burst into her orgasm. As her body slackened with fulfillment, SK planted soft kisses on and around her vagina. He raised his arms and softly pressed both her breasts.

She held his hands and got him up. 'Come into me,' she said.

'No. We do not have a condom,' he replied. 'I will masturbate. Give me a kiss.'

She started a deep kiss but SK soon moved onto her breasts. He squeezed and sucked hard, alternating between the breasts while masturbating with one hand.

The engine room of the steamship deep down within, geared up for action. SK stood on the riveted steel plated floor as the boiler khalasi shoveled more coal into the boiler; red-hot, raw fire. The khalasi closed the lid of the Lancashire boiler. The mercury level rising, rising flames of passion. Unbearable heat. Sweat trickling down the forehead. SK checked the pressure on the pressure gauge; a bit too high, a bit too fast. He pulled down the stopcock lever to release a little of pent up lust; a moment of stillness; a moment of void. He closed his eyes and pulled the lever to start engine. Slowly, the giant machine all around him got going. Twang, clang, clatter, and rumble. He moved around in the maze of gigantic mechanical motions; pressurized steam hissing out every now and then. The large pistons moving up and down, puffing and panting. The crankshaft transferring the motion to the giant wheel; the wheel converting the linear motion to rotary motion. Mechanicality of masturbating changing the hormone pattern in the body: a gush of testosterone to the brain, a metamorphosis of the action from the body to the mind. He held her tight and sucked her breast deep into himself as he ejaculated on the bed sheet, on her.

SK was junior engineer on board of a small steamship that measured the depth of the bed of Hooghly river. Silting used to occur which restricted the entry of the ocean liners into the Calcutta Port. So dredgers, which were ships with huge buckets on two giant wheels, were used to dredge the bed of the river to maintain the necessary depth for the ocean liners.

SK's steamship, White Star, collected the data on the nature of silting. As the ship chugged down the river, two crews stood on scaffoldings lowered from both starboard and portside of the vessel, and alternately threw a big lead ball fixed to a long, thick, rope, into the river. The ball went down and rested on the bed of the river. The rope had knots tied at equal intervals and noting the knot just above the water level, the crew called out the depth in some strange language. It was something like 'ek bom satija', 'char bom atija', etc. The call was in a typical rhythm in continuation of the folk song that they sang through the work. Another man standing on the upper deck with the officers used to translate the depth from colloquial native language to English, as the Second Officer marked it on the chart. A pretty primitive process, but it is 1948.

All the deck officers turned out in starched white gear with pee cap. First Officer noted the path of the ship using a sextant while the Captain guided the ship, often interacting with the Chief Engineer who in turn gave orders to the other engineers in the engine room. SK had to spend most of the time in the engine room in his boiler suit. It was a white dungaree, which hardly remained white by the end of the day due to grease and oil stains. It was only for dinner that he could use his uniform.

It was a much slower pace of life on the ship than it was in the Navy. The river was calm. It only became a little turbulent near the Sand heads; no riding the high waves of the Indian Ocean along the east coast of Africa, or in the Arabian Sea; no tension of being torpedoed by German U-boats. The destroyers providing cover only reminded you of the looming danger. During the World War II days, he had developed the hobby of photography by reading books. He even bought an Agfa camera and recorded the turbulent waters of World War II in black & white. He had an album full of B2-size photographs of torpedoes being fired, guns booming, shells bursting and ripping open the high seas.

Now he explored the calmer waters. The fishermen in their dingy boats throwing nets, the villages on the banks, the sunset at the Sand heads, and portraits of Jyotsna on his cabin bedside table. During his fifteen to twenty days sailing trips, he missed Jyotsna. He kept her close by writing letters. It made him feel as if he was talking to her and the distance vanished. At times, some letters reached even after SK was back to Calcutta; but it hardly mattered to Jyotsna. She read each letter and collected them in a jewellery box.

Jyotsna's career as a heroine had lost its sheen. Both her last films flopped at the box office. She was not worried; she joined the industry as a child artist after her father's death, and matured into a heroine. It was more out of the immediate need of her family that she joined the film world, rather than any fascination for it. She had never nurtured any ambition to be a great heroine. Time only led her to whatever she was today. She had a house, had saved some money, and wanted to settle down as a housewife. SK had not yet proposed but she was sure that he would one day. She was content, and the dwindling offers for films did not bother her.

SK's life also chugged along like his steamship till one day, he brought Jyotsna to his Sinthee flat to introduce her to his mother. And all hell broke loose. Saudamini, SK's mother, did not need any introduction on Jyotsna. She had seen her in a film with her elder son in Khulna, before partition. That was the second of the only two films she had ever seen in her life: the other being on a biography of Ram Krishna Paramhansa, the revered saint of Bengal. She could not believe her eyes when she saw her own son walking in with the heroine of a film. The film was a social drama with Jyotsna playing the role of a bold, modern, young lady. Being orthodox in her outlook, the film left a negative impression on Saudamini's mind and she had decided never to see a film again. She had even scolded her elder son for taking her to such a film. Above all, she hated the heroine. And here she was, walking in with SK.

She did not react in the presence of Jyotsna, but as soon as she was gone, 'What do you mean when you say that she is your friend?' Saudamini burst out. 'Don't you know that film heroines are all spoilt girls? They don't have any character. Today she is roaming with you; tomorrow it will be someone else. You have only grown up by the years, when will your brain mature!'

No amount of explanation or pleading could change the scenario. 'I just don't want you to meet her anymore,' Saudamini spelt out her distaste.

SK continued meeting Jyotsna. He did not tell her about his mother's reaction, but he had to delay his plans of proposing to her.

Saudamini did not delay. She shot out letters in all directions to relatives and acquaintances. The message was clear: 'My son Subodh has grown up and has a stable service. I want to get him married at the earliest. Send in proposals of would-be brides, for me to take immediate decision.'

And proposals started flowing in soon. Every evening Saudamini, SK's elder sister, and her two daughters went through the day's mail. They would read the letter, see the picture, and keep the shortlisted ones separated. One evening when SK came back from office, Saudamini took 20 shortlisted letters and photographs to him. While enjoying the evening cup of tea, he started reading them:

'. . . she is homely, sweet, can cook for 20 people. She has studied till class eight and can even read ABCD in English . . .'

'. . . beautiful, the photograph does not give the clear picture. Allow us to bring her to your house and your son can have a look . . .'

'. . . healthy, actually she is from a well-to-do family. Her parents are keen to tie her knot and ready to offer whatever dowry you ask for . . .'

'her hair runs well beyond her buttocks, she is sturdy and has always lived in a joint family. Will be ideal for your son . . .'

'Matrick pass, can read and write in English, has read Rabindranath, Sarat Chandra. She can cook delicious dishes and is adept at household work . . .'

After bearing through five of them, SK burst out laughing.

'Do you think marriage is a joke?' Saudamini was angered.

'But this sounds like a cattle market. I am not into this,' SK retorted and left for a wash.

He knew he had bought some more time. But how long could he carry on? After every four five days, Saudamini would come over with another bunch of shortlisted candidates. The more the options, the more he grew jittery. He opened up to Jyotsna one evening at the club. She was expecting such a situation. She could feel it coming after visiting SK's mother; she saw him getting restless. She could see her dreams of marrying SK and settling down breaking into pieces. She felt a lump choking her throat. Holding back her tears she said, 'Shu, what can you do? A marriage is not a personal goal. It is a family bonding and you have to accept your elders' decisions. It is always like that.'

'But I cannot think of marrying anyone but you,' SK said.

'It is not what you think. I know we love each other, but we are not destined to get married. You have to think about your family. The bride is not going to be only your wife, but she is also equally a member of your extended family.'

Women are always more rational and restrained than they seem to be. Men are more extreme in their reaction. One would either care two figs, or break down. And SK broke down.

* * *

Chaibasa was a small district town in Bihar. SK got down from the train. The station had only two platforms: one for the 'up' train, and the other for the 'down' train. There were twenty other relatives with him. He was dressed in a white 'dhoti' and a 'punjabi'. He had this strange looking headgear called 'topor' on his head. He felt he must be looking like an idiot, but that's the way would be Bengali groom is supposed to look, an idiot.

The bride's family was there to receive the groom. As they walked out of the station, SK saw a string of cycle rickshaws standing. The leading one was decorated with flowers. A brass band burst into action as he boarded the decorated rickshaw. All the passersby had stopped to have a look at the groom from Calcutta. The procession moved on with the band leading the pack, making an awful noise. The hosts walked by the side of his rickshaw, while SK's relatives followed in the other rickshaws. SK felt like a clown but could do nothing.

The house was down a lane from the main road. It was a single-storey house in 'L' shape with thatched roof, and portions with terracotta tiles. There was a huge open courtyard inside with a 'Bael' and a pomegranate tree in the centre. Under the 'Bael' tree, a tarpaulin had been put up and decorated for the ritual of marriage.

After the groom's side freshened up, they were served tea in small terracotta containers called 'khuris' and 'Britannia Thin Arrowroot' biscuits. Biscuits were a luxury and the Thin Arrowroot was the cheapest available. The ritual of marriage was slated for 12:05 p.m. The time of such auspicious functions were always decided by the priest consulting an almanac called 'Panjika'. SK was escorted to the 'mandap', the venue of marriage under the tarpaulin, and seated on the ground on a rectangular wooden, two-inch high platform called 'piri'. There was another one beside him. He knew it was for the bride.

Suddenly, there was a burst of blowing conch shells amidst a strange vibrating sound being delivered by the women, by moving their tongue in a typical manner controlling the guttural sound that they were blowing out. This was known as 'ulu', an auspicious sound for happy occasions. Together it was like an oral band which reached its crescendo as the bride was brought in sitting on a 'piri' being carried high on their shoulders by her brothers and their friends.

Sandhya, the bride, held two beetle leaves over her face. She was not supposed to look at the would-be groom till the auspicious moment. With the priest chanting the Holy Scriptures, Sandhya was guided to lower the beetle leaf from her face and look at SK.

When the bride's family visited SK's house with Sandhya, he had seen her. She was very fair and beautiful. Now with amateurish make-up, she looked bad. It was all chalky. She was better off without make-up, SK thought. The ritual started and continued for the next hour with the burst of conch shells and 'ulu' at intervals. And at the end of it, Sandhya and SK became man and wife, married.

It was time to take lunch. SK was feeling hungry as he was fasting. The last meal was the dinner in the train last night. The bride and the groom were supposed to fast till the end of the marriage ritual. Now with the lavish spread specially laid out for him, he felt the pangs even stronger. It was truly a meal spread fit for a king; but for a Bengali king.

On a large bronze plate, there was fragrant steamed rice heaped like a hillock in the centre. Around it were a piece of lemon with salt, cooked green spinach, fried delicacies like aubergines, 'papads', fried pumpkin slices covered in rice powder paste, deep-fried head of a big fish—'Rohu'. Around the plate, in bronze tumblers, were pulse cooked with head of fish, two vegetables, a dish of cottage cheese, a large slice of 'Rohu' in gravy, jumbo prawns cooked in coconut milk, mutton curry, sweet and sour preparation of green mangoes, to round off with a plate of assorted sweets.

SK knew he could not even finish quarter of the spread. As he sat down on the floor on a 'piri', his three sister-in-laws sat around him to guide him through this gourmet tour. The youngest of them continuously fanned with a fan made of dried palm leaf to keep SK's sweat away, and the flies at bay. He relished non-vegetarian food, so there was no point in going through the whole spread and started with pulse cooked with head of a fish.

After the afternoon siesta, when SK got up, he saw a flurry of activities in the open courtyard. Bamboo poles were being erected at equal intervals all around the courtyard. He did not understand till it was evening and he found there was no electricity in the house. On enquiring, he came to know that there was no electricity in the entire Chaibasa; even the street lamps were fuelled by gas. There was a person designated for the work, and every evening he had to go around the streets carrying a ladder and light each roadside lamp one by one.

Big lanterns were hung from the bamboo poles, and smaller ones were placed in each room. The cumulative effect of all the lanterns did light up the house and the courtyard quite reasonably. But SK could imagine the eeriness that would creep in the nights but for the festival tonight. Local guests started moving in to see and shower blessings to the newlyweds.

The female members became busy receiving the guests, arranging tea and snacks, while the male were busy laying out the rugs in the courtyard for the reception dinner, backing up the professional cook who was hired for the night. Suddenly, the flurry of activities increased as SK sat with Sandhya by his side, being introduced to all the new relatives that he had acquired through marriage. It was boring and tiring as well. He did not even remember a single introduction and had to bend and touch the feet of all the elders. Quite a task, when the number of guests was more than two hundred.

He looked out of the door into the courtyard. The first batch of guests had taken their seats on the ground and Sandhya's brothers and their friends had started doing the rounds, serving. Back in Bengal, food was served on banana leaf. But Bihar, being the land of 'Saal', here the plates were made of 'Saal' leaf. Otherwise, it was the same routine: Terracotta glasses for drinking water, 'luchi' - a fried bread preparation being served from cane baskets to start the dinner, followed by rice and other delicacies served from brass buckets.

On such occasions each guest was force-fed. 'No, no you must try this.' 'Ok, take one more piece of fish.' 'I know you need more mutton.' Nobody had to ask for anything. There was always excess food on the plates, and there was a lot of wastage as well. The beggars always gathered outside a house hosting a marriage and waited for these wastes to be dumped. They made a big feast out of the leftovers fighting among themselves and trying to keep the street dogs at bay.

It took a few months for the euphoria of being newlywed and carefree fucking, giving way to more realistic adjustments that go into a marriage. Food was not the problem area as both were ready to experiment like they did in sex. SK introduced Sandhya to pork sausages, ham, and Chinese cuisine; while she introduced him to snacks from Bihar like gram flour dough with mango pickle oil, 'litti'—a typical roasted dimsum stuffed with spiced gram flour, etc.

Irritants were the change in habits that one needed to make. SK could no longer walk into the bedroom with his shoes on, while Sandhya had to get habituated to sleeping as SK would snore heavily. He would like to chat away or read books late into the night with lights on as Sandhya would crave to fall asleep; while on the other hand, she would rise very early and start her morning chores, tinkering and tankering, as SK would place the pillow over his face to catch up with a little more of sleep.

Saudamini was of non-interfering type. She had no problem in amalgamating the new bride into the family. She was only too happy to be able to severe his son's relation with that 'wicked heroine'. Sandhya found friends in Meeru and Iru, the two daughters of SK's elder sister. All three were nearly of the same age and when SK went away sailing, they would go out shopping or watch some Bengali film. Life moved on adjusting, pining, bickering, and for some time it seemed SK had forgotten Jyotsna, or at least he had closed the chapter. But time had a different story to unfold.

It was one afternoon in the office. Chakraborty walked in.

'Do you know, Jyotsna's mother has passed away?'

'When?' SK got up from his chair.

Suddenly, he felt guilty for not getting in touch with her for so long. He took a half-day leave from the office, walked down the Watgunge Road to catch a tram to Entaly.

A crowd was waiting in silence at the main door. He walked passed them into the house. She was laid out on the ground covered with a white sheet. A lot of white flower wreaths were placed on her. He had met her only once before when Jyotsna had brought him to this house for the first time and introduced her. Jyotsna sat by her side wailing. There were many people around, some he had met at the sets of shooting, and others were strangers to him. He stood among the crowd, did not dare to go and talk to Jyotsna. The body was raised to carry down to the bedpost ornamented with flowers, kept at the main entrance.

Jyotsna broke down, as other women around came forward to hold back Jyotsna from the body. Her eyes met SK's, and she came running to him and broke down on his shoulders. SK had nothing to say. No word can console anyone being parted from near and dear for life.

'I will be there till the end of cremation,' SK wiped the tears off her cheek and walked out with the body. The last rites are always performed by the eldest son of the departed. But Jyotsna was a single daughter; and women were barred from offering the last rites. So a distant male relative was bestowed with the right. It is a dichotomy in a religion which discriminates against its own women folk in the social context while attributes power to female form, idolizes female entity as goddesses for their power to create, procreate.

SK visited her the next Saturday. The house was still crowded with relatives. He just met her and informed that he would visit after the rituals were over. Though he wanted to be by her side during these tormenting days of grief, he felt it would be difficult for Jyotsna to explain his presence to other relatives.

The times became turbulent for SK. Or was it SK's introspection that was creating the turbulence?

CHAPTER 5

SRINIKETAN BOARDING HOUSE. An old, rusted tin board hanging on the wall of the third floor declared or rather, shied away from declaring the identity of the boarding lodge. A small dilapidated wooden door welcomed me into my new would-be abode.

As I stepped in, a frail voice called out, 'Where to?'

'I have been told that there is a vacancy for boarding in this mess.'

'Yes, there is. But you have to deposit the money in advance and fill up the details in this register.' He drew out a worn out old register from under the table that he was sitting behind and laid open a page with many columns.

'By the way, what do you do?' I had been warned by Ashish, my college friend who had given me this lead, 'Do not disclose that your income is unstable. Nobody will give you shelter.'

'I work at The Grand and study at Umesh Chandra College.' I said as I started filling in the register.

'It costs two hundred and sixty rupees per month. You will have a bed, a cupboard, and a table in a room shared by two other people. For meals, you will get breakfast; vegetarian lunch with one dal, one vegetable, some fries, chutney, and rice; dinner will be same with fish and rotis added. Mutton will be served once a week on Sunday afternoon. Last time for entry in the night is twelve thirty.' He concluded in one breath.

'Understood,' I said. There was no other option but to understand. It was after many days of search and through my friend, that I found this lodge commonly called a 'mess' in Calcutta, which suited my meager budget. It was important to relieve Gule from the extra burden and to let his family regain their space.

'My name is Shaktibabu,' he said while counting the cash that I handed over. 'Shakti' translated to 'power' in Bengali, and I found it to be ironical to be this frail man's name till I heard him call out loud, 'Haradhan'.

Shockingly, it was a resonant, loud call that echoed through the floors of the lodge. And an equally loud reply came back from some corner of the third floor, 'Coming,' and within few minutes, Haradhan arrived at the front office. 'What an effective improvised communication system,' I thought.

Haradhan, the 'man Friday' of the mess; a well-built, middle aged, whitish man in a dhoti worn up to his knees, and a shirt topped by a khaki sweater. Shaktibabu and Haradhan reminded me of Laurel & Hardy. Though not an exact copy but surely two extreme ends of human structure that presented a dramatic visual when seen together. Haradhan did the odd jobs: served the meals to the boarders; fetched them warm water for bath for an extra tip to the only bathroom on each floor; fetched needs of the boarders from nearby shops, again for an extra tip; opened the door for those who came late beyond twelve-thirty at night, again, for an extra tip.

'Take him to Haribabu's bed,' Shaktibabu ordered, and Haradhan led me up the stairs to a second floor room.

'Haribabu was a nice man,' he said opening the lock of the room. 'Last time he went to his village, he never came back. It was day before yesterday that we came to know that he died. He was an accountant in some Marawari office in Dalhousie Square.' Haradhan entered the dark room and switched on the light. There were three beds, three similar cupboards and three tables laid out against three walls. The wall with the door also had a large window, which he opened and a burst of fresh sunlight entered the room. A fresh new life, a new journey, an unknown quest rooted to that three-feet by six-feet wooden bed, will now branch out to the world outside through the iron rods of the window, through the corridor, down the stairs, out of the old door, dingy narrow alley, onto the main road of reality.

'Bipinbabu and Hariharbabu are your room mates.' Haradhan acquainted me. 'Both are above fifty. Bipinbabu is a clerk at the Writer's Building, and Hariharbabu is a representative of Ayurvedic medicines. Both are bachelors, and go to their village every Saturday and return Sunday evening.'

With a bed under my head, a fixed income every month, a band of friends as company, and with Esha by my side, life seemed to be trotting ahead. Morning at the Coffee House after bunking classes, training at the hotel till evening, spending intimate moments with Esha in some dark corner of a park, a chillum or two of hash to round up the day and return to the mess for dinner and sleep. A lot was happening at nineteen; but for art. All I could manage was only a few drawings on some Sundays, when I could not be with Esha due to her Bangkok uncle's visit. But I hardly cared. I had lost my focus, as liking for Esha with every passing day, gradually emerged as passion turning into lust resulting in sex.

I had an off on every Monday from the hotel training. After the Coffee House session, Esha asked me if she could visit my mess. There was no reason to say no, and we took a tram from College Street towards Harrison Road. It was about eleven-thirty. The mess was deserted as all had left for their jobs. I opened the lock and entered the room. It was a small room and nothing to show around. Esha came in, locked the door from inside and sat on my bed. She allowed the pallu of her sari to drop off her chest. Her bosom heaved as she breathed heavily. I moved closer to her, grasped her by hair, bent down and locked my lips onto hers. As I kissed hard, I felt her hand move to my trouser zip. As I licked all over her face, she took off her blouse and the brassiere with ease. I undressed; she lay down on the bed and invited me onto her with open arms. I wildly wriggled over her bare body, pulling up her sari to her waist, pulling down her panty to her knees, sucking on her nipples, and eating her boobs. Suddenly, she rolled me over and got on top of me on her knees and moved down. I stretched out my arm to pull her back but she forced herself further down and bent. And lo, she had my dick in her mouth. She sucked, licked, spat on it and again, licked. Inside a hot dungeon like a Boa constrictor, her tongue was trying to wrap around and squeeze the life out of me. I let go and surrendered to her tongue twirls. I wanted to eject out all my life force and release it into her, but she got up and reached for her purse, fished out a small packet, tore it, and took out a condom.

'Wear it,' she said. It was the first time I was putting on a condom and it was troublesome. The only other time

I came close to a condom apart from the prank in Major Mangy's bungalow in RIMC, was in Pune, when I visited a whorehouse at Budvar Peth.

We were two batch mates in National Defence Academy, Dhir and I, admitted in the Military Hospital, Pune with chest pain. Dhir had the pain and I was shamming. I was trying to be declared medically unfit, to get out of the Academy. Here we befriended a few jawans who were also admitted. We heard their stories of sexual romps. Inspired, we requested them to take us one day. One night, after dinner Lans Nayak Umakant, one of the jawans we knew informed us that they were going out to a brothel and we could accompany if we wished. We jumped to the invite and joined three of them. This 'red light area', as the sex trade zones were called, was out of bounds for all National Defence Academy cadets. We had no idea of the area except for the name, Budhvar Peth. The dingy lanes were lined with four to five-storey buildings. Most of the windows flashed coloured lights. The underlit lanes were crowded by women in garish coloured dresses passing lewd comments, vendors selling fried snacks, and drunk men avoiding eye contact with other passersby, possibly the customers. We followed our jawan friends up a narrow stairway trying to avoid body contact with the girls standing by, giving lewd expressions through eyes and lips. Some sighed as we passed by. We crossed the first and second floor and walked up to the third, and entered a room. It was well-lit and filled with women in different dresses, quite young, though all of them elder to both of us.

Umakant educated us that we were at the best selection of girls in the building. The ground floor is occupied by waning and aged ladies, and as you move up the floors you reach out to the best crop and also the costliest lot. We could pick any one of the women and it would cost us five bucks for a fuck. Dhir did not waste time, he took a girl by hand and she vanished with him behind a thick red curtain. I felt shy to look at the women. Whenever I tried to look at someone, I found her directly staring at me. In the corner there was a woman in a blue dress. Her short skirt exposed her fair tight thighs and I focused onto her. She led me holding my hand behind the curtain. There were rows of wooden cabins with closed doors. Sound of whispers, panting, and gasping filled the air. My chosen woman went walking past the doors tapping on them.

'No', 'More time needed', 'Not finished' came the replies in women's voices till a reply came, 'Finishing.'

She stood at that door and looked at me. 'How old are you?' she asked.

'Twenty.' I lied.

'First time?'

'Yes.' I said the truth.

The door opened as a man and a woman walked out. She took me inside. 'Sit on the bed, I will join you in a minute.' And she walked out of the room.

I sat looking around; there was a calendar with Lord Shiva's painting on it with the Mount Kailash as the backdrop. Shiva, the God and the third in the Trinity as the destructor symbolizing the end of a cycle of creation for a new beginning, sat mute. The dingy cabins functioned as workstations during the evenings till a certain time into night, for the rest they doubled as home for these girls. A little away there was a poster of a nude 'Playgirl', surely a torn page of some Playboy magazine. This was the only familiar thing I could relate to in the room. But I did not feel the gush of blood into my phallus as I usually felt while peeping into Playboy magazines. I was befuddled. The woman in skirt walked in, locked the door and threw a small packet on the bed. She started undressing but nothing was happening to me. She stood naked and tore the small packet and took out a rubber balloon sort of a thing.

'This is a condom, when you are about to ejaculate, hold yourself, pull out and wear this before final doing,' she directed. Those were the days before AIDS spread and as she explained, the condom would allow her to stay clean, without me spilling into her.

Esha helped me put on the condom. She had taken off all her clothes; lay on her back with folded legs spread apart. Gripping her thighs, I dived into her with full tongue stretched out.

'What is your name?' I asked.

'Pam.'

Her round, tight, white breasts bounced as she jumped onto the bed. I undressed and crawled over her. My inner thighs touching hers, my cock sandwiched between our pelvis, belly unto belly, breasts pressed against my chest; I gripped her tight into my arms.

Esha clutched my hair and held me tight into her vagina. I sucked, kissed, licked. Oozing semen from the volcano of her lust was all over my face.

I glided up, tried to take her lips, and Pam moved her head away not allowing me to kiss. I gripped one of her boobs and sucked the other. 'You like it?' Pam asked. I replied by trying to take her whole boob into my mouth. I could not; it was quite large and nicely round.

'Do you like round boobs or the pointed ones?' Esha asked while I sucked her conical and pointed breasts. She did not wait for my reply. 'The girls with pointed boobs are sexier than the ones with the round ones,' she asserted. At this point it hardly mattered to me, whether it was the round ones of Pam or the pointed ones of Esha.

'Put it in now,' Pam said.

Esha held my cock in her left palm and guided me into the vagina. I felt like entering a hot dungeon of gooey lust. I started pushing in and pulling out of the vagina in slow motion, enjoying every moment of the jellied friction. But with every thrust, the primitive animal instinct in every man forced me to go faster and harder. Soon it was so hard that I could feel our pelvis bones crushing into each other. Esha started shrieking, 'Fuck, fuck, fuck harder.' Instead of being shocked at such a raw outburst unexpected of suave Esha, I climbed higher levels of ecstasy every time she screamed, 'Fuck, fuck, fuck me tighter,' clasping my buttocks and slamming me into her. I was sweating, panting, fucking.

'I am coming, do it faster,' Esha shouted. I was also reaching the peak.

'Fuck, fuck, fuck. Oh my God! Oh my God! This is it. This is it. Hold me tight. Hold me tight.'

I slammed down hard for one last time as I ejaculated hot semen into the deep crevices of her vagina.

'You did not hold yourself and put on the condom,' Pam said as she rolled me onto a side. 'See what you have done, it is all in me. Now I have to go and clean it up.' She seemed a bit concerned. 'You stay put. I will wash and come back.'

I planted a few short crisp kisses on Esha's face and laid on her. Felt exhausted and exalted.

Our sexcapedes continued: in the mess room, in Mirana cabins, in dark corners of public parks. During the sex she transformed into a different girl. Wild, raw, fiery, spewing hot lava, using vulgar and abusive language. Every time, she came onto me turning a new leaf of Kamasutra. She was the teacher, I learned; she was the leader, I followed; she abused, I was amused. She knew all that could be experimented in sex, and that too, in perfect style; a bit abnormal for a middle class girl with a humble background.

The mystery called Esha further deepened; but who cared? Not me at least. It was no more about the mystery—it was about sex. I was on the road to discover the manhood in me. Attractions and priorities change with time. We often set out for the journey called life with a goal, at least, an assumed goal. But the all-imposing Time keeps shifting the goal posts without us even knowing it. We saunter, we run; through the winding paths, negotiate the bends, leave a pathway for another, turn left, take a right; thinking we are moving ahead towards our goal, oblivious to the fact of shifting goal posts. Life becomes a journey, without reason, without logic. So why try to analyze? Just walk on, collecting small pebbles of memories along the way, throwing away some, to pick up more down the road. But the beautiful pink pebble that I had collected in my childhood always remained with me through the journey.

* * *

I walked down Kalighat Lane, a narrow lane off Hazra Road. My destination was 52 A, Kalighat Lane. Yesterday I saw an advertisement in the newspaper, inviting applicants for the post of salesmen. The company manufactured consumables. The name was Starlight Industries. The stipend from the hotel training was getting a little short, so I decided to try other avenues. I had taken leave from the hotel and here I was with an application and the CV in hand.

The office was a small room in a by-lane from the main road. There were many, maybe about hundred odd young men crowding the by-lane. One of them guided me, I had to give my application to a person in the room and then wait for them to call me for the interview. I did that. Understanding that it would be quite some time before my turn came, I walked up to the main road and spotted a café, Das Cabin; a small cafe with windows of tin and some old chairs and tables, very basic. Most tables were occupied. I found one in a corner and occupied a chair. On the left wall hang a small blackboard with the day's menu written with chalk. There was a 'Mutton Kobiraji', the most costly item at five rupees. There were mutton cutlet, chicken cutlet, omelet, toast, butter toast, concluded by tea at fifty paisa. A boy with a dirty towel on his shoulder came to my table and asked for my order. I ordered a cup of tea. Looking around I spotted a dark, thin man sitting behind a small table, I presumed him to be the owner, Mr Das. The windows framed a typically Calcutta street scene: trams passing by, clanking at times to clear its track, a sound so typical of Calcutta streets; double decker buses; hand pulled rickshaws; lonely walkers, busy vendors. Whichever part of Calcutta you visit, the scene remains broadly the same.

The tea came to my table in a chipped off white cup on an equally chipped off, if not more, saucer. Also came to my table a young man.

'Can I share your table?' he asked. I looked around. All the tables were occupied by groups.

I shifted to the right, 'Yes, why not.' He took the chair opposite to me.

'Chhotku,' he called out. 'Get me a tea.' I realized that he was a regular customer.

'Dasda, what's the news?' he started a conversation with the owner. Chhotku, the small boy with the dirty cloth, served my tea. The tea looked like what it should, but barely tasted anything close to it. It was sweet hot water with a slight tacky taste and no flavour. I had been crossing this place many times earlier but had never noticed this Das Cabin. It did not cry out its presence loudly to attract attention like most food joints and cafes do. It just existed very ordinarily, just like Mr Das, its owner, blending seamlessly into the backdrop. He was happy selling cups of tea after cups of tea. No tension about 'table turnover', a new term I learnt during my hotel training. Groups kept occupying the tables without ordering any food, only a few cups of tea. Mr Das, content in opening the doors of Das Cabin to these young unemployed men with all the time at their disposal. The business he started to earn a living was no more a need for existence, just an old habit. A mere pastime to avoid being embedded into the dark, damp, dungeon on the second floor, up a flight of rickety stairs with rusted iron railings, called home.

'Are you new to this area?' my tablemate asked.

'I have come for an interview down the lane.'

'I am Khokan, my home is a two-minute walk from here,' he introduced himself. 'Interview, where?'

'Starlight Industries,' I replied.

'Oh! In 'Kelte's office?' I did not know the name of the owner but understood that his pet name was 'Kelte' which implied that he had a very dark complexion. Kelte was a derivation from the Bengali word 'kalo', meaning 'black'.

'If you have any problem, let me know. I will tell him to take you in.'

Unsolicited help was at hand. I thanked him and got up to check the progress at the office.

'This Cabin closes at one. It again opens at four. I will be here again by five. If you need me, you can catch me then.' I thanked him again, paid fifty paisa to Das Babu, and moved out.

It was only at five that my turn came. In the mean time I visited the café and had a mutton cutlet and tea for lunch. There was a tiny sofa on one side, and two tables on the other side complemented by three chairs each. Displayed on the wall shelf were a few packets of detergent powder. So this was the product, I thought. Consumables translated down to detergent powder.

'Please sit down.' A very dark complexioned, thin, man on the other side of one of the tables told me.

'Thank you.' I sat down. This must be 'Kelte', the owner. He was tall, smartly dressed, had sharp, shining eyes. At the other table sat a very ordinary looking young man.

'My name is Abhin Ghosh.' He said in Bengali and forwarded his hand for a shake. I shook his hand. He took out my application and the CV. Silently went through the pages and looked at me. I was skeptical, I had no experience in selling. Will I make it? He looked down into the papers and again looked into my eyes.

'I have a different offer for you.' I was unable to decipher what he meant.

'You see, I need a Manager. I will offer you the job. If you like it you can join from tomorrow, and on joining I shall explain your job profile. I am sure you will be able to handle it.'

I was on seventh heaven but did not express it.

'Your salary will be seven hundred and fifty rupees per month, will that be all right?'

He did not leave any space for a 'no'. I agreed, we shook hands and I left to return the next day. My monthly income more than doubled in a fraction of a second with an enhanced job profile and designation. I walked down to Das Cabin and yes Khokan was sitting there and sipping tea. I told him about my new job.

'So we will meet every day.'

Yes, we met every evening over a cup of tea after my work hours and we became friends. I also became friends with his five more friends who dropped in most of the days to join the adda. Khokan, at twenty-eight, was the youngest of the lot; the rest, much older. I was nineteen.

I did not resign from the hotel training. I just stopped attending with a few hotel trade secrets up my sleeve. I had a thorough knowledge of the various goblets and glasses vis-a-vis the liquor to be served. I knew the laying of a table and cleaning it in style as well. You always serve from the right side of the guest you are serving. The emblem on the plates should always be on the top. You always stretch your legs a little more while walking to give you that graceful gait. But all this did not excite me enough to hold me back from the extra income's lure and I joined Starlight Industries.

I walked into the small room at ten, the next day. Mr Abhin Ghosh, the owner, had not arrived. The other table was occupied by the same young man as yesterday; two others sat on the sofa. We introduced ourselves. The man at the table was Souvik Mitra, the sales team leader. The elder on the sofa was Haripada Das, and the other was Nabarun Sen. Both from Duttapukur, a village in the suburbs, about two and a half hour journey by train from Sealdah. I recalled Bose Kaku; his parental home was also in Duttapukur. Both were part of the sales team. While Souvik had worked for about seven months, Haripada and Nabarun had been associated for more than a year. Mr Abhin entered, dressed smartly in a beige trouser and a black shirt.

'Souvik, take the chair on the other side of the table, and Siddhartha, you occupy his seat,' he said in Bengali. It took me two days to get the real picture at Starlight Industries. Mr Abhin did not know English and I wondered what he was pondering over my CV during the interview. It was a clever posture picked up from various failed interviews that he had appeared in, before starting this venture. He himself admitted it as he soon became a friend to me and opened his heart out, confiding his personal life and the tricks of the trade.

You could not term the venture as fake or fraud, but it surely was not what it was portrayed to be. He had a wife, a child, and an ailing father to support, who lived in the two rooms behind the office. There was one more member in the Starlight family, Beele. He was the manufacturing labour, peon, and the man Friday.

A small open compound at the back of the office, adjacent to Abhin's house, was the production floor. Caustic soda, chalk powder, some parts of cheap washing powder, a little blue colour was mixed in a proportion which Beele knew, was weighed in one kilogram and five hundred gram units, and packed in plastic pouches with printed labels of Starlight Industries. The brand was called 'Surfer', trying to rub shoulders with the all-overpowering brand 'Surf' detergent powder from the house of Hindustan Levers.

The same process was followed minus the blue colour and you had the 'Chamak' utensil cleaning powder. Both the brands were of such inferior quality that shopkeepers had stopped shelving them long back. So they were promoted through direct marketing into the ghettos and lower income group households who had the aspirational brand Surf in their mind but could never afford it. This looked like Surf in colour and feel, with a label that was a clever lift from the original. To seal every deal, a plastic bucket was thrown in free if one would buy both, that is, a kilogram of 'Surfer' and a kilogram of 'Chamak'. There was a smaller bucket for the five hundred gram combo. The offer looked lucrative at half the price of Surf and any other good quality detergent and utensil cleaning powder, till one used it. Hence, the sales team never visited the same area twice. No customer could trace the company to complaint, as the labels did not mention the address at all. Those were the days of ignorance of consumer rights and Abhin, knowingly or unknowingly, fitted into the scenario.

The sales were conducted during the first half of the day. My job profile as the manager was simple. Keeping stock of the products, give a motivational talk before sending off the sales team, sit alone in the office till one when Beele would fetch me my lunch. Four 'luchis', round-shaped flat fried breads with a small bowl of lentils for one-rupee and twenty-five paise. Collect the cash from the sales team when they returned at around two or three, and while away time with Beele till five, when Abhin would again drop in, already under the influence of alcohol—the country liquor 'sixty'— the smell of which was quite known to me. I would hand over the cash and leave for the day. My day's job was done. Spend an hour or so at the Das Cabin 'adda' with my newfound friends, and then take a tram to meet Esha.

It seemed to be a dream job, but two things bothered me: the sales were anything but phenomenal; in fact, they were poor. The other was wiling away time at the office. So on the third day, I decided to accompany the sales team. Abhin liked the idea and encouraged me. On the very first day, the sales increased double-fold. It was not due to any special sales skills that I possessed; in fact, this was the first time that I had gone out selling. At first, I could not assign any reason, and no one was interested in any reason. Everybody was happy and Abhin thought I was a sales maverick. But repeat of the same feat on following days set me thinking. I realised that it was not about my sales skills but my appearance. My polished persona, gentlemanly behaviour, and upper middle-class sophistication translated into an aura of trust around the products. We did not even have to go door to door. Getting the attention of one household would draw in women and girls from other households. We did not have to hard sell. Explaining the scheme, the product benefits, which were completely false, and the price advantage would do the trick. Or was it my persona doing the trick? I could see young girls and housewives picking up our products, ogling at me. I was enjoying this newfound star status as our sales kept increasing.

My sales team of Starlight Industries and I were walking back to office after a day's successful sale. Walking down the lanes of Bhowanipore, as we were passing the house number twenty-two, I asked my team to carry on to the office.

House number twenty-two; I had visited this house many times with my parents during childhood. I pushed open the large iron gate and walked in through the uncared lawn. The lawn had seen better times. I remember there were many flowerpots with various plants, some with beautiful flowers, and the grass was mowed regularly. There was a hibiscus tree near the wooden door at the entrance. The tree was still there, but only dry branches remained of it. The lawn had overgrown grass, and wild shrubberies had taken over most of it. The wooden door had been replaced with a rusted tin sheet.

This was the house of Dadu who had passed away long time back. Dadu was the neighbour of my grandfather— whom I had never seen—at Chaibasa; a small town in Bihar where my mother was from. Dadu had come to Calcutta in the late forties and made quite a bit of wealth and had bought this house. Before marriage, my mother was a close friend of the four daughters of Dadu. Incidentally when we shifted to Khidderpore the eldest daughter lived in the house just opposite to us. She was married to an author with one insignificant book to his credit and many screenplays, which were never filmed. I had never thought then how they made a living. I saw my mother carrying food to them on many days; and our visit to Dadu's house started. The two-floor house was big. I used to spend most of the time in Dadu's ground floor room while my mother spent time with two unmarried daughters, Mintumashi and Phonumashi, on the first floor. I rarely visited the first floor.

Dadu's room was interesting to me. It had collectibles all around which made for interesting time pass. On a table, there was a large brass plate filled with rock collections. It was him who developed in me the interest of collecting rocks. At the end of every visit, he would give me a rock and explain the composition, type, and from where it was collected. Beyond Dadu's room there was another big room, which I never visited. In fact, I was never allowed to go beyond Dadu's room. There was something eerie about that area. At times I could hear a man crying or shouting from that room. I noticed that the room was always locked from outside. It was a secret that I came to know only on growing up. The man crying was Dadu's son, Bikash. He had become lunatic. It was not always like that. He was a budding artist. Dadu being quite rich never minded his son in practicing art though one could not make a living out of it in those days. Even Dadu himself did small watercolours which were framed and hung on his walls.

The Hippie culture invaded India and one day Bikash went missing. Police were informed but to no avail. After two years he returned with long unkempt hair, beard, and a foreigner girl. He told Dadu that they would live together. Dadu was only too happy to have him back and accepted them. The now locked room was cleared and given to the couple. He started painting, and to Dadu things seemed to be normal once again. But there was a secret that Dadu did not know. It was the age of 'LSD', 'hashish' and 'charas'. The couple were heavily drugging themselves at night. They communicated little with the rest of the family except at meal times. Then one fateful day the girl was found lying dead with face down in a pool of blood in the front lawn. It seemed suicide to Dadu, and he informed the police. But he was stunned when Bikash approached him and said, 'Did you know, she knew how to fly? I was with her on the roof. She stood on the rampart and asked me to help her with a little push.' Dadu understood the ramifications of this innocent confession. He rushed him inside the house and bribed the police to conclude the case immediately. Dadu saved Bikash from the police but could not save him from himself. Now alone and lonely, Bikash would stay in the room for days without talking to anyone. It seemed depression was setting in. And soon after, he totally lost the balance of his mind. He became violent, abusive, and uncontrollable to the extent that he would hurt himself by slashing arms and banging his head onto the wall.

Psychotherapy was in a nascent stage in those days in India. Dadu ordered that he be tied up and locked up in the room. The second daughter, in the mean time, got married but died of cancer in the second year of marriage. Suddenly, ill-fate seemed to have struck Dadu. The other two daughters, though well-qualified, never got any job. Slowly they passed their marriageable age. They tried to take tuitions at home, but people were reluctant to send their children, as there was a lunatic at home.

On one of our visit, Dadu expressed interest to visit our house. It was a Sunday, my father fetched Dadu and both the Mashis for lunch. Dadu on finishing a hearty meal said, 'Who knows, this may be my last visit.' He died the next day in sleep.

I pushed open the tin door, and walked in to notice Dadu's room was locked from outside. But the other room had no lock. There was nobody around. I walked up the stairs to the first floor; it was all silent. I walked into the first room. Little daylight poured in. I tried to adjust my vision in the dimly lit room.

'Who, who is it?' some lady shouted. It was Mintumashi. I introduced myself. She was frail; only bone and skin. But that beautiful old hearty smile lit up on her face. 'Arre! Bublu! Come in let me have a look. You have grown so big. How many years has it been since I last saw you? What are you doing now? How is Sandhya?' So many questions in one breathe that I could reply. She took me by my hand and made me sit on the bed. Now I could see well. The room was almost empty except for the bed. A few utensils and a kerosene stove lay at a corner on the floor.

'How are you? And where is Phonumashi?' I asked.

'We are all fine. Phonu has just gone downstairs to the shop. She will be here anytime. Even your uncle will be here. You should not leave till you meet everybody,' she said. 'Let me make some tea for you.'

I could not relate to the uncle at first as a young man walked in. 'Mintu, what are you doing.'

'Arre! Dada look, who has come.'

I realized this was the uncle, Dadu's son, Bikash. But he should be forty plus. He was too skinny and looked frail. But his face was like an innocent child. So he had recovered, I guessed. He came close to me, 'I heard you paint.'

'Yes.'

'I will show you my paintings.' From another corner where now I noticed, there were little bundles of paper. He picked up a few and said, 'Come outside. Still there is some light, you can take a look.'

I went onto the verandah and took the papers. They were all experimental: little colours, a little ink, and at times, pencil strokes. All the paintings were on very small sheets of paper. Poverty was telling but did not restrict experimentation. After all, mind does not need money to think.

'I had shown them to some people. They don't understand them. What do you think of them?'

I was no one to judge his art. I myself did not have much experience except for the little I learned at the Defence Academy on the development of art in the west, and this tremendous urge to be an artist. I drew experimental figurative and had not even developed any style of my own. But I liked them. I did not have the audacity to reply to his question and silently just kept looking at each piece.

He must have realized my appreciation. 'You seem to like them,' he said.

Actually more than appreciation; what must have reflected in my expression was the motivation he aroused in me. If after so many years of hibernation, in the poorest of financial condition, he could still carry on painting without any expectation of recognition, I thought I was right in my decision. Art is a process of self-exploration, a journey, and not a goal.

Phonumashi also walked in after a while. We all had tea together. We talked about my childhood days as the evening turned darker. I took leave promising to come again, only to walk out of the tin gate for the last time. I never went back.

* * *

After seven days at the job, a young man dropped in the morning. Abhin took him out of the office. Soon he returned with him and handed him five hundred rupee notes.

'Next month all your dues will be cleared. Do not worry.'

The man took the money. 'When should I come?' he asked.

'Well, end of next month will be the right time.' My common sense told me that there were debts around. The company did not have any accounting system and I was concerned again. I realized that the daily collection was treated as income by Abhin. There was no concept of capital in his mind. A rough calculation of the past seven days collections projected that if we provide for capital, a month's collection would not provide for our salaries. But Haripada, Nabarun, Bile, and Souvik were all working and getting their salaries. On enquiring, I learned at times the salaries were delayed a few days, but have always been paid. I did not understand the economics, till one fine day a man named Badal Sircar walked into the office in the morning. He carried a cloth bag, from which he carefully took out a parcel wrapped in paper. He opened it. There was a bundle of hundred rupee notes. He handed them over to Abhin and said, 'Here is my security deposit of ten thousand rupees. From when can I join?'

Abhin took the bundle and handed it over to me.

'Just check.'

I counted the notes. They were ten thousand.

'You can join from tomorrow.' Abhin said.

'Will you give me a receipt?' Badal asked.

'Why receipt? I am giving you the appointment letter right away. You will be a company employee from tomorrow. What will you do with a mere paper receipt?'

He took out a draft letter and a letterhead from his drawer. 'Sid, write down his name on a piece of paper and give it to Beele. He will get the appointment letter typed,' and handed me the papers. Beele took the papers and vanished behind the entrance door curtains. I was still not clear about the goings on. I had read the appointment letter before handing over to Beele. It mentioned that he was being appointed as a salesman of the company at the fixed salary of five hundred rupees and a ten per cent share of daily sales. It had no mention of the ten thousand rupees. Soon, Beele came back with the typed appointment letter. Abhin signed it and handed it over to Badal.

He read it. His expression was a mix of happiness laced with skepticism. 'But this does not say anything about the security deposit.'

Abhin seemed quite experienced in handling such situations. 'You are now part of the family. You will be earning much more than ten thousand over a period of time. I hope you are confident of selling, because the job I am giving you is completely dependent on sales. I have interviewed you and I am confident that you will turn out to be a good salesman. Regarding the security deposit, it is because you will be entrusted with products worth thousands. What do we do, if you run away with them? This money is strictly kept in company's locker for safety and handed over to you once you decide to leave. But I am sure you will not leave.' Abhin continued confidently in one breath. 'So tomorrow at ten am sharp.'

Badal got up to leave. The job scenario was bad. He had his parents and siblings back in village to provide for. He thought it wise to accept his fate rather than question company's integrity, lest he loses this hard earned job, selling a few of his mother's jewellery. As he left, a smile spread across everybody's face. Things were falling into place. I was just beginning to understand the business module, the resource of funds for Starlight Industries. What seemed to be drawing the business into a vortex was actually surviving by sitting on a ticking time bomb. It was more of a ponzi scheme garbed as a business. I knew it would not be long before I had to move on; but at present, it was the salary at the end of the month that mattered.

That night, we had a gala party thrown by Abhin. Bottles of sixty, lots of mutton curry cooked at his home, and 'chapatis' fetched from a nearby shanty hotel. All spent from the ten thousand rupees given by Ashutosh. It did not go into any company locker. It assured our salaries at the end of the month, supplemented company's depleting capital, and a bonus to Abhin for his wayward life. He confided in me and soon we were friends in vice. After office hours, I would often spend some time over a few glasses of sixty at some country liquor pub, which he introduced me to, and I introduced him to smoking of hash on other evenings. As I bonded more with Abhin and my friends group at Das Cabin, I started seeing less of Esha in the evenings. Our meetings were restricted to the Coffee House sessions after which I headed for my job. She did not complain as I grew more self-sufficient and now could buy her a gift or two as well.

Badal joined our sales team the next morning. And then Bidyut joined a few days later. Again another party, and it continued. People joined and people left. Those who left were given back a pittance of their security deposit and a promise to pay back in parts. In first few visits they would receive a small amount, but then the harassment began. They came back again and again to realise their security deposit in vain. They had nothing in black and white to prove their legitimate claim. They could not take any police or legal action and Abhin kept handing out more and more appointment letters.

One day, he asked me to stay back. He said he had something to discuss with me. After the sales team had left, he took out a cigarette.

'I think we should make Starlight Industries a Private Limited company. A Private Limited company has more weightage and acceptance in the market.' I agreed. I had no clear idea about formalities and modalities of incorporating a Private Limited company, but I knew that there was a body called Registrar of Companies where it had to be registered, and there were legal guidelines and formalities for the same.

'But how will you do it?' I questioned. 'Will you register it as a new company with a new name?'

'No! No! It will be Starlight Industries Private Limited.'

'But there are no books of accounts or any register. The company needs to function as per company laws, and rules laid down by Registrar of Companies. But we have no records.'

'Why do you worry so much?' he replied. 'We will print the next lot of our order books, chalans, cash memos and letterheads with our company name as Starlight Industries Private Limited.'

He always had solutions which were malignantly simple. 'Nobody is going to go to Registrar or whatever you call it. People believe anything they see in print. So once we get these documents printed, we can say we are a Private Limited company. We will also change our board at the entrance. That is all.'

'But what purpose will it serve?' I questioned.

'We will expand our business.'

'And what area that will be?'

'We will manufacture cosmetics.'

'Come on Abhin, for that you need a plant, machineries and what not. It's a big capital investment.'

'No,' he replied emphatically. 'I have been to Bagri Market and there you get readymade nail polish by litres, in all colour shades. There are empty bottles of different shapes and variety of labels by dozens. We will purchase in bulk and bottle it here and put the labels on. It is that simple.'

'That means you are talking about packaging.'

'No! You did not get me. We will say we manufacture it in our plant.'

'And where is the plant?'

'We will say Howrah. Our plant and warehouse is in Howrah.'

I was really confused about his plans. 'And then set out to directly market them door to door like our detergent and cleaning powder? How many pieces do you think you can sell daily?' I countered.

'You did not get my idea,' he continued. 'We will give out an advertisement in the newspaper inviting distributors. We will give the distributorship to only first time entrepreneurs, because those already in the field will not bite the bait.' He was quite excited as he stubbed out his cigarette butt into the ashtray and lit one more. 'We will select distributors from far off areas. They will have to deposit a security deposit of twenty thousand rupees and we will provide them with goods worth the same amount as per MRP (Maximum Retail Price). So he will easily part with the twenty thousand, as he will be thinking that he has twenty thousand worth of goods at his disposal. He will think that he has zero risk. Now this twenty thousand worth of goods as per MRP will only be about five thousand rupees worth of raw material. We will give him a hefty twenty five per cent distributorship discount. Which leaves us with a clear margin of fifty percent straight in our hands, that too, in advance.'

Now I was reading him right. It was once again about collecting money. I did not comment and allowed him to continue. 'It's a win-win situation. Selling will be his responsibility, and every time he comes back with the money after collection, we will give him more stock. So, the deposit amount remains with us always. Thus if we can appoint just five distributors, we will collect one lakh rupees.'

Here I interrupted, 'But you will have to return the deposit once he gives up his dealership.'

'Somebody else will join. We will take his deposit and return to the distributor who leaves.'

'How are you sure that there will be someone joining at that point of time?'

'These are hard times, and have you not seen people joining our sales team?' He was an incorrigible schematic brat.

A dark woman in her late twenties peeped through the curtain. 'May I come in?'

'Maumita! What a surprise,' Abhin exclaimed. 'Come in, have a seat.'

'I have something personal to say,' she said looking at me and pulling the chair opposite Abhin to sit down.

'Beele,' Abhin called out loud. 'Get three cups of tea. This is Sid, my close friend and partner. You can speak in his presence. By the way, Sid, this is Maumita. She was in my sales team.'

She was good looking, draped smartly in a dark maroon sari, exposing just the right sections of flesh, to make her look sexy yet elegant.

'My husband is suffering from TB. He has lost his job.' She continued, 'I have applied for a few jobs but that will take some time. I need some money to run us through.'

'I told you to continue with me. You would not have faced any problem.' Abhin said. 'But you decided to leave. Anyway, how much do you need?'

'Five hundred.'

'That is a big amount. How will you pay back?'

'I will return it in installments, once I get the job,' she said.

'Do not worry about returning the money. Like old days we will visit your home tomorrow and give you the money.'

Beele served the tea.

'What do you mean by 'we'?' she asked.

'Me and Sid. You see five hundred is a big amount.' Abhin said as he sipped tea from the cup. The conversation was not making sense to me.

'OK, at what time?'

'Tomorrow at one o clock in the afternoon. Will that be all right?'

'All right.' She got up and left without taking the tea. I lit a cigarette and asked, 'What was it all about?'

'Arre, she is a good fuck. And she gives a great mouth too. I have slept with her once earlier.' I was stunned. Here was a woman asking for help and Abhin was lecherously scheming into the situation. I felt pathetic.

'Well I am not interested in it. You can go yourself,' I said.

'Arre, come with me. It will be real fun,' Abhin was all smiles. 'But I will take her first.'

'No! I do not think it is a good idea. You can go yourself.'

'Actually, I want to help her,' Abhin continued. 'She is worth three hundred, but both of us for five hundred is a good bargain. And she gets what she needs.'

I felt utterly disgusted. How could someone commodify a woman and trivialise her pain into a market economy? Well, Abhin could.

'If you are not coming, I will give her three hundred. I do not want to waste money.'

Next day after the sales team left, leaving Beele in charge of office, we took a bus to Anwar Shah Road in Tollygunge. Abhin had visited before and knew the house. It was a single-storey house with paints chipping off the wall, in an area that seemed to be inhabited by people from the lower-income group. Abhin knocked at the door. After a few seconds Maumita opened the door and took us in. Walking in from bright sunlight, it took time to settle into the dark room. The room was lit by a dim incandescent bulb. The only window was closed and in the corner there was a bed. A man slept on the bed, oblivious of our presence. There was a small stool and a wooden chair, which we occupied. On the wall hang an old, framed photograph of Maumita and her husband in better times.

'I have given him a sleeping pill. He will not get up now,' Maumita said. 'Should I prepare some tea for you?'

'No we need to go back to office soon,' Abhin said.

'OK, come with me,' she walked into the house through a curtain and Abhin followed.

I sat aimlessly looking around the room. There was an iron trunk underneath the bed with a padlock on it; an earthen pitcher on the floor next to the bed, covered by a steel glass. A clothesline was fixed from wall to wall and was overburdened with two saris, a shirt, a brassiere and a gamchha. There was a Bengali newspaper on a wooden table at one corner. I picked up the paper and glanced through the headlines. 'NIXON RESIGNS' was the boldest of them all; but that was three years ago, I recalled. All the news seemed to be stale. I looked up the date line on the masthead of the newspaper. It was 9th August nineteen seventy-four. Time stood still for Maumita as her husband's health kept sinking day by day.

Abhin came out and asked me to go in. I pushed the curtain and entered an even more dimly lit room, smaller in size. Maumita stood naked and latched the door behind me. A kerosene stove, and a few utensils lay scattered in one corner. A cane basket with a few potatoes and onions waited to be cooked for the afternoon meal. She had no time to feel the pangs of hunger. She needed the five hundred rupees for her husband's medicines. A rug was laid on the floor, on which her clothes were dumped. She came in front of me and waited for my move. I signaled a 'no' and asked her to dress up. I did not understand what was going on in her brain. I did not want to. I just wanted to get out of here and out of her grim life. Tears rolled down her cheeks as she gathered her clothes and started dressing. We walked back into the room where her husband still slept under the influence of medication.

'You are very fast,' Abhin said as he handed over five hundred-rupee notes to Madhumita. 'Tell me whenever you need money. I am always there,' Abhin kissed her and we left.

But Maumita never came back again. She never again asked for help. 'She must have got the job and had tide over her dark days', I wished.

About a month later in the evening, while waiting to take the tram to my hostel at Dharmatola Street, I spotted Maumita in the crowd. I rushed towards her and called out 'Maumita.' She heard me, stopped, and came to me.

'How is your husband now?' I asked.

'He has passed away. He did not wake up on the day you two had come. I think the sleeping pills were too strong for his frail body. I did not need the five hundred rupees that he gave me any more. I gave it away to a beggar down the street. You should have seen the smile on her face. She was so happy.'

I saw the wilderness in her innocent beautiful eyes as she bade farewell and vanished into the crowd again.

Starlight Industries turned into a Private Limited company with the printing of new order books, challans, cash memo, and the letterheads. A classified advertisement in the Ananda Bazaar Patrika, the leading news daily, brought in many prospective distributors. They found a tremendous potential in our products at the price we were offering. Ready to give the twenty thousand rupees as security deposit, seven distributors were finalized. But there was a hitch—all of them wanted a signed contract on non-judicial stamp paper mentioning the terms and conditions and the security deposit amount. I warned Abhin that this would be a legally binding contract and failing to honour it would expose him to legal prosecution. He did not heed my warning. One-lakh forty thousand rupees to be collected from the distributors was too big a lure to divert his focus. He had never seen such a big amount at one go. The thought of holding one-lakh forty thousand rupees in between two palms sent adrenalin rushing through his veins. He signed all the seven contracts. He collected the money; the distributors collected the product lot.

It was bonhomie at Starlight Industries Private Limited till after about fifteen days, one of the distributors came back with the whole lot of products.

'They are of very inferior quality,' he said. 'I cannot offload them. Nobody is ready to buy them and all those who had bought have returned the whole lot.'

Abhin tried to pacify by saying that his lot will be replaced; but the distributor just would not give in. 'No, you take your lot back and return my security deposit.'

Abhin cooked absurd reasons to defer paying back by ten days.

'I will come back on twelfth of this month and I want my money back.' The distributor warned and left.

Abhin lived in the present moment; he never thought or bothered about the future. What would happen after ten days, would be addressed by him on that particular moment. For now, he was happy with one-lakh forty thousand rupees. And it showed: he bought new clothes, a refrigerator, and a music system; he gave thousand rupees bonus to all employees; he started drinking Scotch whiskey bought from the black market.

But ten days were too long a time away. Other distributors started pouring in one by one with the same demand: individually at first, then in groups of twos and threes, and finally one day, all seven of them together. There was a huge ruckus. All the employees together could not pacify them. They broke the samples, hurled abuses until Abhin declared that he would need a little time to arrange the money. He would return all the security deposits morning of the next day. The distributors left. Abhin left, and being the manager, I declared off and asked all employees to come back the next morning to decide on future action.

As I walked into Kalighat Lane next morning, Khokan was standing at the entrance of Das Cabin. 'Sid,' he called me. 'Do not go to the office. The crowd is very violent. They have pulled down the signboard and broken down the door. And Kelte is missing.'

I looked towards the by-lane leading to my office. A huge crowd had gathered and was shouting slogans. I sat down with Khokan in Das Cabin over a cup of tea and waited for events to unravel. An hour later, the slogan shouting became louder. I looked out of the window. There were about half a dozen policemen who had arrested Abhin and coming up the lane with the crowd following. I saw Badal—one of the ten thousand rupees deposit salesman at Starlight—suddenly break into the police cordon around Abhin and landed a few punches on his face. Abhin's nose was broken, and the face was completely splattered with blood. The crowd cheered and Badal felt like a hero taking on Goliath. With the eclipse of Starlight Industries Private Limited, Badal would once again face the uncertain world of millions of unemployed, and I too, had to move on looking for new pastures.

Life is a like a trek. Every bend opens up new terrains, new mysteries, and new excitement; the joy of learning, the pain of learning; beautiful memories, and sad longings. As you walk on, and the day tends to fade out, the shadow grows longer, reaching out behind you once again trying to reach out to the past, the smiles, the tears, only slowly to fade out as the night sets in. But the pink pebble walked on with me.

* * *

I met Esha at eight in front of Elite cinema. She had really worked on herself. A beautiful sari, clinking ornaments, a light yet prominent make-up. She looked beautiful.

'Are you going somewhere?' I asked as generally she sported an understated look.

'Not exactly. Let us walk down. I want to have some golgappas,' she said. 'The ones near the Globe cinema are great.'

Golgappas or 'phuchkas' as they are known in Calcutta, are a favourite outdoor snack particularly for women. It is also known as panipuri. Whoever invented it would have been a billionaire if he had patented it. But of now it is popular all over India and churned out in millions every evening. It is a crisp spherical hollow ball of flour, the size of a golf ball. A little portion is crushed and a mixture of boiled potato, spices and herbs placed inside, and filled with spiced tamarind water. It's that simple, but tasty. The ones being served from the vend near Globe were much bigger than a golf ball. In fact, one had to really stretch one's mouth to put it in. You have to do it in one go because if the ball breaks, the tamarind water spills out and it is no more a phuchka, and no fun.

I had five while she continued till ten. We walked into New Market, the old one, before it was razed due to a fire and a new concrete multi-storied structure came up in its place. It gave a modern look but never matched the aura of the old market with slanted, tiled roofs built by the Britishers in the nineteenth century.

We walked hand in hand till suddenly, she stopped and pulled me inside a shop. It was a ladies undergarments shop. I felt slightly awkward.

'What are we doing here?'

A man walked in and with a smile on his face told Esha, 'Having a good time?'

I didn't know the man. Esha seemed to be slightly taken aback. 'Just roaming around.'

'Who is he?' the man questioned looking at me.

'A college friend.'

'What time are you coming? He was asking me. I told him that you will be there in the evening.'

'Yes! Yes! I will be there.' And the man walked out.

'Who was he?' I questioned.

'Arre, he is my uncle's manager. But he shouldn't have seen us. He is not a very good man.' Esha replied. 'Anyway let us forget it.'

'Are you going somewhere in the evening?'

'I forgot to tell you, my uncle from Bangkok is here and he has brought some stuff for us. But he will be busy in meetings, so I will go to collect them from him. In fact it is already time. I will meet you tomorrow in the evening at six in front of Elite.' She seemed to be a bit in hurry. 'Most probably, I might not come to college tomorrow.' She waved her hand at me and walked away.

Something was bothering me, particularly the stranger. Why a girl so bold felt disturbed on confronting this man. Was she too afraid like all other Bengali girls being spotted with a boyfriend? I could still see her at a distance. I slowly started walking in the same direction. She walked out of New Market. I kept my distance, as she boarded a rickshaw. The rickshaw-puller slowly got into his rhythmic gait, clinking the small bell on the handle to clear the pedestrians on road, and picked up speed. I walked fast enough to keep pace but the distance was increasing. I couldn't run, as that would raise suspicion among the people around. I walked even faster keeping my eyes fixed on the rickshaw. It moved down Hogg Street passing the Aminia restaurant, onto SN Banerjee Road, and took the right turn on Chowringhee Road.

Why was I following her? I was clueless myself, but an inner instinct pushed me on. The rickshaw took a right turn into a small lane and vanished. The lane was not any posh locality. It had a few rundown hotels, old buildings where mostly Anglo-Indians and a few Chinese families lived. It had a few of those shoe shops owned by the Chinese. I had been through this lane once before. Not exactly a place I expected her rich uncle to stay or even have an office. I walked into the lane, it was all quite, badly lit and no sign of the rickshaw. I stood for a while feeling defeated. Suddenly, there was this clinking of the rickshaw bell and I saw a rickshaw moving out of the entrance of a hotel. Yes it was the same rickshaw-puller.

I moved in through the entrance of the hotel. A very old building dimly lit with no one around. A tin plate signboard identified the building as Hotel Bluestar. A wooden staircase with worn out carpet greeted me. I walked up the stairs trying to be normal with no clue as what to reply if confronted and questioned by somebody. The stairs led to an even more dimly lit corridor on one side of which there was a sort of a reception, unmanned. A row of doors, which seemed to be the rooms spread out on the other side. The doors had a glass paned ventilator on top, as in colonial period architecture. Light trickled out of only two rooms. Seemingly, the rest were unoccupied. I walked up to the first occupied room and placed my ears on the door. There were two men talking in a language I felt was south Indian. I stood for a while. Yes there was no third person in the room. I moved onto the next room. There was a man speaking in Hindi and there was Esha also fluent in Hindi. I was stunned. I never knew she knew Hindi so well. And why was she conversing with her uncle in Hindi? I walked onto the next door, and slowly pulled it open. It was not locked. I wanted to hear their conversation; but standing on the corridor was not feasible. Anybody could question me. I entered the nearly dark room. Nearly dark because there was one-foot wire mesh partition near the ceiling between the rooms, and light came through. The rooms were small and had wooden partitions in between. Everything could be heard from the next room. I looked around. A small bed with only a mattress, a small table at a corner with a stool in front, a mirror on the wall, was all that was there. Surely, not the place where Esha's rich uncle would put up. Suddenly, the voices in the next room turned into whispers. Did they feel my presence? I slowly opened the door and peeped out. Everything seemed as it was. I closed the door and now hardly anything could be heard. I placed the stool on the bed and climbed up to peep through the wire mesh.

Sometimes how strongly we try to see the truth otherwise. We build a world of our expectations on the basis of our experiences, knowledge, and feelings. We believe the world we have built to be the true existence, the reality. We like to feel safe in this make-believe world. But the truth of life, the actual reality does not exist thus. It is as it is. A fact in time and space not dependent on human expectations, aspirations, dreams. *It just is.*

There was this bald Sikh stout man embracing Esha. They were entwined in a deep kiss. The man's hands were moving all over her. She started unbuttoning his shirt as he removed her pallu and tightly gripped one of her breast. I could not take it anymore. I got down the chair, rushed to their door and banged on it.

'Esha open the door,' I shouted.

There was calm and I shouted again. The door opened and the Sikh came out with Esha behind. They had undone the undressing.

'Who are you?' the Sikh questioned.

'Esha come with me,' I told Esha instead.

'Who are you?' he questioned again, irritated and angry. I just ignored him.

'Esha come with me!' I shouted. The Sikh looked at Esha.

'He is a college friend.' She told him; calm and ignoring the fire raging within me.

'Aren't you coming?'

'Why should I?' She replied in a cold voice. 'You go back and leave me alone.'

I broke down. I lost all senses. The world was falling apart. I banged my head on the wall again and again. She stood still, not taking notice of my madness.

The hotel staff arrived, caught hold of me, pulled me down the stairs, and threw me out of the main gate. The stranger who met us in the New Market was standing in front of me as I lay on the street.

'Don't ever try to meet Esha,' he threatened. I looked up at the corridor. Nobody was there. The Sikh and Esha must have returned to their room, entangled in a kiss, immune to my failing world.

I pulled myself up, or could I? I moved to the footpath by the side and sat on it. I cried and cried. I do not know how much time had passed, but surely it was late. There were few vehicles on the main road at the end of the lane. I got up and walked aimlessly.

Whatever Esha's dialectics may have drawn me into, though not analytical then, it was the first time I felt possessive about her. Love makes you possessive. But was this love? Or was it the beastly feeling of owning her?

I walked on, not knowing where to go. Surely I did not want to return to my mess. Clueless of the night ahead and life itself, I walked on. As I wandered through the by-lanes of Park Circus, I noticed a few people coming out of a shanty quite drunk. I walked in. There were two women in their fifties serving liquor in small glasses to men sitting around. I knew it was one of those illegal joints were they sell illicit liquor. I asked for a glass.

'Four annas,' the lady said.

Though the anna system of currency had gone with the British Raj, yet it was still colloquially used for twenty-five paisa. I took out a coin and paid. I kept drinking as the men around me kept fading in and fading out like a Francis Ford Coppolla film. I was quite drunk, when I and the two others who were there were asked to leave. I walked out of the shanty and dragged myself onto the footpath. It was all empty. The street dogs were barking out their territories. They are very possessive about their defined territories. In fact, every living being is. It is a way of realising one's own existence, making one feel, I am. But here was I—no territory, no one to belong to, without any existence. I felt powerless, weak, and defeated. There was a handcart on the roadside tied to the street lamppost with an iron chain. I sat down on it.

It was the cawing of the crows next morning that woke me up. It was a usual early morning ritual of the crows in Calcutta. We never heard a rooster breaking the dawn; it was always the crows. I was lying on the handcart. I do not remember when I fell asleep. I was stinking with last night's liquor smell. I got up and walked towards my mess. It was afar. The first tram from Park Circus to Sealdah was passing me. I ran and boarded it. The conductor made a face and walked away from me, and did not even ask for my ticket.

When I reached the mess, some of the early birds had already started their routine. I walked up the stairs to my second floor room. My two other roommates were sleeping. Bipinbabu opened the door as I knocked.

'Where were you last night?'

'With a friend,' I said, and dumped myself into my bed.

It was late afternoon that I could get up still reeling under a hangover. The lunch plate lay as cold as me on my side table. I did not feel like eating but the hunger pangs made me gulp down a little rice and dal, and the piece of fish. I went down, made a phone call to my office to inform that I was sick, and came back again to go to sleep. Next two days I cut off myself from the rest of the world and stayed back in the mess. Nobody came inquiring about me, as only Esha knew this address. Even my office had my parent's address. I did not even think of that evening's happenings. May be I was emotionally drained out, exhausted.

It was the third morning; I lay in the bed after breakfast behind locked doors. My elderly roommates had left for office. There was a knock on the door. I reluctantly got up after quite a few knocks, opened the door, and Esha was there. Words failed me; I retired to my bed and lay on my face. She walked in and sat at the edge of my bed. I felt her palm on my back. Suddenly, I felt reassured. There were many questions, many complaints, but that very touch made me feel that I belonged. My world was not a void like the past two days. I turned and looked up into her eyes. She was looking straight into me as well.

'Why did you follow me?' she asked softly.

'I don't know. But why did you lie to me?' I questioned.

'Because I knew you could not face the truth. I feared you would end our relationship. And I did not want that,' she explained. 'You can call me selfish, but we all are selfish, and I have no qualms about accepting it.'

With her by my side, strangely, I was not feeling defeated like that evening. Even the kissing scene was not on my mind. I just wanted the truth from her.

'Will you break our relationship?' her eyes seemed glistened.

'What if?'

'I will face it, what else.' She got up from the bed. 'I will always cherish the moments spent with you.'

I reached out for her hand.

'Why hold on to the past,' she said. 'You go back home. That will be good for you.'

I caught hold of her hand and pulled onto me. I held her tight as I caressed her hair and planted tiny kisses on her face.

'Why? Why? Why?'

CHAPTER 6

Haradhan Chatterjee was a clerk in a British private firm dealing in jute products. He had migrated to Calcutta with his parents from East Pakistan after Independence and creation of Pakistan. He is tall, handsome, and energetic. At twenty-seven, he got married to Purnima Devi, a working nurse in an Indian Railways hospital. It was an arranged marriage. Purnima left the job after marriage, and soon three children followed: Devika, Gita, and Barun; two girls and a boy.

Life continued at snail's pace with neighbours, and a few old nursing friends of Purnima dropping in for occasional company. Shanti, one of the friends still unmarried, visited them quite often. She would always bring some toffee or sweets for the children and was their most favourite aunt. She was not beautiful, but had a suppressed attractiveness. It could be the way she wore her sari, talked, and carried herself. Whatever the reason, Haradhan was getting emotionally attracted to her by the day.

It was a late morning on a Sunday. Purnima had gone to the nearby Shiva temple with the children. Haradhan was carrying out minor errands at home. There was a knock at the door. As he opened it, Shanti walked in.

'Come in,' Haradhan said. 'They have gone to the temple and will be back soon.'

'What are you doing?' Shanti asked.

'Just petty things, which get left out over the week. Would you like to have some tea?'

'I will, but then if you allow me to make it.' She sat on the bed.

'Why? I can prepare tea.'

'Purnima always prepares it for you. Now that I have got this rare chance, why don't you taste me?' she laughed out intending pun.

'Should I?' Haradhan walked towards her and held her by the shoulders. Shanti got down from the bed. Haradhan pulled her close.

'Leave me,' Shanti whispered. 'They will come back anytime.' Haradhan held the back of her neck with his right hand and pulled her into a deep kiss. Shanti did not resist and opened her mouth to invite him in.

Haradhan and Shanti were sipping tea when Purnima came back with the children.

'Here's your Cadbury.' Shanti took out three small Cadburys from her vanity bag and gave them to the children. 'He said you had gone to the temple.'

'Yes,' Purnima replied. 'There was this puja today. So I took the children for blessings.'

'I have prepared an extra cup of tea for you,' Shanti said. 'It is in the kitchen.'

Gradually, Shanti's visits became more frequent. Purnima took a long time to feel the under current between his husband and Shanti. Though she never pointed out the small but tell tale overtures of Haradhan towards Shanti, she started bursting into fits of rage on very petty issues. It was the inner turmoil, which she could not share. The small outbursts slowly gave shape to petty quarrels and metamorphosed into full-fledged violent fights. The children did not have an inkling of what was happening. They watched helplessly as their parents went through these verbal and physical abuses. Barun used to cry while Devika and Geeta sat with him in their lap in one corner of the bed.

Suddenly, Shanti's visits decreased and gradually waned off. Once again there was quiet, and the children were happy like before. They missed Shanti aunty, as she was the one who always got gifts for them. They often asked about her, but Haradhan and Purnima always gave some vague reason.

A year passed with Haradhan's office timings slowly extending. Generally, he returned home by seven in the evening. It extended to eight, then nine, and finally he started coming home beyond ten in the night. Purnima often asked about the extended period of work and Haradhan would explain about some shipment that his company was making, increasing paper work. Life went on but Purnima noted that at times, Haradhan became quite irritated over petty queries. She thought it was the increased workload. She kept her cool and tried to avoid any confrontation.

It was a Saturday. Always a half-day at Haradhan's office, but he did not return till ten in the night. Purnima started worrying. She served dinner for the children and packed them to bed. There was no way she could communicate with Haradhan's office. They did not have a telephone. It was a luxury then, and there were no local public call offices at street corners either. The local shops, some of which did have a phone, had downed their shutters. She walked out and sat on the doorstep, waiting. Wait is all that she could do. She never realised that it will be a never-ending wait. Haradhan returned in the morning. The children had gone out to the local park to play. Purnima prepared a cup of tea for Haradhan.

'So much work?' she asked innocently.

'I want to talk to you,' Haradhan said.

'Yes, tell me.'

'No it is . . . how I should put it.' Haradhan tried to get his words together. 'I am going to marry Shanti.'

On a new-moon night suddenly you wake up after a nightmare and look around to reassure yourself about your own existence, and it's all dark around; your orientation all gone wayward. You don't recall where the door is, or which side of the bed you had slept. Was there a window on your right or was it behind your head? You reach out and grapple with the bed sheet to ensure that you exist.

Haradhan just walked out of Purnima's life. Purnima was too dumbstruck to protest. No divorce, no alimony. She sat on the bed as Haradhan packed his clothing and odd personal belongings in a suitcase and walked out. She sat, still believing it was a nightmare and soon she will get up at the cawing of the crows and Haradhan will be by her side with side-pillow tucked between his legs. She knew he could never sleep without the side-pillow. Till Devika was two years old, Haradhan would use Purnima as his side-pillow. It was only when Devika started growing up that Purnima went to the local bedding fabricator and got a side-pillow made. On the first day, Haradhan refused to use it. He accused Purnima of not liking him anymore. But over a period, he also realized that Devika was growing up and accepted the side-pillow.

The children came back.

'Hasn't Baba come back?' Gita asked. Purnima did not know what to reply. She walked into the kitchen to prepare the lunch.

'You all go and take your bath.'

'When will Baba come?' Gita asked again.

'After a few days.' Purnima cooked up. 'He has gone out of Calcutta for office work.'

A faint ray of hope passed through her mind. Truly it could be that he would return after a few days. 'No I will not tell him anything. I will not question him,' she thought to herself. A faint smile wafted through her mind. 'I will wait.' And she waited, opening the door at every knock hoping to see Haradhan standing there with that big smile. It is strange, Purnima never shed a single drop of tear. It took a whole week for her to realize the truth and the tears had dried up by then. She had to rear the children, pay the house rent, and pay for the school fees. There were too many demands of reality to find time for the luxury of emotional breakdown.

Years passed like the flowing waters of Ganges, never to touch back the shores once crossed. The times had changed; Purnima's nursing certificate was old. She could manage a job of midwifery at a private nursing home. It was tough with her low salary, but at least she could manage through nine long years. Yes it was a very long nine years. Devika had eloped with a CISF (Central Industrial Security Force) jawan who stayed in the neighbourhood. Purnima never resisted realising it was best that could happen to Devika. She had left studies after class nine, and Purnima was in no position to find a good suitor for her. Gita was in class nine, and Barun in class seven. Gita did not excel in studies but seemed to have interest in continuing education. Purnima always backed her by purchasing second hand books for her; but of late, she had to borrow books from classmates.

Rising inflation and mounting needs of two growing children made Purnima look for additional income. She was good in embroidery. During off-duty hours, she picked up embroidery work from the tailoring houses in the neighbourhood. It did help, but did not augment the need. A skirt for Gita, when she was small, cost about twenty to thirty rupees. Now she is grown up, and needs to wear a sari to school. The most ordinary of them cost seventy rupees. Then there was the brassiere, panty, petticoat, and the blouse. The package most ordinary had an expenditure of hundred and thirty to hundred and fifty rupees.

Purnima often skipped a meal to save. The overload of work combined with low food intake was telling on her health and looks. She looked much older than she really was. She realised this when one afternoon, Kanan came visiting. Kanan was a colleague nurse during Purnima's stint at the Railway hospital. They were friends, though not of the intimate kind. Kanan was beautiful and always dressed well, used make-ups, and always had the extra money to enjoy life's little pleasures. That was eighteen years back. Purnima was taken aback; Kanan had not changed much. She was still beautiful, didn't look her age, had make-up on, and draped the sari tightly hugging the body. When they used to go out of the hospital, many male would stare at Kanan and it seemed Kanan liked it. Even today many would stare at her, Purnima thought. There was not much communication between the two except one or two occasional visits, and a few letters exchanged. That too was a decade ago.

'Come in. What a surprise,' Purnima exclaimed.

'I was passing by, so thought why not visit you,' Kanan said.

'You are still working? How many children do you have?' Purnima asked. 'They must have grown up.'

'Children?' Kanan showed surprised. 'I never married.'

'Achha! But why?'

'Ah! It is better to be single. Why should I lose my freedom?'

'But don't you feel lonely?' In her heart of heart, Purnima thought maybe Kanan was better off. Kanan had come after a long time. Some sweets must be served with tea. And that would be an extra expense over the budget. Such petty things, but Purnima had to worry.

'You wait for a while; I will get something to eat.' Purnima left for the corner sweet shop. When she came back, Gita had already returned from school. Barun would follow soon. Kanan had introduced herself to Gita and was already into a tete-a-tete with her.

'Gita, my daughter.' Purnima introduced her daughter once again. 'And Barun will come soon. He is younger to her by two years.'

'Where is Devika?' Kanan asked.

'She got married three years back.'

Over a cup of tea and a few sweets, the friends talked on. Kanan said she organised parties for the rich, but Purnima did not understand the job. Purnima told about her poor times and poverty. It was then that Kanan suggested.

'Why don't you make some extra money?'

'I do some embroidery work, but they hardly pay anything.'

'I'm not talking about you, I'm talking about Gita.'

'What can she do? She is so young and moreover, has her school.'

'Look, I organize parties. And I hire hostesses who look after the guests. I can hire her as well.'

'But she has her school and studies.'

'Aha, parties are held in the evenings. It won't disturb her school and you will have some extra earning.'

'I don't know what is to be done there and will she be able to do them right.' Purnima showed her apprehensions. 'She has never been into something like this. She doesn't even know what a party is.'

'She will learn if she attends a few. Moreover, if she picks up well, you can earn a lot.'

'What do you mean by a lot?'

'If she is good, she can even earn in thousands every month.'

'You are joking. Thousands, I don't believe it.'

'Why should I lie?'

Thousands. That was a big illusion to sweep Purnima's mind. So much hard work and she could only earn about eight to nine hundred per month. And this work had potential of getting thousands. So Gita accompanied Kanan for the next party.

Before the party day, Kanan had taken Gita out and got blouses custom-tailored, bought fancy undergarments, and two chiffon saris. And on the day, there was a total makeover of Gita supervised by Kanan. Her greasy hair was shampooed. They never used it before. Washing hair once a week with soap and oiling was all that Gita did. Gita giggled to herself while putting on the fancy undergarments in the kitchen. They revealed more than they covered. The blouse was tight fitting. The neckline was deep. Not the readymade type that she wore to school. Kanan helped her with the sari and make-up. Gita looked at the small mirror on the wall. She was a changed girl. She felt grown-up.

She remembered a few times when Ma was off to work, exploring her own sexuality with her friend Tina. They undressed and went under the bed and touched each other's tits and felt a strange feeling creeping in. She did not know what it was but she liked the touch and the sensation. The coming of menstruation and mother teaching her to pad up with old cloth wrap ups, and telling her, 'Now you are a woman.' It did not mean anything to her then. But today, she could relate the sensation to her own self. She understood her sexuality. She felt she had turned into a woman from a girl. Kanan said Gita was a backdated name and would not be perfect for the party circle. So Gita metamorphosed into Esha.

Kanan squeezed in two hundred-rupee note into Purnima's palm before leaving.

It was a big house. Kanan walked in with Esha. The door opened into a big hall. There were already many people around. Men, young guys, women, and she felt she was the youngest of them all. In fact she felt that she did not fit into the scene. There was nobody from her age group. There was music on and most of the people were holding glasses in their hands. Esha saw that Kanan was known to most men and particularly to all women around.

'You be around,' Kanan told Esha. 'If somebody comes and talk to you be polite and talk, and watch around what is happening. You will learn this way.'

She took to a corner as Kanan left her. The music became louder and as time passed, Esha saw the people behaving strangely. Everybody was speaking in loud voices. Some couples danced to the music in the centre of the hall. Some men retired to the couches and sofas with a woman, and some even with two in arm. Nobody felt ashamed as kissing and embracing continued openly. For once Esha felt afraid. She felt lost in a strange, bizarre world, with no one to reach out for.

A man of thirty plus walked up to Esha. 'You are all alone.' He had a glass in his hand. He could not speak clearly.

'Yes, I am new to this place,' Esha replied.

'What is your name?'

'Gi..... Esha.' She corrected herself.

'Come take some snacks.' He led her to the table spread with variety of vegetarian and non-vegetarian fare. He picked up a plate and handed it over to her. She picked up two small pieces of mutton, which later on she learnt was called kebab.

'Take more,' the man said.

'No. That's all.'

'OK. Come with me, we will stand on the balcony.'

She followed him. It was dark outside and the balcony overlooked a private lawn. Here, too, there were a few couples entwined in intimate postures. Esha felt shy to face the man with all happenings around. He took her to a corner. 'I am Abhijeet.' he said. 'Do you know you are very beautiful?'

She felt a flush on her face. She could say nothing. Abhijeet raised her hand to touch her cheek. Esha liked it but moved away.

'Why are you feeling shy? You are truly beautiful. I just want to touch you.'

She saw the couple standing a little away engaged in a deep kiss. She could feel something strange was happening to her. She liked every moment, but there was this fear of the unknown. Abhijeet held her face in both hands and softly squeezed. He caressed her hair and came close to her.

'I want to kiss you,' he said.

'No.' Esha broke loose and ran inside the room.

It took two more parties for Esha to get into the groove. She kissed a few young men. Cuddled with some. Allowed some to explore her body all over, but only over the dress. She enjoyed good food, learnt their names, never drank, but learnt about them. She enjoyed this whole new experience and started looking forward to attend such parties, but never told the details to Ma. Purnima was happy with parties happening quite often, and a few extra hundred rupee notes rolling into her palm. She felt relieved of the stress that she was going through.

Another Saturday, another party. Kanan had stopped coming to pick her up. She used to give her the address and time for the next party at the end of the ongoing party. Esha did not need any more guidance on dressing up. She had noticed other women and knew how to dress to attract men. She started feeling the power of being attractive and being craved for. The excitement did not end with the parties. Often in bed at night she would conjure up the fantasies.

Slowly put her hand down through her panties and rub on the vagina as it slowly got moistened.

The address was one of Camac Street. It was a multi-storied building. The party was on a seventh floor flat. She took the elevator and knocked at the flat number 704. A lady opened the door. In most of these parties, there were always new faces to be encountered. Only Kanan Aunty and the hostess women were mostly the same; same loud music, flowing booze, and mindless anarchy. Esha walked up to Sweety, another hostess she knew.

'There are no young men this time,' she said.

'This is a party of all old hags. Even some of their wives are here.' Sweety replied. 'Just wait and see. These parties with old hags are terrible. They just tear you apart.'

'What do mean by 'tear you apart'?' Esha questioned.

'Just wait and see.'

Esha became slightly apprehensive about the evening.

As she picked up a few kebabs and a little salad on a plate, a man walked up to her. Stout, short, pot-bellied, bald, aged about sixty.

'I am Razdan, what's your name?' the man asked.

Esha was repelled by the very look of the man. He smelt badly of whiskey.

'Esha.' she replied curtly.

The man caught hold of her hand and said, 'Come.'

'Where?' she asked.

'Don't be silly, come with me.' He pulled her along with him. As he was getting into a curtained room, Esha pulled herself clear and ran to Kanan Aunty.

'Aunty, that man is misbehaving with me.'

'Which man?' Kanan asked. Esha pointed out to the man near the curtained door.

'Do you know who he is?' Kanan shouted at her, caught hold of her hand and pulled her back to the same man.

'Razdan Saab what's the problem?'

'Ask her. She is not ready to come with me. She is good, but why do you get them here if they don't want to oblige.'

'Don't worry, she is new. I will talk to her and she will be yours.' Esha shivered within. She had never seen Kanan Aunty in such fiery state. And she was the only one whom Esha could fall back upon in case of trouble. But . . . Kanan pulled her to a side.

'Bitch! Do you know I gave five hundred to Purnima? For what? Just for you to enjoy good food and fool around.' Esha felt lost. She could not relate five hundred rupees, Ma, the party, Razdan.

'Just go with him and do what he says.'

Kanan pushed her and Razdan into the room and closed the door. Mr Razdan caught hold of Esha's face tightly in his palms. So tight was the grip it pained her lower jaws.

'You are beautiful,' he said. Esha heard this as the opening conversation many a times in the last few parties, but then she liked it. But today she felt repelled. He opened the door slightly and asked for a glass of whiskey. Esha stood still as he came in with the glass, locked the door, and sat down on the couch that was there.

'I like to see women undress. Will you do it or should I tear your dress apart?' he said, sipping the whiskey. Esha shuddered at the thought of going out of the room with torn dress. She wanted to cry out for help. But there was no one.

'Will you do it or should I come?' Mr Razdan growled. Esha slowly took off her pallu and started taking off her sari.

'Bitch, open the blouse.' She started unhooking the blouse.

'Take it off.' She did.

'Do I have to tell every step? Take off the petticoat.'

She untied the petticoat knot and let it slip down. She stood like an inanimate object in her bra and panty looking down. Mr Razdan suddenly rushed to her, caught hold of one of her breast, and started biting it. It pained, but she had lost her voice. He caught hold of her by the hair and licked her face again and again. It was filled with his saliva as he pulled open her bra. Esha felt nauseating with all that gooey saliva on her face, his armpits stinking, and his dirty teeth biting into her body. He pulled her to the bed, and threw her onto it; pulled out her panty, and pushed in a finger into her vagina. It was dry and his rough cracked fingers added to the pain. He undressed to reveal a hairy body and stood in front of Esha looking voyeuristically down at his own cock. She had never imagined a man so ugly. He caught hold of his black wrinkled erected cock and came closer to Esha. She closed her eyes.

'Bloody fuckin whore, get up.' He shouted.

She got up and sat on the bedside with eyes closed. She felt she would throw up as Mr Razdan caught hold of her hair and pulled her face to his piece of pride.

'Bloody suck it. You will never get a better one in your mouth,' and tried to push it into her mouth. Esha kept her lips tight and bit them hard from inside so that nothing could open it. Mr Razdan, failing in the endeavor, pulled her by the hair and slapped her hard on her cheek. She opened her eyes and mouth in shock and pain. Semen was dripping and there was some dirty looking white stuff around the tip of the penis. It smelled like rotten egg. He pushed it straight into her mouth.

Esha could take no more and literally vomited on him. Suddenly his erection dropped down. With all the vomit on his pelvis he stood stunned for a while and then started slapping Esha hard with both the hands, on both cheeks. She cried out in pain and ran away to a corner. Mr Razdan sat down on the bed. Esha picked up her dresses, moved to a corner, dressed, and walked out of the room.

'I will not go to any party anymore,' Esha told Ma.

'Why?' Ma asked.

'I don't want to talk about it, but I'm not going.'

'So where is the money going to come from?' Purnima was cold and harsh.

'Ma, I know that you know everything. You cannot do this to me.'

'I have reared you so long. Now I cannot work hard anymore. How long will I continue?' Purnima tried to reason out. 'If tomorrow my job goes, where will the money come from? You have a duty; you have to look after your brother and me.'

Esha loved Barun from the bottom of her heart. She knew Ma was being unreasonable but for Barun, she could do anything.

So parties continued: new men, new experiences. Arindam, Mr Kalsi, Kohli, Abinash, Mr Roy, and slowly the names did not matter anymore to her. Their figure, smelly armpits, nostril hair, greasy hair, cracked palms, nasty feet—nothing mattered anymore. She picked up the fine nuances of the art of seduction and sex, talking to other hostesses, and Kanan Aunty. By fifteen she was one of the most sophisticated and sought after hostess in the circuit.

Things at home were changing, too. The old transistor was replaced by a record player. The bed now had a comfortable mattress. The wardrobe was quite full with fashionable saris and dresses. Esha's undergarments were all top of the line. Ma had five silk saris. Barun boasted of jeans and sports shoes. The family started dining out at restaurants. And an engraved wooden puja counter with Shiva idol, adorned the eastern corner. And Esha spent fifteen minutes every morning before going to school performing puja.

Esha did not leave school. She continued her studies. It was here that she found the child in herself among the class friends. In the parties, she lived as a woman. Here she was a kid, still running out of school for that ten-paisa stick ice cream, looking at the boys from afar and commenting among selves, laughing aloud from the heart on the silliest of jokes. She started living a dual existence and it seemed she managed well. Kanan did not pay out a few hundred rupees to Purnima anymore. Esha had taken control. She struck deals at parties directly and passed on a cut to Kanan Aunty.

It was the winter of 1974; a party at a Theatre Road flat. Nothing was different except that there were a few new guests from Bangkok. Kanan Aunty had briefed all the hostesses that they were rich and influential. Any deal should be struck with them keeping the fact in mind. The party was on. All the hostess were introduced to the four new guests from Bangkok. Esha found nothing extraordinary in them; they were all in the late forties or early fifties. Two were Sindhi, one Sikh, and one Gujrati.

She picked a glass of whiskey and settled down on a sofa. She never took more than two drinks at such parties. She actually did not like drinking, but it helped her in becoming impersonal. After the first drink she noticed the Sikh from Bangkok, Mr Singh stealing glances from her. She consciously tried to avoid locking eyes with him. She had learnt the tricks of the trade. She knew men like to go after women who are hard to get. Male chauvinism gives them this false sense of achievement. She was right. Soon the Sikh walked down to her.

'Can I sit here?' he asked.

'Of course, Mr Singh.' Though not needed, she shifted a bit as if to make place for him. 'And what do you do?'

'My name is Ranjit Singh and I have an export-import business running from Bangkok.'

'And what do you import or export?'

'Well that depends. Sometimes electronic items or saris, or at times even gold jewellery,' he replied. 'What is your name that the lady introduced you with.'

'Esha.'

'That's a nice name.' *'Why these men use the same rotten opening lines in a conversation?'* Esha thought.

'You are very young. You must be attending college.'

'No, I'm about to complete school. Of course, I will join college thereafter.'

'I heard you are the most sought-after hostess in the party.'

'Well, the most expensive surely.'

'Do you go out? I mean do you meet outside the circuit?'

'Well I have not as yet, but I can make an exception for you if I like your offer.'

'Actually I don't like this hullabulla of the party. I will like to meet you personally.'

'What's on offer?'

'You are quite direct.'

'After all, it is my profession. Why be vague about it.'

'Well for a night, I will give you five hundred.'

'Night out is out of question. You tell me any other time and I will spend two hours with you. The offer remains the same. Do you agree?'

'OK. Then tomorrow we shall meet at Hotel Bluestar at seven in the evening.' Mr Singh jotted down the room number and the address of the hotel on a piece of paper, and handed it over to her.

Esha knew she was entering into a new arena; the freedom of being on her own. But there were risks too; in the parties it was in a circle where there were known people around. The guests were known to Kanan Aunty, or someone in the circuit. The parties allowed people only with references. So there was a tab on their background. In going alone, there was this risk of landing up at the wrong places with wrong men. But there was this lure of not sharing the commission. Moreover, Mr Ranjit Singh came to the party through reference only. The risk was a calculated one, Esha thought.

It was ten minutes past seven when she reached Hotel Bluestar. She was in a blue jeans and a red top. She walked up the stairs and knocked at the given room number. Mr Ranjit Singh opened the door. Esha could not recognize him. He did not have his turban on and there was this bald head. She had never visualized a bald Sikh. With their turban on it seemed they all have this huge flowing hair tied in a bun on top.

'Come in,' Mr Ranjit Singh said. She recognized the voice and moved in.

'I did not recognize you at first. I thought I was at the wrong place,' Esha said.

'I too did not recognize you. Yesterday I saw you in a sari and you look so different in jeans and top. But you are looking good and smart.'

'Thank you.'

Mr Ranjit Singh closed the door. Esha sat on the bed.

'Would you like a drink?' he asked. 'I have a good scotch.'

'I will try one,' Esha said. Mr Ranjit took out a bottle of Johnny Walker Black Label from a leather bag and rang the room service bell. A bell-boy knocked at the door.

'Get us two glasses, soda,' and looking towards Esha asked, 'What would you like to have?'

'Any sort of snacks. Of course I prefer non-veg.'

'OK, they make good tandoori chicken just nearby,' Mr Ranjit ordered the waiter. 'Get us one full tandoori chicken.'

Esha was waiting for the usual. Most of the men do the same—a little wait, and then the grab. But the usual did not happen. In fact, Mr Ranjit just talked the whole two hours, learnt about Esha's background; spoke about his wife and children in Bangkok, about his Indian experience, etc. At nine, he took out five hundred rupee notes from his purse and handed over to Esha.

'But you did not do anything.' Esha was astonished.

'May I ask you a favour?' Mr Ranjit asked.

'Yes, tell me.' Esha felt sure that this man could not ask for some undue favours.

'Will you have dinner with me?' Mr Ranjit proposed.

'I will be delighted.' And they walked down to Elfin, which was nearby.

During dinner Mr Ranjit informed that he was staying in Calcutta for the next two days and proceeding to Delhi thereafter, before leaving for Bangkok. He requested Esha if she could drop in both the evenings.

'Of course I will pay your fees,' he assured. Esha had nothing to lose, she agreed.

Next day started on the same note too—a drink, few snacks, gupshupping, and then dinner. It was during dinner that Mr Ranjit became more personal.

'Why are you in this trade?' he asked. 'You said your mother is a working lady.'

'But her income is meager. It does not suffice for our family's needs,' she reasoned.

'How much money do you need per month?'

'Why are you asking? Will you give me a job?' Esha enquired. 'But I cannot work. I am continuing school and want to study further.'

'No it's not that. Tell me how much is your family's monthly need?' Mr Ranjit insisted on knowing.

'Three thousand to three thousand five hundred.'

'What if I give you four thousand every month?' Esha was shocked. 'Will you leave this circuit?'

Esha could not believe her ears. Why is the man doing this?

'You will have to leave the circuit and visit me the three or four days when I come to Calcutta.'

Esha could not decide on the spot.

'Let me talk to my mother.'

'OK. Tomorrow when you come, let me know.'

There was a long discussion between Ma and Esha after Barun went to sleep. It was a win-win situation for both. As if, it was a God Shiva send boon, Esha thought. She did not have to face all those idiosyncratic guests, and that no new ones with new demands every time, in every party. Ma found the income to rise by minimum a thousand rupees; so a better life, and maybe, a little to save for future as well.

Next evening, Esha gave in to Mr Ranjit's proposal. The evening changed its hue. Ranjit came closer, got her in an embrace and kissed her. After dinner he asked her to stay back. Esha relented. They had a wild night. For the first time, Esha felt different while having sex. She felt she belonged to someone. It was no more the pseudo appreciations followed often by violent sex. Ma knew it was a big deal, and did not worry when Esha did not return home. She told Barun that Didi had gone to Mona Aunty's house; she will stay the night there. In the morning as Esha prepared to leave, Ranjit handed over four thousand rupees to her.

'When will you be coming back?' she asked. She felt she will be missing him. It had never happened to her.

'My manager, Mr Mehta, will contact you at your home and let you know when I'm in Calcutta.'

'Can I write letters to you?' she felt emotional.

'No,' he replied. 'But soon I will have a phone installed in your house. We can talk then.' Esha thought she was living in a fairy tale. Nobody in their colony had a telephone. She hugged Ranjit, kissed him and left; waiting for the day when he would return.

As months passed, Ranjit and Esha got real close emotionally. At least, Esha thought so. There was the telephone at home. She made international calls to his

Bangkok office to be in touch. He always brought lots of gifts whenever he came—American georgette saris, fancy lingerie, electronic gizmos, chocolates. Esha called him Kaka, which meant a child in Punjabi, and ironically Uncle in Bengali. Times were so happy, a dream germinated in Esha's mind. She started nurturing the fantasy of getting married to Ranjit one day and become Mrs Esha Sandhu. He was much elder to her but why should that matter, after all she loved him and he loved her too, at least that's what she thought. Esha even discussed this with Ma. She liked the idea but was more cautious. 'Don't speak of marriage to him now.'

And more months passed. Esha came to know that Ranjit was not an exporter-importer. He was a big fish smuggler. He had a network of carriers who would bring in contraband goods through Bangladesh and Nepal borders. He had well oiled distribution channel in the grey markets of Calcutta and Delhi. He had a wife, and two grown-up children in Bangkok, and another paramour in Delhi. Esha's dreams were not only shattered but she felt used. She had only switched the mode of operation. She was still peddling her body. She was only a keep for his pleasure. But she did not get an opportunity to cry out her pain as all this revealed over a period of time. She adjusted herself to the new realization. She behaved the same way as before, only that now she faked it once again. She felt like the party days, emotionless while kissing Kaka or having sex with him. Mr Ranjit Singh never realized it. So the relationship continued and Esha's home flourished.

CHAPTER 7

THERE WERE THESE two gigantic trees in front of our education block. I never found out the English name but I knew it bore round fruits double the size of a cricket ball. It was called 'Chalte' in Bengali and was used to cook 'chutney' or added in 'dal' preparation to add a citrus taste. I loved it whenever Mamoni cooked them. One vacation I collected six of these fruits and carried them home, thinking parents would be happy, only to find out they cost peanuts in the market back home and the effort was fruitless. Further down towards the rows of our dormitories was a Magnolia tree. In a particular season it bore large flowers. Whenever we passed below it, there was this beautiful fragrance all around. One day I picked up one that had dropped to the ground and could not resist the temptation to breathe in a lungful of its fragrance. To my astonishment I felt like throwing up, felt giddy. The smell was too strong from up close.

Growing up far away from parents' caring influence had its pros and cons, but was interesting. Always a new experience, self acquired. It was like discovering the world all by oneself and believing all the little things to be inventions. It was fun rediscovering the wheel. RIMC had a vast sprawling campus with nature nurtured all around in more than fair doses. There were the tall Eucalyptus trees that shed its bark in winter; the large mango trees which bore fruit in summer to be ripped off by cadets, never allowing any to ripen; the short bushy guava trees with fruits that always tasted alkaline.

One afternoon, Mehta and I even discovered a grapevine in the backyard of our Commandant's residence. It had tiny black pepper-sized grapes on it; we tasted a few, and they were extremely sour.

But nothing to beat the small brook that passed by our campus; It was always dry except during the rainy season when ankle-deep, clear water lazily sauntered down over the pebbles of various hues and shapes. Often on Sunday afternoons we walked down this brook, out of our campus, behind backyard of many dwellings prospecting small nothings: a broken alarm clock, an odd shaped glass bottle, a piece of ornamented broken crockery; all thrown away as valueless junk, which landed up in our cupboards as priceless treasure. When the water flowed, we waded barefoot, with the shoes and socks in our hand. There were a few spots where the water would stabilize to form a small pool within the running water. We would stand around and watch a few tiny fish playing in it before zipping into the moving stream and vanish. Our shooting range was also by the side of this brook. It had a rugged terrain apart from the cleaned flat shooting wall. All around were soil and sandstone upheavals with huge boulders. Here we played the fight scenes of Bollywood films on many Sunday afternoons. Punching in the air, making the big punch sound 'dishuum' vocally, would feign to fall off a ledge, hang from it with firm ground under our feet, do handsprings, cartwheels, as taught in our physical training classes, and bring in action into otherwise lazy Sunday afternoons.

Those days, most Hindi films had the same basic storyline. There was a hero, who fell in love with the heroine. And there always was a villain who plotted against the hero and finally would nearly be successful in harming the heroine. But hero always arrived in the nick of time and a fight would follow. Though the same tale was picturised with different dressings, the climax would always be clichéd. The villain, through flying punches and lot of incomprehensible gymnastic acts, would get the hero off the edge off a cliff. But the hero cannot die, so he hangs on to the ledge as the villain keeps trampling his fingers with his heavy boot. Suddenly, the miracle happens. Well, the hero was always expected to be a super human being. He gets hold of the villain, pulls him off the ledge, down the cliff, and climbs up to hold the heroine in his arms. The families and the police arrive. The END.

However silly the storyline may sound, they were very dear to our hearts and we not only made sure we saw all of those that were released in this small town, but at times repeated, some even thrice. Films were an integral part of my growing up. So were many other life's experiences. It was in class eight that I started smoking occasionally when we went out on leave or cut bounds in the night for a movie. It was not only I, but seven in our class had started occasional smoking. While others experimented with every new brand that was launched or with the longest available, I started on Charminar, the brand of the then intellectuals of Bengal. It was a strong brand, which I got used to through lot of coughs and palpitations. Moreover, it was the cheapest brand available, thereby allowing me to smoke more cigarettes than my friends at the same cost. Some of my friends were also lured to try the brand due to the cost factor but drifted to lighter brands because of its strong flavour and the bitter taste that it left in the mouth after smoking. It seemed equally important to learn the vices as fast as the virtues that we were being taught officially.

'Have you ever tried 'ganja'?' Gazmere asked, getting down from the bicycle. We were in town on a weekend leave. 'It is also called grass.'

Gazmere from Kurseong in north Bengal was a Nepali and a semester junior to me. Over a period of time we had found a common bonding through poetry and music. He was adept in playing quite a few musical instruments and had a guitar of his own. Often, in free times, we would sit together in the dorms and try to put music to the poetries that I was writing as an ode to Lipika. I had not heard the term.

'What's that?' I queried.

'It's a bud of a plant. You crush it and fill in a cigarette and smoke. It gives a high like nothing else in the world.'

'Have you ever tried?' I asked.

'Yes, quite a few times. I have some on me today.' I could not be left behind the James and Joneses in experiencing the high like nothing else in the world. I agreed to give it a try. We bought two tickets of a film and walked into Moti Mahal for lunch. As usual, the tomato ketchup bottle was immediately removed from our table. We ordered a plate of 'Chhole Bhature'. Gazmere asked me to follow him to the lavatory. We locked ourselves in the same loo and the preparation of 'ganja' started. It seemed Gazmere was quite adept at it. He rolled out the tobacco from a cigarette. Took out some very dark green dry leafy stuff, crushed it and mixed it with part of the tobacco from the cigarette and refilled the cigarette. We went back to the table, had lunch, and it was only after watching the film on our way back that he stopped at a secluded spot.

'Let's have it here. You cannot have it everywhere as it has a strong smell.' He lit the stuffed cigarette and puffed on. Soon I saw his eyes turning red and slightly swollen. He passed on the cigarette to me. I took a drag. The first one hit my gullet and I started coughing badly.

'You are trying for the first time. Take in small puffs.' So did I. Soon, I was feeling a little dizzy and the vision became a little blurred. I felt a little numbness on my fingertips. Truly, it was a feeling I had never experienced. A few times that I had taken a peg or two of rum, I had something of a similar feeling, yet this was different. The numbness was now growing into my brain. There was a feeling of euphoria but I could not stand any longer. I sat down on a big boulder by the roadside.

I could not gauge how much time had elapsed when Gazmere tapped me on my shoulder. 'Sid, let's move, or else we will get late for evening roll call.'

We biked up and down the serpentine roads to reach our college in time. Soon after, Gazmere's stock of grass had finished. We could not wait till the vacation for him to bring in the next consignment. It did take some days for Gazmere and I to source 'grass' locally. A talk with the daily wager grass cutters who came into the campus to keep our lawns trimmed, revealed they quite knew the stuff, and were even willing to smuggle it into the campus for us. Thus started our occasional Sunday afternoon short sessions of grass smoking.

I could not keep the secret for long from my other friends Jayant, Tirtha, and Roy. They soon joined us in this newfound pleasure. On Sunday afternoons, five of us would smoke the grass in the empty gym, laze around for a little while, and walk back to the kit room with our coffee kit. With many cadets gone on leave to the town, some loitering around the campus, and some taking the afternoon nap, the kit room was generally empty. Even the seniors never peeked in. This was a room with large wooden boxes assigned to each cadet. The box was used to keep the used clothes, which we sent out for laundry on Sunday mornings. The room was also used for changing dresses, which we needed to do quite a few times through the day. Our coffee kit consisted of a tin of 'Milkmaid' condensed milk, a packet of 'Nescafe' coffee, our mugs, in which we had our morning tea, and the heater. The heater was a unique improvisation inspired by our physics lessons. Two wires had two metallic keys attached at one end. The wires were tied to a stick to keep them at a distance. The bare ends were plugged into a socket and the keys were dipped into a mug full of water, making sure that the keys did not touch each other or the mug. Switch on, and in a few minutes you have boiling water ready for the coffee. Sometimes, a tin of canned sardines, luncheon meat or pork sausages, which we bought from the college canteen, accompanied this afternoon picnic after the drag. We ate them raw straight out of the brine in the can. Though the luncheon meat and the sausages were fine, the canned sardines or tuna really never tasted great. Being from Bengal, land where fish was a staple diet with every meal, the pickled salty taste of canned fish was nothing to write home about. But nevertheless we savored it because eating processed canned products was totally a new experience for all of us.

It was the early seventies; the age of 'flower power', 'hippie cult', 'free love', and psychedelic drugs. Though we were not part of this movement, we heard about them and spotted 'hippies' in saffron vests and pyjamas, with dirty lousy backpacks when we went to town on leave or back home during vacation. The numbers were increasing by the day. Even a small town like Dehradun was soon flooded by American and European hippies. Every tenth passerby would be a hippie. Though we did not understand their philosophy of disdain, we picked up knowledge about the various drugs in use and their effects through hearsay. At the high end there was 'LSD', then there was 'Mandrax', and then at the bottom was the 'grass'. I was already occasionally smoking 'grass', so it was time to graduate to the next, 'Mandrax'. I wanted to try 'LSD' as well. But no knowledge about its sourcing and the idea that it was costly put me off. On the other hand, 'Mandrax' was openly available as a medicine at all chemist shops. Though a restricted drug to be sold on a licensed medical practitioner's prescription, it was available to the adults for the asking.

Like many occasions, I had shammed into the small Military hospital in our campus. I had complained about chest pain, which was never there in the first place. Preliminary examinations by the resident doctor failed. So I was supposed to be sent to the Base Military Hospital in town for x-ray and some more tests. So I managed three days of rest at the college hospital and escaped from the rigors of the daily routine. On the very first evening, I asked the orderly serving us at the hospital if he could get me a medicine from outside. He agreed. I wrote 'Mandrax' on a piece of paper and gave it to him and waited anxiously for my experiment to bear fruit. It was after we had finished dinner and I lay in the bed reading a James Hadley Chase book that the orderly arrived. He handed me a small brown paper envelope. I opened it to find the tablet in it. Tore open the foil, took out the white tablet and gulped it down with water. I waited for about ten minutes, but could feel nothing. Another five minutes, yet nothing. I felt fooled and took up the book to continue reading. After about reading two pages I started feeling sleepy. I decided to go to the loo for a piss before sleeping. I climbed down the bed and to my sheer surprise I just fell flat on the ground with a thud—like a lump of soft clay. None of my joints were functioning and there was hardly any sensation in my limbs. Other cadets rushed to me from their bed, 'What happened?' I could see them all but could not respond and kept lying on the ground. I knew that the Mandrax was working. They picked me up like a beanbag and dumped me onto my bed. I passed out into oblivion.

Mandrax was a costly affair at sixty paisa a tablet; cigarette cost six paisa; and a packet of grass, twenty paisa. One packet of grass was enough for two jaunts. Naturally, Mandrax was only for rare occasions. I did experience the high quite a few times and slowly found my feet on the ground with this new drug. My joints no more gave way and I could feel the high instead of passing out. But being a costly affair, I stopped indulging soon after.

* * *

It was the end of class ten vacations. Lipika had joined college. This was the first time we had decided to meet outside her home. We could, as she no more had to commute by the school bus. She would be on her own while going to college and back. She could bunk a few classes without her parents knowing it—the small liberties that one gains on joining the college.

I took the tram number 31 that went to Khidderpore, to Lipika's home. It was ten in the morning as I pushed open the door and stepped into the courtyard. They had three stately swans as pet. Shefali Mashi was attending to them at the other end of the courtyard.

'When did you come from Dehradun?'

'Yesterday.'

'Shona is getting ready for college. Why don't you sit in that room while I finish with their bath? I will just join you.'

I walked into the room where I always met Lipika in the vacations. Lipika walked in. We looked at each other and blushed. It was always the same. And the silence followed. She took a few seconds to come out of the stupor.

'When did you come?' she asked.

This was the first time I was seeing her in a sari that generally grown-ups wear. Till the last vacation, she wore skirts and blouses. In the sari she looked so beautiful, so woman.

'Just few minutes ago,' I replied. 'Can we meet outside today?'

'I will leave for college in some time. Why don't you leave now and tell me where I should meet you.'

It was the first time we were going out. I didn't have much idea about what we should do. With my Rimcollian friends, it was different. We could see a film, go window-shopping, go to 'Rover's Music House' and try a few LPs (Music long playing records) for free, or just loiter around New Market watching Anglo girls in short and tight skirts. That was a guy thing. It was easy and came naturally. But taking Lipika out was a different ball game altogether.

'Can we go for a movie?' I suggested the only thing I could think of doing with her outside the home.

'Which one?' she asked.

'Yaadon ki Baraat, it is a new film that released last Friday.'

'And in which cinema hall?'

'At Bharati Cinema. I will buy the tickets and wait outside the main entrance.'

'But where is this Bharati Cinema?'

Though she was in Calcutta for a much longer period than me, as I visited only in the vacations, she did not know the location of the cinema hall. After all, it was recently that she started moving out of the home environment alone.

"Take the tram No. 31 and get down at the Hazra More Stop, ask anybody for Bharati Cinema, it is just in the neighbourhood.'

Shefali Mashi came in as Lipika walked out. 'Will you take some tea?'

I was now in real hurry to move out. 'No, maybe some other day. I just came to meet you all. I have to go to my friend Jayant's house, I will leave now.'

I was at the cinema hall at eleven, too early for the noon show. I bought two tickets and stood at the entrance. It was a long wait but it became threateningly longer as it struck twelve. The show had started. It was not House Full.

Generally, the noon shows were never House Full. Still few people were buying tickets at the counter and moving in. I kept looking at the tram No. 31 stop. Each tram brought in hope of her alighting with her smile, but moved on leaving me more resigned. Interval between my cigarettes started decreasing and when puffing the fifth I saw it was one thirty. It was interval and people started coming out for snacks and beverages. I presumed something had terribly gone wrong. Could she have been unable to find out the place? Did I tell the right tram number? Was she wandering helplessly in a maze in some other area? Or worse, did Shefali Mashi find out our plan? Sweat started trickling down my temples. I lit another cigarette and started walking towards the tram stop and there she was waving from the window.

Verdant meadow sprinkled with dewdrops glistening in the clear sunlight. Carpet of soft grass under my bare feet, and blue sky dotted with cotton ball clouds above. I was running into the horizon in ecstatic joy.

CHAPTER 8

THE ALARM BELL kept ringing. It signals danger and all miners were supposed to move to the pit bottom for evacuation. But nobody cared and continued working. The bell had rung many times in the past; always it had been a mischief of an errant labour or short circuit between the 'bell wires' at some point with heavy seepage. Nobody expected any mishap in this sleepy colliery, producing merely fifty tonnes of coal per shift. Siddhartha was not alarmed as well, but as the shift supervisor, thought it appropriate to check. He moved out from the face and kept walking towards the pit bottom, looking out for any possible short circuit among the bare wires running along the tunnel walls. He reached the first haulage point. The alarm was ringing there too.

'Any idea?' He asked Haren, the haulage driver. Patting out the lime dust from the 'khaini', a dry tobacco variant, he said most disinterestedly, 'Who knows?'

He held out the khaini for Siddhartha. 'Khaini' was always to be shared among those around. Whenever a group of labourers were together, only one prepared the khaini and the rest would pick up a pinch from it. Next time, somebody else prepared. This system of sharing helped build camaraderie. Siddhartha picked up a pinch and carried on towards the pit bottom. Sharing of 'khaini' with the labourers was a good management move. The labourers felt that Siddhatha was one amongst them, a part of the team, and not some officer imposed on them. But it was not this aspect only that made him share khaini; it was a necessity as well. He was an avid smoker, and smoking was banned underground for the risk of explosion due to presence of methane gas. So this khaini gave his needed shot of nicotine. He was a hands-on manager. It was during his training after graduating from the mining school, that he quickly realised that more than the mining technology theories he had learnt, he would need people management skills to succeed. Even more than what he had learnt from a few HRM chapters, it would be inter-personal skills, ground zero communication techniques that would bring him results. And he had to develop all these through observation and innovation in this totally alien world. Siddhartha also discovered during training that there was a common thread that weaved through the psyche of all workers. Awe and respect for the characters that were portrayed by the hero in the Bollywood films. The style, the panache, even a truck driver hero on screen left an indelible dent on their aspirations. This phenomenon translated into high esteem and respect for anybody with slight resemblance to these bigger than life characters on screen.

Actually it was the then Manager, Vinay Dubey, in his early forties who helped Siddhartha conclude this observation. Not good-looking, dark, tall with twisted wrists, broken in some earlier labour unrest, always invited more respect; and patient listening by the workers, even more than the top boss, the colliery Agent himself. He always talked in a baritone voice, stood with a deliberate tilt, walked with an accentuated gait, slow, yet a lot of hand gestures during conversation. It seemed to Siddhartha that subtly, Vinay Dubey was copying the super star of the day, Amitabh Bachchan, and was successful in creating an impression on the workers. The first step in the direction was to revolt against the system by wearing jeans and canvas trousers to work instead of the half pants, which were the norm. It was not Siddhartha alone, but his three friends Mihir, Kunal, and Rajat, who passed out together, trained together, and now joined together in the same colliery revolted. When questioned by management, they cited that as per Mines Safety Rules, there was no ban on trousers. It was mentioned that no loose clothing to be worn to work and by any standards the half pants that others were wearing were much loose than the jeans they wore. So the workers had a new breed of supervisors who, at the first instance, were different by looks itself. Siddhartha and his friends had made the initial impact.

Eighty percent of the workforce was illiterate. The hot, humid, and treacherous mining conditions, in an all black world somewhere 500 feet below ground level made them haughty, stubborn, and alcoholics. Every shift, even the morning one starting at 8 a.m., with a workforce of about thirty people, would have at least eight to ten labourers smelling of liquor. The strong smell of either country-made liquor or 'Mahua', a locally homemade hooch distilled from a round extremely sweet fruit by the same name. Mahua was extremely popular with the indigenous tribals like the 'Santhals', 'Mundas', 'Koles', etc. The smell did not bother Siddhartha. Though now he drank rum, at one time he had consumed a lot of 'sixty', a country liquor.

A 'loader', the one who collected the coal from the face and loaded them into the tubs, which were coupled together in a train and finally hauled out of the face, had to fill two tubs for his daily minimum wage. There was an incentive system on further loading, but low motivational level and with heavy debts to the moneylenders, none went for it. At the first go it would be difficult to understand why a man in debt will not try to earn more, the scope being in place, and get out of the debt. The moneylenders, who were either the union leaders or the local grocery and liquor shop owners, had slowly spread vice-like tentacles into the lives of these labourers. Every labourer had an identity card which one had to present at the cash counter to withdraw one's salary. Whenever a moneylender gave money to a prospective borrower, he kept this card as security. Most of the labourers, being illiterate, had no idea of the percentage of interest being charged or calculations leading to the final amount to be paid back. Once a moneylender got hold of the card, the borrower's salary income would totally be in control of the money lender. On salary day, moneylenders would stand at the cash counter, make the borrower put his thumb impression on the register to officially record that he had withdrawn the salary, collect the total cash in connivance with the disbursing clerk, and hand over a pittance back and direct the borrower to withdraw his daily needs from a grocery shop with allegiance to the moneylenders mafia. The quantity of daily needs to be allowed to the borrowing labourer differed from one to the other, and was predetermined by the moneylender. He would allow just the needs to keep the family living at its barest minimum, and the labourer would continue serving, earning a salary for him. They were the golden geese. And thus ages would pass without the loan being cleared. In some cases, even offsprings would join the colliery; hand over their identity cards to the moneylender to continue clearing loans that their father had taken. So the labourers had no reason to earn extra. They would rather prefer a shot of Mahua and enjoy life playing 'Madol', a tribal drum and sing their life away after loading two tubs.

Siddhartha kept walking towards the pit bottom. Even a brisk walk took about forty minutes to reach the pit bottom from the face. Sound of a flute started flowing in from a distant gallery. Siddhartha knew it was loader Sankarsan Majhi nee Shanku as everybody called him. He always had this bamboo flute tucked in his 'gamchha' tied around his head. Whether waiting at the pit top to go down for the shift or at the face to start loading coal or anytime else, he always played a tune to himself—tunes with an earthy thumping rhythm, tunes of hope and happiness. Shanku was a small, docile looking man. His eyes always red and seemed lost in another world under the influence of Mahua. He had no words or anecdotes but only a lovely smile and the tunes to share. He spoke very little, mostly with 'Haw' or 'Naw' implying yes or no. But he proved himself to be a picture in contrast when it came to the big bad criminal world of moneylenders.

Shanku was not reporting to work for two days. Siddhartha asked Birsa, who lived in the same cluster as Shanku's, about his well-being.

'He has decided not to work anymore,' was Birsa's reply to Siddhartha's astonishment.

'What will he do?' Siddhartha enquired.

'He has a fighting cock. He said he will earn from it.'

'But how much can he earn from a fighting cock?'

'I don't know. He has put up a hearth in his backyard to distill Mahua. I had gone to see it and he said he will not work in the colliery anymore,' Birsa said. 'He will prepare his own Mahua and live on what his fighting cock will earn.'

'Strange are the ways of these people,' Siddhartha thought. 'The earnings from a fighter cock could never match the salary of a loader even at the minimum level. Of course he does not have a family to look after, but still . . .' Siddhartha remained dazed and decided to visit him soon.

It was a dusty summer evening. The sun had not yet gone down. Siddhartha had just come out of the colliery. He lit a cigarette; the first thing he always did on coming out. His canvas trouser dusted with coal dust, hands all black. There were coal dust streaks on his face as well. He physically participated in pushing tubs along with the 'Thelwans', the miners who handled the coal-laden tubs underground. He did not have to do it. In fact, no other shift supervisors ever did it. And all of them came out clean after a shift. But here was Siddhartha, all blackened. Looking just like any other miner of his shift apart from the smart dress that he generally wore. He was happy looking more like his co-miners than like his co-designates. So were his shift miners. He was building his team.

He took off his helmet and took the headlamp off it; opened his belt, taking out the battery pack from it, and walked towards the 'lamp room'. Depositing the lamp and battery, Siddhartha went to Mihir, standing in front of the pit-top office.

'The right side of the roof at face one is slightly loose. I've put up a temporary prop to support it,' he told Mihir.

'Keep a check on that, and the seepage at face 2 has increased substantially. I've moved the idle pump at level 3 to the face. Send your pump khalasi immediately to take charge from Rati. I've left him there.'

'How many empties are there?' Mihir asked.

'Nine tubs at level four, and six at the pit bottom,' Siddhartha replied.

Walking away from the colliery, he looked back. The sun had gone down but the western sky was still golden orange. The winding engine room and the black head-frame with its huge wheel like pulleys formed a graphic silhouette against the horizon. It was a beautiful scene, but Siddhartha had moved away from painting realism. In his spare time he often experimented with figures and forms trying to create new expressions. Three of his water colour experiments adorned one of the two-room flat that Siddhartha, Mihir, Kunal, and Rajat shared; a two-room flat with kitchen, bathroom, a small dining space, and an enclosed backyard, with two in each room.

Siddhartha walked down the winding, dusty road, weaving through barren open stretches, passing by abandoned inclines. It was getting dark. Some of these inclines were on fire, and in the darkness of night, walking amidst these fire billowing pits gave one an eerie feeling. It was like walking through a cremation ground with huge funeral pyres all around. It was a four-kilometre walk from the colliery before one reached the outskirts of the colliery colony. There were no streetlights till one reached the colony. On new moon and cloudy nights, one had to depend on the torch that one carried, and on one's own instinct. One soon got used to it. Siddhartha also got used to it.

Just before the row of colliery flats started, a small road diverted to the left, into a small settlement of tribal miners; a cluster of about ten to twelve mud hutments. Siddhartha knew that Shanku lived somewhere in there. Sound of 'Madol' was blowing in with the wind. He asked a passer-by about Shanku.

'That house on the left, at the end of our village.'

'So they called this small settlement a village, and that too their own,' Siddhartha thought. 'One needs to learn from these simple people how to be happy with the smallest of things.' He crossed the house from where the 'Madol' beats were coming. Three men sat on a cot outside the hut. While one played the 'Madol', others sang on. Shanku was sitting outside his hut on a similar cot, drinking Mahua. As soon as he saw Siddhartha, he got up and greeted him with folded hands and a bow, 'Sahab.'

The British had left India, thirty-seven years back, but certain legacies continued, some even without any logic. During the British Raj, most of the senior officers were Brits. So the junior employees called them 'Sahab', which was colloquial synonym for white foreigner: for that matter, not only British but also French, German, or any white foreigner, was a 'Sahab'. There was nothing wrong in the nomenclature, but the psychological burden that reflected in the way one said it, was demeaning. It reflected the two hundred years of British ruthless rule that converted the ordinary Indian merely to a slave. Millions of ordinary Indians, particularly the economically weaker section, lost their self-respect through the gradual dehumanization process unleashed by the British Empire. Standing on two unsure feet, bowing down and greeting a white foreigner 'Sahab', came as naturally as he bowed to his God or Goddess. And the legacy continued; and Shanku was no exception. Indian officers replaced the white foreigners and became 'Sahabs'.

'Shanku. You are not coming to the shift?' Siddhartha questioned.

'Sahab, please have a seat.' Shanku took off the 'gamchha' from his shoulder and dusted the cot off some imaginary dust. It was more of a gesture of respect and concern than actual dusting. Siddhartha sat down. The 'gamchha' which Shanku tied on his head as a headgear with the flute tucked in, was a unique piece of one and a half-meter handloom woven cloth. Not only Shanku, but most of the tribal miners carried one on the shoulder. Though the main utility was that of a towel, it also acted as a headgear to save oneself from the scorching sun. It was used as a carry-bag at the market place wherein one tied the purchases at one end and slung it over the shoulder. And underground, it acted as a bed sheet, which they laid out on the floor to lay on for a little rest during idle periods in a shift.

'Will you take a glass of Mahua?' Shanku asked.

'Oh yes.' Siddhartha did not want to miss the opportunity to get up close. Shanku went inside the hut.

Siddhartha looked around. There were four streetlights erected by the colliery. Not enough, but nevertheless it was better than complete darkness. There was no electricity in any of the homes; kerosene lamps served the purpose. The huts had paintings on the walls. It was typical of such tribal houses. Figures of peacocks, deer, flowers, and women adorned the walls. They had a typical style of their own. The womenfolk painted them to decorate their house, and the art has been passing on from mothers to daughters for generations. Shanku's walls were blank. He was unmarried and hence had no family to paint. He was on his own, colouring his world with his flute instead.

Shanku came out with an earthen pot, a small tin plate with cut onions and an aluminium glass. He sat on the ground and poured Mahua into the glass and offered it to Siddhartha.

'Why are you not coming to work?' Siddhartha asked, taking the first sip.

Shanku dipped his thumb and the middle finger into the glass and sprinkled a few drops on the ground before taking the first sip. It was an offer to Mother Earth thanking for good times he will enjoy.

'I am fine,' he replied. 'I have Jhumu, I can prepare my own Mahua, and I have brinjal, pumpkin, and gourd plant in my backyard. I don't need to work. Whatever little money I need, Jhumu can earn for me.'

'I thought you had no family. Who is Jhumu?'

'Oh, you have not seen him. He is a very brave fighting cock. He has won many amateur fights, but now I will take him to the betting circuit at the weekly market. I know he will earn me good money.'

'But you can earn much more from colliery's salary.'

'No, I do not.'

'What do you mean Shanku?' Siddhartha was astonished. Shanku had finished his glass of Mahua and asked, 'Sahab, if you finish it, I will pour one more for each of us.'

Siddhartha emptied the glass and gave it Shanku. 'But how do you say you do not earn more from the salary?' He could not find the logic. 'How much will your Jhumu earn?'

'He can earn my weekly need of rice, flour, and pulses. Oil I need to purchase once in a month. So why should I work?'

'But with your salary you can do a lot more.'

'No I cannot. My card is with Bhisam Seth.'

Siddhartha knew about Bhisam Seth. He was a grocery shop owner and ran an illicit liquor business. He was a moneylender and infamous for brutal tactics for realizing loans. Whisper had that he was related to one of the coal mafia dons of Ranigunj. Nobody knew for sure but the rumour helped Bhisam Seth to be ruthless with his defaulters. But still, Siddhartha did not understand the link between borrowing money from Bhisam Seth and Shanku's decision to leave the colliery job.

'He takes whole of my salary and only gives me my weekly ration of rice, flour, pulse, oil, and toothpowder. It is all right; because I had taken loan, he takes his interest. But ten days back some guests came to my house from a far off village. I was meeting them after six years. I told Bhisam Seth that I needed good quality rice, chicken, and country liquor for my guests.' Shanku continued, 'It was not for me but for my guests. He was very rude and did not give me anything. I had to serve them Mahua, rice, pulse, and brinjals from my garden. I was so humiliated.'

Shanku picked up his gamchha and wiped the rolling down tears as Siddhartha sat listening. 'On that very day I decided that I will not work anymore. Because, even without working, I can still have my rice, pulse, and Mahua. But where will he get his interest from?'

A logic even Siddhartha's institutionalized education could not counter. He could feel the sense of revolt in

Shanku. When you have nothing to lose, you can stake it all.

Two weeks later Siddhartha once again found Shanku sitting amidst other miners with flute tucked in his gamchha around his head at the pit top of the colliery.

'Shanku.' Siddhartha called. Shanku looked back, got up and came over with that wide innocent smile.

'Sahab.'

'You said that you will not work anymore.' Siddhartha questioned.

'Bhisam Seth has agreed to give back my card. I have to pay him only one more month's salary.'

'That is about three thousand rupees. And how much have you paid him earlier?'

'Two month's salary.'

'And how much had you borrowed?'

'Two thousand rupees.'

'That means you are paying nine thousand rupees for borrowing two thousand rupees for just three months?' Siddhartha was shocked at the rate of interest would stand out to be, if calculated.

'Sahab, you are forgetting. He is also giving me my ration and all needs for these three months.'

'But how much that will amount to?'

'Can you calculate the cost of life? He gave me life for three months.'

Siddhartha was dumbstruck; so innocent, so naive, so simple, yet so philosophical.

'Anyway after this month I will get my whole salary.' Shanku beamed with that wide smile. 'Sahab, you must come to my house, this time I will get English for you. Last time you kept my honour by drinking Mahua. This time I will honour you with English.' By English, he meant IMFL (Indian-made foreign liquor) like rum, whiskey, etc.

Siddhartha nodded a yes.

The sound of the flute had faded into the background and the lights from the pit bottom were streaking in. Siddhartha walked up to the pit bottom cage khalasi,

'Balbir, what's wrong? Why have you wrung the emergency bell?'

'Sahab, an accident has happened in the East Section.'

'What accident? Who informed you?'

'Raghu was coming from the face, he told that a blast has injured someone.'

'Methane blast?' Siddhartha was worried. Methane was a dangerous killer in these dark tunnels. Though Jambad was a Degree II mine with lesser chances, but a little carelessness could cause a methane blast disaster. As coal had its genesis in decomposition of vegetation, methane was produced during the process, which got trapped in the crevices of the coal seams as they moved down the earth's strata. The gas was highly flammable and was released into the mines as coal was extracted, opening up the crevices to the atmosphere. Any contact with fire or spark instantly ignites the gas, which, unless controlled under permissible limits, would spread rapidly, engage in a blast, raising a storm of residual coal dust which further is ignited like gunpowder and triggers huge explosion engulfing the mine. There are safety measures to localize such blasts but damage control depends on accumulated methane volume. Siddhartha had read about methanometers in the mining engineering books.

But here, everybody depended on age old Davis Safety Lamp to check methane emission.

'No,' Balbir replied to Siddhartha's relief. 'The coal blasting at one of the faces.'

'It is a local accident. Why are you ringing the emergency alarm?' Siddhartha disengaged the alarm. 'Where is Mukherjee Saab?'

'He has gone up to the pit top. I have told Raghu to inform him,' Balbir said.

'I am going into the East Section. Inform pit top to arrange and keep a vehicle ready. You continue tub traffic from my section. Nothing to worry.'

Siddhartha started walking into the East Section. Thelwans sitting on the tracks and having khaini, greeted him 'Salam Saab', as he passed them. There was no tub movement. During the beginning of any shift it was normal that there was not much action at the pit bottom except for raising the residual tubs from the last shift. The action began at the faces. But this was three hours into the eight-hour shift. Such stillness was indicative of abnormality.

The main haulage station was empty. The haulage driver and the thelwans were missing.

'Must have moved into the face.' Siddhartha thought. There were voices coming in, he moved on. There was a huge gathering near the intermediate haulage station. As he reached, silence fell.

'What has happened?' Siddhartha asked. A deafening silence.

'Will somebody tell me what has happened?' Siddhartha asked again.

A short dark man came out of the crowd. 'Saab, I think somebody is dead.'

'What do mean by 'somebody is dead'?'

'I was at the face pump. I saw someone going into the face and this blast. He must have died.'

'Who is the Mining Sirdar in charge?' Siddhartha enquired.

'Netaji,' someone from the crowd replied.

'Where is he?'

'We don't know.'

'He is a duty-bound Sirdar. He never leaves the face at these moments.'

Siddhartha had spent quite a few evenings with him over drinks. His real name was Manohar Thapa. A stout and healthy, fair, Nepali with above-average intellect and a sense of morality much above his colleagues. He was popular among the labourers and had earned the reputation of always advising the right solutions. The labourers, as a mark of respect, called him Netaji, meaning 'leader'. And the name stuck. He lived alone while his family resided somewhere in the north-eastern hills of India. He would visit them twice in a year. He always talked about his daughter, Tanna who studied in class seven. Siddhartha had seen her photo, which Netaji always carried in his wallet.

'He is not the type to desert his team at this moment of crisis.' Siddhartha thought.

'Has anyone of you been to the face?'

'No.'

'Who is the exploder in the shift?'

'Antu Majhi.'

'Where is he and his helper?'

As if some invisible force dissected the crowd with a sharp chef's knife to reveal Antu Majhi sitting on the explosive container. Terror struck white eyes flashed against cruel darkness as he looked up into Siddhartha's cap lamp.

He rushed to Siddhartha; fell on his knees, 'Sahab, save me. I have not done anything.' he started crying catching hold of Siddhartha's hand.

'OK, come with me.' It was not a time for emotional attachment. Siddhartha caught hold of his hand and walked towards the face.

'Which face did you fire?' He asked.

Antu Majhi led him into the fifth level, turned into the left gallery. The smoke had not cleared as yet. The raw smell of gelatin explosive sticks was still in the air. Siddhartha's boot hit into something; it was soft. He unplugged the cap lamp from his helmet and pointed it towards the object he had hit into. It was a battered right palm of someone, smeared with coal dust, thick dense blood still oozing out slowly. The smoke diluted. Siddhartha saw someone lying flat on his back at a distance of five metres.

'Mahato!' he called out loudly as he moved towards the body to check for life. 'Four / five men come in!' He called again.

He bent over, focused the lamp onto the face. It was caricatured with gaping flesh, facial muscles burrowed by coal splinters, gooey mix of oozing blood, and coal dust. The face was battered but Siddhartha recognized he was Netaji. The torso lay with one leg and both arms torn off. He put his hand close to the nape to feel the pulse beat. No movement. No hope. Netaji was dead.

Most of the labourers had run into the face hearing Siddhartha's call. The smoke had cleared and in the light of all the cap lamps, the tragedy unfolded. The limbs and pieces of flesh scattered around, the abdomen torn apart, the torso dumped like a mound of soft clay. The wallet lay a few feet away. Tanna's photo tucked in.

Helping her mother collect dried clothes from the clothesline fixed in the garden outside the house, she asked 'Ma, how many months more for Papa to come?' The night was setting in.

* * *

Jambad, a sleepy little colliery with a hibernating population and a rusty production system, twenty kilometre from the nearest railhead and district town, was miles behind the contemporary world. It had its own attitude, pace, and a coal production rate which defied any mining engineering logic. It produced, on an average, only fifty tonnes of coal per shift from each of the two sections, with a work force of about one hundred fifty. It contributed well towards the mounting losses of government-held public sector behemoth, Coal India Limited, to which it belonged. The Agent, a colliery designation above Senior Manager and below General Manager, Vijay Singh, whose name in Hindi means victory, had totally failed to initiate change. Yet he was a happy man. Stands five feet, five inches, stout with large bulging paunch, did not look forward to promotion. There was enough income from illegal channels to compensate for stagnation.

Jambad had no rail connection. The coal was transported out in trucks. One had to bribe the area General Manager heavily to get a posting at such collieries. There was a fixed income per tonne of coal being transported out for the Agent. Even after handing over a percentage to senior in the Area Office, an Agent made a cool income which was in addition to his official salary and perks. Apart from this fixed illegal income, the icing was pilferage of coal. Trucks were allowed to load more than sanctioned at a price much lower than the government rate which the Agent pocketed, along with local mafia dons who helped running this scam. To manage the figures, a small dump of coal was fired off in the dump yards and a larger volume was reported as loss due to in- situ firing in the yard. Nobody cared to check as everybody gained in some form or the other through this corruption, except for the Public Sector Undertaking - Coal India Limited, the government, and in actual context, the nation. Nobody cared. Since independence, nationalism was gradually sinking into the abyss. Nothing moved in any department to do with the government without pushing in currency notes into the palms of concerned officials under the table. Such bribing, trading without raising invoices, and various other ingenious methods of evading taxes had evolved a parallel economy of 'black money'. Even the government being aware, did little to contain this fiscal damage to the nation. So Jambad Colliery, instead of being shut down for being a loss making unit, continued guzzling public money and filling the coffers of a corrupt few.

Mihir, Siddhartha, Kunal, and Rajat got down from the rickety bus that seemed would breakdown at every jerk but made through the barren, dusty road to nowhere. Jambad Bus Stop. A small hutment for tea stall, cigarette, and pan shop, which also doubled as a grocery store. It's 10:30 in the morning. Five people sat in various poses on the two wooden benches sipping tea. A charpoy, which was laid out under the shade of a banyan tree by the hutment was occupied by a burly, dark-skinned, paunch wielding middle-aged man. A child of about twelve years washed glasses and a kettle under a tap that seemed to suddenly jut out of nowhere from the ground. The shopkeeper sat behind a counter with glass and plastic jars displayed on it, reading a newspaper. The moment seemed to be frozen in time only to be jerked out of stupor by the honking, clattering, bus that left a whirlpool of dust and black smoke to vanish behind it.

As Kunal walked towards the shopkeeper, everyone seemed to have taken note of the four. Those drinking tea straightened up while one even got up and stood by the bench. The one on charpoy who seemed to be snoring away had got up too, and was putting his vest on. The shopkeeper folded the newspaper and kept it aside as Kunal approached. The four felt amused at the attention being showered.

'Which way to the Jambad Colliery?' Kunal asked.

'This is Jambad,' the shopkeeper replied. 'But if you want to go to the colliery, you take that road, straight down. First the office, and about four kilometers down is the colliery.'

'Let us have some tea and then we will move on,' Kunal called out to his friends.

'I am Rajbir, I own this shop,' the shopkeeper introduced himself. 'Hey Chhotu,' he called out to the young boy washing utensils. 'Make tea for the Sahabs, and make it special.'

'Chhotu' which means 'small,' was a generic name in the region for any little boy. Children came to work in these industrial hot spots to earn a living for themselves and their families back home. They came from the wilderness of rural Indian poverty and they came in hordes. Every shop or household had these 'Chotus' running errands, making tea, manning shops—earning a living. Child labour? It's survival necessity for those trying to make through another dark night.

So Chhotu started preparing tea, the 'special', as the four settled down on the worn out benches. Tea is not brewed in this region; it is cooked. Water, milk, and sugar are placed in a saucepan or kettle and put on fire to boil, and boil well. Spoonfuls of tea leaf dust is added and boiled further to get a thick, light caramel colour consistency. And the tea is ready. Well, 'special tea' was a step ahead in culinary experimentation: bay leaves, cardamom, cinnamon, and ginger were added in the concoction of water, milk, and sugar, and boiled till a fine aroma of a well-cooked meal filled the air, and then the tea leaf dust was added. After draining down a glass of this 'special tea', one had to reach for a glass of water, just like one often washed down a richly cooked meal. Kunal often joked, 'Why don't they add some garlic and red chilies as well?'

Armed with appointment letters for executive training from ECL headquarters at Dishergarh, after the graduation years, once again the four were thrown in together in the same colliery with a huge three-room house to call their own. Jambad was a dream beginning of the long journey called career. Siddhartha had initiated them to liquor and ganja at the mining engineering hostel. Here, he initiated them to the art of cooking. They had to cook their own meal, wash clothes, and do the complete housekeeping. All four were close friends in the hostel. They became buddies in Jambad, and got Debu on board as well.

Debu, a small-time contractor making a living out of executing small civil repairing works of the colliery; he came as a 'Chhotu' to work errands at the colliery manager's home at the age of sixteen. He had passed secondary education but had to truncate further studies to support medication of his father's failing health. His father died just seven months after Debu came to Jambad, and Debu stayed on. Mr Mukherjee, the manager in whose house Debu worked, spotted the spark in the teenager and helped him to get a few colliery civil repairing works. He executed them satisfactorily. So when Mr Mukherjee was transferred to another colliery, Debu stayed back becoming an entrepreneur as contractor for minor repair works.

Walking down the dusty road, they reached the office to locate the house they had been allotted. The house, a bungalow of the colonial period, was really huge. As they entered the boundary wall, they were delighted to see corn shoots with little corns sprouting from them all over the front lawn. The open door invited them to a huge hall, which had two equally large rooms on both sides. The bathroom was attached to one of the rooms while there was another small room attached to the other. Dislodging their belongings at one corner of the hall, they decided to have a look around the area. Locking the door, they moved out. They had the whole day to themselves, as it was only on the next day that they had to report for training. Asking directions from the passers-by, they headed towards the colliery.

It was a long walk in the hot sun but a new beginning kept them going. Past the office building, the semi-tarred road twisted and turned through dugout excavated old mines. A few trees with dried brown leaves at remote distances added a flourish to the rustic landscape. During their graduation days, they did go through short term training programmes at collieries near their institute. But here, nothing seemed to match their experience. Those were large, professionally managed modern mines. Here they were in a land with its dugouts, crevices, cave-ins, and dark tunnels of abandoned mines which could only be compared to a macro photograph of skin with eczema. And the colliery?

'Look, there it is!' Rajat exclaimed. Yes, the giant black wheel on the headgear above the pit top was gradually rising above the horizon as they approached.

'Seems to be a small mine,' Mihir commented, gauging the size of the headgear.

'Who cares?' Siddhartha retorted. 'I am here to have a good time. The smaller the mine, the lesser to be engaged in, and more time to have the time of your life.'

'Will you never take anything seriously in life? We will be building the foundation of our career through this training.'

'Career? In mining? Get fucked by life if you want to, get imprisoned by a career,' Siddhartha replied. 'I want to be an artist. Painting the myriad nuances of life from angles never explored. Just look around. What a rustic landscape that can be the perfect metaphor for the dance of death.'

Mihir did not prolong the argument. There was no point. During the college days too, Siddhartha enjoyed what he described as life in its full. Bunking classes, heavy drinking, smoking charas and ganja, living in the hostel with walls plastered with nude posters, kissing the idol of Saraswati—the Hindu goddess of education—and even declaring that she was sexy and the idol had attractive, full bosoms to dive into. There was always an extreme nihilistic touch in whatever he did, or ideas he expressed. He was an accepted atheist. Only thing that intrigued Mihir was that with so little studies and so much disregard to God, how Siddhartha always came second in all the exams. Mihir was always first; but he was an extremely studious student and a devout worshipper as well. Both were poles apart but were bosom friends. Mihir was his roommate as well and hence knew him quite well, and did not argue any further.

The colliery had no gate. Only a slope led them on top of a plateau, the pit-top of the colliery. An iron frame held up a worn out iron board with JAMBAD COLLIERY painted on it. The 'J' had long been lost and read 'AMBAD COLLIERY'. The Lamp Room was there followed by Manager's and Agent's office, if that is what they were to be called. Both the rooms had a wooden table, a few folding iron chairs, and an earthen pitcher on a wooden stool at one corner. They walked towards the pithead. It was around one in the afternoon, and supposed to be peak production hours for the first shift that starts at eight in the morning, but there was hardly any activity. Thelwans, as the labourers on the pit top handling the tubs were called, pulled out the two coal filled tubs from the cage, and pushed in two empty ones. Another two thelwans pushed the coal filled tubs to the tumbler and tumbled the tubs empty into the chute, under which the dumper waited to be filled and carry the coal away. A bell clanked, giving signal to the engine driver. The huge steam engine woke up ranting and roaring, taking the cage with empty tubs down the shaft while pulling up two more filled ones. The process was the same as what they had seen in other collieries during short-term training—or that they had read—but at a pace that they had never imagined. Mihir was disheartened; Siddhartha was overjoyed; Kunal and Rajat thought it was time for lunch.

* * *

Sitting opposite veteran mining professionals and teachers, Siddhartha had to prove that he was not only intelligent for the mining engineering course—which he had already done by passing the written entrance examination—but also prove that he would make a fit mining engineer and will not be blocking one of the only twenty coveted seats of the institute from another deserving candidate.

'I'm Dr Dhar, Principal of this institute,' the man in the centre of the panel of interviewers with thick specs introduced himself. 'You left National Defence Academy after two semesters, studied Accountancy Honours for one year, and left it. And now you are here. What makes you feel that this will get you the right career?'

'I don't know if this is the right career for me,' Siddhartha replied. 'In fact, I had no option. I have crossed the age for attempting competitive exams for other professional courses. This had a higher age limit and so I am here. And without any professional course under my belt I won't have any home to call my own.'

'What do you mean?' The bald man at the extreme right in a tweed suit expressed surprise. 'What do you mean by 'you won't have any home'? By the way, I am Dr Bhar. Vice Principal of the Institute. Your parents are not going to disown you if you fail in this interview.'

'Not exactly, but that's another story and not related to this interview. Actually, I want to be an artist of repute.'

'Then you should attempt to join the College of Art,' quipped Mr Sen, Manager, Ningah Colliery as he introduced himself.

'I don't have that option due to my age. Also I did not say that I wanted to make a career out of art. I want to be an artist and that can be along with being a fine miner. In fact, the mines in the secluded, far-flung areas will open a vast new canvas for my art.'

'I don't get you,' Mr Biswas, the professor of Survey, articulated well using his hands to express his confusion. 'You want to be a Mining Engineer to provide you a scope to be an artist.'

'And also a respectable career with a sound livelihood, which will be very necessary if I am experimenting in art and not selling paintings to make a living. In that case, the market would command my artistic expressions and I will not be able to experiment, or in simple terms, I will not be able to do something different, something path breaking.'

'What do you paint? Portraits? Sceneries?' Dr Bhar asked.

Siddhartha could gauge the panel's level of knowledge in art.

'Not exactly. Art has gone much beyond just portraits or sceneries. A whole new grammar is being written every day. It is about experimenting with form, colour, deconstructing perceptions, etc. At present, I experiment with forms and long to slowly master in abstraction.'

Nobody understood, and Siddhartha joined the Institute of Mining Engineering in the late winter of nineteen seventy-nine.

At the office, he was guided to Block A hostel. He walked down the football field with a sling bag on the shoulder and a cheap suitcase in hand. The two-storey building was just behind the field. As he entered the building, he could hear roars of laughter coming from a room at the end of the corridor. There was nobody around, so he headed towards the room.

'Here comes one more mining engineer,' said someone.

Before he could enter, one of the students came and relieved him of his luggage.

'Get into the 'murga position' mother fucker,' another shouted. Being from the defence institute background, it did not shock him. So it was ragging time. He quietly put his hands through the leg, sitting down, and caught the ears. There were seven more students in the same position. 'All freshers,' Siddhartha thought. He tried to look up at each of his batchmates as a big thud on his head made him fall flat on his face.

'Sala, trying to be smart. Go to the 'seventh heaven',' the senior in an uncanny green pullover growled. 'Don't know what 'seventh heaven' is? Mihir show him.'

One among the seven rose from the 'murga position' and walked towards the window as Siddhartha got up and waited to unravel the mystery of the 'seventh heaven'. He had a good stock of such treacherous positions from his earlier military school experiences. It was punishment there; it is ragging here. It was all through boarding years then. It will be only for the first month now. 'Not a big deal.' Siddhartha told himself as Mihir started climbing the iron grill on the window. He got into a position, which can only be performed to explain and not described. Siddhartha could understand that the body weight will slowly start telling on the shoulders and the blood will start flowing into the brain as body hanged head down on hands clasping the iron grill—something similar to 'legs up hands down' of the yonder years but a more innovative, complicated, brutal version. Siddhartha followed and went up the 'seventh heaven'.

By evening, all nineteen of the twenty new entrants had reported in. The ground floor was completely for the first year students. The dining hall, store, and the kitchen was also on the ground floor. The first floor was allocated to the second year students. The third and the fourth year students stayed in the Block B hostel and they were supposed to be Gods. Rooms were allocated. Siddhartha had Mihir and Biman as his roommates. It was only after dinner, when the seniors went off to their respective rooms on the first floor, that the newcomers sat together and introduced themselves. There was Ashok, short and stout, broke down crying, said would leave, could not take the ragging; Ramtanu swore that first thing in the morning he would walk up to the Principal and complain; Ghoshal looked up at the ceiling and called out the weirdest of foul slangs, though in a low voice.

'Cool down, it is only a matter of a month,' Siddhartha said, and took out a small paper packet from his sling bag. He had carried some stock of ganja and charas from Calcutta. He pulled out a small piece from the black lump and rolled it into a small ball, stuck it to the end of a matchstick, fired another, and heated the ball. After crushing it into powder, mixed it with the tobacco taken out of a cigarette, and refilled the cigarette.

'What's that?' Kunal asked.

'Charas,' Siddhartha explained, lighting the fag and taking a deep puff as others watched astonished. There were a few smokers, actually five of them, apart from Siddhartha. But Charas, none had any idea.

'Want a puff?' Siddhartha asked Kunal.

'OK, let me try.' Kunal took a light puff, afraid of the outcome. All the five smokers followed, but with one puff each only. Initiation into yet an unknown world had begun. And with Siddhartha's ways, there was so much more to explore.

Following days unfolded the pattern of the hostel life to the newcomers. Classes in the morning, lunch at the hostel, classes in the afternoon, evening tea at the hostel, a few hours of ragging in the last room of the ground floor, and then dinner. After dinner, all the five smokers, namely Mihir, Kunal, Ghoshal, Rajat and Ramtanu, huddled in Siddhartha's room and shared charas before going to sleep.

Ragging was painful, but there were lighter moments as well. At times, even the freshers burst into laughter at some of the batchmate's follies and foolish acts. Every evening during the ragging period, a heater was brought in religiously to the room. It was the most terrorizing element in ragging. Anybody who broke down or failed to do the tasks was warned that he would be given the 'shock treatment'. The heater would be switched on and the fresher in question would have to piss on it. The thought itself was quite agonizing. Through the month of ragging, the heater made its holy presence but was never used. It was never used in the history of the institute and will never be used in the future as well. But every year, when the freshers turn second year students, they introduce this ritual learnt from their seniors; and the tradition continues. There were many such traditions, which were passed on from seniors to juniors year after year; like seniors were called by their name suffixed with 'da', which was short form of 'dada', meaning elder brother in Bengali language.

It was on the evening of the fifth day that Gautamda, who occupied the room above Siddhartha, walked in to the room designated for ragging a little before other seniors. All the freshers seated on the three beds rose, bowed, and greeted in one voice: 'Pranam Pitashree' —'Salutation to you O Father'—that was how freshers greeted seniors during the ragging month.

'Pranam, pranam,' Goutamda replied. 'Tell me how many of you smoke?'

There was a chilling silence. Smoking was a no-no during ragging.

'Don't worry.' Goutamda tried to bring in a semblance of confidence. 'This is just for my knowledge and I will not tell other seniors.' Siddhartha could smell a fish. He picked up his hand.

'I knew it,' Goutamda smiled. 'Any more?'

Kunal raised his hand. Rajat followed, and then Ghoshal, and then Mihir. Ramtanu, who did smoke, did not own up thinking it to be a ploy to extract truth and use it for further ragging, for breaking rules.

'How many of you have smoked Ganja?' was the next question from Gautamda.

Siddhartha's suspicion was falling into place. 'Gautamda must have got the smell of Charas,' Siddhartha thought. He raised his hand as others put theirs down.

'Come with me.' Gautamda took away Siddhartha from the room. A little later, other seniors started pouring in. It was ragging time. But Siddhartha did not come back.

The dining hall was huge, with two long tables lined with wooden benches. One table was for the first year students and the other for the second year. There was a head-cook and a helper who alternated as the waiter to serve meals. Meals came in thalis, stainless steel large plates with good serving of rice, two chapatis, a serving of seasonal vegetable, a small bowl of dal, and another with fish curry. The Mess was run by the first year students, one by one in rotation. The Mess Manager, as per rotation, had to collect the fixed Mess charges from all, plan the menu and budget, do the daily marketing, and run the show for one month. A slice of fish was a must in each meal, mutton or chicken a must for Sunday meals, and a big feast was a must at the end of month. The fish, mutton or chicken, and the vegetables, were served one helping only; while one could ask for rice, chapati or dal as much as one needed. There was a fixed time for all meals when one had the privilege of being served by Anjum, the helper-cum-waiter. Beyond that, the thalis were lined on a shelf in the kitchen, and it was anybody's guess how the singularly tasting meals could taste once cold. Yes, the vegetable tasted like the fish curry tasted like the mutton curry day after day through the year. The only differentiator was the dal. Pulse cooked in a gravy form tasting horribly different as the head cook had an innovative form of using less pulse, and yet making it thick by adding the rice broth extract in it. The current batch would also take up this responsibility after the month-long ragging period culminating in the 'Fresher's Welcome'. The other side of the hall had a table tennis board and a carom board with a few sofas spread around.

All on the fresher's table ate silently and anxiously as Siddhartha walked in. His eyes were red. 'Must have had a tough ragging session', all thought but nobody asked. It was only after dinner that all were stunned to know that Siddhartha was smoking ganja with Goutamda in his room. Goutamda, son of an Indian Railways officer from Dhanbad, had failed in the second year and was repeating the semesters with his junior batch. His classmates respected him for two reasons: the obvious one being that he was their senior; the other that he was the rebel kind. He bunked classes, smoked ganja, and was friend with the local hooligans. In every hostel, his kind—the defiant kind—invited awe and respect. Every student aspired to be as defiant but never had the guts to do so. There were no proven benefits of being defiant but at that age, everybody always hero-worshipped all those who broke the institutional norms, even though eventually, might turn into great failure stories in life.

Gautamda had taken Siddhartha, another rebel in the making, under his wings. No more ragging for him. He would spend the evenings smoking ganja, sharing his stock of charas with Gautamda and other seniors, while his batchmates were being ragged down under.

On the morning of Freshers Welcome Day, surprise awaited the first year students. All the seniors descended from the first floor and greeted and hugged the freshers. It suddenly seemed the past one month never existed. The celebrations would begin in the evening. The Gods, as the senior most batch was referred to from the other hostel would arrive and would be introduced. Many alumni employed in nearby collieries would also pay visit. There would be a gala dinner, music, and dance. The sound system was already being tested for its volume and pitch. Siddhartha had already informed his batchmates that all would have to drink 'Shiddhi' in the evening as learned from his seniors during his evening sessions in Gautamda's room. 'Shiddhi' or 'Bhang' as it is known in many parts of India, is an intoxicant drink made by mixing paste of 'Bhang' leaves in sweet milk. It is taken by many during holy festivities; but here, 'Shiddhi' was on overdrive.

The kitchen helper was busy from morning preparing the paste. A few seniors were seen rubbing one paisa copper coins with water on stone blocks to add the residual copper liquid into the concoction. It was believed that it made the concoction more intoxicating. Gautamda sat on the bench in the dining room and supervised the process. It seemed all accepted his authority and knowledge on the subject of intoxication. But Gautamda himself differed.

'Sid,' he called out. 'Come here and check the 'Shiddhi'.'

Siddhartha came in, took a small sip, gurgled lightly, waited for a few seconds and said, 'Gautamda add some more sugar and few more copper coins.' Some expert, he seemed. And truly he was an expert: he had started ganja and alcohol, though in limited extent, from class eight onwards. At this point he had experience of Mandrakes tablet and even Brown Sugar under his belt. He knew the evening dose of 'Shiddhi' would be a rather weak shot for him and he had already kept a pint of rum handy in his cupboard.

By the end of the first month, Siddhartha realized he was in a boring place; not the hostel, but the Institute with boring classes and professors and lecturers who were even bigger bores. The subjects were new and not boring, but the way they were taught was. Most teachers came to class prepared with a chapter or part thereof from the book and repeated the same in the class. Siddhartha found no reason to attend the classes when he could learn the same thing just by reading the books, that too, at his convenience. First, he started raising questions beyond what was being taught in the class and met with stern replies: 'I will get back.', 'Listen to what I am saying.', 'Focus on what I am teaching.' and so on.

Then he started pointing out the deficiencies, 'Sir, you are giving us the Bengali translation of the definition given in the book,' he got up and interrupted Mr Choudhuri. 'We are not here to learn Bengali translation, we are here to learn mechanics.'

'You may understand the English, but not everybody,' Mr Choudhuri retorted.

'But to make us understand you need to simplify through examples and not just translate it.'

'If you don't like my way of teaching, you may leave the class,' and Siddhartha walked out. Finally, he started walking out of most of the classes after making his presence felt. Nobody objected, as having him in the class could turn out to be a bigger embarrassment than to accept his disdain for their way of teaching.

There was an exception: T. K. Roychaudhury, the Lecturer of Geology. 'TK', as per Institute's weekly classes schedule on the notice board, and 'Tiku' among the students. Tall, dark, and handsome with salt 'n pepper back-brushed hair, was a bachelor at forty-six; commanded a baritone yet friendly voice; dabbled in theatre; had lunch and dinner at the 'B' Block student's hostel, and was often spotted with a group of students in the corridors of the Institute, chatting away from pin to pint.

Siddhartha had some knowledge of rock types and even had a small collection of rocks at his home in Calcutta. Though he did not find the geology textbook very interesting, it was obvious that he would attend the first few Geology classes like all other—the Geology class was to be held in a separate lecture hall than their regular class room. There were large tables with high chairs. As they entered the hall, Siddhartha started singing a popular song from a Hindi Film that was running successfully. Kunal and Ghosal started giving the beat on the table. Mihir backed up with vocal rendition of various musical effects. Actually, this was their favorite pastime in the evening at the hostel over a 'chillum' of ganja where the mining helmets also substituted as drums. The tempo rose as Ramtanu and Ashok also lend their voice. And then Tiku walked in. There was silence.

'R. D. Burman,' Tiku said. 'Fantastic music director and even Gulzar the lyricist has done a great job.'

The students never expected any teacher to react in the manner.

'Do you all know that RD often composed music at night and often would wake up Gulzar, his friend, in the wee hours and go for a drive to share his new composition?' Tiku continued. 'Even Gulzar has composed some of his best lyrics during such drives. Now let us come back to Geology . . .'

He articulated well, had an overbearing body language and brought the most inanimate of objects, the rocks, to life through his facial expressions—a good improvisation of his knowledge of theatre brought into teaching. Siddhartha got engrossed and got hooked to his classes. He attended all the Geology classes and had a lot of questions, too. Tiku always had an answer.

Another class Siddhartha never missed was that of Dr Dhar, the Principal of the Institute. He took one class every two weeks and it was not on any curriculum subjects. It was an orientation class for mining industry; lots of stories, anecdotes, and case studies. Other than these two classes, Siddhartha would either be at the hostel reading books, smoking ganja, or exploring the city just sauntering around. Another place he frequented was the library. Alokesh, the lanky librarian, had already succumbed to Siddhartha's persuasion and pressurizing tactics. He issued him up to five books for hostel whereas only one was allowed. The main subject, Mining Technology, was taught from three books by an Indian author. But from the seniors Siddhartha learned, as his batchmates did, that the book in three volumes written by Statham, a British author was the Bible of mining. The second-hand old version cost three thousand bucks and only five in the hostel possessed it. Others borrowed those five or referred the one at the library.

Mr Statham did not impress Siddhartha. With a dark brown, hard cover overcoat, it seemed to be a direct lift from some under lit alleyway of some British period film. The text layout was outdated and uninviting. The illustrations were too academic—the photographs, black and white, and only informative like catalogues. Even the content did not impress Siddhartha. Whereas India followed the Metric system of measures, the book followed the old British measure units. Whereas Indian coal seams were thick, the book stressed on thin seam mining that are prevalent in the United Kingdom. And a particular typically complicated Mine Tech mathematical problem still took forty minutes or more to solve just like the Indian book's demonstration of the same problem. 'Boring, back dated, bull shit Bible.' Siddhartha concluded. He soon discovered translations of books by Russian authors in the library. Metric system measures, more about thick seam mining with more updated technology, and above all, reduced the particular problem's solving time by about ten minutes through a different approach and reduction of steps.

This particular problem on haulage was very dear to all the students because when they appeared in the second year exams of the National Council, they had to answer or solve five out of six questions or problems within three hours. The question paper among the six questions always had two problems, one being the haulage problem, and students never missed both. Done right, being mathematical in nature would fetch full marks. Whereas answering other questions gave the examiners a subjective scope in marking, even on being correct. And the haulage problem took away a minimum of forty minutes, raising the pressure in completing the other four. So reduction in time by ten minutes was a great discovery for Siddhartha. Full of enthusiasm, he demonstrated the method to all his batch mates. All noted the benefit of time, but when the first year annual exams came which also had the same problem, though in a slight simpler form, all approached it in the conventional method except Siddhartha and Ghoshal. All scored twenty out of twenty including Siddhartha. Ghoshal got it wrong and scored a zero. When the results were declared for the first year final, Mihir came first and Siddhartha second—a trend that continued through the four years at the Institution.

Six months into the second year, National Council declared that 'scientific calculators' would be allowed to be used for the annual exams conducted by National Council. Mihir was the first to buy one, and slowly a few more followed. Though there were a plethora of mathematical functions in this version, Siddhartha found only a few functions that would be of use to them, in addition to the functions of the basic calculator. With a fast and good calculative strength, he decided against investing three hundred bucks on the gadget; but it was catching up as a fad and most students gradually bought it. So even without buying, Siddhartha always had one handy from anybody's study table. One afternoon, bunking classes, sitting in his hostel room, and smoking ganja with Ghoshal, he was going through the user's manual of Mihir's scientific calculator. The calculators were smuggled in products and the manuals were in some European language, probably in French or Spanish or even could be in Italian, as Siddhartha thought, but not in English. Intriguing, and hence interesting to Siddhartha, he started decoding though vaguely, by relating the numeric and graphical representations with the text in the manual. By the second day, he was able to do a few mathematical steps by a single tap of a key, which was not the case in a basic calculator. Thrilled, he got deeper into it. Next few days it was ganja, the manual, the calculator, and more ganja. There was no goal, no quest but he found new horizons evolving. By the fourth day, he had some fluid formulas in solving three to four mathematical steps through one tap of a key of the scientific calculator. He did not know the logic, neither the detailed function of the gadget nor what the key graphically depicted, but it was happening.

Room number ten. Room shared by Mihir, Siddhartha, and Biman. Ghoshal pushed open the green wooden door. A strong, sweet yet caustic smell hit his nose. The wall facing the door was Mihir's domain with his bed and the study table, and a cupboard. On top of the cupboard, a clean piece of cloth, was laid over and a section was dedicated to the Gods. There were two framed pictures: one of Saraswati, the Goddess of education and intellect, and the other that of Radha and Krishna. Krishna, the avatar of Vishnu, one of the Trinity of Hindu mythologies, Brahma, Vishnu and Maheshwar. Siddhartha revered the character of Krishna, not as a God but as a mythological character created very close to what he thought should be the ideal man. Complex, intriguing, intelligent, and full of shades of grey. Unlike other Gods, Krishna had many traits, which ideally could not be referred to as truly ideal.

One such parable was that of Radha. The picture depicted Krishna playing the flute consorting Radha under a 'Kadam' tree. The tree had large leaves and bore tennis ball-shaped golden yellow flowers. Unlike other flowers, 'Kadam' flower was a solid sphere blooming in the monsoons. Radha was supposed to be one of the gopis and married to a milkman of the village of young Krishna, and also portrayed as elder by age. There are many romantic stories on the duo establishing them as lovers. The relationship, though not socially accepted and incestuous by nature, became a symbol of true love and was raised to the podium of being pray-worthy. One of the many grey shades of Krishna, authored the sad end of this love story: mythology has it that Krishna left for the great epic Mahabharata, he had promised to return to Radha once his role in the Mahabharata ended. Radha would wait every evening with an oil lamp under the Kadam tree for his return. Mahabharata came to an end. Krishna married Rukmini and moved to Dwarka as the king, and never returned. Though many esoteric religious explanations are given to prove that Radha and Rukmini are the same, Siddhartha believed that these were futile attempts to create a God out of a truly human character, the greatest human character ever portrayed through the ages. He liked the idea of Radha still waiting with the oil lamp under the Kadam tree and Krishna enjoying the spoils as the king of Dwarka, with Rukmini and other consorts. And at fleeting moments, sitting alone in leisure, when a wild breeze brought in a whiff of the fragrance of the Kadam flower, a sweet pain, and a few flashes of the days in Vrindavan passed his mind. How he longed to go back, meet Radha, and keep his promise. But time had decided it was never to be. Siddhartha thought, 'so lifelike'—like you think of your first love, lost somewhere in the recess of the past, long to meet again, turn back the clock for once, but it never happens. Time, too powerful a dimension to be manipulated even by one idolized as God.

There was a brass incense stick-holder with a burnt out incense stick jutting out of it in front of the picture of the Gods. On the other side, books of various shapes and sizes were stacked. There was a small wooden photo frame with his parents' black-and-white photograph shot in some small muffasal town studio. The bed was neatly laid out with the mosquito net hanging from the four iron rods attached to the four corners of the bed. The sides of the white mosquito net were rolled up onto the roof of the net and were only brought down and tucked under the mattress while sleeping.

On the wall right to the door was Biman's bed followed by his study table and the cupboard. His table, apart from books, had a glass and a bottle of Ayurvedic concoction. Religiously, he would have two spoons of it, mixed with a glass of water every morning as he rose from the bed. It was for his stomach, he had said, and everybody was well aware of this. He belched and farted every now and then and was nicknamed 'live, moving methane gas chamber'. He contributed quite much to the ambient smell of the room. Mihir's incense, Siddhartha's ganja, and Biman's fart; no room could boast of such exclusivity. There was also a framed picture of a 'Guru'—those who claimed direct contact with God and the lesser mortals prayed them as God; middlemen who facilitated in achieving salvation and be one with God.

Siddhartha's bed was on the left of the door. The mosquito net hanged from three corners of the pole, with the fourth being on the bed. He never rolled up the net. He would pick up the fourth corner and slide inside; that saved him the double task of rolling the net up and down every day. The study table had more books than his roommates: it also had Debonair and second-hand Playboy magazines; packets of cigarettes, matchboxes, and a terracotta 'chillum'. The 'chillum' was a hollow, cylindrical object, with a wider hole on one side gradually ending in a smaller hole at the other end used to smoke ganja. The wall in front of the table had a large collage of nudes. It was not just posters pasted on the wall; it was true piece of artistic collage created from cutouts of nudes from different magazines. Ghoshal ogled at the new addition at the bottom of the collage—big boobs and a great buttock.

'You got a new Playboy?' Ghoshal asked Siddhartha as he sat on the edge of the bed.

'Yeah.' Siddhartha replied, still engrossed in the calculator with the Mine Tech book open in front.

'What are you doing? Want to smoke some ganja?'

'The packet is on the first shelf. Prepare a great shot.' Siddhartha said and continued with what he was doing.

Ghoshal took out the packet, prepared the shot, and forwarded it to Siddhartha to fire.

'Just a few minutes, I am just going to crack the code.'

'What code? What are you up to?'

Ghoshal kept sitting with the chillum as Siddhartha kept looking at the book and tapping the calculator keys. He tapped on a key as if it was the masterstroke and 'Yeah got it. Viola! Mother fucker haulage problem?' He threw the calculator on the table. 'Sala, will shove the problem up this terminal exam's ass.'

'Arre, it is a costly stuff, don't throw it like that.' Mihir, concerned about his calculator, retorted from his table.

'If it was mine I would have broken it into pieces.' Siddhartha turned his chair towards Ghoshal and took the chillum.

'Fire it.'

Mihir got inquisitive. He put a page marker in the book he was studying and closed it. He pulled his chair towards Siddhartha and Ghoshal.

'Give me a puff. What is it that you are so thrilled about?'

Siddhartha handed over the chillum to Mihir, 'Sister Fucker haulage problem?'

'What haulage problem?' Mihir asked, blowing out a lungful.

'The haulage problem can be solved in five minutes.' Siddhartha looked at Mihir after pulling in a lungful. Ghoshal stood up in disbelief.

'Are you crazy? OK last time you were right with the Russian procedure of solving. I got it wrong in the exam, but you were right with the process. But five minutes?'

Mihir followed the conventional method to solve the problem in the first year annual exam but knew Siddhartha was right even then. He knew in the second year National Council exam that the problem was always much tougher. It could be a great help if truly the problem could be solved in five minutes as Siddhartha claimed.

'Are you sure?' he asked.

'I am sure to the third decimal, and we have to give the answer up to the second decimal. I have checked it up five times with five different problems.' Siddhartha beamed, picked up the calculator, and handed over the Mine Tech book to Mihir.

'Take up any problem.' Mihir pointed to one at random. Siddhartha read the problem, fifty seconds. Tapped in a figure, tapped the plus sign, tapped in another figure from the book, tapped the multiplication symbol, pressed 'equal to'. Sixty seconds. Pressed one of the keys, first of the discovered mysterious formula, tapped in a few more figures from the problem interspersed with general mathematical symbols. One minute twenty seconds. 'Equal to', more figures from the book, again a magic formula key, 'equal to'. Two minutes. More figures, more mathematical symbols, more magic keys, 'equal to' and then the answer. Three minutes forty seconds and Siddhartha forwarded the result on the calculator screen to Mihir.

'Check it out.' Mihir picked up the Mine Tech book, turned the pages to the 'Answers' section at the end. He looked at the printed answer of the particular problem, looked at the calculator screen, looked at Siddhartha, once again looked at the calculator screen, looked at the printed answer, and exclaimed, 'I don't believe this.'

In the second year annual exams everybody used the 'scientific calculator formula' to solve the haulage problem but masqueraded it by writing the solution in the conventional method and using the formula to speed up actual calculations only, utilizing one whole page of the foolscap answer sheet as earlier. But Siddhartha went a step further. In the first line he wrote 'Note: As permitted by the National Council, a scientific calculator is being used to solve the following problem.' Then he wrote a few lines explaining the theory and logic of arriving at the answer. Followed by five lines of figures interspersed by graphical representation of the keys of the calculator being used by him, and in the sixth line he wrote 'Answer = 1142.24 secs. i.e. 19 min. 2.24 secs.', utilizing only one third of a page of the answer sheet and even lesser time than his batchmates to solve the problem. After the exam, when he related his approach, most of his batchmates expressed skepticism and the rest were confused.

A month later, the results were declared. Everybody but one had got full marks in the problem and Siddhartha too got twenty out of twenty in it. Ghoshal again got it wrong and got a zero. Mihir was first, Siddhartha second, and Ghoshal just managed to scrape through to the third year.

CHAPTER 9

'AT THE CRACK of the gun, Zishan bolts out but Allah Rakkha takes to the rail and sets the pace followed by Zishan, Superstar, Valentino, Zubido, Calypso, Debonoir, and Class Apart bringing up the rear. Four hundred metres and it is still Allah Rakkha setting up a scorching pace, with Zubido catching up, followed by Valentino, Calypso, Debonoir, Superstar, Class Apart, as Zishan falls back. Six hundred metres and Superstar takes over the lead as Calypso challenges on the outside, followed by Valentino, Debonoir, Class Apart as Zishan wears out, and Allah Rakkha brings up the rear. Two hundred metres from the finish, it is Superstar, Calypso neck to neck, Debonoir making a strong challenge, and it's Class Apart blazing the trail on extreme outside; it's Calypso and Superstar with Class Apart on the outside; Calypso, Superstar, Class Apart; Superstar, Calypso and Class Apart stretches and comes up to challenge on the outside. It's Calypso, Class Apart and Superstar. Superstar, Calypso and Class Apart. It's Calypso and Class Apart. Calypso, Class Apart. Calypso, Class Apart. Class Apart stretches out. What a finish. Class Apart wins by a head from Calypso, followed by Superstar, Valentino, Debonoir, Zishan, Zubido and Allah Rakkha.'

As the horse racing commentary finished, I got up from the bench at the stands and could feel a hot flush running through my veins. I had betted 1000 bucks at 6 to 1 on

Class Apart and was now richer by 6000. I was instinctively confident of his win. In the jackpot ticket too, I had only Class Apart as the winner on the fourth leg. Jackpots were drawn on five races and each being known as a leg. There were 46,000 bucks for the fourth leg but one had to wait to see how many tickets survived, as the money would be divided among the surviving tickets. If 40 tickets survived each would get a share of 1150. I had to wait a little. It would be announced before the next race, the last for the day, and also the last leg of the jackpot. The jackpot stakes for the day were something around two lakhs twenty thousand plus. I had two horses on the fifth leg and with anyone winning, I would be a claimant to the jackpot booty. The size of the booty again depended on the number of surviving tickets, but that was yet a race ahead. As I walked towards the bookie's chamber to collect my win from the race, it was declared on the public address system that there were only two surviving tickets on the fourth leg. It translated into another 23,000 win for me, and a less competitive fifth leg of the jackpot.

It is astonishing how prying eyes and murmurs spread news in the racecourse. As I collected my 7000, 6000 for the win, and 1000, the amount I had betted. A man in sixties, dressed in white pajama and 'punjabi' with white hair walked up to me. He was about five feet, four inches, short, healthy, and seemed to be a veteran to the races. There were a few more of his friends in different shapes, sizes, and age groups behind him.

'Do you have the other fourth leg winning ticket?' he asked. I was hesitant to reply. Why on earth was he interested in my winning ticket? But their looks and the polite approach rested my apprehensions about their intention.

'Yes, I do have,' I replied.

'Which are the horses you have marked on the fifth?'

I took out the ticket. 'Jolly Boy and Fedora.'

'That's great. We can come into a contract,' he said.. 'Of course, if you agree.'

'What great? What contract?' I thought.

'We have the other winning ticket and we have marked Desire, Hallehluiya and Distant Dream.' I listened as he explained. 'The fourth leg win remains with us and you, respectively. Now if you agree, and we come into a contract, then in case any one of us wins the jackpot, we share fifty-fifty. The plus point is that you have two horses and we have three covered in the next seven-horse race. Chance is, one of us will surely win. And whoever wins we get about one lakh plus each.'

I thought for a few seconds. It was a good hedging tactic. I will lose over a lakh if my ticket wins but I am also assured of a lakh plus even if their ticket wins. However, I might justify myself that I crunched through fractions of seconds of previous race records, went deep into pedigrees to spot the winners; at the race course, it was pure gambling. And this offer was not blind gamble but a calculated risk. I agreed.

'There is some time before the next race. Let us celebrate the contract at the bar.'

The bar was reminiscent of the British colonial period. Built behind the 'First Class' stands, it was an open space with very high ceiling and number of large columns. Round marble top tables with some old, wooden, and some later addition steel chairs were strewn all over. The waiters dressed in white with red sash running across the chest, and an eloquent turban as the headdress looked direct lifts from the

Raj era except that time seemed to have taken away the sheen. The white dresses had turned quiet dirty with curry stains at the pocket edges. The worn out leather belt holding the sash loosely hanged under oversized bellies, and the red sash had turned into an unrecognizable dark colour. Well, the bar, the waiters, and the ambience seemed perfectly matched for each other. Anyone with a better presence would stick out like a sore thumb. It was not just the Bar, but the whole of the Race Course, as it is commonly known, laid out in 1820 and officially taken over by Calcutta Turf Club in 1847 for running the races, and managing the club seemed to have frozen in time. There were separate enclosures for separate people keeping the discrimination policy of the British. The Club enclosure was segregated and its stands were exactly opposite the finish line, providing the best view of the finish of every race. This was only available to elite members of the club. The next was the First Class enclosure. It had an entry ticket priced higher than the Second Class enclosure, which followed. I visited the First Class stands as that gave the best view of a finish without being a club member. From the Second Class enclosure, one always saw the butts of the front running horses and waited for the announcement to know the real winner.

'I would like to order a beer,' Mohinda, the burly short man said. We had introduced ourselves. Mohinda was the owner of the famous 'Punjabi' (Kurta) tailoring shop, Akhnoor on Bow Bazaar Street. Many film stars, famous personalities, and even a star cricketer had a set tailored from his shop. He was rich: he had two palatial houses, one on Amherst Street and one in Park Circus; had two cars, one the Ambassador and the other Fiat Premier Padmini.

The Maruti revolution was yet to happen. He had two wives, one traditionally married living at Amherst Street, and the other, a live-in mistress living in the Park Circus mansion. Like betting, drinking was a passion for him. He never kept straight after three scotch shots, but never stopped even at seven. He would come loaded with bundles of cash stashed in his 'punjabi' and 'payjama' pockets every racing day, and would leave empty. He always lost but never saw him disheartened and would again come the next day with fresh hopes and more bundles to lose. Every racing season, losing four to five lakhs was a habit with him.

'Same for me,' said Subhashda. Very dark complexioned, hugely built, and always wore 'Hawaian shirts' over his bulky belly with trousers and buckled shoes. He worked in some West Bengal government office and betted only a few hundred through a day of racing.

'Me too,' followed Duttada. Very fair, good physique and handsome, he was past forty five. He ran a leather unit and was into manufacture and exports of 'Shantiniketan' style leather bags. Had made good money but with tastes changing world over, he was going through a dwindling phase. Racing for him was a supplementary income-generating avenue. He generally betted on favorites and always happy with a little that he made at the end of each racing day.

'I will go for a large whiskey,' Sourenda broke the monotony of orders. 'The sun will set soon, why waste on beer?' Sourenda, the youngest of the group at thirty-six, did nothing for a living. His father owned a hotel on the Bow Bazaar Street near the Sealdah Station end, and lived in a spacious floor of their huge ancestral mansion on College Street. The other floors were occupied by his uncles and their families. Sourenda was married, had a son aged five, and got a pocket money of ten thousand rupees per month from his father. The family which translated to Sourenda, his parents, wife, and his son, was maintained by his father; leaving his pocket money for racing and evening drinks.

'I will take a rum.' I agreed with Sourenda's point of view, why waste a beer?

Drinks served, Mohinda ordered for 'Fish Kabiraji' for all, a typical Bengal culinary experiment—fish marinated in herbs, coated with egg batter, and deep-fried; it tasted great, particularly with a dash of mustard sauce, and tomato ketchup. The bar served only drinks. The food was brought in from the Bijoli Grill stall just opposite the bar. Bijoli Grill, they had a take away counter at the Bijoli Cinema at Bhowanipore. I had many times bought fish rolls from there to take home.

'Cheers', and the last race of the day started. There were loud speakers placed at all vantage points, which blared out the running commentary. For the first six hundred metres, we were well placed. All our five horses were well placed just behind Chaitanya, who set the pace; while Startrack, the seventh horse was way behind to cover up the ground. We all looked at each other, as the jackpot seemed to be a cakewalk. The pace setter generally tired out, which meant any of our five horses could be the winner. It was a twelve-hundred metres race and at eight hundred mark, still Chaitanya held his ground well. Desire was making a strong challenge on the outside and we were ecstatic. 'It's Chaitanya and Desire as the others failed to keep the scorching pace set by Chaitanya. Thousand metres, and it is Chaitanya and Desire neck to neck; Desire giving a strong challenge. It is

Desire and Chaitanya. Desire and Chaitanya. But Chaitanya is not giving up. It is Desire versus Chaitanya. Desire versus Chaitanya. Last ten metres and Chaitanya breaking loose with a final burst. It is Chaitanya versus Desire. Desire versus Chaitanya. And Chaitanya stretches out and what a finish. Chaitanya wins by a head. It is Chaitanya.'

We all had stood up in excitement and what a fall. We sat down. Mohinda ordered one more drink for all. We did not win the jackpot but I won a new group of friends.

We met at the racecourse on each racing day. Some lost, some won. Most placed their bets on the favorites while I backed the offbeat dark horses with high odds. At the end, of most of the racing days, we would huddle into Mohinda's car and head for some bar for a tete a tete evening. When due to some reason the races were cancelled, we drove to Mohinda's Amherst Street residence and gambled on 'flash', a playing cards game. I had played 'flash' a lot in the mining hostel, but the stakes then were fifty paisa, to maximum of a rupee per bet. Here, the stakes were high, starting at hundred rupees and sometimes reached five thousand bucks. I restricted myself to a maximum of five hundred. I never won in card games, be it in the mining hostel or at Mohinda's house. It was just a pastime for me, though a costly pastime.

Racing was more interesting. There were racing almanacs which were published a day before every racing day. I would religiously buy a copy and spend the night before calculating timings, checking pedigrees, and referring to past races. I had over a time built up a large collection of such almanacs to refer back to. It was during these late night exercises that I fished out the dark challengers. Betting on the horses with high odds was a high-risk game; but slowly I mastered to select one or two high odd horses in a day, which won. This developed a racing day system for me, where I would make some or a lot of money even on losing in three or four races. But it was a tiring and tedious process burning the night oil. On one such night, I had focused on Aberdine as the upset horse in the fourth race of the next day. On checking earlier almanacs, I found she had run five racing days ago and the comment against her finish was 'burst into a sprint to finish a close fourth'. That bolstered my view and the next day I confidently placed a thousand bucks at an odd of one is to twelve. It was one of the least fancied mares. If it won, I stood to win twelve thousand bucks risking only a thousand bucks. The twelve hundred metres race started and till half the way it seemed to be one of my very adventurous choices. But from the six hundred-metre marking, things started changing. Aberdine suddenly seemed to get energized out of the blue and spearheaded a strong challenge on the outside. It seemed to be a miracle when it won by a length from the favourite horse. The Race Course fell silent as I cried out loud. My racing friends and the crowd around me stared at me in astonishment. I was the lone person at the betting stands to collect the winning amount. Not a single one had betted on Aberdine. The 'Bookie' asked me if had a tip. I replied that it was a gut feeling.

Twice more it happened that I noted the same sentence 'burst into a sprint to finish a close fourth' in the earlier racing day comment. I was close to short listing one, 'Stargaze', but was not even close to selecting 'Yours Faithfully' on another day with the same tagline in the earlier race, but on both days I backed the two. 'Stargaze' won at an odd of one is to eight, and 'Yours Faithfully' made a last-minute challenge but was declared second. I thought my reading between the lines was childish. I had betted two thousand at one is to nine odds, and was about to tear the betting card as the loudspeakers declared that jockey Aslam on 'Yours Faithfully' had raised an objection against jockey Mike riding the winner 'Well done'. A ray of hope flashed in my mind and I kept the card back into my pocket. 'Well Done' was the second favourite and the crowd was confident that the Stewards would overrule the objection. It was really a long three minutes before the loudspeakers blared that the objection was upheld and 'Yours Faithfully' was declared winner. I had won; I was happy not just because of the win but stumbling upon a secret code or simply a mysterious link between the text in the almanac and a dark-winning horse. The textual comment used to be identically the same, 'burst into a sprint to finish a close fourth' without even a shift of a word. Racing days continued and slowly, my long nights became shorter as I spent less time calculating, waiting for the code to appear for some other horse in some other race. I continued betting on all races but more on hunch and betted heavily on the coded horses, which appeared continually after every second or third week. I shared my choice with my racing friends but kept the secret to myself. They tried my choices of dark horses, sometimes winning and sometimes losing. But they never dared to touch the mysterious sure shot winners as they were always on odds higher than eight to one and were the most unfancied horses. It was happy racing, great winning, and a gala time.

One evening, over the drinks at the Astor on Elgin Road, it was decided that enough time had passed and we should go for an outing with our families. The place was decided,

Digha. A sea beach in the southern part of West Bengal that most Bengali families had visited, some time or the other; a few hours drive, a good weekend getaway. I had been to Digha when I was in class nine, along with my parents. I had lovely memories of a pristine beach with Hotel Sea Hawk, the only hotel of class, right on the beach. Bapi had presented me his Russian camera 'Zorky' and I used it to the hilt on this beach.

There were sea snakes, which floated onto the beach sands with the incoming waves and were stranded till the next wave came in. I caught such snakes by their tail and spinned over my head and threw them back into the water. The snakes lay still in the water as I took their pics and after a few seconds they wriggled back into the sea. I had read somewhere that spinning a snake stretches their spinal cord and leaves them numb for a few seconds. I had also noticed that unlike other snakes on land, the sea snakes had a flattened tail. Then there were hordes of Olive Ridley Turtles all turned on their backs, shell side down so that they could not move. Large turtles all waiting to be loaded on trucks to be carried away to various markets. Their flesh was supposed to be a delicacy in many parts of India and there was no notification of ban on fishing these turtles, which came much later. All these made good photographic subject. In fact, everything makes for a good photographic subject when you get your first camera.

So Digha it was. While all of us came with our wives, Mohinda came with his second wife or mistress. Subhashda's two children had also accompanied us. After two nights of revelry, we left Digha on the third day, promising to meet with families more often. But back in Calcutta, only Sourenda and I got closer; it could be the less of age difference that bonded us. I was twenty-eight, Sourenda forty one, his wife Aitreyi thirty one, and my wife Anjali, at twenty three. We visited each other's home quite often, watched video films on VCR, and went out for dinner together. Those were the days of VCR, the Video Cassette Recorder, a prized possession of many families—a one-by-two-feet black box that changed the way families watched movies. The films came in video version, in four-inch by six-inch black cassettes. Many video libraries mushroomed in all localities, who would rent out VCRs as well if you did not own one. People stopped going to cinema halls and while the video business boomed, the mainstream cinema suffered. The video revolution also brought in a fresh air in pornography. Earlier, soft porn like Playboys, Playgirls, Hustler, and other hard-core porn magazines were available in dark corners of street side bookshops at a high premium. But now, the foreign porn films—categorized X, XX, and XXX—were readily available at these video stores, but only rented out to regular trusted customers. Many times I had brought in a cassette or two along with other movies and watched them with Anjali. Some were fabulously shot while some were pure trash with no style. But it was all about watching hardcore sex in your bedroom and it did give new dimension to our lovemaking and in many other homes.

CHAPTER 10

T HROUGH THE HISTORY, religions have clashed either to establish its domination, or to survive. Though founded on the principles of universality of being with a purpose of providing a meaning of life to its followers, in the long term, religions became typecast in the materialistic logic of Herbert Spencer's phrase 'Survival of the fittest'. It was no different in India. Particularly after the traumatic 'Partition' and independence of India and Pakistan, the followers of two major religions, Hinduism and Islam, never trusted one another. Under the visible calm of secularism in India, there was a tinderbox, which could ignite at the slightest provocation. It happened in nineteen fifty and now, once again in nineteen sixty four, riots broke out between the two communities in Calcutta. Some relic went missing from an Islamic mosque in Srinagar. Muslims in Pakistan attacked the household and business establishments of the minority Hindus. And the backlash happened five and a half thousand kilometers down east in Calcutta. Hindus attacked Muslim residential areas and business hubs. Muslims retaliated, too. It was mayhem and state government declared curfew.

Twenty-two Monsatala Row, the house where Bublu stayed with his parents, was the last house in the row of houses resided by Hindus. Across the road was a Muslim populated ghetto followed by houses of Muslim families. SK lived with his family on the ground floor of the house on rent. On the ground floor, there was another tenant family, the Kapoors. These two families were most vulnerable to a probable Muslim attack from the ghetto across the road. The house was owned by 'Lal Jethu', as Bublu called him, because of his extremely fair pinkish complexion.

He was the landlord and had a towering personality. In his heydays, he had hunted down a pair of man-eaters. Framed photographs of this achievement adorned his wall. Also, the double barrel gun with which he had shot down the man-eaters was also hung beside the framed photographs. Bublu, studying in class two, heard the word 'curfew' for the first time, and he saw the streets being empty, military convoys and contingents moving up and down the road at intervals. He did not have to go to school. SK had gone to the office in the morning and there after the curfew was declared. The day passed quietly. Just before evening, he saw 'Lal Jethu' come down with his double barrel gun and took him, Sandhya, and the other family, upstairs to his home. As evening came down, all the families moved to the roof and with baited breath, awaited the night to unfold the unknown.

Bublu looked over the parapet: there was a military jeep standing on the road. Four army jawans had positioned themselves at the corner of the street. There was a carpet of silence spread over the neighbourhood. As darkness descended on the streets, a burst of light flashed on the horizon beyond the rooftops. A large bang followed. 'Must be crackers,' Bublu thought. Lal Jethu moved restlessly with the gun on his shoulder, often looking down on the streets. Sandhya started getting worried as time passed. SK generally came home by seven in the evening; it was eight and still there was no sign of him. Sandhya expressed his worries to Lal Jethu. He called up office to be told that SK had left in time. He had to cross Watgunje, a predominantly Muslim area, to reach home. The worries mounted; Lal Jethu called up the police station and informed them about SK. Bublu, unaware of the growing tension, enjoyed the adventure-filled evening behind the shield of innocence and ignorance. No studies, more time to play with Lal Jethu's younger daughter Kajal, and an evening away from the routine. It was around ten as he was having his dinner, a siren pierced through the silence down the road. A few minutes later, a knock on the door. Lal Jethu carefully opened the door with his finger on the trigger.

'I am Inspector Sen,' a voice was heard. SK walked in escorted by two policemen. Sandhya sighed relief. Lal Jethu bursted out at SK and Bublu felt amused seeing Bapi being scolded by someone.

Curfew continued for the next day. SK did not go to office and the night was again spent at Lal Jethu's home. But once lifted, it seemed nothing had happened. Everything was normal. SK even sent Bublu to fetch a packet of cigarette from the shop at the corner of the street, owned by a Muslim. The barbershop where Bublu took his haircut opened. The Hindus and Muslims walked in without any prejudice to take a hair cut from the Christian barber. The Muslim hawker of bakery products once again walked down the streets with his iron trunk on his head, calling out 'Cakes, pastries, patties . . .' in his typical tone.

Lal Jethu passed away a year later. Bublu knew Bapi was searching for a new house. He looked forward to the change as disturbing facets like the cigarette butt in the wall almirah, passing away of grandmother, and continual clash of Bapi and Mamoni overshadowed his treasured moments in the house.

The school and moments spent in Shefali Mashi's home were his only windows to a breath of fresh fun. Promoted to class four, he had to shift to the senior division of the school. It was a new address on Moira Street with a large building and a huge playfield. It was a place where Mrs White, the English teacher, would be someone with a very dark complexion; Miss Cummins, the History teacher, would be anything but adorably inviting. She had the typical punishment of putting the pencil in between the two fingers and pressing the fingers hard. It was unbearably painful. Then there was this large auditorium, where Bublu watched his first Hindi film, Sant Gyaneshwar, a black-and-white biopic on a Hindu religious saint.

SK shifted to the new house in Gopal Nagar in the October of Bublu's class four. Though not drastic, there were a few changes in Bublu's world. The LPG gas cylinder was just introduced and SK, being forward thinker, subscribed to one. The big wood and coal-fired oven at the Gopal Nagar house became redundant. Even the back-up kerosene stove also was used rarely. Sandhya was advised against use of LPG by her well wishing newfound neighbour friends. They feared that cooking on a gas stove would generate gas in the stomach and thereby cause high acidity. A logic even young Bublu failed to understand, and Sandhya ignored, having trust in SK's decisions. The LPG (Liquefied Pertroleum Gas) system was not only a little cheaper option but also a much cleaner fuel with a clean cooking system. Bublu could himself operate it easily. With Bapi sailing out, and Mamoni being asthmatic, Bublu could prepare simple rice and dal on the gas burner for himself and Mamoni before leaving for school, whenever she had an acute attack. It would be impossible with the wood and coal fired oven and quite tedious with the kerosene stove. Life had become a little easier with the introduction of this new system.

A new world also opened up in the house next to their building. A single storey house where Mashima, as Bublu called her, meaning aunt, lived with her husband and a son elder to Bublu by four years. Meshomoshai, husband of Mashima, worked in some senior capacity in some government office and the son, Khokada studied at Ballygunge High School. They were the descendants of the 'Zamindars' of Serampore. Zamindars were appointed by the erstwhile British government as landlords of large tracts of land for which they were responsible for management and collection of tax on behalf of the government. Zamindars were a rich class and many were despots, too. Khokada had become a good friend and introduced Bublu to the interesting collections in the house: an air gun, a long telescope, collection of books like Ripley's Believe It Or Not Omnibus, National Geographic magazines, Reader's Digest, Sandesh, a children's magazine launched by Upendrakishore Raychoudhury, the grandfather of Satyajit Ray, the Indian film doyen and Suktara, another children's magazine which introduced Bublu to the cartoon characters of 'Handa and Bhonda' loosely inspired by the characters 'Laurel and Hardy' of Hollywood. He did not mingle with the other children of his age in the area; instead he would spend the after-school hours in Mashima's house delving into these newfound treasures, or nature in the large garden at the backyard of the house. At the corner of the garden was a 'Hashnuhena' tree with small fragrant flowers blooming in the evening called the 'Queen of the Night', of which a few sticks with flowers would end up in Sandhya's flower vase on many evenings. At the edge of the wall, there were four pinapple trees, which bore fruit in the season; Mashima would cut these and give one to Bublu. Next to it there was a kafir lime tree. Bublu would often be asked to pluck a few leaves of this tree to be put into lentil preparation for flavour. In the centre there was a 'Shiuli' flower tree, which bore 'Night Jasmine', small white flowers with orange stem which bloomed at the advent of the autumn. They would bloom in the night and in the morning the bed of the tree would be decked with a white and orange carpet of the fallen flowers. Sandhya often collected a large quantity of these, pluck out the orange stems, dried them in the sun, and stored in glass jars to use them as natural colouring agent for pilafs, biryanis, and other rice preparations. Then there were the ferns, aloe vera, and crotons; the colourful seasonal flowers and variety of creepers that Mashima would lovingly nurture through the year. For Bublu, it was like 'Alice's Wonderland', growing up amidst newfound fragrances, plethora of colours, texts beyond textbooks, and delicious snacks and sweets prepared by Mashima.

SK's world had no change. It was a fifteen to twenty days sailing on the steam ship to the Sand heads down Hooghly River, followed by a week on land with office duty. Evenings would be spent reading books, listening to the radio news, overseeing Bublu's homework, or chatting with Bose Kaku whenever he dropped in after his office. Bose Kaku lived in a rented room nearby in Alipur. Unlike before, he did not have to leave early and sometimes joined the family for dinner before leaving. One such evening, SK returned from office and after freshening up had just turned on the radio for the news, that there was a knock at the door.

'Sandhya, see who is knocking.' SK called out Sandhya who was in the kitchen.

'There is somebody asking for you,' Sandhya said opening the door.

SK turned off the radio and walked to the door. There was a person whom he could not recognize.

'Yes, tell me.'

'Jyotsnadidi asked me to hand over this packet to you.' SK was taken aback. There was no contact with her after her mother's death. All the memories lay unattended, entwined in cobwebs in some corner of a locked storeroom. SK had even lost the keys.

'Where is she?' SK asked on taking a thick white packet from the stranger's hands.

'She died fourteen days ago. She had given me your address and had asked me to hand over this packet to you after her 'Shradh', which was yesterday.'

Shradh was a religious ritual performed for the dead as per Hindu religion, to relieve the dead of all worldly attachments and preparing the soul for the final journey into eternity. SK stood dumbstruck for a while. He unconsciously found the key to the storeroom, which he had consciously lost. He opened the door and struggled through the darkness, frantically trying to clear the maze of cobwebs with both hands to reach the treasure trove of memories. More cobwebs and more darkness, and at the end it was all blank. She was gone.

'What happened to her?' he asked trying to hold himself together.

'She was suffering from cirrhosis of the liver for a long time,' he said 'and I will take your leave now.'

SK tore open the thick packet and found all his letters to her neatly tied together with a violet ribbon.

'Who was he?' Sandhya came out from the kitchen and asked. She took the packet from SK's hands to have a look. He did not resist. She kept the packet on the corner table and untied the ribbon and picked up a letter. 'That bitch! Again!' she screamed. 'What does she want from me now?'

Bublu sensed the brewing storm from his room. But there was no storm. Nobody talked that night. Dinner at the table was quiet. Bapi wished him 'Good night' before going to bed. Next morning, before leaving for school Bublu saw Mamoni burning a bunch of papers in the kitchen. For SK, Jyotsna did not exist for a long time, but time asserted her existence to him and Sandhya will never know that Jyotsna, the 'bitch' did not exist anymore.

As SK became quiet and indifferent, Bose Kaku's after-office visits increased, particularly when SK was out sailing. From a day or two per week over tea, to three to four per week over tea and evening snacks; to everyday over dinner except weekends, when he visited his relatives in Duttapukur. As the interval of visits decreased, Bublu's resentment against Bose Kaku increased. Indifference gave way to dislike. The nondescript dark, on the fatter side man in Dhoti, and Kurta or Half Shirt with a receding hairline was now the black, fat, bald man who had the dirty habit of pushing snuff, a powdered form of tobacco, into his nostrils and blowing out loud into the handkerchief. He sang Rabindra Sangeet, playing the Harmonium on some evenings. Mamoni appreciated his singing capability but Bublu thought he was very nasal. He took part in dramas organized by his office club and did a few roles in the radio theatres. Mamoni thought he was a brilliant actor; Bublu thought that the stage shows were boring and the radio theatres had 'you answer someone's call and you miss the line' roles.

Bose Kaku tried a lot to woo Bublu but in vain. He started getting gifts and chocolates. He started taking Mamoni and Bublu out, to Dakhsineswar, Victoria Memorial, but to no avail. Bapi was so vibrant in such outings. He used to engage Bublu completely with activities, stories, and small anecdotes. And here Bose Kaku would sit with Mamoni and they would keep talking among themselves, while Bublu had nothing to do but to roam around close by. During these outings, Bapi would be out sailing or even if at home, would give some excuse and stay back. Bublu felt Bapi had changed but could not gauge as to why.

In the winter of nineteen sixty-eight, Sandhya fell ill with a heavy asthmatic attack. Doctor suggested a long stay in some seaside town. The sun and the salt water would help clear her lungs off congestion naturally, the doctor advised. Every year, SK vacationed outstation depending on Bublu's school's summer, or Durga Puja holiday schedule. Coming summer he planned for Puri, a seaside town on the Bay of Bengal, in Orissa. It was an overnight's journey and a favorite vacation spot for Bengalis. Bublu was excited as he had been to the mountains, historical cities, and jungles, but had never seen the sea. He had read in the books about the huge waves, the golden sands, and the beautiful shells on the beach. Now he will have the opportunity to experience it all. As his school closed for summer vacation, the plan for their holiday became clearer. Bapi had booked a two-room cottage, right on the beach. Bose Kaku would accompany Bublu and Mamoni. Bapi would finish fifteen-day sailing schedule and join them in the last week of the twenty-day holiday. Bublu felt a little sad, he had double the fun with Bapi around than Bose Kaku. But the call of the mighty waves, the golden sands, soon overshadowed his feeling of loss.

On the night of the journey Bublu got down from the taxi at the Howrah station as Bose Kaku appointed a 'coolie' to carry their luggage. Travelling for vacations was not light. To keep the budget in control, SK travelled 'third class three tier' with the complete bedding arrangement, cooking utensils, the kerosene stove, and of course, clothing for the vacations. Every vacation, Bapi would wash clothes early in the morning and Mamoni would prepare the breakfast and package meal for consumption during the daily sightseeing. Dinner was cooked once back in the hotel. SK saved on laundry and eating-out. SK's holidays would not be relaxing and luxurious but all encompassing about the place—the sights, sounds, the people, the markets. Planning economy holidays, SK could travel more. He travelled at least once, if not twice, every year and every time, Bublu would return home with fond memories and richer by experience.

There were two 'hold-alls': one iron trunk, a cane basket, and Bose Kaku's leather suitcase. Bublu looked around. He had experienced the chaos of a railway station, particularly of Howrah, many a times. It was no different this time: Hordes of people, vagrant street dogs, piles of rubbish at pillar corners, inaudible speakers notifying train schedules, pushy vendors; it was all the same. Bublu went to sleep as soon as his bed was laid out on the top wooden berth. He woke up in the morning to a chatter of many people he had not seen in the compartment the earlier night. Many strangers had boarded the train and they all wore identical dress. All were dressed in a white—some quite dirty— dhoti and sandow, or half-sleeve vests. Many had 'gamchas' around their neck or on their shoulder, and were trying to build up a conversation with the travelling tourists. Bublu learnt from Bose Kaku, they were 'pandas'. Puri was famous for two things: one was the sea, and other, the Jagannath temple. The 'pandas' were the priests of the Jagannath temple. They boarded the train a few stations earlier to Puri and tried to hook customers, whom they would take to the temple, get them the best 'darshan' and do the puja for them, so that they are showered by the best blessings of Lord Jagannath, an incarnation of Lord Vishnu. The legend goes, as Mamoni had told Bublu before the vacations, that Lord Jagannath was originally worshipped by a tribal chief named Viswavasu. Having heard about the benevolent deity, King Indradyumna sent Vidyapati to locate the Lord. Vidyapati failed but managed to marry Viswavasu's daughter Lalita. On repeated request of Vidyapti, Viswavasu took his son-in-law, blind folded, to a cave where the Lord Neela was worshipped. Vidyapati was very intelligent. He dropped mustard seeds on the ground on the way. The seeds germinated after a few days, which enabled him to find out the cave later. On hearing from him, King Indradyumna made a pilgrimage to Orissa to worship the deity, but the deity had disappeared underneath the seashore sand. He observed fast unto death when a celestial voice cried 'thou shalt see him'. Afterwards, the king performed 'Ashwamedha Yagna', a horse sacrificial religious ritual, and built a magnificent temple for Vishnu, who was pleased and blessed the king with a vision of Lord Jagannath. Also, an astral voice directed him to receive a fragrant trunk of a tree on the seashore and make idols out of it. Lord Vishnu himself appeared in the guise of a carpenter to make the idols on condition that he was to be left undisturbed until he finished the work. But just after two weeks, the Queen became very anxious. She thought that the carpenter was dead as no sound came from the temple. She requested the king to open the door and check. Lord Vishnu abandoned his work leaving the idols incomplete. The three idols representing the Lord Jagannath, his elder brother, Balabhadra and their sister, Subhadra are only torso upwards and with no palms. Bublu found it intriguing. God, who was all-powerful, was helpless and had no option but to appear before his devotees as an incomplete self.

The cottage on the beach that Bapi had booked was complete with two rooms with wooden beds, a kitchen, a bathroom, and a courtyard with a hand pump for fresh water. The roof was thatched with dry hay and stood on a raised cemented platform from the beach. It was on a higher ground giving a clear view of the complete beach in front, and the ocean beyond. One had to walk through sand to reach the cottage. A cool breeze flowed in from over the sea and there was continuous background melody of the breaking waves. Bublu stood in awe in front of the cottage as Bose Kaku and the rickshaw pullers, who ferried them from the station, carried the luggage inside. In ecstasy, he ran in short bursts, jumped digging his heels deep into the sand.

'Bublu, do not do that,' Mamoni called out, 'Your shoes will get filled with sand. First change your dress, wear your slippers, and then come out and play.'

It took a lot of time in unpacking, setting up the kitchen, and laying the beds. While Mamoni was getting Bublu dressed up after a bath underneath the hand pump, Bose Kaku went out to search for some food for the afternoon. He came back soon.

'There is a good hotel nearby. We can have lunch there.'

Every eating joint was called a hotel in colloquial language. Mamoni was also ready, Bose Kaku locked the cottage, and they walked through the sand towards the hotel. It was not far; it was also on the beach about five minutes walk from the cottage. A low rise, long mud hut with thatched hay roof. It was lit by natural light flowing in through the doors and windows. There were long tables and benches made of wooden logs. The meal was common: a plate of rice, dal, fried potatoes, seasonal vegetable, and a fish curry. The type of fish changed every day as per best fresh catch available on the day. It cost two rupees and fifty paisa and except for the fish, one could ask for extra portions of all items. The day's fish was 'Pabda', a delicacy for all Bengalis. The food was tasty, Bublu loved the Pabda as it had fewer thorns.

For the first time, it was a long, lazy holiday for Bublu. Jagannath temple visit was scheduled after Bapi arrived. So it was rolling in the sands, bathing in the sea, collecting shells, and long walks on the beach. Though located on the beach, the cottage was at a secluded spot away from the popular spot where major tourists bathed. Taking a long walk in the evenings with Bose Kaku and Mamoni to the popular spot,

Bublu had to cross 'Anondomoyee Maa's Ashram' next to their cottage, a few hutments with coconut groves and a spot encircled by a low height, cemented wall. Every time he crossed the spot he found a pile of wooden logs burning. Sometimes, it would be one and at other, it would be two to three. Sometimes, there would be a group of people around the fire and sometimes there would be none.

'What do the people burn there?' Bublu asked one day.

'Garbage,' was Mamoni's reply.

'So it was a large open litter bin,' Bublu thought. True, a large open litter bin.

The anomaly was, the litters here were dead bodies—it was an open-air crematorium. Bublu had never visited a crematorium or had witnessed any cremation ceremony. Even when his grandmother died, a simple explanation that 'God had taken her as she was suffering here' sufficed. It was not that in the last five years after SK's mother's death, nobody died among relatives or acquaintances, but Bublu was kept in the dark. So for Bublu revisiting the explanation of 'God taking away someone' did not arise. Though oblivious of one of the major truths of life, Bublu got enlightened about another facet of existence, the Time, the continuity of time. In the afternoons, when Mamoni and Bose Kaku took their siesta, Bublu sat on the bed near Mamoni's shoulder and looked out of the open window into the continuous breaking waves. His world always had a beginning and an end: the day began, the day ended; the night came down and it vanished the next morning; rain poured and it stopped; winter came and it went away. For Bublu, everything that started had an end. His concept of a cycle was limited by his age. For the first time, he was witnessing something that never had an end. The waves kept coming and breaking on the shores. Be it morning, afternoon, evening, and night, or beyond into the next morning. There was no beginning and there was no end, he realized Time was not limited to the circular dial of the timepiece that lay on Mamoni's dressing table or Bapi's wristwatch. There was something much more humongous than anything he had ever experienced. He could not fathom or define its existence, only kept watching the breaking waves in awe.

Dinner was cooked by Mamoni every night. Late in the evening, on the way back, they took a detour of the local market where Bose Kaku bought vegetables and fish. Once back in the cottage, the evenings were a little boring for Bublu. Mamoni got engaged in cooking and Bose Kaku got engaged in talking to her, standing at the kitchen door, leaving Bublu to watch the dark beach outside. After dinner Bose Kaku sang Rabindra Sangeet after stuffing snuff into his nose, sitting on his bed. Mamoni listened and Bublu, after every hectic day, would feel sleepy and retire to his bed. He would fall asleep much before Mamoni joined him by his side. One night, Bublu woke up to find that Mamoni had not yet come to sleep by his side. The lights were off, and the room was dark. There was no sound from the next room as well. He looked out of the window: moonlight glistened on the breakers; the litters were burning far away; the sea groaned, and the wind whined. He got a little scared. Getting down from the bed he walked towards the next room. The door was open, the curtains drawn. He peeped through the curtain. It was all dark. He stood still as he heard soft groans and whispers. 'Should I call Mamoni,' he thought, but did not. He tiptoed back to his bed and pulled the bedcover over his head and closed his eyes.

One fine morning Bapi joined in. Bose Kaku left the next day and the holidays became more vibrant.

On returning to Calcutta, everything went on like before. Bose Kaku kept coming. Sandhya kept listening to his Rabindra Sangeet. Bublu kept unraveling little mysteries in Mashima's house. And Bapi sailed out, sailed in, did land duties and on Saturdays after a half-day office, visited the RCTC Race Course and placed petty bets.

* * *

SK passed away in the January of eighty-four. Bublu, now better known as Siddhartha, was in the mines when he received a telegraphic message that Bapi was hospitalized after a massive stroke. He rushed to Calcutta to find his father in coma on a bed in CPT Majherhat Hospital.

His Mamoni had passed away two years ago. Shefali Mashi, Mamoni's friend, was a nurse at the CPT Hospital when Siddhartha last walked out on Lipika. She was the Matron now. She took personal care and came into SK's cabin every now and then to check his condition, but never talked to Siddhartha. He could feel the pangs of a mother betrayed, the pain of watching her daughter's dream slowly fade away. SK lay in the vegetative state for three days, and passed away. Doctors had told Siddhartha that even if he did come out of the coma, he would surely be majorly paralyzed. Siddhartha could not imagine Bapi, a self-made, strong-willed man, being dependent on others through the rest of his life. He sighed relief when Bapi died. Bapi's office friends arrived on getting the news. Relatives poured in and Antara, Lipika's younger sister, dropped in too after school. Amidst all the crying and chaos, Siddhartha took Antara to a corner and asked, 'What is Lipika doing? I last heard she was doing Masters in Archeology.'

'That was years back. She is married and has a lovely one year old daughter.'

Siddhartha knew time waits for none, but felt it for the first time. Even during his affair with Esha, many a times he would board the trams and buses that generally he and Lipika travelled by or the ones she took to college, in the hope that some day, by chance, he might come across her. He yearned that he came face to face with her and believed everything would be just like the past. A time span would be completely wiped out. But in vain.

'So what is she doing now?' Siddhartha questioned her again.

'Of course she is nurturing her daughter and running her home,' she replied.

She made Siddhartha feel real stupid. Of course, a lot of water had passed under the bridge and she was happily married, having a child, running her home, putting the past and him behind. Of course, she must have wiped out the name Siddhartha from her life. Her husband must not be aware about him. The letters that she cherished and kept in her secret closet must have been torn and trashed into some dustbin. Siddhartha was a non-entity in this happy household.

The air-conditioned vehicle to carry the dead body arrived from Hindu Mission, white flower wreaths and garlands were arranged, white sheet of cloth to cover the cadaver was there. The body was covered by the white sheet, white flower wreaths on top and was placed in the vehicle. Two flower vases with white Rajanigandha flower sticks were placed on both sides of the head. Siddhartha was asked to accompany the dead body in the vehicle while others would reach the crematorium by other means. He sat beside the dead body. Underneath the white sheet of cloth there was Bapi, a cigarette between his lips, burning away fast.

The joker of the Russian Circus raising his fool's capped head through the sheet creating a snowy mountain peak. The peak kept rising. Lipika stood in a white sari with a white Rajanigandha stick in her hand, ankle deep in the white snow. A cold breeze lashed past Siddhartha's face. He walked down the slope towards her. A snowstorm started. It became grey all around. An avalanche began. He could see a crevice develop behind Lipika. He started running to reach her. Bapi called out from a higher ground, 'Bublu do not try to hold back Time. You will never succeed.' Siddhartha looked back. It was too dark up there and he could see nothing. He slides on the snow and stretched out his hand to Lipika, but in vain. She slowly slides down into the dark crevice. The Rajanigandha stick lay before him. He picked it up.

The driver opened the cadaver-carrying vehicle. Siddhartha sat with the Rajanigandha stick in his hand.

'We have reached the crematorium,' the driver said. Siddhartha placed the Rajanigandha stick into the flower vase and got down.

'It was quite a chill in that vehicle,' he told his sister on getting down.

The thirteen-day mourning ritual began with Siddhartha wearing a single-piece, coarse, white cloth in the 'Dhoti' style, a typical Bengali dress from waist down. He had no liking for this ethnic dress and never mastered the art, or so to say, the craft of wearing it, so somebody else would dress him up for the next thirteen days. The ritual did not end with the dress. He could have only one meal after sunset, which he had to cook himself. A clean combination of rice, potato, and green plantain boiled in an earthen pot over a jute plant sticks called 'patkathhi' fire. The rice and other vegetables must be given as alms by relatives and neighbours. The only luxury allowed was a spoon of 'ghee' or better known as clarified butter. During the day, he could have fruits brought in by relatives. After two days of such diet meals, not only Siddhartha's palette started revolting, it was getting on to his nerves. So he started going out on the pretext of a walk in the evening and reached Shaktida's Roll Corner at Kalighat More. It was not far; a five minutes' walk over the Alipore Bridge to the other side of Ganga canal. A mutton roll was a welcome break. Skewered mutton kebabs rolled into pin-rolled flat bread, shallow fried in oil, called 'parantha'. Though non-vegetarian food was a strict no during this period, it hardly mattered to Siddhartha.

It was on the fourth evening during this period that an envelope arrived by post in Siddhartha's name. It was a white envelope with no sender's name mentioned on it. He tore open the envelope to find a card, a condolence card. There was a poem on 'death' by Mark Twain on the cover. He read the poetry. 'Touching, meaningful,' he thought, 'but who could send this.'

He opened the card and he was shocked. The message in green ink read '*Mon, my heartfelt condolences. I know what it feels when you lose your loved one.*' Signed, '*Lipika*'.

'Mon', that is what Lipika called Siddhartha. He sat down on the bed, looked up at the ceiling fan, rotating, the wall clock ticking away. He read the poetry again, and read the signed message again and again and again. He thought he should write back, and then he thought he should not, and realized he did not have the contact address in any case. Suddenly, his RIMC days came to his mind; Lipika's writing of 'I love you' with the backside of a pen, which was not visible directly but could be read once slanted against the light. He picked up the card towards the light and slanted it. No, there was nothing; a chapter of life so close, yet so far. How many times you meet people after ages and say, 'See, the world is round after all.' Siddhartha hoped one day he would be able to tell the same to Lipika.

Losing Bapi was painful but what followed was yet more painful. The legal processes of succession; the visits to the court, and Estate Duty offices. Siddhartha was unaware of all these procedures. Bapi's office friend Ghosh Kaku came forward to help but with a condition.

'There is a 'Mohur' in your father's locker. SK told me, he had promised to give it to me but he passed away before that.' Ghosh Kaku said. 'Do not worry, I will help you in all the procedural matters but will you keep your father's promise?'

Mohur is an antique gold coin used in the earlier days for financial transactions. The older it was, it would be more precious. Siddhartha had learnt from Mamoni that they got this Mohur in heirloom and was of Bahadur Shah Zafar's period, which meant it was a priceless antique. Siddhartha agreed, and procedures became clearer—procedures became clearer, but not easier. Taking leave from colliery, coming to Calcutta to attend court hearings, and getting yet another date instead of a verdict. Date after date after date. That is how Indian courts work. The Estate Duty's office, since abolished, was not easy to handle either. Ghosh Kaku took Siddhartha to the Deputy Commissioner in the Estates Duty Department who was the final authority in Siddhartha's case. An appointment could be set up, as Ghosh Kaku knew one of the relatives of the said officer. Otherwise, one had to start at the bottom of the pyramid, doling out bribes, which keeps increasing as one rise up.

S. Chakravarty, Dy. Commissioner, was mentioned on a shining brass plaque on his closed door. A message was sent in through his peon and both Ghosh Kaku and Siddhartha were called in. After the preliminary sympathies and concerns, Mr Chakravarty came down straight to the point. He had asked Ghosh Kaku to bring in all the papers regarding all movable and immovable assets. SK lived in a rented house and apart from a single bank account, had no assets. There was a locker in the bank but the matter was *sub judice* and hence, was not his concern. He called for three cups of tea. The person seemed to be nice and gentlemanly to Siddhartha. He went through the two passbooks in detail for some time, and tick-marked two entries. There were two withdrawals from the bank by SK within two months before his death.

'What did he buy with these two amounts?' Mr Chakravarty enquired.

'He was having physical problems so must have spent for medicine or some devises relating to that,' Ghosh Kaku tried to justify.

'If it was for some purchase, there must be some bill,' Mr Chakravarty said. 'I need to see them.'

'What bill?' Siddhartha thought, how could he know what his father spent the money on. He could not talk to a dead man. And that was the loophole Mr Chakravarty was trying to find out while scrutinizing the passbooks.

'See, I am not interested in how much money has been deposited into the account or its source of income. That is the job of Income Tax Department. My job is to see how much a person has in assets. So when an amount is drawn from the bank, unless you substantiate with spending documents, I will assume that the money has been utilized to acquire some assets,' Mr Chakravarty asserted. 'And once you acquire assets, my department is supposed to tax it.'

'But this amount cannot get you a land in the remotest of places,' Ghosh Kaku tried to justify.

'I agree, but you could buy jewellery which again will be treated as an asset creation.'

'How do you expect us to provide you proof of something, about which we do not have any knowledge?'

'I do not expect. So I will treat this amount as asset creation and the Estate duty on the amount will be just a sec,' he took out a calculator and after a few taps said 'Fifteen thousand rupees.'

'You mean to say that this poor boy will have to pay fifteen thousand rupees to the government for no rhyme or reason.'

'You are right, there is no rhyme, but I have clarified the reason. On the other hand, you can give five thousand rupees and I will overlook these entries.'

Siddhartha was astonished at the way, who a little while ago he was thinking to be a gentleman, could even have the audacity to ask for a bribe in such blatant manner.

Ghosh Kaku knew the system, looked at Siddhartha and agreed for the deal. It was decided that the next day, they would come and bribe him and get the file cleared. Five thousand at a go was a big amount for Siddhartha. He borrowed from friends and relatives, and collected five thousand rupees. The next day, Ghosh Kaku and Siddhartha visited Mr Chakravarty's office and handed over the cash in an envelope.

'Look sonny,' Mr Chakravarty said. 'Do not think that you are giving me five thousand rupees. It is me who is giving you ten thousand rupees. Now you are parting with only five thousand, otherwise officially you would have to part with fifteen thousand. So I am giving you ten thousand.'

'What a nauseating logic,' Siddhartha thought.

It was after seven harrowing months that Siddhartha got the court order of inheritance to certify what actually was his. He collected two cheques from the Calcutta Port Trust Accounts Department on Strand Road totaling to rupees two lakhs and seventy thousand. He also got the custody of the locker in United Bank on Taratala Road. The locker was a treasure trove of gold jewellery, gold guineas of British period, and of course the 'Mohur' from Bahadur Shah Zafar's era. All coming down the generations and being added to by each generation, even by SK, and now they are all Siddhartha's. But Siddhartha did not add any, instead he soon encashed them and spent it all away in times to come.

Suddenly, Siddhartha became the most eligible bachelor for his relatives and families that knew him. Good looks, a secured job with Coal India Limited, and now the inheritance. Of course, the 'Mohur' was gifted away to Ghosh Kaku and that was the last Siddhartha heard of him. Even knowledge of Siddhartha's jointing and drinking binges did not come in the way of incoming proposals for marriage. Siddhartha did not contemplate about marriage, family, and life beyond. He was disoriented, lost. He had walked out on Lipika, who wanted to ride along into the wilderness, the unknown; and Esha had walked out of his uncertainty for a more secured reconciled reality after Ranjit Singh wound up his Calcutta operations.

The relatives found something to rally around, a purpose for their otherwise staid insignificant life. A responsibility that would bring in a sense of achievement and Anjali was finalized as the right choice; and Siddhartha accepted.

But according to the Hindu customs, he could not marry until a year passed after his father's death. The girl's family couldn't wait that long, having hooked a good potential groom for their daughter, who was strictly against taking any dowry, a one year wait was too great a risk. Little did they know that he was a wanderer, and soon he would wander away into uncertainty risking their daughter's security that they so confidently sought

CHAPTER 11

Walking down Park Street, or maybe I should say walking up the Park Street, moving away from Jawarharlal Nehru Road, suddenly the razzmatazz of lights, hotels, bars, restaurants, and the crowd abruptly ends. The buildings on the roadsides are the old colonial ones. The lights are only the streetlights, which are unable to carry the mantle of glamorous Park Street. But it was still Park Street. I had not visited this part before. Esha was engaged as Ranjit Singh was in town. I had the evening to myself to aimlessly saunter around. As the road became narrow, a dilapidated wall stretched along the footpath. The plaster less, weathered bricks, giggled to establish the presence of the past. I walked along side. I had no idea what lay within. Suddenly, there was a crumbled down section. There were two bricks well laid to create a stair. 'So people must be going in,' I thought. I peeped in. It was dark, bushy, and tall large trees in the silhouette. I stared in sharper. There were some manmade structures. What were they? I climbed the make shift brick stairs to enter the walled arena.

There was tall grass, bushes all around, a thin pathway seemed to exist, created by repeated walking. I followed it, to be led to a large stone, masonry, and marble structure. It was a tomb. So this was a burial ground. It was not maintained, which meant it was not in use. I lit a match and tried to read the tombstone. 'Sacred to the memory of Elizabeth Jane Barwell,

(The Celebrated Miss Sanderson), Married the Thirteenth September Seventeen Seventy Six.' I was taken aback. Taken back in time by two hundred years. I read on. 'Richard Barwell Esqr., (The Friend of Warren Hastings), Member of Council of the Hon. East India Co., Died the 12 November Seventeen Seventy Eight., Aged about Twenty Three years.'

I had read about this lady in some old book on Calcutta of the East India Co. period at the National Library. She was the cynosure of all eyes from the very moment she landed. She was said to be beautiful beyond compare and raised many a siren. But later married a gambler and womanizer whom today I knew was Richard Barwell Esqr., the friend of Warren Hastings, the first Governor General of India. I walked amidst the bushes looking at the tombs in myriad shapes and sizes. One of them shaped in the form of a small temple and also having a Hindu deity carved on it. The stone read, 'Major General Charles Stuart, (Known as Hindoo Stuart), Quarter Master of the First Bengal European Regiment and later commanded the Tenth Andes Regiment'. I failed to understand why was he called Hindoo Stuart till later when I delved into the resources at the National Library. He was an Irish and an officer in the army of East India Company. On being posted to India, he adopted Hindu customs and rituals. He bathed in the Hooghly every morning and allowed his Indian soldiers to wear the 'Tika', a Hindu colour adornment on the forehead. He also prodded British ladies to wear 'sari', a typical Indian women wear. He also believed in the multiple deity worship of the Hindu religion and had a large collection of these deities. Though follower of Hindu customs, he had not renounced Christianity and was buried in this cemetery along with his collection of deities.

I kept lighting the matchsticks and kept reading the tombstones. It was like walking through history, understanding and relating to some and imagining some. One thing struck me that most of the dead died at a very young age. There were many children tombs; there were ladies and men who died in their twenties. While many of the men might have died in the frequent battles fought between the East India Co. army and the rulers of undivided Bengal and Bihar, others must have succumbed to the many diseases prevalent in the hot tropical climate like cholera, malaria, kalazaar, and typhoid.

I lit the last matchstick over a large horizontally laid tomb. The marble plaque read 'In memory of Henry Louis Vivian Derozio. Born Sixteenth April Eighteen Hundred and Nine. Died Twentieth December Eighteen Hundred Thirty One.' The matchstick blew off. I could not read further. But I had read about Henry Derozio. I walked down to the next tomb and sat on it. Henry Derozio, is how I knew him. He was an early nineteenth century free thinker and a poet. Though he was an Anglo-Indian, he considered himself to be Indian and wrote many patriotic poems. He was the English teacher at the renowned Hindu College where he promoted radical thinking among his students. Soon he provoked the ire of the Managing Committee, who felt that the basic tenements of Hindu thinking were being challenged, which in turn, would reduce their influence on the society. He was ousted from the College and soon after he died of cholera.

Something glistened near my neck. I felt a cold hard metal on my skin. I looked back. A dark boy of my age stood behind and held a sharp knife onto my neck.

'Where is the girl?' he questioned.

'Which girl?' I was astonished.

'I know what have you come here for. Everyone comes here for a fuck.'

I was bewildered. By now he had grabbed my hair, pressed his knees onto my back and pressed the knife tighter on my neck.

'Tell me where the girl is or else I will slit your throat.'

I feared his move but had to tell the truth. 'There is no girl with me. I am alone here.'

'Take out your purse and give it to me.' I realized he was a petty snatcher and bore no threat to my life. He was here for some easy buck. I had no purse. I hardly had any money at any point of time and never felt the need to carry the extra baggage of a purse. It was month's end. I had three rupees in my pocket. I took the notes out.

'I have three rupees,' I said. 'I need to last till my salary. So you take one and I will keep two.'

Suddenly he burst out laughing and sat down beside me. 'What happened? Here is one rupee, you can take it.' He put his arm around my shoulder. 'You are a bigger destitute than me,' and kept laughing. 'I make about ten, twenty rupees everyday and sometimes if luck is good, it could be even fifty or hundred. It depends on how rich the catch is. But I have never come across anybody who has only three bucks in his pocket.'

He had shed his ferocious pretence and seemed to be a friendly young guy.

'What about this girl thing?' I asked.

'Men bring prostitutes in here,' he said.

'Here?' I winced, aghast at the irony, bringing prostitutes into a graveyard?

'Yes, they do not have the money to go to a hotel. They cannot afford the prostitute quarters as well. So they pick up cheap street side prostitutes and come here for a quick fuck on some tombstone. You see the one there,' he pointed out to a flat human size tombstone. 'That is the favorite spot for most.' He again burst into a hearty laugh. 'But they too have ten or twenty bucks with them. Unlike you, who has only three bucks and no girl. But why did you come here?' he asked.

'I just stumbled into this this place. The place is quite interesting,' I said.

'What is so interesting about an old graveyard?'

There was no point in explaining, he would not understand. Instead I enquired, 'Why do you snatch for a living? You are young and fit. You can take up some work.'

'It is not easy to get work these days and particularly if you are from the ghettos.'

'What do you do with your earnings?'

'I give a part to my mother for my daily food at home. The rest I spend on drinks and an occasional fuck. I know most of the street prostitutes in this area. Some of them even tip me beforehand about their customer to help me prey. But for fucking, I have to pay. There is no free fuck.' I was dumbstruck at this new facet of life.

He took out a bundle of 'bidis', a hand-rolled tobacco leaf cigarette, lit two, and passed on one to me. I drew in a lungful and looked at him. 'I understand getting job these days is tough. But why don't you save some from your everyday haul and once you have a sufficient kitty, you can start a small business. Like a cycle repair shop or something like that.'

'Yes I am fed up with this life. I think it's a good idea. I have even worked sometime in a cycle repairing shop, so I have a little idea of cycle repairing.' His eyes brightened. 'It is time I move. If you need any help in this area, just ask for me in the 'pan cigarette' shop across the road. My name is Arif, and I know a few police constables in the area police station as well.' He vanished into the darkness through the bushes as silently as he appeared.

I liked the spot and visited on many evenings and sat on the tombstones at times, writing poetry. One always had to enter through the broken wall. The main Iron Gate on the front side was always locked. I saw an old man sitting on a 'charpoy' with a dog at his feet behind the gate. Must be the caretaker cum sentry. A marble plaque had 'South Park Street Cemetery. Seventeen Sixty Seven dash Seventeen Thirty' engraved on it. I never met Arif again. I did see men fucking prostitutes on the tombstones and on realizing my presence, just covered themselves under the prostitute's 'sari' and continued fucking.

Three months and half, a diary full of poetries, I walked down to the 'pan cigarette' shop across the road from the graveyard. I bought a 'Charminar' and asked, 'Do you know Arif?'

The aged, bald shop owner looked through me. 'You cannot be his friend,' he said.

'No, I met him a few months back,' I explained. 'He told me that you would be aware of his whereabouts.'

'He was a nice boy. He always brought bread from home to feed the street dogs.' He pointed to a building and continued, 'Last month he broke into a house in that building and carried out a big robbery. He and his accomplices were all caught. The police beat him up badly. They have sent him to jail.' He looked pained. 'He was doing well with small snatchings. I do not know who gave him this idea of robbery, becoming rich at one go. Poor little fellow.'

He started preparing the next pan for a customer. He did not know who gave the idea. Maybe nobody gave the idea of robbery. But, maybe I knew the idea germinated from—the cycle repairing shop. I walked further up the Park Street to reach Lower Circular Road, now renamed Acharya Jagadish Chandra Bose Road. I took a tram to Sealdah and reached Sriniketan Boarding House in time for dinner. I walked by the South Park Street Cemetry many a time later, but never crossed over the broken wall.

As Starlight Industries Private Ltd. closed down, I became jobless. I was sure to find another one but that would take some time. Whatever little savings I had could last me a month. But before I decided my course of action, Esha offered me to move into their home. It was a pleasant surprise. I had to pay one hundred fifty bucks every month to her mother for food and that was all. Lodging was free. I would save about a hundred bucks from what I was paying at Srinekatan Boarding House. I gladly accepted it.

So one fine day I packed my baggage and left the mess. Forty Three, Beniapukur Road. That was the address. A wide road commencing from CIT Road opposite Chittaranjan Hospital, stretched for about three hundred metres and distributed into three narrow lanes. At this very point, the right hand walled corner plot was the Forty Three, Beniapukur Road. So this was Esha's house. The wall had been whitewashed long ago, but portions were freshly done up to paint political slogans and graffiti. There was a huge, wooden framed tin plate gate. I pushed open one of them. An open courtyard led to a red coloured, brick finished two-storey building. As I walked in, on my left there were two single storey large halls with asbestos sheet roofing. Seemed to be later add-ons and were rented out as workshops. First was an iron tool-forging workshop, and the second was a corrugated cardboard packaging factory. Heaps of boxes in various sizes lay stacked in the courtyard. Labourers moved in and out of their respective workshops, giving me indifferent glances.

'Esha's house?' I asked one.

'Go straight by that building, it is just in front.'

I walked on. Esha had mentioned that they did not live in the main building. What she had not mentioned was that they lived in a large room at the rear end of the plot with tiled roof.

Esha came out of the room to greet me. An aged lady followed her. Must be her mother, I presumed.

'Ma, this is Siddhartha,' she introduced me to her. 'And Siddhartha this is my mother.'

I touched her feet in typically true Bengali tradition.

The house was owned by veteran footballer Anil Dey. He was the captain of the Mohun Bagan team from nineteen forty-six to forty seven. Those were his hay days. A top Bengali heroine had fallen for him and gifted this house for him to live in. This was the love nest for the two. Hearsay has it that when she died, her next of kin tried to take over the property but failed. Anil Dey, with his clout and goon power, usurped the estate. But the title was not in his name. So neither he could carry out any transaction against the property, nor could he sell it. He was a bachelor and brought in one of his distant cousin brother to live with him on the first floor. He rented out the ground floor to two tenants, built the workshops and the room where Esha's family lived, and rented them out, too. He collected a handsome rent, which sufficed his need for booze, non-vegetarian fair, and occasional visit by a prostitute. At seventy-one, he had a burly physique but misbalanced by a huge paunch.

There was a large Pipul tree in front of Esha's house. Its canopy created a mesmerizing chiaroscuro on the tiled roof. It also provided shade, which kept the house cool even in humid hot summers of Calcutta. I entered. It was not a house, only a large room modestly laid out with two beds, an almirah, and a few clothesline criss crossing the room with clothes hanging. One had to sideline the hanging clothes to move around the room. There was a phone, a tape recorder, a dressing table, laid out with imported perfumes and cosmetics. A paradox of kitschy indigence and affluence. I was not perplexed knowing the background. I had accepted Ranjit Singh in Esha's life for I could not provide a better solution at that point. I struggled within and without, hoping for a day to unchain the present from the grim reality. A small extension, partitioned in between, functioned as the kitchen and the bathroom. The toilet was at the opposite corner of the plot, a small room with tin roof and door. It was forenoon and I found only Esha, her mother, and elder sister, Devikadi, in the house. Though a single room, it felt quite spacious. As the day rolled on, other family members started moving in. At twelve thirty, Esha's brother, Barun, came in—a very tall guy, about six feet two, fair, and with a strong build. By one 'O 'clock, Devikadi's five-year-old daughter, Sweta, returned from school; one fifteen, Devikadi's husband Ranjan, a jawan in the Central Industrial Security Force, walked in for lunch. With all the family members in, the room that seemed to be spacious turned claustrophobic.

The thought of so many people sleeping in this room during night bothered me. I tried lot of combinations but failed to find a clear solution till the night solved it all. Mashima, Sweta, and Esha shared a bed. Barun and I were on the other bed. Ranjanda and Devikadi went underneath one of the beds. The rest of the room was occupied by the hanging clothes on the clotheslines, swaying to the swirling breeze churned out by the creaking ceiling fan. The silence of the night was not only broken by the creaks of the fan—there were the squeaks of the beds, the snoring noses, few whispers from below the bed, and meows of a cat outside on its night prowl.

New environment, new neighbourhood, and new people as friends. Barun was reclusive, but he introduced me to some of his local friends. One of them was Bhaja who heard me singing one day in the bathroom while bathing.

'You sing quite well,' he said. 'Why don't you come for practice in the evening?'

'Practice for what?'

'We have a band,' he explained. 'We practice on weekend evenings and perform stage shows in local functions.'

'I am not a professional singer.'

'Hardly matters,' Bhaja gave me confidence. 'You have a good voice and you have sense of rhythm.'

So that very evening I accompanied him to their practice session. It was in a small first floor room nearby. There were five others apart from us. The room was packed with musical instruments: guitar, set of drums, piano-accordion, saxophone, flute, tabla, and what not. After preliminary introduction, each picked up his instrument and started tinkering with it. It was all noise, which slowly started shaping into a rhythm as each one complemented the other.

Bhaja handed over the microphone to me. It was the first time I was holding one.

'Which song?' Bhaja asked.

'Aise na mujhe tum dekho,' I said. A peppy Hindi film song and a favorite of mine.

I started right but faltered every time I had to take cue from the music to start again after a gap. I had never sung with an orchestra. I did not understand the discipline. But the group was supportive; they helped me to understand the nuances. Bhaja taught me how to position the microphone for various effects. After two weeks, I was as good as Bhaja, a singer himself. I performed in two shows with them and got fifty bucks for each show. My prospecting for job had not borne any fruit yet. I was getting a bit restless, as three weeks had passed since my last job. My savings were dwindling. And once again, Mirana crossed my path. There was live music on the first floor, every evening at Mirana Restaurant. Bhaja was going to audition for the singer's job there. He asked me to accompany him and also try my luck. He performed live in front of restaurant guests and so did I, one song each. Robida, the owner, and his wife stood through the performance. Then I, Bhaja, and Robida walked down to the cash counter.

'How much do you expect?' Robida asked Bhaja.

'Eight hundred per month for two hours every evening.'

'We already have a lead singer, we only need a filler guy during his breaks,' Robida said.

'I can offer you four hundred.'

'No,' Bhaja replied. 'I want to be the lead singer. Why don't you try Sid for filler?'

Robida looked at me.

'I have seen you here earlier, is that right?'

'Yes.' I replied.

'You also sing quite well but you seem to be new to this line.'

'That is true. I started singing professionally just some time back.' I felt a strong pinch on my buttock. It was Bhaja.

'I will offer you three hundred per month to sing between eight and eleven every evening, during Amit's breaks.'

'But he should have a weekly break,' Bhaja interfered. He seemed to know the profession.

'OK, he can have a weekly break but that has to be on a predetermined weekday.' Robida put in his terms. I was delighted even if it would have been without the weekly break. I had landed a job before the month had ended.

Robida asked me to collect the appointment letter the next morning after eleven, and join in from that very evening. I sang my way back to Esha's house with Bhaja.

Hindi film songs blared loudly from inside the compound. I pushed open the gate to see a joint puja celebration in process by the two workshops. It was Vishwakarma Puja. He was the God of everything technical and engineering in the pantheon of Hindu Gods. The establishments that performed the puja remained closed on the day and nobody touched the tools or machines. A big makeshift mud oven was put up in the courtyard and there was something cooking in a large vessel. Tabuda, a supervisor of the corrugated box factory, walked up to me.

'Have dinner with us. Rice and mutton curry,' he said. 'I will send dinner for Esha's family once it is cooked.' He stopped for a while and asked, 'Do you drink?'

I said, 'Yes.'

'I will get you a glass.'

I knew he was already high on drinks. So was everybody around.

'I will leave a few things at home and come back,' I said and left. Mashima, that is, Esha's mother, did not allow me to leave home.

'They are all drunk. Let them send our dinner, we will all have it together at home.'

Suddenly, there was a loud noise of breaking glass bottles. A din followed. We all came out of the room and stood trying to ascertain the situation. Suddenly, we saw Tabuda leading the factory crowd armed with iron rods and other large metal tools and rushing upstairs to Anil Dey's residence.

'Sala, it is yours or my dooms day.' I heard Tabuda yelling. 'Mother fucker, throwing glass bottles at us? We will kill you today.'

Esha pushed her mother, Devikadi, and her daughter, into the room and locked the door from outside. It was Esha and me; I was confused as minutes later I saw the crowd rushing out of the house. Tabuda also came out and stood still.

He looked at us and said, 'I did not kill him. I do not know who had hit him with an iron rod. He is dead upstairs, lying in a pool of blood.'

Esha suddenly sprang into action. 'Tabuda, run away, immediately. Tell all others to leave the compound and switch off the sound system and all lights.'

I could not fathom her plans. Tabuda obeyed her like a lost child. Once Esha heard the gate bang close, she caught my hand, rushed out, and took a rickshaw to the Beniapukur Police Station. It was close by. He pulled me into the police station and rushed to a desk with a board marked, Station House Officer.

'Sir, some people rushed into our house and went up to Anilda's residence. There was huge commotion and suddenly it is all silent now.' She lied without even blinking an eyelid. 'Sir, can you come and please check the matter?'

Next morning it was front page news, and by afternoon, when the body arrived after post mortem, a crowd had gathered to pay their last respects to a legend of football of yesteryears. A vehicle with ornamented glass case to carry the body arrived. I could not fathom who were organizing all this. More people were trickling in. Many dressed in white for the solemn and sad occasion. It always intrigued me as to why the east adorned the white to mark the end of the journey of life, while the west adorned the black. Two exact opposites: white, the resultant colour of amalgamation of the seven primary colours, while black was absence of all. Around five o'clock, the procession started moving with the dead body for its last journey. 'Bolo Hari, Hari bol' 'Take the name of Hari, repeat Hari' chants resonated in the air.

'Look at his destiny, nobody cared through his life.' I overheard somebody standing in the crowd, 'and now so much concern after his death.'

I was born in a rational Hindu family and evolved into an atheist by belief. So the word 'destiny' was not there in my dictionary. But it was exactly the opposite with Bengalis at large and with my friends at Das Cabin. They were content, very content—content in failures, content in being short-changed, content with the present state of their existence—because they believed that it was destined to be so. No stress of underachieving, no pain of failing to achieve the goal, in fact, there was no goal at all. Just moving on from day to day, living as time passed by, intellectualizing life in debates at the street corner addas and tea stalls. It seemed to be an offshoot of the philosophy of renunciation, and seemed to be working quite well with the unemployed youth of the late seventies in Bengal. Being content helped them being happy even in these grimmest of times. Believing in destiny, one would be more enthusiastic to know what was there in their destiny, than being enthusiastic about creating the future. And some etched out a profession from this enthusiasm— palmistry, horoscopy, numerology, and a number of other methodologies had developed through the ages to determine destiny. While some tried to explore these knowledge streams in true earnest, majority of the practitioners had turned them into hoax and exploited the fear of destiny among the commoners.

Pratap, a medium-built, tall guy, with a receding hairline, belonged to the second group. He was one among our friend circle at the Das Cabin. Palmistry complemented by pseudo spiritio-religious rituals was his profession. He charged five bucks for a palm reading at his residential chamber but would be happy to collect a buck or two for reading of the palm at the Das Cabin or other tea stalls. He would also offer remedies in the form of planetary gemstones or 'maduli', a silver or tin mini drum-shaped medallion stuffed with herbs, leaves, and flowers sanctified by holy chants. The remedies were the larger part of his earnings because the gemstones he sold ranged from poor quality to fake, and the 'maduli' had only the cost of buying the medallion. Whatever his methods, he did make two ends meet. I was witness to many of his clients even vouching for the remedial effects of his solutions. I did not believe them. I knew sometimes these remedies worked like a placebo effect; but what interested me was his ability to match happenings in the past of a client's life, to more or less the same period without even knowing him or her. Nobody had seen the future; so predicting the future was something like shooting in the dark. One could not verify it until one reached the time of the predicted future. But the past had already happened and he could read that in the lines on the palm. So was there a true connection between the lines on the palms and events in our life? From Pratap's description of past events in his client's life through reading of palms, it seemed there was. So if the past was marked on the palm lines, could the future be also encrypted? After all, past or future, they were events. Many a times I tried to engage Pratap into a dialogue on the subject, but he would not relent. He would hold the secret close to his heart. After all it was his bread and butter. But I would not relent, too. So one fine day I landed at the Oxford Book Store on Park Street and searched through the palmistry section for a book with detailed information on the subject. I found one: 'The book of Fate and Fortune – Cheiro's Palmistry'.

William John Warner, known as 'Cheiro', was an Irish self-declared clairvoyant. He had visited India during his teens and learnt the ancient science of Indian palmistry from a Konkan Brahmin. His works were the most concise documentation and knowledge of the ancient Indian palmistry. 'The book of Fate and Fortune – Cheiro's Palmistry' was a voluminous book. With only late evening engagement at Mirana for my living, I had all the time to delve into it. I stretched out my own palms as the drawing board to learn the technicalities. I learned about the hand types, finger formations, nail shapes, the lines and the mounds. I understood the planetary effects and the signs, the destructive cross, the benevolent triangle, and the square signs. As I read on I realized that reading the book was not enough. One needed to practice to predict. And where could I find a better lab than Das Cabin to experiment? Thus my palm reading sessions started, for free. I talked little but talked well; but palm reading taught me to be a good listener as well. Everybody who opened out his palm for reading opened out his heart too. Behind the façade of contention there was pain, fear, apprehension, and little wishes. Wants deprived of being fulfilled slowly turned into little wishes. Aspirations scorched in the hot summer of deprivation into minute hopes. Confidence metamorphosed into doubt. 'I can' transformed to 'Can I?'

As an unexplored wonderland started unfolding before me, I found palmistry was not only about following the rules; it was more about empathizing with your client. The more you knew your client, the better you could feel his circumstantial existence and hence you could predict more accurately. Studying about twenty to twenty five palms a day gave me a lot of confidence. I could pinpoint events in one's past and confidently predicted the events to happen in future. At times it was no more about a line from the mound of Venus crossing the lifeline at a certain point, or the headline stooping down to the mound of Moon. It was a maze of life events that stared at me like an abstract painting on a canvas. Prediction of the future and depiction of the past came like intuitions—all of a sudden, out of the blue, but always with the logic of palmistry as its backdrop. I predicted Mamoni would die before being fifty. She passed away at forty-six. I predicted Devikadi would be pregnant the next year, but there would be danger to both the mother and the child's life. She did get pregnant and it was a tug of war between her and the newborn's life. Finally she gave birth to a stillborn child, herself having a close shave. I had become quite a celebrity at Das Cabin and among those who knew me. I kept on rolling out predictions for free, or sometimes for a cup of tea. Pratap felt the pinch. All his clients gradually shifted to me. He still kept coming in the hope that someday I will falter. But I did not. At least, till the time I continued practicing palmistry.

So had I perfected the practice of palmistry? Was palmistry itself so perfect? I thought to myself. It could be that the right predictions were just coincidences. It could be that my wrong predictions did not get reported to me. I needed to test the ground for a stronger belief in the subject. As per palmistry, the lifeline was the most sanctified of all the lines on a palm. It predicted the life tenure. Some schools of palmistry believed that all lines changed during the lifetime except for the lifeline. My lifeline depicted that I would live for about sixty-two years. I was only twenty, so I could challenge the veracity of palmistry if I could end my life here and now. But how? Only by suicide, I realized. My headline drooped sharply towards the mound of moon at the left-hand side bottom of the right palm. This symbolized that I could suicide or even turn lunatic. It was the effect of moon's characteristics over the brain. Like the tidal effects caused by the moon, extreme turbulences were created in mind and thought process. This made a person's mind highly vulnerable to extreme polarization, which naturally made the subject incompatible to take rational decisions. This would end up in lunacy at the worst, suicidal tendencies for some, or bouts of depression at the least. But here it was me taking a conscious decision to suicide to challenge palmistry.

I needed a full-proof plan. Ranjit Singh was in Calcutta, so Esha was staying away at night. I reached Esha's home late at eleven thirty, when all had fallen asleep. I knocked the door and Devikadi opened the door for me and went to sleep. I had informed earlier that I had some work for a few days and would come late. I would not take dinner. It was dark with all the lights put off. I did not switch on the lights and moved to my bed and slid beside Barun to fall asleep. This was a dry run. Yes, everything was working. So if I consumed poison and fell asleep without anybody's knowledge, by morning I would be dead. The poison would get enough time to take its irreversible toll.

Just opposite Das Cabin there was a chemist shop. Kamala Medical Stores. I studied a few palms, refused cups of tea to keep my stomach empty for the poison to act fast. None from my friend circle had arrived yet. At about eight, I walked down to the chemist shop and asked for a bottle of 'Tik Twenty'. It was a chemical generally sold over the counter for eliminating bedbugs. It was fatal on human consumption. I focused onto this product for two reasons: First, because it was easily available at all chemist shops and commonly used by many families; secondly, I had read in many newspaper reports that there had been many suicide cases in the countryside by consuming this chemical. I held the bottle in my hand and walked up to a taxi.

'Beniapukur Road,' I said.

As the taxi started and moved a few metres, I unscrewed the bottle and drank the whole liquid. I looked at the rearview mirror. The taxi driver was busy weaving through the traffic and had not noticed me. The liquid tasted nauseatingly odd and smelled like cockroaches up close. I felt like throwing up but refrained. I was used to taking neat rum; that helped me. The liquid settled down after about fifteen minutes and I felt normal by the time I reached Beniapukur Road. I got off a little distance away from Esha's house and walked down. Slowly, I started feeling drowsy. It was just like having three large pegs of neat rum. It was nine o'clock. I sat down on a wooden bench of a tea stall, a few metres away from the house, and waited for the clock to strike eleven. The drowsiness was slowly giving way to a completely drunk feeling. I did not expect the chemical to act so fast. Suddenly, a bike screeched to a halt just in front of me. I looked up with half closed eyes. It was Khokan and Nepal, my two friends from Das Cabin. I could not speak and soon passed out.

I woke up next morning in a bed at Nilratan Hospital. Khokan was sitting next to me, and Esha stood at the end of my bed. I looked around. It was a long dormitory with two rows of beds. All the patients seemed to be aged and queer.

'Your father has come,' Khokan said.

'Where is Bapi?' I asked.

'Outside, with one of his office colleagues. He will not meet you he said.'

'That is all fine.' I was having a severe headache, just like heavy hangover after a binge of excessive drinking. I smelt like a thousand cockroaches, felt nauseating. A nurse came and gave me some intravenous injection. I had a temporary amnesia. I could not recall the last night. Esha gazed at me with a lot of questions in her eyes, but said nothing.

'A police officer has come and he is talking to your father,' Khokan said. 'Your father told me to tell you that just do or say as the police officer says. Or else you will land up in legal problems. Suicide is a criminal activity and punishable under Indian Penal Code.'

'Suicide?' I thought myself. Slowly, things started falling into place. The whole sequence of last night's events flashed in my mind like a short film. So I had not died. This proved that predictions as per palmistry were right. I would live till I was sixty-two.

The police officer walked in. He pulled a stool and sat by my bedside.

'If anybody asks you, say that you drank 'Tik Twenty' by mistake. It was dark and you mistook it for the bottle of cough syrup.' He laid out a few papers and asked me to sign on them. There was no point telling the truth. My purpose was served. It was not that I desperately wanted to die. I wanted to test the sanctity of palmistry and that had been achieved. I signed the papers.

'But how did you come to know about my plan?' I asked Khokan.

'Doctors will keep you under observation for the next seventy-two hours. You are still not out of danger,' Khokan replied. 'Your stomach was washed clean last night to save you. I will tell you everything once you get completely well.'

For two days, I passed urine that smelt like 'Tik Twenty'. I passed black liquefied stool that smelt like 'Tik Twenty'. It was only on the third day I felt better. The cockroach-like smell of 'Tik Twenty' was fading away from my body and from my mind, too. Everyday, my friends and Esha would visit me during the 'visiting hours'. Bapi would also visit every evening and enquire from the doctors about my progress, but he never walked in to meet me. I did not feel hurt. Both of us were holding on to our terms of reference on engagement.

I continued reading palms for some time, on a stronger foothold, and with a firmer belief. I stopped, once I was in the second year of Mining Engineering. Requests came even after I had stopped predicting. But I shunned by telling that I had forgotten it all. And truly, as time passed by, I found the lines and mounds on the palms merely had names, I could not read into the intricacies. I could not predict. I found palmistry just like Mathematics. The more you practice, the more you perfect yourself. If you do not practice, only few basic principles and formulae remain with you.

I was accosted by palmistry once again years later. It was in the early nineties. I had shifted to Delhi along with my wife, Anjali, and living in a 'barsati' at New Friends Colony. I had once again plunged into uncertainties and was working as a creative faculty with Centre for Cultural Communication, a NGO. Two families, Shekharmama, with his wife Pinku; and Mithu, with his wife Anjana, visited us. We had a great time hopping and shopping across Delhi during the day and sat over a bottle of rum in the evening at my residence. After a few pegs and whole lot of hearty chat, Shekharmama said, 'Sid just have a look at my palm. Nothing is going well for me.'

'Shekharmama, I had told you earlier also that I have completely forgotten the subject.' I replied.

'I do not believe you. You must be remembering something.'

'Actually, no.'

'Just try. You might remember a little if you see the palm,' Mithu insisted.

I was fairly drunk. I took his palm and stretched it out in front of me. Suddenly the lines, the mounds, crosses, and stars all came to life. It was a three-dimensional world of events talking to me. I followed a line from the mound of Mars as it pierced the lifeline at a certain point. I calculated the age of the point of intersection on the lifeline. It was the same as Shekharmama's current age. I looked up at him.

'Shekharmama, you will have a big accident very soon. It will not be fatal but it will leave a deep scar on your body and mind.'

The room fell silent.

'You will soon have your own house,' I continued in one flow, 'and a car as well.'

Everybody burst into laughter.

'Sid, I am having a hard time to make two ends meet with my business and you are talking about a house and a car.' Shekarmama retorted. 'Look at the prospects of my business. What will be my position one year hence.'

'If I am saying you will have your own house and a car, surely your business will pick up and do well. That is what I will conclude.'

Shekharmama lived with his family and parents in a rented house and ran a business of water pump installation. His father had established the business and had seen good times, but in recent years it was not doing too well. Under his current circumstance, even I, felt the prediction of the house and the car was a bit too over the top. And we forgot it all the next morning. About two months later the telephone rang. I picked up the heavy black receiver. It was a STD call from Calcutta.

'Sid, it is me. Pinku.' Shekharmama's wife spoke loud and clear from Calcutta.

'How are you all?' I asked.

'Your prediction has come true.' Pinku continued, 'Shekhar has met with a serious scooter accident. His right leg has been badly fractured and a steel rod had to be implanted.'

'How is he now? And why do you sound so happy?'

'He is fine, will be in bed for three months. But imagine,' she continued, 'when this prediction of yours has come true, that means your other two predictions will also come true. We will have our own house and our very own car.'

For a moment I was astounded by the irony of joy emanating out of pain. Pinku trying to fantasize little wishes coming true in the reality of today's grief. I wished Shekarmama a quick recovery and a good luck to Pinku's dream. I did not read much into my drunken predictions and took the accident to be a coincidence. But another three months later, it was Shekharmama on the phone.

'Sid I have bought a house. Your prediction has come true.' He said, 'I could not have ever imagined of buying a house with my income. But our landlord offered four lakh rupees for leaving our rented accommodation. I accepted the offer and with that money I have bought a house in Santoshpur. You must come. We must celebrate.'

I was taken aback but was happy and waited for the news about the car. Seven months later he phoned again and informed about buying a Maruti Suzuki Alto. Business was doing well and he sounded happy.

CHAPTER 12

ONCE AGAIN, SIDDHARTHA was in Delhi on his own for the third time. First, when he ran away from RIMC, inspired by Bollywood movies to etch out a life of his own; second, to appear in the UPSC written examination for National Defence Academy; but this time, it was for a career shift. Calcutta had become boring. Though a job as art director in a small advertising agency, part time earning from photography of export house products and a visiting faculty status at Careers Incorporated for commercial art, provided a fairly good life, but there was nothing exciting happening. Even painting had taken a back seat. So when Mrs Jayanti Chakravarty, the owner of Careers Incorporated confided in him that she was leaving Calcutta and moving to Delhi, and if he would like to shift base with her, Siddhartha grabbed the opportunity. The plan was to open a similar institute in Delhi where he would be the faculty for commercial art. It was not tough on his part to leave a settled twelve thousand per month income and agree for a three thousand offer topped with a place to stay for free. The excitement of the unknown well compensated for the loss in financial earnings.

Siddhartha reached Delhi leaving his wife Anjali back in Calcutta. It was the winter of nineteen ninety. He had the address. It was somewhere in New Friends Colony. He took an auto and moved on to find the address. It was not difficult as the auto driver was quite aware of the area. As the auto entered New Friends Colony zone, Siddhartha realized that this was a posh locality in South Delhi. C-146, the house was a two storey building with a 'Barsati' built on the rooftop. 'Barsati's are a common phenomenon in Delhi. A one room, self-sufficient tenement built on many rooftops in Delhi and rented out.

The ground floor had some Mavlankar nameplate on it, so Siddhartha walked up to the first floor and was greeted by 'Didi', as he used to call Mrs Chakravarty. This was her parent's house and he met them, too. 'Bapi' a.k.a. Mr Chakravarty, the father, and 'Meshomoshai' to Siddhartha, was a retired Research Doctor from the Indian Medical Services. He had to his credit, eradication of 'Kalazaar' from India, which was a fatal epidemic in India till early sixties, particularly in hot and humid regions of eastern Indian states. He liked to share dirty jokes on the sly and he had a huge stock too. He made sure his wife; 'Mashima' would not be around at such times. In his early seventies, he was a frail man with a vibrant mind basking in the glory of past attention that he had enjoyed. Every day at the breakfast table he would read aloud all the gory news of the day like rape, murder, dacoity and rue, 'See what has Delhi come to be. In our times . . .' and it continued while others finished their breakfast and moved on.

The institute was started pretty soon. It only took a classified advertisement in the newspaper to have prospective students walking in. The 'Barsati' room was the office by the day and Siddhartha's abode by night. He had a mattress on which he slept, which was shoved into the kitchen during the day. For the first batch, sixteen students registered. The classes were held in classrooms at the Indian Sociological Institute, hired on daily basis. Things started rolling; Mrs Chakravarty was not street-smart, but knew how to use her beauty and charm to get things done. She had contacts in high places due to her Delhi Public School background. It did not take her much time to revive the contacts with top bureaucrats like Aman Khurshid and Jaindra Ramesh, who were a year senior to her in school. While meeting them, Siddhartha realized that Didi was a siren in her schooldays, and these men still had a crush on her. Penetrating the Ministry of Tourism of Government of India was a child's play. Funds were released to the institute for research work in no time. 'Sustainable Wildlife Tourism Potential of West Bengal' project took off with funds from the Ministry.

By February, Anjali joined Siddhartha in Delhi, selling off all their belongings in Calcutta. She was the third member of the institute. For the project, it was decided that Didi would hold fort in Delhi for about twenty days, while Siddhartha and Anjali would travel to West Bengal. They prepared themselves for the all-paid trip. It was a new experience—freedom to travel, and getting paid for it, too. From Calcutta, both of them moved into Sajnekhali Wild Life Sanctuary, popularly known as Sunderban Tiger Reserve. They took the West Bengal Tourism Department package tour of Sunderban by launch. After being transferred to Sonakhali by bus, they boarded the launch at early noon and breezed down the river Hooghly. It was a weekend and it was a full board with mostly Bengali families from Calcutta. Bengalis love talking, and that too talking loud. Soon the launch was abuzz with 'Ore Pintu, edike aaye, dekh dekh . . .' 'Pintu come here, look. Look . . .' intercepted by honks of some passing launches.

The launch had already turned away from the main Hooghly and entered a wide tributary. The demography had drastically changed: large tracts of open land, widely spread rice fields, villages at a distance, and clusters of palm and coconut trees; a few children in short pants, and bare-bodied, ran along some distance waving at the tourists in the launch; women folk taking bath, and fishermen netting in the shallow water near the bank.

One thing that Siddhartha noticed, is that the rural scene had changed. There were metal roads winding from village to village; solar powered streetlights on the roads; and tractors ploughed in the fields. A lot had changed which he was unaware of. Maybe reason enough for Communist Party of India Marxist winning elections term after term in West Bengal. By four, the waterway had even further narrowed. The serene village scene slowly gave way to 'Goral' tree and 'Sundri' tree bushes by the riverside. 'Sundri' is a short deciduous tree typical of this region on which the name Sunderbans was coined. It is the only tree with deep roots, which survive high and low tide water level fluctuations and the saline and sweet water mix of the delta. A jackal was spotted; further down the river, a crocodile suddenly woke up from his slumber in the sun and swooshed into the waters, prankster monkeys jumping around. Even baby monkeys jumping down from trees into the river and swimming back to the bank, presented quite a unique scene. Parrots, herons, and other smaller birds flew past the launch, chirping on their way back home as evening set in. The launch docked. After dinner on board, Siddhartha and Anjali walked down to the Sajnekhali Guest House late in the night. The guesthouse was a wooden lodge raised on a high wooden platform amidst dense jungle by the bank. In the pitch dark of the night, they did not realize how dense the jungle that they were in was.

As the early morning lights trickled in through some of the wooden planks of the wall, it was time to move on. Siddhartha had explained their purpose of the visit to the tour supervisor, who was to manage a local boat for Siddhartha and Anjali to travel further deeper into the Sunderbans, while the launch would return back to Calcutta. After breakfast on board the launch, both bade farewell to all and got on to their boat. Siddhartha explained to the boatman the purpose of the visit and asked him to take them deep within the jungles rowing through the narrow tributaries. More than documenting facts, Siddhartha and Anjali travelled to explore what a tourist would like to enjoy during a visit to the Sunderbans. The Tourism Department launch trip was too staid. As they steered through the deep forest, they spotted variety of birds, jackals, deers, and monkeys. There were no tigers, but one had the fear at the back of one's mind of tigers lurking somewhere behind the dense Sundri bushes. It could peek out and dive into the waters to attack the boat. And the boatman continued with tiger stories adding to the thrill. Siddhartha had understood from the forest officials that tigers rarely came out of the core area of the tiger reserve, which was deep within the jungle. Tourists were allowed only in the periphery where tiger spotting had little chance. Only some aged or wounded tigers strayed into the peripheral villages for an easy prey and at times create mayhem. As the sun came down and the darkness started crawling in, the boatman lit the 'harricane', a glass covered oil lamp, which barely made Siddhartha and

Anjali visible to each other. It was more of an assurance, a sense of safety than actually lighting the surroundings. Even the boatman at the helm was rarely visible, but he knew his way through the waters and steered them back to the lodge. This boat trip became one of the many observations in the report. So was the crocodile breeding centre on the Haliday Island, the biosphere reserve on the Lothian Island. Journey continued criss-crossing West Bengal through Bethuaduari, Ballabhpur, Jaldapara, Buxa, all reserve forests, and finally submitting the report in Delhi to the Ministry.

Siddhartha was happy to migrate to Delhi. His earnings were meager, but he could manage to buy a canvas every month and could continue painting. More so he loved history and was mesmerized by Delhi—there was a monument, fort, tomb or mere ruins from the past at every bend.

Soon Siddhartha discovered that Delhi was a city where, to succeed, one needed talent and connection; or hard work and connection; or luck and connection. Connection was a must. It was a city that had a flair for flaunting connections with people in high offices. Caught on the wrong foot, the most common reaction of most Delhites was, 'Don't you know who I am?' Even Tom, Dick, and Harry tried to wriggle out of tight spots with the same question. In the distant past, it might have worked but with over indulgence it had been reduced to a 'statement non grata', a bad habit, which does not even warrant any reaction; but like all bad habits, it continued.

But Mrs Jayanti Chakravarty did have real connections in plenty, at the right places with the right people. She was ambitious and had a weird drive to be rich and independent. It was not that the thinking was absurd, but the extremity of the want was. It was the sole reason to break out of her twenty-two-year-old marriage into an orthodox rich Brahmin family, leaving behind her teen daughters. She was ready to go to any extent where she sensed a financial windfall. She was, one would say not rich yet but made more money than she could have ever imagined by running her institute 'Careers Incorporated' in Calcutta. She would flirt and allow others to flirt with her as well in the parties she attended. Getting physical with strangers was not a taboo for her if that could milk out some big bucks.

So when she was introduced to Rishi Raj as a business tycoon in one of the social gatherings, she did not let the opportunity slip out of her hands. Her opening line on being introduced was, 'You are extremely handsome.'

'Thank you,' replied Rishi, a well-built, fair, and good looking gentleman.

'You are not taking any drinks?' Mrs Chakaravarty asked.

'Yes, I will. Wait, I will fetch one.'

'I will call one for you,' she said and signaled a waiter. 'What will you prefer?'

'If there is good champagne I would like to raise a toast to you.'

Mrs Chakravarty felt flattered and ordered the waiter to fetch one.

'By the way what are your business interests?' she asked.

'I am into international trading.' Mrs Chakravarty moved a little closer in the pretext of giving way to another guest at the party. Rishi took a step back being the gentleman that he was. Mrs Chakravarty kept trying to make Rishi feel comfortable and drop his inhibitions. But Rishi was warm and replied in short sentences while maintaining the space in between.

'Can we meet tomorrow for dinner?' Rishi suddenly asked.

'Why not,' Mrs Chakravarty thought her charm was working, 'Where and at what time?'

'Maybe at LeMeridian,' he said. 'Eight o'clock, if that is fine with you.'

'That will be a pleasure for me.'

'Where should I send the car?'

'No. I will make it on my own. Let us meet at the Le Meridian lounge.'

'Fine, I will wait for you.'

Mrs Chakravarty felt a sense of achievement, but she knew that she had not broken the code yet. Rishi was the same reserved self that he was when introduced. 'Maybe I should prod a little more,' she thought. But before she could start the conversation, Rishi excused himself, waved at another guest and was gone. Mrs Chakravarty tried to track his movements but failed as if he had vanished into the guests.

The next evening, Mrs Chakravarty left home early. She did not own a car. She had to travel in an 'auto', a three-wheeler public transport, and she did not want Rishi to know this. 'You never know these men after a few drinks.' She thought to herself and asked Siddhartha to accompany her at the last moment. They were at Le Meridien half an hour before schedule. Rishi was staying at the same hotel. He walked down to the lounge sharp at eight to be taken by surprise to see a young man in his twenties sitting beside Mrs Jayanti Chakravarty. He walked up to them.

'This is Sid,' Mrs Chakravarty introduced Siddhartha to Rishi. 'He is like my brother, my colleague, and my man Friday.'

'A smart and handsome escort cum bodyguard.' Rishi commented and Siddhartha smiled back.

'Not exactly.'

'I get the message. No one messes with Lady Jayanti Chakravarty.'

'He seems to be more casual than yesterday,' Jayanti thought.

'Let us move to Le Belvedere for dinner. It is a nice place with a great view.'

All three moved towards the elevator. Le Belvedere was a Chinese fine dining restaurant on the topmost floor of the hotel. It had bay windows that overlooked the expanse of Lutyens' Delhi. Rishi selected a table with the Rashtrapati Bhawan and the India Gate as the window view. It was dark except for the streetlights, and the few shimmering lights of the Rashtrapati Bhawan. Moonlight from the crescent moon added a mysterious blue hallow over the landscape. 'Delhi looked mesmerizing from the viewpoint of the rich,' Siddhartha thought as he pulled in his chair to settle down.

'What would you like for a drink?' Rishi asked.

'Any refreshing bubbly,' Mrs Chakravarty was moving in high social circles but had little knowledge of wines.

'I think you will like a Chardonnay Pinot Noir. And what would you prefer young man?' Rishi looked at Siddhartha.

Siddhartha had been drinking only Indian rum. With a short experience in the hospitality he had some knowledge about whiskies and other hard liquors, but wines were Greek to him.

'I will take the same,' was Siddhartha's smart move. Rishi looked at the wine list and ordered a bottle of Jacob's Creek and came down to the point.

'I was told that you have good connections at high levels.'

'It depends on what you mean by high levels,' Mrs Chakravarty replied.

'In Delhi it would translate into politicians and senior bureaucrats.'

She did know many bureaucrats but no politicians at all. She could sense an opportunity in the offing and did not want to nip it at its bud.

'Yes, I know many senior bureaucrats and I do have approach to some politicians.'

'How well do you know them?' Rishi realized he was intruding into her privacy too fast. 'Do not understand me wrong. I am just trying to understand if you can help me.'

'What are you looking for?'

'Well, I will make myself even clearer.' Rishi relaxed on the backrest of the chair, as the wine was uncorked. 'The Government of India has opened up the skies to private players.'

Jayanti had read a few editorials on the subject. 'You have three months to prepare your groundwork. DGCA, the Directorate General of Civil Aviation, is the nodal body to give the licenses.' Rishi raised his flute. Jayanti and Siddhartha followed.

'To the health of India's open sky policy.' Rishi raised the toast. 'I will like to establish Swan Airways as one of the first private Indian airlines.'

'But the policy allows private operators to run only air-taxis.' Jayanti informed.

'I know,' Rishi replied. 'But soon it will be for airlines and we must get the first mover advantage.'

Siddhartha did not fathom Didi's role in Rishi's scheme of things. If Rishi wanted to open an airline, his company would need to fulfill all criteria laid down in the Government's policy. 'It was all a procedural work' Siddhartha thought.

'You will have the next three months to identify the decision makers, the contact points in DGCA, and the influencing nodes in the Ministry of Civil Aviation. You will have to get informed about the procedures, and apply, and get the license' Rishi took a sip from the flute and asked for the 'A La Carte Menu' from the Captain.

'If you allow me, I will set the course for dinner. I was told you are a Bengali and I presume he is too.' Rishi deviated from his discourse. 'You will love the whole pomfret schezwan style.' He described eloquently all the dishes he planned to order, placed the order for dinner and continued.

'What do you think?' Rishi asked.

'I think we will manage this,' Jayanti replied.

Rishi fished out a card from his wallet. 'This is my office at Nehru Place. Mr Rajesh Chopra sits here. Every month end, you submit a progress report and the expenses incurred. You can collect twenty thousand as your retainership per month and the expenses from him in cash.'

'May I have your phone number?' Jayanti asked.

'No, you do not contact me,' Rishi said firmly. 'Anything you need—documentations, certificates—Mr Chopra will provide you. I will monitor your reports and I have the right to stop this arrangement at any point of time.'

It was a well spent evening not for the lavish dinner spread but more so for the opportunity unveiled.

The assignment turned out to be a cakewalk. Jayanti worked her way into the Ministry of Civil Aviation through her network of contacts in the bureaucracy. A word from the Ministry to one of the Joint Director General in DGCA was enough to set the playing field. Siddhartha was the man on the ground and received a warm welcome from the Deputy Director in the Licensing Department of the Directorate General of Civil Aviation, when he introduced himself with a reference from a Joint Secretary in the Ministry. It took him only a little more than a month to get familiarized with not only the procedures, but also with the officers concerned and the class three and class four staffs of the department. The Deputy Director, Mr Srivastava, was more than willing to guide and help. Once the policy was announced, the Nehru Place office provided the reams of documents that were needed with the application, and Siddhartha tracked every stage of the file movement. Often, some palms had to be greased to speed up the process and be privy to inside information. In the second week of the sixth month, the license was granted to Swan Airways. The assignment completed, Siddhartha stopped communicating with the Nehru Place office, but to Siddhartha's and Jayanti's surprise, Mr Chopra called up on the second of next month and asked Siddhartha to come and collect the retainership.

'There is nothing that we are working on,' Siddhartha asked Mr Chopra counting the cash at the Nehru Place office. 'So why this retainership is being paid to us?'

'We build long term relationships' was Mr Chopra's reply.

Jayanti and Siddhartha were more than happy with the long-term relationship. Every month, Siddhartha collected the cash religiously on the first of every month. It was an extra income. Ten percent of the retainership, that is two thousand bucks, was given to Siddhartha by Jayanti. She was fair in sharing the spoils. Careers Incorporated ran the Advertising Agency and Commercial Art classes while Rishi's work was an added income for Jayanti Chakravarty and Siddhartha.

When Siddhartha visited the Nehru Place office on the first of February nineteen ninety one to collect the 'long term relationship' retainership, Mr Chopra said, 'Tell Madam Chakravarty that Mr Rishi would like to meet her over dinner on the third. Confirm with me over the phone and I will tell you the venue and time.'

'It seems some assignment is coming,' Siddhartha told Jayanti.

'This time we will ask for more,' Jayanti suggested. 'Maybe thirty thousand. You bloat up the expenses account as well.' They were well prepared with reasoning out the raise. It was the same place and at the same time, Le Meridien, eight o'clock.

Rishi was dressed in a black suit. He pulled back the chair for Jayanti to sit down and ordered the wine straight away.

'The next assignment is more crucial.' Rishi continued, 'India is facing defence spare parts shortage.'

'He seemed to be a man who knew too much,' Jayanti thought.

'After the disintegration of USSR, there is a shift in the power centre in Russia. India's contract with Russia has also ended, but India cannot wait for the renewal of the contract as it is facing acute crunch in spares supply, particularly for T72 tanks and the Mig 21. A lot of these spares are now lying with some of the confederation countries, which they are eager to sell. I am representing Slovakia. The spares that India need immediately are there with us and fit to the tee. I want you to make inroads into the defence establishment and establish contact with the right authorities and find out their eagerness to acquire the spares. If they are interested, they can pinpoint the needs and quantum of supply. We will confirm the availability, and then you can set up a meeting between the defence purchase committee which will be authorized to handle the case and the Slovakian counterpart committee. The Slovakian team will be headed by a minister in the Slovakian government.'

Siddhartha looked at Jayanti. She took out her handkerchief from her vanity bag. In the pretext of cleaning something that had got into her eyes, she wiped the drop of sweat that trickled down her temple.

'What do you think about the assignment? Will you be able to deliver this time?' Rishi asked.

'You have not started the airlines as yet.' Jayanti tried to divert the topic to get a breather. At the back of her mind she tried to check on her network of contacts. 'This is big business, really big.' she thought. 'May be I can demand forty thousand as retainership.'

'I have dropped the idea of the airline.' Rishi said.

'But you have spent quite an amount for it,' Siddhartha said.

'Yes, but it does not make sense to invest big in this sector for want of clear policy guidelines from the Indian government. I think it will not be profitable. So why dig one's own grave?' Rishi explained.

'Jai is in Planning Commission. He will be able to give some lead in the Defence Ministry,' Jayanti tried to chalk out the action plan at the back of her mind. 'I think I should ask for forty thousand as retainership. This seems to be big money business.'

'I will pay a retainership of seventy five thousand per month for this assignment and bear all expenses.' Rishi declared. It was like dropping a bomb. To Jayanti and Siddhartha, it was an atomic bomb. A neat seventy five thousand per month earning was unimaginable to both.

'Let me give it a thought,' Jayanti tried to get her appearance right.

'Either it is a 'Yes' or it is a 'No',' Rishi said. 'We do not meet again.'

'Of course it is an 'Yes'.' Jayanti could not allow such big money to slip through her fingers. Machinations can be planned later.

The assignment started over a cup of coffee with Colonel Dhir in the lounge of the Oberoi Hotel on Mathura Road. That was the only meeting that ever happened but for the final meeting, seeking which was the goal of the assignment. Siddhartha briefed Colonel Dhir the antecedents of Vectors, the company owned by Mr Rishi and their interest in supplying spares for T 72 tanks and Mig 21 aircrafts. Colonel Dhir understood the importance of the offer and particularly at this juncture. He asked Siddhartha to jot down a phone number. The number was supposed to be of somebody in the Defence Ministry. He did not divulge the name.

'You can call him tomorrow anytime before lunch.' Colonel Dhir said, 'He will be briefed about the Vector's expression of interest and he will guide you to the right contact.'

Siddhartha called the next morning and after that, it was call after call from one number that led to another. Most officers on the other side of the line did not disclose their names but were completely aware of the Vector's offer in detail. Some did divulge their name but Siddhartha did not believe them in true earnest. It was a maze of telephone calls, fax transmissions, new voices, and new requisitions. From Defence Ministry, to the Army and Air Force Headquarters, and finally back to Defence Ministry; all through a maze of cables. Siddhartha felt communication cables growing out and into him. He was completely wired felt weird and then he saw a ray of hope.

'The meeting will be off the record,' the voice on the other side of the line said. 'We cannot offend the Soviets.'

The Soviet Union had disintegrated but the term was still in use for the Russians.

'If the deal goes through,' he continued, 'then only we will blow the lid off. Otherwise, the meeting never took place.'

'Let me consult my boss and I will get back to you tomorrow.' Siddhartha replied.

'I will not be available at this number tomorrow.' He said, 'If it is OK with your principal, fax us the delegate's details along with their identity proofs to . . .' he gave a new number. 'Remember, all foreign delegates identity proof must be their passport. And also fax us your contact number for confirmation.'

Siddhartha collected the details from the Nehru Place office. There were five in the delegation with two Indians. Mr Rishi himself, and one retired Brigadier Kadian. The other three were of Slovakian nationality. Documents submitted,

Siddhartha waited at their New Friends Colony office for the confirmation. It was he who was always asked to call back at the given numbers. Nobody ever called back. This was the first time somebody from the other end was to call up.

And the call did come. The meeting was confirmed for two thirty at the South Block. He was directed not to go to the main entrance. Instead he was asked to lead the delegation to a small entry at the back of the South Block.

At one forty five, two black Mercedes cars left with the five delegates and Siddhartha, from Nehru Place for South Block. Siddhartha was asked to note down a number, which he had to flash to the sentry of the parking lot. On seeing the number, both the cars were guided to a particular parking slot. As directed over the phone the earlier day, he led the delegation to the small entry at the back of the building. A bureaucrat in white safari suit stood in waiting to receive the team. Security matched the original identity documents with the photocopies of the ones that Siddhartha had faxed and let the five delegates in. Siddhartha saw them vanish behind the main door along with the bureaucrat. His job was done. He walked back to the main road, took an auto and headed towards his office. It took four months to achieve the goal. It was peak summer in Delhi. Hot, dry wind lashed onto Siddhartha's face as the auto sped through the traffic. Neither he nor Jayanti ever came to know if India did buy the spares from Slovakia through Vectors. But they were soon informed that their retainership was being stopped.

CHAPTER 13

Having lost a substantial amount in the 'coal for bricks' business after walking out of my mining profession, I was on the lookout for a new source of income. It was at this time that I met Rajiv Chopra through a common friend. He was handsome with a sparkle in his eyes. If you had one word to describe him, it was 'charmer'. He ran a security agency by the name of Smartguards. A small agency, which enrolled the unemployed, trained them to be gaurds, and supply them on contract basis to various organizations for security. It could be a lone guard at the gate of a private house, or could even be twenty plus guards, working in shifts at some industrial installation. His was not a big set up but did not do bad either. He ran his office from a mezzanine floor room on Kareya Road. He won work contracts by filling in tenders of companies, hired people by advertising in the classified section of the newspaper, trained them a little in army drill, and placed them at designated locations. Most of the workforce was temporary and floating. He had a former Lans Nayak in Indian army as his permanent staff who ingrained the discipline and drill into the new recruits. The footpath in front of his office was the training ground. Every day morning at five, the neighbourhood would wake up to marching orders of ex Lans Naik Bharat Singh.

'Savdhaan, Vishram, Savdhaan, Tez chal, Left, Right, Left, Right . . . Peechhe mur, Left Right, Left, Right, Squad tham' and so on. The uniforms of most security agencies looked the same. They were purchased readymade from the wholesale market of uniforms at Chandni Chowk and only altered to fit the individuals. What differed was the monogram, which also had many readymade options with the company's name only to be stitched onto it. It was a simple business and Rajiv did quite well to make more than just two ends meet.

In the very second meeting he expressed his interest in opening another company. This was where I fitted in.

'Supplying security guards is at the bottom of the pyramid of security business.' He said. 'Actually there are many more areas where we can function which provide higher remuneration.'

'Like?' I enquired.

'Like getting court orders implemented, collecting information about people or organization, etc.,' he replied.

I did not understand much but believed in what he said. He wanted me to be a partner in this new venture. It would function from his present office and his current office staff, which was a lone girl receptionist, would service the new company as well. So there were no extra overheads. I had to invest twenty thousand rupees as capital.

'And what will you use this money for?' I enquired.

'I will buy a second hand car.' At first I was taken aback.

'You only can get this sort of business if people believe that you have connections in high places,' he explained. 'Connections can be developed, it is all about money. But nobody is going to pay you unless you can convince them that you can accomplish his job. The car is the first step in this direction. When you go to someone's office in a car, it does make a difference.'

I could not agree less. In Calcutta, a low percentage of people owned cars and they were perceived to be the privileged.

'The twenty thousand will remain in the company as your share. On my part, my current establishment will be my contribution.'

Thus the 'DAMAK's Security Agency' was established and started functioning. The name was given by Rajiv; he said that he had read the name in some James Hadley Chase novel. I too had read many of those books but did not remember coming across something like DAMAK's Security Agency. An extra table and chair was organized and I started attending office. On the second day, we visited a second-hand car dealer on Lower Circular Road. Rajiv focused onto an 'air force blue' Fiat. Calling price was twenty seven thousand. After a little negotiation and persuasion, the deal was sealed for twenty thousand. I handed over the cash and we drove back to office in the second-hand car.

* * *

The races were cancelled due to rain. We, five racing buddies, stuffed ourselves into Mohinda's small Fiat. He drove to his home and organized card party just like any other race cancellation day. We gambled with liquor being served intermittently. I lost about a thousand bucks and excused myself out of the game. I wanted to leave when Sourenda said, 'Sid you said Anjali has gone to her parent's home.'

'Yes.' I replied.

'Then why don't you come and have dinner with us?'

I liked the idea. It would save me from cooking dinner.

'But it's a long way back from your house,' I shirked and got up.

'Tomorrow is Sunday. You can stay with us for the night and go back home tomorrow morning.' Sourenda tried to reason me out and the idea was not bad either.

'I am also leaving,' Sourenda got up too, and we took the tram to his home. We got down at the College Square tram stop and had to walk a little to reach his home. It was a palatial building, built maybe two generations earlier. We walked up the stairs. The ground floor was let out to two families; the first floor was occupied by a cousin brother of Sourenda's father. The second floor belonged to Sourenda. In fact, it belonged to his father. His father's hotel on Bow Bazaar Street was very basic in character. It was mainly for the traders who thronged from the suburbs to do business in the city. As Sourenda rang the bell, Aitreyi came and opened the large collapsible Iron Gate. We had met in Digha.

'Arre, Siddhartha, you?' Aitreyi was surprised.

There was a large hall with a six-seater wooden dining table at one corner. It was dimly lit by light flowing in from another room. Aitreyi switched on the neon tube. A child of about five years came running and clutched Aitreyi's sari.

'Our son, Babun.' Aitreyi introduced.

'My parents are visiting my uncle in Darbhanga. That is their room.' Sourenda pointed to a dark room beyond the dining table. 'Our room is on this side.'

There was a long verandah on the right and the first room was Sourenda's room. There were other rooms down the verandah but they seemed to be locked and not in use. It was a really big house for just five occupants. The house must have seen more resonating times in the past when joint family system was the order of the day. Times, when nearly the whole family tree alive lived in the same house and had meals prepared in a common kitchen. I entered Sourenda's room. In fact there were two rooms. The first, which I entered into, was a sitting room. Nothing elaborate. At one corner a divan was laid out for sitting. On the other end there was a small table with a colour television on it. A video record player rested on the lower rack of the table with a few Bengali film video cassettes beside it.

Another door from this room led one to their bedroom.

'Aitreyi, it is quite late for Babun. Why don't you give him his dinner and pack him into his bed.' Sourenda told Aitreyi.

'Would you like to freshen up?' Sourenda asked me. Calcutta in June is hot and humid. I always took a bath in the evening to get rid of the grime and sweat.

'I will like to take a bath,' I said.

Sourenda fetched a towel from the bedroom almirah and guided me to the bathroom. It was at the end of the verandah. After a bath, I came back feeling fresh and found Aitreyi sitting on the divan watching the television. Sourenda was pouring whiskey into a glass.

'I do not have rum for you,' he said. 'Hope whiskey is OK with you.'

Unlike me, all my acquaintances preferred whiskey. Earlier in the evening also, I was taking whiskey at Mohinda's place as well.

'That is fine,' I said.

He prepared three drinks and handed over two glasses to Aitreyi and me. Aitreyi looked at me to gauge my reaction to her drinking. It was not anything unusual for me.

'It is perfectly all right for you to enjoy a drink.' I tried to put her dilemma to rest.

We raised and clinked cheers. Babun had been tucked for the night in his grandparents' room. Sourenda switched off the television and put on the video cassette player.

'Have you watched a XXX film?' Sourenda questioned me.

'I had. Many times.'

'Aitreyi get that cassette from the bedroom,' Sourenda said. And as Aitreyi went in to fetch the cassette, 'Let us watch one; I have a very good one.'

Aitreyi came and sat next to me as the video cassette started. We sipped our drinks as Sourenda put off the light and the film started. I felt a little awkward watching 'blue film' in company of a lady; with my wife Anjali, it was a different ball game. But Sourenda and Aitreyi did not seem to be perturbed. The XXX films were filmed around a weak storyline. This one started with two couples biking down to a Texas-style cottage for a weekend holiday. One of the girls wore micro jeans short and a red-and-black check shirt tied in a knot under her bosom. The top buttons were open to reveal her cleavage and round fleshy boobs. The white lace bra was also partly visible. She had a rustic brown cowboy hat on. The second girl wore a shocking pink, skin-hugging, spaghetti top and a sunshine yellow mini skirt. Her nipples poked out to declare that she was braless. Her mini skirt occasionally blew in the wind to reveal her shining red panty. She was a fluorescent buff.

The men wore jeans and while one had an unbuttoned black shirt on to expose his hairy chest, the other wore a round-necked green vest. Both were muscular and handsome. Both the bikes move into the camera and come to a grinding halt as the camera closes onto the front wheel of one of the bikes as it kicks up dust. Cut. A low angle shot of the leather boot of Pamela, the girl in micro shorts, as it hits the ground, and pans upwards over her smooth legs to caress over her protruding buttocks. Camera zooms out and revolves around the group. Cut. Mike, the one with the bare chest, grabs Sasha, the one in mini shirt, by her waist while Jack lifts Pamela into her arms and moves towards the cottage. Cut. Inside the room. Camera pans the room to show the Texan interior and close in on Mike and Sasha who were on a leather sofa kissing. Cut. Extreme close up of vigorous lip-locking, and licking. Camera follows Mike's arm to his palms, which was on Sasha's buttocks squeezing hard and his fingers kept trying to creep into her satin red panty. Cut.

Aitreyi had moved a little more closer to me. I could feel the warmth of her thigh against mine. The jeans at my crotch had tightened. I could feel the hardness within and small spurts of juice being released occasionally. Aitreyi rested her left hand on my thigh. All our eyes were glued to the television.

Jack untied the knot of Pamela's shirt and took it off. He sat on a stool and made Pam sit on him with legs apart. The lace bra was tight and Pamela's boobs seemed to be bursting out of it. Jack softly bit on one as he held the other in his right palm and squeezed hard as the camera closed in. Cut. Mike skinned off Sasha's top to let another pair of boobs gush out in freedom. She took off Mike's vest. Mike lay down on the sofa and Sasha got on top him. Camera zooms onto their vigorous kissing, hands trying to grasp a pound of each other's flesh.

Aitreyi softly rubbed her feet on mine.

'I know what you both are feeling about each other,' Sourenda's voice broke out of the background music of the video. 'Go to the bedroom, spend fifteen minutes together, and then come back. But keep the lights on.'

I felt kinky. Aitreyi caught hold of my hand and led me into the bedroom. She locked the door behind and sat down on the bed. She looked up invitingly at me. I was confused. She took my hands and placed them on her cheeks.

'Sourenda will mind it.' I said.

'He will not mind at all,' she said. 'He only told us to enjoy.'

'But . . .'

She put her arms around my waist and pulled me towards her. I caught hold of her by her nape, by the left hand, and plied my fingers through her soft silky hair. I pulled her up onto her feet and grabbed her by her waist onto me. I felt her heaving bosom on my chest, her churning stomach on my lower abs, and my rising cock in between her warm thighs. I felt like tearing her clothes apart and get into a straight fuck. But I only planted a soft kiss on her trembling lips. I planted one more. And again. And again. In short bursts. She caught hold of my head and pulled me into a deep kiss. I ran my hands down her to take off her nightdress over her shoulders. She stood naked in front of me for a second before she started stripping off my shirt. I placed my right palm on her crotch. She was clean-shaven. I pressed my palm deeper as she loosened her thighs. She was all wet, just like me. She held my head tight as I ate her breasts. I grabbed her buttock. She groaned as we fell on the bed. Cut.

There was a knock at the door.

'Your fifteen minutes are up.' Sourenda's voice interrupted our lovemaking.

I got up. She put on her nightdress and opened the door. Sourenda was standing at the door, naked. I was shocked. He was dark and broadly built of about my height. Some white hairs interplayed with the dark ones on his chest. A slight paunch protruded out of his waistline. Bushy dark crotch, home to a five-inch long, stout, dangling penis.

I took my vest to put it on. Aitreyi pulled it away from me threw the vest and my shirt to the other end of the bed. Sourenda pulled her close, 'Did you enjoy with him?'

She looked into my eyes, 'He caresses nicely.'

'I know. I saw it all.' I was taken aback.

'There is a gap between the door planks,' Sourenda explained. 'I was watching you both all the time.'

'So that was reason why he wanted us to keep the lights on,' I thought to myself. 'He was enjoying live pornography. But using his wife?' I had no answers.

It was really getting kinky.

'Come Sid, now we will have some real fun. Take off your trousers.' Sourenda said as he pulled off Aitreyi's nightdress and switched on the sitting room light

The video played on as we sat next to each other. My cock had lost its steam and shrunk to its two-inch normal self. I looked at it and felt inferior when compared to Sourenda's five-incher. 'My two inch grew to a stout six inches when aroused.' I thought, 'How long and stout did Sourenda's grow?'

Sourenda made another drink for all three of us. I needed one to get out of my inhibitions. I took off my trousers and the brief to expose my small little embarrassment.

'Look, he has such a cute one,' Aitreyi told Sourenda pointing to my cock. I felt a little emboldened. She liked it. She did not scoff at it.

'Does it grow any longer?' Sourenda asked.

After a few sips and Aitreyi's observation I had the confidence back in me.

'Yes,' I replied, 'it grows more or less to your size.'

'What,' it was time for his surprise, 'that small thing grows so big?'

'Yes.'

He finished his whiskey and cuddled Aitreyi. 'Come let us play with her.'

Aitreyi wriggled out her left arm from Sourenda's embrace and signaled me to come close. I moved closer to her while Sourenda lay on her and sucked the breasts. It was only her face that was not covered by his body. I took her face in between my palms and planted a kiss on her cheek. She parted her mouth for a kiss. I penetrated my tongue deep into her throat. She sucked it hard. She caught hold of my head by her both hands as did I and we engaged in a wild kiss. My tongue explored the inside of her mouth; I licked her face, her cheeks. She lightly bit my lips, spat on my cheek and licked the saliva all over my face. She turned my head and took my ear into her mouth. Her tongue penetrated deep in. It was face-to-face sex and I hardened again.

Sourenda suddenly crawled and stood up. His cock was perpendicular to his body. It had grown a little stouter but the length was nearly same. I understood why he was astonished to hear that my two inch grew to a six-incher.

'You are not taking interest in me,' he complained to Aitreyi. He seemed a little drunk.

'Siddhartha is also here,' she replied as I moved away from her face and she sat up.

'Who brought Siddhartha here?' Sourenda was irritated.

'Of course, you.'

'So come here and give me a good mouth.' Aitreyi moved on her knees to Sourenda and took his cock in her mouth. He grasped her hair and pulled her face into his pelvis to thrust his cock down her throat. Aitreyi pulled back on being choked.

'Suck it, bitch.'

Aitreyi glanced at me and got down to her job, the blowjob. She started softly but soon sucked tight, licked his balls, spat at the cock and continued sucking hard again. I sat as my cock slowly shrunk to its original. Sourenda caught hold of her hair and kept moving her head in and out against his cock. I could see suppressed anger and a sense of triumph as he looked at me. He was reaching the climax. He pulled Aitreyi back by her hair and started masturbating with his left hand. And he came, ejaculating on Aitreyi's face. He splattered his semen all over her face, which gradually dripped down her cheeks onto her shoulder and breasts.

'Now go and get fucked by Sid.' he left for the bedroom. Aitreyi picked up her nightdress and started cleaning herself.

Way back in prehistoric times, sex was recreation, a way to keep warm and just incidentally, a means for propagation of species. The club-wielding caveman gave it an added spin, when he discovered that sex was also about domination, about power, about triumph of the strong over the weak. Power was not only about physical strength. It was also about the 'haves' and the 'have nots'. The 'haves' traded kinds to have sex with the 'have nots' and sex became a commodity giving rise to the oldest profession in the world, prostitution.

Like the Stone Age even today, sex is same. It is about keeping warm. It is recreation. It is a procreation process. But above all, it is about power.

* * *

Two weeks had passed, sitting on the desk at DAMAK's Security Agency. Elena, the receptionist, attended a few calls that rarely came in. Rajiv dropped in once or twice during the day in his newly acquired Fiat to enquire about any fresh calls and spent some time chatting with me. I just did nothing. I was beginning to feel that I had hit a dead end when one afternoon Rajiv walked in with a big smile.

'We have landed up our first job.'

I got up from my chair. 'Yes this is working,' I said to myself.

'What is the assignment all about?' I asked.

'Mr Harshvardhan Bagri is the head of a Hindu Undivided Family.' Rajiv elaborated, 'They own a big chunk of land at a prime location on Hazra Road.'

I knew the area.

'The land has been encroached by a Bengali family who run a motor garage and service unit on the premises.' Rajiv continued, 'They have been occupying the land for the last twenty years. Mr Bagri had been fighting the case in various courts to get the possession for the past thirteen years. Four years back, a district court had given the decree in his favour. But when he went with the bailiff to take the possession, a shock awaited him. The bailiff opened the big Iron Gate to be affronted by a huge brick wall blocking the way. Mr Bagri told the bailiff that he could organize labourers to break down the wall in front of him and then take possession. The bailiff refused. His logic was that court had ordered him to hand over the possession of the land to Mr Bagri. Court had given no direction to break any wall. Without breaking the wall he could not enter the land and hence could not hand over the possession. Mr Bagri's repeated requests fell on deaf ears. The bailiff said he was helpless and he would go back to the court and report the matter. He suggested Mr Bagri take recourse to court, again.

This time, Mr Bagri is over cautious and does not want the situation to go out of control. He has a High Court decree in his favour and he wants to manage it professionally.'

'So what will be our job?' I asked.

'We have to provide security to the bailiff so that he can hand over the possession safely.'

'That is all?' I tried to reassure myself.

'Of course.' Rajiv said, 'I will temporarily shift my guards from all posts and deploy them on the spot. It will be a matter of minutes and then they take on their original posts. So we do not incur any extra expense for this operation.'

'How much will be paid to us for this?'

'Fifty thousand.'

I was shocked; fifty thousand rupees for deploying private security guards just for a few minutes? But it was not as simple as it sounded. Slowly, the twists started unfolding. The D-day was a week later. First we visited the bailiff's home who was designated the duty by the court. Rajiv cut a deal with him. He would be paid two thousand five hundred on the D-day before the job and a similar amount on successfully completing the job. Next day, we visited the local police station. Rajiv asked me to wait outside and went into SHO's room for a long discussion. He came back and informed me that he would take thirty thousand to be present and would ignore any violence from our side while acting promptly in case the accused used violence.

'We will be left with only fifteen thousand.' I told Rajiv.

'Are you mad?' He retorted. 'Harshvardhan Bagri will pay all this. We are negotiating probable hot spots on his behalf. We are providing him our professional service for which we will be paid fifty thousand.'

'So it was not merely deploying private security guards' I realized. The astonishing amount started justifying itself. Next stops were the local leaders of two opponent political parties, the CPM and the Congress. It was cakewalk for Rajiv to make sure that there would be no political support to the accused at the ground level on the D-day. I did not know when he discussed with the leaders but later told me he had promised twenty thousand rupees to both their party funds. There was a small unit of CPI (ML) active in the area also. They were handled for five thousand rupees.

Three days before the D-day, we went to Harshvardhan Bagri's house. It was in the Bara Bazaar area. It was an old five-storey building built in the old style with an open courtyard at the centre, and the house encircling it. Mr Bagri lived on the second floor. We climbed up and walked down the corridor. An inmate directed us to the corner room at the end of the verandah. Many portions of the house were rented out as was evident from the nameplates on the doors. The rest were being inhabited by various Bagri families from the same family tree. Mr Bagri was the head of this Bagri Hindu United Family. In most cases, there remained nothing united about such families. Every Bagri family lived an independent life. The Hindu United Family façade was only for tax benefits and other legal advantages.

'You tell him about the amount needed to bribe all the people,' Rajiv whispered into my ear before knocking the door. A man in his late fifties dressed in 'dhoti' and a half-sleeved vest, opened the door.

'Namaskar Bagriji,' Rajiv wished. I understood this was our man.

'Namaskar, aaiye, aaiye.' He greeted us in.

He was a Marwari. The first thing that struck any Bengali about Marwaris was wealth. Yes, they were a wealthy class in Bengal and controlled major trading activities of the state. The amount of money Harshvardhanji was ready to spend further confirmed my idea of Marwaris being rich. But Harshvardhanji's room did not spell wealth. With a bed at the end of the room and two chairs, it seemed to be a humble existence. As we took to the chairs, he climbed the bed and sat with folded legs.

'Aur bataiyen.' He spoke in Hindi. He also spoke fluent Bengali as was revealed later when he spoke to me. Well, most Marwaris did. They held on to their culture strongly but adopted the culture of Bengal with open heart as well. This seemed to be their trade secret of their trading success in West Bengal.

'Everything has been settled. The local police, political parties, the bailiff, are all on our side,' Rajiv gave a pause for me to pick up.

'We need to pay eighty thousand rupees to them in total.' Harshvardhanji seemed to be struck with a bolt from the blue. At least his facial expression translated thus.

'Eighty thousand?'

'Five to the bailiff,' Rajiv took over from me, 'thirty to the police, twenty each to party fund of CPM and Congress, and five to the Naxals of the area. You don't have to worry.' Rajiv continued without giving any chance to Harshvardhanji for second thoughts. 'We will be paying fity per cent before action and the rest after successful completion of the operation. You surely don't want to mess up like last time.'

'You are sure that it will be done. I will get the possession of the land?' He asked.

'We are professionals. This is the fourth case of eviction that we are handling.' Rajiv lied.

'So I am giving you forty thousand now.' Harshvardhanji said as he got down from the bed.

'No.' Rajiv quipped, 'You can pay fifty per cent of our fees, that is twenty five thousand but the bribe money you will have to pay upfront. So you have to give us a total of one lakh five thousand rupees.'

'I will give you a lakh now and rest on completion.'

'Done.' Rajiv closed the deal and Harshvardhanji walked out of the room.

He came back with a jute bag, which generally is used for shopping vegetables at the morning markets. He took out ten bundles of hundred rupee notes and laid them on the bed. Rajiv collected them and put them in the bag and got up. I got up, too.

'Remember you should be there on Tuesday sharp at eleven at the second crossing from the spot.' Rajiv reminded while moving out. 'We will start action at twelve. It will be noon, so there will be less people on the road. And make sure they do not spot you before the action.'

We walked down the corridor, down the stairs, into the Fiat, and drove down to our office. It was past office hours and Elena had left. The guard at the gate had been waiting for us to return. Once inside, Rajiv locked the door from inside and took out two bundles of hundred rupee notes from the bag.

'Our company's first earning.' Rajiv said holding the bundles in his stretched out hands high up in the air. He broke open one bundle, counted the notes and handed over half to me.

'Out of twenty thousand, I will keep ten thousand in company's account and the other ten we will divide amongst us.' He said. 'Similarly we will share the next installment as well.'

I counted my five thousand. This was getting more interesting than I had ever imagined.

'You may leave for home. I will distribute the fifty percent among those whom we have promised and then return home. See you tomorrow.'

On the D-day, I reached office at eight in the morning. Rajiv was already there. So was Bharat Singh with his team of twelve guards in uniform. There were three taxis in waiting as well. One guard was not in uniform and there was a locksmith as well. It seemed Rajiv was well prepared for the occasion. He briefed his team. The plan was to transport the team and station them at the second crossing from the spot. They would position themselves so that they were not visible from the main road. The guard without the uniform will position himself at the same spot on the main road. He will be the communicator between Rajiv and the hidden team. The taxis were flagged off at ten thirty and Rajiv, I, and the locksmith, drove in the car. At eleven, we all assembled at the second crossing from the spot. Harshvardhanji and the bailiff had also arrived. At eleven thirty Rajiv and I walked down the main road and made a recce. There were two police vans stationed about ten meters from the Iron Gate, on the other side of the road. As we crossed the gate, we noticed that the gate was locked with a big padlock from inside. There were a few pedestrians walking up and down the footpath. A few people waited for the bus at the bus stand down the road. We walked back to our team. We asked the bailiff, the locksmith and Harshvardanji to follow us at a considerable distance so that it did not seem we were all together.

Down the road, as we approached the gate, Rajiv and I slowed down to let the bailiff, locksmith, and Harsvardhanji to take over. On reaching the gate, the bailiff looked helpless as he found the gate to be locked from inside. Rajiv ran in and ordered the locksmith to break open the lock. It took him less than two minutes. Rajiv signaled his team and we moved in. The inhabitants were taken by surprise. A man in his fifties and two young men rushed towards us shouting,

'Dacoits! Dacoits! Help! Help!'

The team had rushed in. It was a large walled open space with a small room built at the other end from the entrance gate. A middle-aged lady rushed out of the room and started howling. The team, as instructed, pushed away all resistance and started lifting all furniture, goods, and dumped them on the pavement outside the premises. There was utter chaos. The two young men ran out to the street and started screaming for help. I noticed a few pedestrians stopping at the gate. I could sense trouble. I informed Rajiv. He rushed out and signaled to the police. A contingent immediately rushed to the spot and disbursed the onlookers and encircled the bailiff. The bailiff took out the court order and read it aloud.

Most of the things had been dumped on the pavement outside the premises when a guard came running to Rajiv, 'There is a wooden temple with gods on it. Nobody is ready to touch it.' Legally, Harshvardhanji could only take possession of the land and no other belonging of the accused. So everything belonging to the accused had to be removed before taking possession. And this had reached a dead end with nobody wanting to invite the wrath of the Gods.

'Do something.' Harshvardhanji pleaded Rajiv and me. I ran to the room and found the lady sitting in front of the small wooden temple and screaming.

'All your children will die. God will see to it that you people suffer with leprosy. Just touch my 'Radha Keshto's temple and your hands will start burning.'

The room was empty but for the temple. Five of the guards stood helplessly and listened to the shit that she was spouting. I walked up, picked up the temple with both hands and moved towards the door. The lady caught hold of one of my leg and would not allow me to exit.

'She is no God. Just take her away from my feet.' I howled at the guards.

As they relieved my feet from her clutch I ran out of the gate dumped the temple alongside other goods.

Harshvardhanji ran to me with a wide smile, 'Dhanyabad, Bachalen amay.' 'Thank you. You saved me.'

Things started calming down. The accused family realized they had lost the ground under their feet. The land, which provided them shelter and livelihood for the past twenty years, had vanished. They had to start afresh, they had to move on and so did I have to. The crying lady sitting on the dumped furniture on the roadside remained photographically in my head for years to come. I realized that I had no business in being in the business of uprooting families.

Rajiv handed over twenty thousand that I had given to start the company and another twenty thousand as the remaining share of this assignment and said, 'You could give it a second thought. We had an auspicious good and successful beginning.'

* * *

The horses stopped whispering to me. Suddenly one day, the mysterious line 'burst into a sprint to finish a close fourth' stopped appearing in the racing almanac. I went through the history of past races in the almanac again and again. It was not there. Once again I started my calculations like earlier days to pick out dark horses. But over a period, heavily relying on the mysterious hint had taken its toll. I was confused. I could not track even a single dark horse that I was confident of winning, like I used to before. I had lost my calibre to unravel a winner from the maze of text, timings, and pedigrees. I had lost my capability of intuition and I started losing at the races. I started losing interest in the races. The only interest that drew me to the races was the allure of a threesome at Sourenda's house after the races. I did not like the way we three had sex, but it was getting addictive. There was suffocation, not enough freedom, and the quintessential emotional bonding that I longed for in sex, was missing. But not for long; an emotional longing started developing between me and Aitreyi. A new silent language was evolving through the glances, passionate touches, a gentle yet assertive squeeze on the buttock, boobs or the cock. It said 'I long for you, in person, in seclusion, just the two of us.' It went unnoticed by Sourenda and one evening while I was leaving, Aitreyi shoved a piece of paper into my hand. It read 'Do not go to the races next Saturday. Nobody will be home. I will wait for you at three o'clock.'

It was an autumn afternoon. The six seasons had lost their distinct characters. Though the sky was clear, there were no cotton ball clouds that I read about in Tagore's poems in the childhood. The wind did not have the hint of the chill of the approaching winter. It was hot. I tiptoed up the stairs. Instead of ringing the doorbell, I slipped my hand through the iron collapsible gate and knocked the big hanging padlock on the gate. Aitreyi came to the gate and opened the lock. I helped her push open the heavy gate. I could see her breathing heavily under the pallu of her sari. And so was I.

'You betrayed me.' Sourenda caught hold of my hand and brought me closer to him at the racecourse next day. I suddenly started sweating thinking about yesterday afternoon. 'It must be about something else,' I tried to solace myself and remain calm.

'You had sex with Aitreyi yesterday afternoon,' he said. I was hit by a powerful thunderbolt.

'She told me,' he continued. 'Why didn't you ask me? I would have happily allowed you, but behind my back?'

My palms had turned cold. I did not look at him. The horses were running, the race was on and I wondered 'Why? Why did she have to disclose it to Sourenda?'

I wanted to immediately face Aitreyi and demand an answer. I could not. I left the racecourse for good.

The question kept harping on mind as I went along with my daily routine of designing logos and folders at the advertising agency that I worked for.

Was it to take a revenge on some count that I was unaware of? Or was it to express her individuality, which many women lose as a wife in this male-dominated society? Was it her declaration to Sourenda, 'I am, beyond what you make of me. Before and beyond being Aitreyi Mukherjee, your wife, I am.'?

Not many days had passed since I had stopped going to the racecourse in the weekends. It was about two weeks. Anjali had gone to visit her parents in Bashirhat. I had just returned home from the agency. There was a knock at the door. I wondered who could it be and opened the door.

Aitreyi stood there with a large sling bag on her shoulder and a suitcase. I felt a little hesitant to let her in without Anjali being at home, but had no option either.

'Aitreyi! At this time!' I exclaimed. 'Come in.'

She walked in as I took the bag off her shoulder, helped offload the suitcase. It was a little too heavy. We did not have a drawing room. Those days, most Bengali families rarely had. There were two bedrooms, one large and one small, and there was the dining room, which doubled as the sitting room. I pulled out a chair off the dining table and asked her to settle down.

'What brings you here?' I asked.

'I cannot take it anymore,' she said.

'What is it that you cannot take any more?'

'From the day you stopped coming, he has been bringing different men from the race course to the house,' she paused for a while and looked up straight into my eyes, 'and he wants me to sleep with them, just like we did.'

I was taken aback. I do not know how many minutes passed as I kept looking out of the window and she sat dumb. An unusual cawing of a crow at this odd hour of the night got my feet on the ground.

'Let me fetch you some water.' I walked into the kitchen but did not switch on the light. For the past few days I had wanted to question Aitreyi about her confession to Sourenda about our sexual encounter. Unfolding of the current scenario pushed that into a back burner. I stood confused, aghast at the lightning strike against a violent dark blue sky. I did not know how to react. Light flowing in from the dining room was enough for me to pour the water from the terracotta pitcher. I walked into her reality with a glass of water in my hand.

'I am going to stay with you, Sid.' Bolts continued and thunders followed. 'I have got my few belongings for the time being, you need to give me shelter.'

I could not turn away someone with whom I had an emotional bonding, however licentious it may have been. I had physical relation with her and it was not paid sex. It was not love, but it was not a cold jerk it off physical need either.

But I could not give her shelter. I was married. Forget about social conditioning, Anjali would not accept it. And I too realized it would be wrong to Anjali. I pulled myself together. There was time to think about the future but what about now, present? What about tonight? Anjali was not home. Would it be appropriate to allow her to stay the night with me? What would Anjali think once she learned about it? Aitreyi's expectant eyes did not allow me to reason within me. I took her suitcase to the small bedroom and asked her to settle down.

'Stay the night,' I told her. 'We will decide the course of action tomorrow.' I allowed myself a breather.

It was not a cold night but I found the physical passion that we shared in the past, had abruptly turned cold. We did not talk any further. After dinner I retired to my bedroom, leaving her sitting at the dining table. About ten minutes had passed as I lay looking at the ceiling fan that the lights in the dining room went off. I squirmed at the thought of her walking into my bedroom. But she did not and silence followed. I turned off my bedroom lights and lay on my bed in the darkness of confusion.

The lights through the window woke me up the next morning. The crows were cawing, a tingle from the small 'ghungroo' in the hand of the rickshaw puller faded into the distance as he alerted the passersby, honk of a taxi horn came in from the main road. It was all silent within the house. I got up and walked to the small bedroom where Aitreyi slept last night. She was not there. The door to the balcony was also latched and then I noticed that the front door was open. Once again I went into the small bedroom to look for her luggage. That too was not there. I realized that she had left. Aitreyi was gone.

CHAPTER 14

1995. GOVERNMENT OF India had eased the procedures to avail home loan and also introduced tax incentives for the same to boost the housing sector. Apart from the public sector banks and financial institutions, many private finance companies also started offering home loans to seek a pie of this newly opened booming sector. It was not that Siddhartha never thought of buying a house, signing eleven-month tenancy contract and changing homes after every eleven months had become disgusting. Leaving bag and baggage in less than a year and again resettle in a new home in Delhi had become a pain. Though there was a clause of ten per cent increase in rent after the eleven-month period to get into a fresh contract, owners preferred new tenants, as there was always someone ready to pay much more than the ten per cent increase. There was also the hassle of finding a new house in a decent location, deal with the brokers and paying brokerage. But he knew his savings were meager and he had never weighed the option of taking a loan. The advertising business that provided him his bread and butter was also not running too well. So the new home loan scenario did not excite Siddhartha much.

A past experience had also left a bitter taste. Some years back, he had applied for a Delhi Development Authority (DDA) flat. He had paid ten thousand rupees as the application money. The allotments of DDA flats were always through draw of lots. Everybody he knew in Delhi gave him the impression that being allotted a DDA flat was a rare opportunity. Also, he had no resources to finally acquire the flat worth four lakhs. It seemed he applied to test his luck; and he was lucky. He got a two-bedroom duplex apartment in Narela drawn in his name. Anjali, his wife, was overjoyed. Siddhartha needed to deposit another ten thousand rupees as confirmation money. The catch was that one could withdraw at this stage and get back five thousand of the application money. But once you deposited the confirmation money and did not pay the final amount when possession was given, the total deposit of rupees twenty thousand would be forfeited. Siddhartha checked his resources. He knew he could not raise three lakhs and eighty thousand in any which way. He decided to cancel his application to Anjali's dismay. When Anjali discussed his decision in one of her kitty parties which had much elder ex-army officers' wives, they persuaded her to make Siddhartha see sense.

'Arre, DDA allotment is once in a lifetime opportunity.'

'Even if you do not want to take over the flat, it always goes with a premium. You take the allotment letter, sell it in the secondary market and you can make some good money.'

'Nobody lets go an opportunity like this.'

'You are so lucky.'

All her kitty party aunties were gung-ho about this DDA opportunity and Anjali coaxed Siddhartha to deposit the confirmation amount. They were sure that they will not be taking the possession of the flat as their resources would not allow them, but were happy that there would be some windfall earning. As per all aunties' suggestions, Siddhartha confirmed the allotment by depositing another ten thousand. They hired a cab one day and with much enthusiasm ventured out to visit the DDA property allotted in their name and find out the market premium that the brokers could fetch. Being in Delhi for only about four years, they did not have much knowledge about the city's spread. They started early having a vague idea that Narela was on the western border whereas they lived in Noida, which was on the eastern periphery. It was a long journey. Till Rohini, it seemed they were within city limits but beyond that, soon the landscape started changing. The asphalt roads gave way to uneven bumpy roads. The concrete structures faded away to expose wide, dry fields, and small cottages with a few brick and mortar two-storey houses.

'Are we in Delhi?' Siddhartha thought wiping the sweat from his forehead on that hot summer noon. Anjali sat silent as the non air-conditioned cab made its way through the Wild West. After some while with the midday sun on top, the cab climbed onto an asphalt road once again. Siddhartha and Anjali could see row of concrete houses on the horizon. A ray of hope rekindled. Following the asphalt road, they reached the DDA colony with a tin board declaring it to be the DDA Apartments of Narela. Both of them got down from the cab and looked around. There was not a single sign of humanity around. All the houses bared their brick structures like the ghastly teeth of a scarecrow in a dry barren field.

'This is a new colony.' Siddhartha consoled Anjali, 'It is still under process of completion.'

'Must be.' Anjali found it horrifying to think otherwise.

'Let us find our flat.' Siddhartha tried to bring in a little childlike adventure to make their long journey into hopelessness a little more interesting. They had a confirmed house number. All the houses were numbered on a square tin plate nailed above the main door. They moved from one dusty lane to another trying to locate R190, their house number. It was a surreal world. With the sun on top, a shadow less landscape of brick and mortar structures with no doors or windows fitted looking like uncovered toilet pans ready to swallow both of them like pieces of shit. Complete silence was rarely broken by the caw of a restless crow. They tracked down R190 and entered it. Siddhartha tried to understand the space. Slowly, a beautiful, small home emerged from the structures.

'This is the drawing cum dining room, and that is the kitchen. But the drawing cum dining is too small. We have two bedrooms upstairs. We need only one. So we can convert the second one, which is on top of the kitchen into our dining room. We can have a hole through the floor of the dining room and have a pulley system installed to get our food from the kitchen to the dining room.'

Anjali listened in awe and saw the raw bare space taking shape of a beautiful little home of theirs. What a wonderful feeling.

'But we cannot buy this house. We do not have the finances,' Anjali came out of stupor.

'I know,' Siddhartha replied, 'I am elaborating what we could have done to transform this small place, if we could have owned it.'

'Come, let us find a broker.' Siddhartha helped Anjali out onto the reality of the dusty road ahead. It took them some time to trace a human. A labourer, who had made one of these structures his home, directed them to the end of the asphalt road where a few broker shanties were there.

Being afternoon, most of these corrugated tin shanties were locked up. The brokers had left for home to avoid the fiery heat. Only one was open. Siddhartha moved fast towards it to make some sense of this journey. There was a man having his lunch from a tiffin box.

'May I come in?' Siddhartha asked.

'Yes,' the shabbily dressed, burly man looked up, 'How can I help you?'

'I have been allotted a house in this colony by DDA. How much premium can I get by selling the allotment letter?' Siddhartha came straight to the point.

'Premium?' It seemed the man fell from the sky. 'This area has been like this for the last ten years. Nobody comes here. And why should anybody come?' He continued to explain. 'There is no transport, no electricity, no water. So how can people take possession of these houses?' Siddhartha felt a shiver down his spine. Whatever the man said translated into a straight loss of twenty thousand rupees for him.

'Sir,' the man continued, 'I would advise you not to deposit the confirmation money and withdraw your application. Nobody knows when DDA will actually complete these houses and this area will become livable. DDA does this every time. They advertise these houses with other properties, allot them and when nobody falls for them they do it again the next time thinking someday some people will bite the bait. But are people fools? They will surely come here to check the locality and facilities before confirming their booking.'

Siddhartha did not think about other people but knew that he was a fool of the first order.

It took many more years for Siddhartha to muster up courage to buy an apartment. He realized the fact that it would be difficult to survive in Delhi in the long term, without having his own roof above his head. But deciding on a house was no easy task. First, he had to organize his resources. His savings completely churned out would fetch a lakh; he organized another lakh as loan from acquaintances. He thought if he took a loan of five lakhs as home loan for fifteen years, he had a kitty of seven lakhs. Going through the advertisements and calling up the builder's offices he found Gurgaon was out of question. There was nothing decent available in that price range. There was a Greenfield area coming up on the eastern periphery of Delhi border, Indirapuram. It was just across National Highway 24 from Noida where he lived in rented accommodation. There was only one project, the Alpine Riviera. On visiting the builder's office he found that two-bedroom options were available between six to ten lakhs. Having options within his range, he decided to visit the site with Anjali. By now he had a second hand non-airconditioned, white Maruti car. So on an autumn Sunday morning they drove from Noida to Indirapuram. The distance was not much but as soon as they crossed the NH-24, the scenario was similar to the journey to Narela for the DDA flat. A 'kutchha' road ran beside an irrigation canal into Indirapuram. On the right it was all barren as far as the eyes could see apart from a few green grassy patches. On the left by the bank of the canal there was this bushy spread of three-metre tall wild Kans grass with their conical, fluffy, white flower heads at the tips. They bloomed in the autumn. The scene reminded Siddhartha of one of Rabindranath Tagore's poem in his class three Bengali text book.

Loosely translated, it read:

> *Our little river flows in graceful loops*
> *The summer heat dries her to a gentle flow*
> *Both cart and cattle travel across with ease*
> *Her banks are high, her depths are low*
> *The sand bed glitters, no trace of mud*
> *The far bank shimmers with Kaash flowers white, where flocks of mynas chirp busily all day*
> *And jackal calls arise at night.*

There was this small river, albeit the irrigation canal, the 'Kaash' flowers, the chirping mynas. Siddhartha braked hard to a grinding halt. Two wild brown rabbits with long ears ran across the dusty road.

'This place is just as forsaken as Narela,' Anjali said. 'At least there were some standing structures there, here it's only wide open spaces.'

On the horizon, structures of buildings started rising as Siddhartha drove further down.

'This place is equidistant from Connaught Place as our home in Noida.' Siddhartha affirmed. 'It will take me the same time to drive down to my office as it takes me now.'

Though uninhabited, there was something more to the place that invited Siddhartha than just mere distance and logistics calculation. They arrived in front of the complex, which was being developed. A fast pace of construction was in progress. All the buildings were of four-storeys. The executive from the makeshift office informed that apartments in the range of six to seven lakhs were already sold out. Before they were disheartened the executive said, 'Why don't you have a look at the new constructions that are going on at the other end? These houses are reconstructed on structures of old GDA constructions. The ones I am talking about are completely new constructions with much better specifications and planning.'

Anjali and Siddhartha followed the executive to the other end of the complex. Unlike the earlier buildings that were finished, these were being freshly constructed. While some buildings were complete with walls raised, others had the RCC structures being worked upon. Both followed the executive to a second floor apartment with only plastering and woodwork being left. It was a nice four-side, open apartment, with large bedrooms, two attached bathrooms, and the balcony opened out from the drawing cum dining room to a large open space. The afternoon autumn sun moved into the drawing room through the balcony. Anjali and Siddhartha both looked at each other and nodded in consent.

The executive must have sensed the smile within them and said, 'The price of this apartment is a little higher. It is eight lakhs and twenty thousand only. But be rest assured it is worth it.'

The incoming autumn sun through the balcony was too strong an enchantment to be avoided. Anjali and Siddhartha moved into their new home on the same day as the Chaterjees. They became close neighbours.

Chaterjees. Father Chaterjee, retired technical government employee with a torrid passion for music. His spectrum was real wide, classical Indian, Tagore's songs, Hindi light music, which even included Hindi film songs, English Pop, Rock—to the extent of Hard and Acid Rock—took every opportunity to force the pleasure and at times the pain of listening to his wide collection of audio cassettes onto every guest. Of course, this pleasure or pain did not last long as it was soon interrupted by his explanations, and the music only worked as a background score. It was tough for everybody to refuse him. But Siddhartha learnt through his management experiences how to deliver a tough 'no'. It was only he who could have a pick at what he wanted to listen though a dialogue on the same was a foregone conclusion. Happy, satisfied, a really good human. He was to become Siddhartha's new Meshomoshai.

Mother Chaterjee, Urmila, became Siddhartha's Mashima. Mashima had been holding the reigns of Father Mukherjee's homefront, and quite aptly. Raising a daughter and a son with perfect élan and quite proud about it too. And why not, both settled well in life. Quite confident and happy about her style of home management, she still held the reign tight. When other actions failed to achieve results, she flashed her ultimate weapon, 'We will go away to Kolkata. Then you all can do whatever you feel like.'

This was mostly for Kallol, her son—Siddhartha's new friend—a happy go lucky efficient officer with a smile always on the face. Quite impatient, became tense at the drop of the hat. Well Arieans were supposed to be so, and he was one. Never taking any snide remarks deep into the heart, always ready to forgive and forget. A nice simpleton with an odd enough stubborn streak which flashed at times.

And there was Jaya, Kallol's wife, and Sambit, his son. So they were the Chaterjees, Anjali and Siddhartha's close neighbour. After being married for fifteen years and relocating in Delhi in 1991, first time Anjali and Siddhartha could call a house their own, though mortgaged against a huge loan under the new relaxed home loan policy of the government.

So was the case of twenty odd families that moved into Alpine Riviera. Apart from a Colonel, all were in their early forties. All were from a background where people thought of owning a house only after retirement. For the time they were the new generation and the pride reflected in their attitude. This was a proud lot. Though each had to come clean of a huge loan in the coming days, they knew that they were the trailblazers and were looked up with respect by their near and far relatives and acquaintances. It showed in their behavior. Quarrels would break out on petty issues trying to prove that one had arrived in life. But more often, each would also come forward to lend out a helping hand to one another. The subconscious feeling of living in a place marooned in an isolated desolate place, developed strong bonds of friendship. But that would not be for long. With more families moving in and priorities changing for the families, the bonhomie of the earlier days gradually started waning and new equations of friendship emerged.

Siddhartha and Joydeep, an artist became friends. Joydeep had a Masters Degree in Arts from Uttarakhand University and worked part time with a magazine group to do their magazine layouts. Before this engagement, he worked as a graphic artist for a daily newspaper, which wounded off. Siddhartha had seen Joydeep's paintings and he highly appreciated them. They were abstract, chiaroscuro representation of colours of nature.

Kailash, another resident who was also a graduate of the same university, also painted acrylic on canvas. Kailash had won plethora of awards whose list ran through two A4-size pages. Siddhartha did not hold Kailash's paintings in very high esteem. He used a technique, which Siddhartha thought was only an extension of commercial art. But he never expressed his views to him. He liked the freedom in which Joydeep applied his colour while he considered Kailash to be very mechanical. Joydeep saw the paintings and drawings that Siddhartha was doing and thought that there was potential in him to get into the mainstream art world. Siddhartha had evolved in doing abstracts. He had come a long way from his cubism inspired figure defragmentation.

'Why don't you participate in the exhibitions?' Joydeep asked.

'What exhibitions?' Siddhartha had no idea of the professional art world. He was a self-taught artist who pursued painting without ever thinking, how to get his creations to the world.

'There are so many regional, State level, and National exhibitions,' Joydeep explained. 'All professional artists participate in these exhibitions. You can give it a try; but be ready for rejection. There are thousands of artists across India who participate, most of them professionals, and many quite established. Only a few hundred are considered worth exhibiting by the judges.'

'I was not aware of it.' Siddhartha said, 'How do I participate?'

'Well, the UP State Lalit Kala Akademi exhibitions are coming up two months from now. Both Kailash and I will be participating. I will get you a form. You select your painting and join us.'

He selected one of his paintings, a four by three feet canvas and sent it along with Joydeep and Kailash for the exhibition, as advised. He was ready for rejection. A month and a half later, a letter arrived from the UP State Lalit Kala Akademi. To his amazement, his painting was selected. He informed Joydeep and Kailash. Their paintings had also been selected. Joydeep was wholeheartedly happy for Siddhartha's success, but Kailash seemed a little confused. No degrees in art, no past exhibitions, he did not expect Siddhartha to jump into the league of the established artists so soon. But he too congratulated Siddhartha for his journey into the world of art. At least, that is what Siddhartha thought, too. The beginning of the journey into the world of art. Little did he know what time had to unfold?

Coming days saw Siddhartha and Kallol, the son of Meshomoshai, and Mashima Chatterjees, also get closer. Kallol was five years younger to Siddhartha and called him Sid'da, the way Bengalis called an elder brother. In addition to being close neighbours, they had their offices across the street at Patel Chowk, and Kallol went to and returned from office in Siddhartha's car. Siddhartha did not have a fixed time of return due to his nature of job. On such days Kallol would have to take public transport and return home. The earlier get together of the early bird residents in the evenings at the parking lot always ended in a drinking session. Liquor was contributed for, and everyone drank. Some got high on a peg; some consciously drank little, while some drank a lot. Siddhartha and Kallol belonged to the last category. Siddhartha drank much but stayed in control while Kallol had to be guided to his home every night. There were others too, who had to be guided home: Virender, Rajiv, and sometimes Ramalu as well. But with disintegration of the group and reorientation of friendship bonds, the drinking sessions also shifted from the parking lot to various locations. Some splinter groups got together on rooftops, some huddled into a patronizing member's drawing room, while others moved to the nearby liquor vend. Siddhartha maintained a bar at home and had no problem to continue drinking. He was a regular drinker; but for Kallol, drinking was banned at home. Earlier, he did go home drunk but that was late in the night. Meshomoshai and Mashima would already be sleeping and Jaya would quietly open the door and assist him to the bed. Kallol had to find a new circle for drinking and he did it soon. It was his office colleagues. He worked as a Section Officer at the Election Commission. He joined a group of colleagues who would drink after office hours at the 'pan vend' on the lane behind their office. Siddhartha soon found that Kallol would come drunk to take the lift back home in his car.

'It is not yet sundown and you are already drunk.' Siddhartha often advised against drinking at this early hour but to no avail. Kallol's drinking rose by the day and it became a problem for Siddhartha. Kallol would ask to stop the car, buy bottles of water and pour it on his head in the hope of reducing his inebriated state before reaching home.

Sometimes he would vomit by the roadside and sit on the pavement to gain some time. He was turning into a nuisance for Siddhartha, but he did not withdraw himself. Being a close friend, he decided to get deeper into it, to try and nip it from the roots. He decided to join the drinking sessions with Kallol's office colleagues.

Kallol was too eager and happy to invite Siddhartha into their fold. The day Siddhartha expressed his wish to have drinks with Kallol's office colleagues, he got a call at five o'clock.

'Come over to the 'pan and cigarette' vend behind our office.'

'But it is too early.' Siddhartha replied.

'We are going down in five minutes. Join us there.'

'But isn't your office till six pm?'

'It hardly matters. Join us in five minutes.'

Siddhartha had work in hand and he did not like to leave office so early. 'OK, you start; I will join you as soon as I am done with my work.'

At six thirty, Siddhartha took the elevator down and crossed across to the red Election Commission building. He took the side alley to get to the backside of the building. As he took the next turn, he could see a 'pan and cigarette' vend at the other end of the street, under a huge tree. It was crowded. There were small groups of six to eight people jostling around the vend. As he moved closer, he realized that the different groups that had assembled there were all for the same purpose, drinking liquor. Passersby did not bother them. Even a police constable at some distance did not bother them. They all had small plastic glasses in their hands from which they drank. Kallol waved to Siddhartha as he walked up to the group. He was given a plastic glass with whisky in it.

'With soda or water?' One of them asked.

'Water will do.' Siddhartha replied. He was not here to enjoy drinks. He wanted to get deeper into the conundrum of Kallol's attachment to the group and lead him out of it. As he was introduced to the group members he found that addiction had found a common ground to break all hierarchy. Kallol was a Section Officer. There was an Under Secretary, another Section Officer, three clerks, two peons and even a driver in the group. All drank pouring from the same bottle, cracked jokes, and passed lewd comments on female colleagues, just like pals. The hierarchy of the office stayed back behind the iron gates of the Election Commission.

'How could this work?' Siddhartha was intrigued, 'Or, did it really work?'

Joining the street corner party, that is what they used to call it, was just the tip of the iceberg of the larger scenario. Soon Siddhartha started getting calls for joining afternoon parties.

'There is a party today at Rawal's place.' Kallol phoned one day, 'I am going with Ramesh, Nikhil will come to your office and pick you up at twelve thirty.'

'Twelve thirty?' Siddhartha was stunned.

'Yes Gurung will cook meat for all. Rathore's allotted flat is empty. We are having the party there.'

'But afternoon is no time for party.'

'Any time is party time. Join us and you will have fun.'

Siddhartha did not join the party. He noted the details of the flat from Nikhil so that he could pickup Kallol after office hours. When Siddhartha arrived at seven in the evening, the party was nearly over. A few from the group had left and few lay drunk on a bed sheet on the floor. Siddhartha shaked Kallol out of stupor, splashed some water on his face and helped him into the car. The journey back was a lonely one as Kallol snored away slumped into the car seat by his side.

Soon Siddhartha found that these afternoon parties were not an exception. There were at least four to five such outings every month. 'How does the office function with such people?' Siddhartha pondered, 'And how does the government work with such employees? Or was it that government was so overstaffed that dereliction of duty by some hardly affected functioning?' He had no answers.

It was time for 'Delimitation', a process by which the electoral constituency boundaries were redrawn as per demographic and sociograpic changes reflected in the latest census. A 'Delimitation Commission' was created from within the office of the Election Commission to carry out the task. Kallol was deputed to the Commission after his promotion to Under Secretary. There was a set of rules laid down for the process and no one could tamper with the outcome. Only in case of rare disputes, a committee of top officials took decision on the final outcome.

But for many in the political class, who were used to manipulating every process, believed that it could be done in this case as well. One had to have the right connections at the right places. At least Omkar Tomar, sitting MLA (Member of Legislative Assembly) from Indore in Madhya Pradesh, believed so. He had a hunch that his area could become a reserved constituency for Scheduled Caste/Schedule Tribe. He had to stop that from happening to contest the next election from the same constituency. He had nurtured the criminals and the muscle power in the region that he believed would help him win the next election. He had invested heavily in the region's power equation to let the constituency turn into a reserved constituency and leaving him fending for himself in an uncharted constituency, and he found the right connection. At least he thought so. He found out that the son-in-law of a long retired party colleague had been deputed in the commission, who was also in charge of his State, among others. It was Kallol Chatterjee. And soon a contact was made with him through an emissary, Nagesh Bishnoi, who had met Kallol on a few occasions at the Indore Guest House.

It was a sultry summer afternoon, the phone rang in Kallol's office.

'Hello.'

'Mr Kallol Chatterjee, please.'

'Speaking.'

'Arre Kallolji.'

'Who is speaking?' Kallol asked.

'Kallolji, this is Nagesh from Indore.' Kallol still could not recognize the caller at the other end. 'You are now such a big officer, how will you remember us small people.'

Kallol tried to place the caller in the context of Indore but failed.

'Remember I had got the Scotch bottle to your Guest House at Indore? Omkarji had sent his wishes.'

'Oh ya, MLA Saab.' Kallol recollected Nagesh's face. 'How is he? All well?'

'Ya, ya,' Nagesh continued, 'Omkarji was talking about you the other day and asked me to give you his good wishes.'

'Thanks.'

'How are your wife and daughter?'

Kallol could sense that there was some favour to be asked of him.

'Yes, everybody is fine.'

'I will be coming to Delhi soon, will meet you at your office.'

'Sure, just give me a tinkle before coming.'

Kallol was now very sure that there was some favour to be asked of him. After winning elections, politicians only remembered those who would be of some use and only at the time of need.

Nagesh did not waste time. On the very third day from calling Kallol, he landed up in Delhi, met him at the Election Commission's office, and invited him for tea the next evening. These matters are never discussed in the office. Though he had invited Kallol for tea, the little he knew about Kallol, he was sure it would be over a few drinks. He was not worried about the expenditure. It was an all-expenses-paid venture sponsored by Omkarji, the MLA. Kallol shared the development with Siddhartha and asked him to accompany him for the tea next evening.

It was about six forty five when Siddhartha parked his car in the inner circle car parking of Connaught Place. United Coffee House was finalized as the venue. It was Kallol's suggestion. Siddhartha had introduced the restaurant to him and he liked the food. As Siddhartha and Kallol alighted from the car and walked to the restaurant, Kallol spotted Nagesh at the entrance of the restaurant and waved at him.

'Good evening Kallolji.' Nagesh walked up to greet and looked warily at Siddhartha.

'Good evening Nageshji,' Kallol shook hands, 'this is Siddhartha, my best friend.' He understood Nagesh's concern, so continued, 'Everything is open with him. He is not in Election Commission; he is not in Government. He runs a private advertising agency. So you can relax and discuss everything in confidence.'

Siddhartha also shook hands with a smile and all walked into the restaurant.

On settling down on a corner table, Nagesh asked, 'What would you like to have?'

'Black Label.' Kallol said. Whenever it was for free, Kallol always preferred anything pricey. It is not that he loved refined scotch; he drank only to get drunk. But on this occasion he wanted to squeeze out the maximum.

'And you?' Nagesh asked Siddhartha.

'A large rum, Indian dark rum with water at room temperature.'

Nagesh ordered accordingly and a beer for himself, and got down to business.

'Omkarji is very worried about the delimitation process.' He explained the MLA's concerns and asked for Kallol's help.

'It is very difficult.' Kallol said after one peg.

'Difficult, but not impossible.' Nagesh said, 'Particularly when you are part of the process.'

Understanding the process from Kallol, Siddhartha knew it was just impossible but sipped his rum as a silent observer.

'Let me see.' Kallol, after two pegs; and after the third, 'I will do my best. How can I disappoint MLA Saab?'

Liquor has an unexplained effect of shedding off inhibitions.

'But what will I get in return?' Kallol laid his cards.

Siddhartha was astonished at Kallol's unabashed hint at a quid pro quo. In other words, his demand for a bribe; knowing that Kallol had no control over the process. He was a mere organizer and an observer of the process.

'You tell me.' Nagesh thought he was close to the deal. 'You know Omkarji is very generous. You tell the amount and it will be delivered once the job is done.'

'Arre Nageshji,' Kallol interrupted, 'I am an honest Government servant. I do not take cash.'

Nagesh knew that liquor was Kallol's weakness.

'Tell me the brand and the number of bottles that I should bring to you.'

'Bottles are OK. But this is a big task. And it's not only me; I have to influence my boss as well. The bottles will go to him and what about me?'

Siddhartha was a bit confused. He believed that Kallol was an honest officer. He knew liquor was his weakness, but he could not fathom what Kallol was hinting beyond the bottles.

'Kallolji, you just spell out your demand and it will be met.'

'How about some fun in the bed?'

Bolt struck Siddhartha from the blue. Nagesh burst out laughing. 'That's it?'

'But don't get some prostitutes.' Kallol clarified his demand.

'I will send you a sexy housewife. It will be an experience of a lifetime for you.'

Nagesh looked at Kallol with a mischievous wicked smile and forwarded his hand to clinch the deal.

'But where?' Kallol wanted to iron out the details.

'Once the job is done, I will deliver the Scotch bottles to you in Delhi. But for the other part you have to come to Indore.' Nagesh said, 'And it will not be difficult for you. You get an official tour sanctioned. Rest I will take care.'

'I love official tours. That will not be a problem.'

Nagesh put forward his hand, 'So I take it to be final.'

Kallol took his hand, 'It is done.'

And Siddhartha sat stunned. There was no point in talking to Kallol while driving back home; he was drunk. Next morning while driving to office, Siddhartha wanted to clear his apprehensions.

'Kallol as you explained the Delimitation Process to me; you have no role in influencing the outcome. Why did you get into this deal? And how could you demand such a thing?'

'Have you not slept with unknown women? It is such a great fun. During most of my official tours, I have slept with different women. But they were all call girls and prostitutes, for which I or somebody else paid. It will be an experience on a different level to sleep with a housewife; the unprofessional coy approach. Wow.'

Kallol fantasized. 'And about getting the job done? I am going to do nothing. If his constituency becomes a reserved constituency, I get nothing. But in case according to the process if his constituency still remains a general one, I will have the information much before it gets to him. He will only get to know once the list is officially released. I only need to call him and say that the job has been done before the official declaration. That is it. I have nothing to lose but I stand a chance to gain.'

An unknown facet of Kallol unraveled in front of Siddhartha. He did not go into the morality of sleeping out of marriage, but what stunned him was the shrewd streak in the otherwise gullible looking human.

Omkarji's constituency remained a general one after delimitation. Nagesh came to Delhi to deliver a crate of Johnnie Walker Black Label. Kallol went to Indore on an official tour. On returning, he described his misdemeanors to Siddhartha in graphic detail. How he savored the voluptuous housewife for two days in every way and in every orifice.

It was a Saturday afternoon and Kallol's gang had a party at another colleague's flat. There wasn't much for Siddhartha at the office. Around three, he decided to join them. By now he was aware of all the venues where the parties were held. This was in a government flat in the Sarojini Nagar area. He had been there to pickup Kallol on an earlier occasion.

Parking the car inside the boundary wall of the complex, he went to the ground floor flat and knocked at the door. Loud laughter and haughty voices came trickling out of the closed windows and the door. Gurung opened the door.

'Welcome, welcome.'

There was a joint welcome by all. The room was lit by a sixty watt bulb and was empty but for a small table on which a television ran in mute. A few bed sheets were spread on the ground on which all relaxed with their drinks in their hands. Siddhartha was shocked to see that a XXX movie was being played on the television and all were leeching over it passing loud lewd comments. Shankar handed over a glass of whiskey to Siddhartha as he sat down in a corner and looked around. There were more surprises waiting for him. There were two more men in the group whom he had never met earlier and there were two fat, dark-complexioned women also sitting. Ramesh was lying with his head on one of the woman's lap. Both wore garish loud make-up and undersized dress that revealed more than they covered. Siddhartha felt uncomfortable.

'Look at the size of the cock, fuck.' Daljit exclaimed pointing to the TV screen.

'I have a bigger one than that.' Ramesh replied.

'Let me hold it and check,' one of the women said, as she moved her hand to Ramesh's trouser fly and gave a tight squeeze to his erection.

'Haan, it is big.'

Ramesh got up. 'Come, I will show you how big it is.' He pulled up the woman and walked into the next room with her as all cheered loudly. Siddhartha never felt nausea in his life. But now he could not describe to himself what he felt like, but surely he was feeling deep suffocation. He got up.

'I need to leave,' he said. 'Kallol I came to tell you that I am going to Gurgaon on an official work. You will have to return home yourself.'

All pleaded with him to stay back as according to them the fun had just started.

But Siddhartha left.

It was early winter, four forty as Siddhartha walked out. The sun was near the horizon; bright golden-orange rays layered over the city. There was a cool refreshing breeze. But Siddhartha had trouble breathing. He felt his lungs were straight jacketed. He tried to take a deep breath but the air intake hardly sufficed. He lit a cigarette and took a deep puff before getting into the car. He turned the key on, pressed the clutch and pushed the gear to the first. Suddenly, heavy gloomy clouds darkened the horizon and the orange flares on the sky turned fiery red. In a flash it was dark all around. A heavy storm swept in. He looked outside the window; visibility was near zero.

He switched on the headlights as a smell of raw flesh tickled his nostrils. The smell was coming from his left and as he turned his head towards his co-passengers seat, there was a beheaded, skinned carcass of a goat on the seat. It sat like a human with its fore legs stretched in front like a man exercising. Clotted blood glistened on its sheared neck from the dim light of the dashboard. Siddhartha moved to the second gear and then the third. The shining raw flesh started loosening from the bones. Siddhartha pushed the gear to the fourth and to the fifth. The smell started altering. He pressed on the accelerator. Fifty, sixty, eighty. The smell was transforming into stench—stench of rotten flesh; flesh that was loosening, and slowly coming off the bones. A few maggots started creeping out of the carcass flesh. Small white jellybean maggots ate into the flesh and grew bigger, fatter, laid eggs and multiplied. The smell became unbearable.

Siddhartha opened the window to let in fresh air, only to let a stronger stench burst into the car. And whooshed into the car a swarm of flies—large blowflies glowing metallic green and blue in the dashboard light. Siddhartha quickly rolled up the window but the car was already filled with thousands of these buzzing menaces. Battle ensued between the blowflies and the maggots over the largesse of rotting flesh. Siddhartha pressed the brake pedal. He wanted to stop the car and get out. Brakes had failed, did not function. He rammed on the brake pedal again—once, twice, thrice.

Speedometer whizzed from hundred to hundred twenty. Siddhartha pulled back his feet from all the pedals. The car speeded on. The blowflies and the maggots had finished off the carcass and turned to him; moving into his jacket, inside his trouser, underneath the shirt, and the vest. Creeping into the private parts, into the nostrils. He kept his lips tight as he realized in the headlight he was getting lost. Lost in a jungle. The creatures kept pushing into his eardrums, deep into the anus. He closed his eyes. Crash. Bang. Crash.

CHAPTER 15

'I T WAS DARK, very dark. Then I realized that my eyes were closed. I opened my eyes to see a high ceiling above me with patches of cobweb. I realized I was lying down. A priest sat beside me and was chanting something that seemed to be in Sanskrit. He sprinkled some water on my face from some leaf that he held in his hand. And as he looked at my face, he shrieked and fell back. I raised my head to see some thirteen, fourteen people standing around. I was lying down on some wooden frame that hurt my back. I was wrapped tight in a white sheet. An elderly couple was crying while two tried to console them. I did not know anyone in the crowd. As the priest fell back from his low-height stool creating a cankering noise of the brass utensils lying around him, all hell broke loose. Everybody looked into my eyes for a fraction of a second and clamored towards the door. I looked to my left. There were two more bodies wrapped in white cloth, equidistant from me surrounded by some people. The reverberating canker and the shrill voices of the fleeing crowd caught their attention. Again there was uproar and the rest dashed towards the two doors.

I lay for a few seconds trying to grasp the circumstance and the situation. I realized I was in a crematorium. Slowly but doggedly, I tried to wriggle out of the tight white sheet like an escape artist. First I got the hands free, and then the rest was easy. I sat up and looked back. There was this big

351

cylindrical Lancashire boiler like cauldron with its circular lid open. Within danced the orange flames. I got up on my feet, wrapped the white sheet around my naked body and walked out of the gate to find my red car just in front. I got in and drove back home.'

'You did not recognize any one in the crowd?' Vivek asked.

'Not a single person.'

'Even Anjali was not there?'

'That is the strangest thing. If I was dead and was being cremated, Anjali surely would have been there.'

Vivek took a long drag from his cigarette and looked at me.He was confused and so was I.

'Where did you meet Anjali next?'

'At home, upon returning. She opened the door and asked me if everything went fine at the crematorium. And I replied, yes.'

'You did not tell her the crematorium story.'

'No, she would not have believed it.' Vivek took a sip from his whiskey glass as I did the bottoms up and left for home.

At the onset of the stairs to my home, the mobile rang. It was an unknown number, and I picked up the call.

'Hello.'

'Remember me?' A female voice questioned at the other end. 'You painted me on your canvas.'

I did paint a few nudes long back, but had never used live model. It was all from imagination.

'Who is this?' I queried.

'Anwesha, your favourite blue nude.'

I recalled the blue nude that I had painted ten years back. Yes, she was my favourite among the five nudes that I had ever painted. I could not recall the face, but I remembered she was dark blue and voluptuous. While brushing on the highlights on her curvaceous tight bosoms, I wanted to dive into the canvas, hold her tight and suck her cyan nipples. All I did was go to the washroom and masturbate.

'Are you there, Siddhartha?' She tried to confirm my presence.

'Yes, but ...'

'Come over to my apartment. I am lonely and need you to complete me as a woman.'

Strange things were happening of late. First, Siddhartha off and on walking into my studio from nowhere, and vanishing away in the thin air. Then the crematorium incident, and now Anwesha calling. The reality was becoming mysteriously confusing.

'Apartment number 2008,' and she disconnected.

I changed my course. Instead of taking the stairs I took the elevator to apartment number 2008.

As she opened the door I saw her standing in the nude. Absolutely the way I had painted her. The same bleary face, shining dark Prussian blue skin, a few shades lighter tight rounded bosoms exuding muliebrity, tiny cyan nipples, strokes of white accentuating her cleavage and the curvaceous buttocks, short black curly hair neatly painted above the azure blue vagina, which opened up to a fathomless aquamarine world of untamed pleasure.

'Welcome, Siddhartha, to your real world. The world of your art,' she said.

I stepped in, into a pool of fluid colours. She closed the door and led me into a hall with canvas walls; paints dripping down endlessly, into the pool we were standing in, knee-deep.

'I am Anwesha, the one you have been searching all your life,' she confronted me and said. Then taking a palmful of vermillion from the pool, rubbed it on my face. With her left hand she took another palmful of viridian and poured it on my head. The paints trickled down.

'Let us play. The game of life, in colours you paint and with colours I shall reveal,' Anwesha said.

A sense of rejuvenation electrified me. I splashed the pool colours on her and she did the same. We cavorted like two children, splashing and touching, painting each other. Gradually, the innocent touch transmuted to passionate caress and thereon lust inflamed. I pulled her close, skin to skin. She held my shoulders and hinted me to get down on my knees and I did. The aquamarine world awaited me and I dived deep into the abyss.

CHAPTER 16

S IDDHARTHA HAD JUST settled into his large chair at the office when his mobile rang. He looked at the number. It was not any of the saved numbers. He picked it up.

'Bastard, where are you?' somebody screamed at the other end.

It was not the voice, but the tone and the language triggered a spark in his subconscious.

'Jayant,' he exclaimed. 'Where are you calling from?'

It was Jayant Ghosh. His cadet guardian at the RIMC who had famously declared to shove the painting brushes up his ass. It was Jayant, the first one to buy his painting. He had paid in kind through two bottles of Red Knight whiskey bottle from the CSD canteen. It was Jayant, who, every time Siddhartha would get lost in this convulsive world, like a magician's hat trick would fish him out and get in touch. Siddhartha never made any effort to keep in touch with others. He never cared for a both-way communication to build relations. He was not an introvert, but happy to be as the present self. Hence, only those who kept in touch with him were the only ones he had, and which was always only a handful of people in the present. But this was Jayant. Here again, he was there on the other end after twenty-three years. Siddhartha was overwhelmed.

'How did you get my number?'

'That is a long story,' Jayant said. 'I am coming to Delhi next week. Tirtha and Roy are in Delhi. I will get in touch. Keep your evening free on the seventeenth, let us get together.'

'Sure,' Siddhartha confirmed. 'But where are you now?'

'Mumbai. Are you still painting? Become famous?'

'Painting, no; famous, no. See you on seventeenth for the rest. Bye.'

On the seventeenth, Jayant, Tirtha, Roy, and Siddhartha got together at the Air Force club at the Race Course Road. Tirtha and Roy had not changed much, only Roy had put on a bit of weight. Jayant was the shortest among them and with his potbelly and slouching shoulders, he seemed to have grown even shorter. He grabbed his belt at the waist and wriggled his trousers above his paunch as he welcomed the three. He was serving the Indian Air Force as a Group Captain. Roy was a Colonel in the Army and Tirtha who did not join the National Defence Academy was a General Manager with the Taj Group of hotels. The three had been in touch and even met once or twice in a year. Siddhartha was the odd man, lost.

After the initial brouhaha and ordering drinks, Jayant said, 'Bastard you have not changed your habit of getting lost.'

'We always talk about you whenever we meet.' Tirtha said.

'It's a wonderful feeling to be lost in this world.' Siddhartha said, 'So many people know you yet you cannot reach out to them, a feeling of solitude. Not just me but most people in this world are lonely. Lonely is not a fearful state to be in.'

'You and your painting, I never understood them and never tried to either.' Jayant said.

'But how did you get my number?' Siddhartha asked.

'Hah. Now you see, you cannot hide from me,' Jayant laughed. 'Actually all my efforts from all my contacts failed. Nobody had any clue about your whereabouts. Then one day I Googled your name and voila there was your website.'

'Oh, that old website I had put up at the behest of Rohit.'

'That had your number and here we are.' Jayant took a sip from his glass. 'By the way, I still have your painting on my drawing room wall.'

'I am honoured.' Siddhartha replied.

'But this time you have to present me one of your oil paintings. Some current work.'

'I have stopped painting ten years back. You can take the one for which I got the award in 2002.'

'Which award?'

'Camlin Art Foundation Award.'

January 2002. Lalit Kala Akademi hall. It was packed with people, the night of Camlin Art Foundation Award. The veteran artist Krishen Khanna was the chief guest and would be handing over the awards. Siddhartha sat in a corner with his wife.

A few days back, a call had come from the Foundation intimating him that his selected painting for the exhibition had won the award. He could not believe it. And there was reason for it. It had been just two years that he had started participating in the exhibitions in the professional circuit. Last year, the same award was given to Kailash, his neighbor, recipient of innumerable national and state level awards.

And he was just a self-taught artist with least exposure among those who had participated.

'Are you sure?' Siddhartha tried to reconfirm.

'Sir, the list is in front of me. You have been awarded and the official invitation has been sent by post.' The official at the other end continued, 'The function will be held at the Lalit Kala Akademi on the 16th January, Sunday, at six thirty in the evening.'

Siddhartha did not disclose the fact to anyone, even to his wife Anjali. He wanted to have the official invitation in hand before making it public. But days went by and only two days were left with no trace of the official invitation. He called up the foundation again.

'Sir, there must be a postal goof up. I am confirming that you have been awarded the Camlin Art Foundation Award. Letter or no letter, do come to the function. In my official capacity I am inviting you.'

So Siddhartha came to the function with Anjali and took a corner seat, apprehensive. The function started with inaugural speeches and niceties. The awards followed. First the award for drawing was declared and then the one for water colour.

'The award for oil on canvass goes to Siddhartha Sircar.'

Anjali gripped Siddhartha's hand. He got up and walked to the stage.

It was a piece of dream receiving an award from Krishen Khanna, one of the veterans whom he revered. The function concluded with a declaration that three selected artists from among all award winners will be sponsored for European Art Gallery Tour.

Having his paintings selected in nine consecutive exhibitions, Siddhartha felt confident, Joydeep felt he had given the right direction, and Kailash though apprehensive, started to take note of his work. Not in appreciation but to understand elements in Siddhartha's paintings that impressed other senior artists. Often, he would suggest applications without understanding the mental processing that went into Siddhartha's paintings. Both painted abstracts. Whereas Kailash's paintings were technically planned, Siddhartha's were spontaneous outbursts. Kailash was schooled in art. He had a Bachelor's degree and a long list of awards. Siddhartha did not learn art and hence he did not have to unlearn to create. There was an undercurrent of tension building up in their relationship, but that was beneath the surface of visible existence. Apparently, the three artists became greater friends.

Joydeep asked Siddhartha to accompany him to various art exhibitions and events that he would attend. This brought Siddhartha in contact with a large group of artists in Joydeep and Kailash's circle of contact. Most of the events would be in some art gallery or adjacent auditorium, if any existed. The events would follow the same pattern. Drinks would be served with snacks. After exchanging pleasantries, the conversations would continue appreciating each other's works. Though not unsocial, Siddhartha was not overtly social either. After a few introductions he would enjoy his drinks looking at the paintings on display. It was not a world of art or artists that he had envisaged. He could not put them on a higher pedestal than himself. All had different professions for living like himself, and art was a means to earn some extra buck, unlike himself. All of them were schooled in art but with very little knowledge of world art. Their world of art began and ended with what they and their friends were doing. Alternately, they would be the judges and participants, doling out awards to each other in turn. For Siddhartha it was a nepotistic club of opportunistic artists. It did not end here. There were rival groups and there was the politics of vote. Vote for controlling the Lalit Kala Akademi and thereby power politics to control the funds of this autonomous organization. Whichever group controlled the Akademi, the perks would flow down to their buddies and sympathizers. And perks were many: paid foreign trips with cash packet in tow; camps with financial benefits, and of course, references to collectors. It was a world no different than other walks of life. Siddhartha did not care. He enjoyed his drinks and continued painting. He thought art spoke for itself and believed his works were proof enough.

It was one such art function of inauguration of Gautam Dhir's art exhibition at the Gunjan Art Gallery. Siddhartha had received the Camlin Art Foundation award just two weeks back. The artists who already knew him, congratulated and some praised his work. He felt his works were on the right track and his belief in himself vis-a-vis art gained more ground. For the first time he felt his dogged pursuance of art shunning the normal trajectory of life was in right earnest. The party continued. He sipped his rum looking at the displays. He was walking past Kailash who was in a huddle with a group of artists in one corner of the gallery. He saw Raghubir Singh, one of the judges for the Camlin Art Foundation Awards in the group.

'I cannot believe this Raghubir.' Siddhartha overheard Kailash speaking in an annoyed tone. 'How can you give the award to such a new comer? He is a novice.' Kailash continued.

'His work was good,' Raghubir replied. 'And I was not the only one. Kashmira and Mohane were also there as judges.'

'Siddhartha is just an apprentice with me. I received the award last year and this year you people give it to him.' Kailash continued vehemently, 'You people put him at par with me. That is not fair. He could have received the award after seven, eight years. But just the next year after me is not done. I do not know Mohane well, but you and Kashmira could have asked me.'

'His bio-data did not have your reference. In fact it had no reference from any of our friends or acquaintances. He was fresh out of the blue and his work was different and that impressed us.' Raghubir tried to justify the decision; but Kailash did not see reason.

'Do not further complicate situation and select him for the overseas art gallery tour. He does not deserve it.'

Siddhartha moved on. He appeared before the selection committee for the European Art Galleries Tour a week later. They were the same three judges from the award jury. Siddhartha was confident he would make it; but soon, he realized otherwise as the interview progressed. It started on a cold note and ended with Kashmira's comment, 'You should be obliged that we gave you the award. You have to do a lot more to be distinguished to be selected for the tour.'

'Do what?' Siddhartha thought as he left. 'Be a sycophant for the 'we are the ones' coterie?

On reaching home, he grabbed the award memento and smashed it on the ground. Again and again. It was made of brass. It did not break but he battered it beyond recognition.

'Obliged? For what?' He looked up at his painting on the wall. The colours started melting and creeping into each other, defying gravity, defying reason, slowly metamorphosing the canvas into a muddy, flat, lifeless rectangular mass.

Anjali stood silently and watched Siddhartha disintegrate, As days rolled on, she witnessed a gradual and slow change in his behavior and colour palette. He earlier talked little, but now he talked incessantly and at times even incoherently. His bright vibrant colours gave way to somber crimsons, Prussian blue, and charcoal black. It happened sometime back as well, but Anjali did not take notice of as Siddhartha had a world of his own which was incomprehensible to her.

'Nothing alarming.' Anjali thought, till one day Siddhartha asked for coffee to be served with a lot of salt.

CHAPTER 17

I PICKED UP AN oil paint tube, unscrewed the cap, and squeezed out some crimson. It dropped on the canvas on the floor and settled like a dark red centipede. I looked at the wooden box filled with oil paint tubes and picked up the vermillion, and squeezed out some of it. It settled into a question mark. I fished out the Prussian blue tube and prepared half a cup of it, thinning it down a little with the linseed oil and varnish mixture, and poured it on the canvas. I took my rubber roller and spontaneously rolled it vigorously over the splattered paints on the canvas: forward and backward; left to right and at all angles, whimsically. The different hues merged into each other at different points at varied densities and created new hues of mixed tones. New forms evolved from the centipede, the question mark, and the splattered Prussian blue—forms with spontaneous vignettes and solid patches. I picked up the three by four canvas and rested it by the wall and sat back looking at it.

Siddhartha walked in. For the past few months, Siddhartha has been often walking into my life out of the blue. He walked in, stood with folded arms, a little twist on his lips, and a sarcastic look in his eyes. He always walked in, observed me, and faded into thin air as silently as he came in. He never spoke. But today, he spoke.

'What are you doing?' he asked.

'Painting, of course.' I replied.

'I can see you are painting, but why?'

'Because I am an artist. I want to create. And I have taken up this visual medium of painting to create.'

'To create?' he questioned and continued, 'If you want to create, you will agree that you have to have knowledge of creation.'

'Of course,' I said. 'Why only creation, anything you want to do, you can only if you have its knowledge.'

'Then let me ask you, what is creation?'

It was such a simple question. 'Creation is developing anything new.'

'Developing something new. So creation is a process of development.'

'True.'

'Can you develop something from nothing?'

'How can you develop something from a void?' I questioned.

'So you need something to develop something. You agree.'

'Of course.'

'So in case of your painting, you need something to develop it. And what are they?'

'Paint, oil, canvas, brush, etc.'

'You missed out the major some things. Your emotional and practical experiences from the past. Reality that touched you and illusions that moved you.'

'Yes, yes.' I could not agree more.

'So what you say you create, the painting, is only a collage of bits and pieces of elements that were already present in the past. There is nothing new in it. It is not a creation as you will like to believe it to be.' he continued. 'Thus, you cannot create. Face the truth, no humans can create.'

'Then what is creation?' I had a question.

'Creation is us, and the world we exist in, that we know and that we do not know.'

'So you conclude that art is not creativity.'

'How can something be creative when you do not create it? Assemblage can be art but surely not a process of creation.'

I did not mind in the past, Siddhartha being mum and observing me. But speaking out today, he was confusing me. He was loosening the very foundation on which I ventured out to be an artist. I could not push him out of the studio. So I tried to ignore him and concentrated on my painting. I wanted to brush aside his dialectics. I wanted to reassure myself as an artist.

I splattered liquid yellow ochre, chrome green, and viridian on the canvas. Raised it above my head, gave it good vigorous shake and rested it against the wall. The colours dripped down the canvas. I turned it on another side and the drippings changed course, the negative spaces taking amoebic forms, slowly reaching out for me. Enveloping, they tried to pull me into the canvas. I resisted but failed and slowly got drawn into the abyss of colours. Siddhartha's loud laughter gradually dimmed away.

It was a dark world—narrow, lonely alleys criss-crossing each other; danger lurking at every corner. I kept running from one to the other. Then again to another, and another, trying to run away from the unknown fear. There was something, someone, chasing me. I ran and ran till there was this staircase in front of me. I ran up the stairs, two at a time. There was this door. I banged on it and Meshomoshai opened the door.

'Come in Siddhartha, you have run out of your breath.'

I rushed in, 'Please close the door. They are after me.'

'Who are after you?' Meshomoshai asked on closing the door.

'I think Siddhartha is with them. They want to kill me.'

'Have you gone mad?'

'I am telling you it must be Siddhartha.'

'Which Siddhartha?'

'Previously he used to come and just watch me. Nowadays he talks a lot.'

'OK. Relax on the sofa. Would you like to have a cup of tea?'

I sat down and tried to catch my breath. 'No. I would prefer a jug of salted coffee.' I said.

'Salted coffee?' Meshomoshai seemed to be confused. Mashima walked into the drawing room.

'What happened?' she questioned.

'Siddhartha is trying to kill me.' I said.

'Urmila, you prepare a cup of coffee for him.' Meshomoshai told Mashima.

'With lot of salt.' I added.

'Coffee with salt?' Now Mashima got a shock.

'Yes prepare his coffee with salt.' Meshomoshai confirmed. 'Let me hear and understand what happened.'

'It has been quite some time now that Siddhartha has been coming into my life time and again.'

'Who is this Siddhartha?' Meshomoshai asked, 'We only know about you. Who is this other Siddhartha?'

'He comes in from nowhere and vanishes away similarly. Previously he used to quietly stand and observe me, but nowadays he has started talking.'

'What does he talk about?'

'He talks about me, my paintings, my beliefs. He questions everything I do. In fact he has started threatening my existence.' I paused to take a long breath, 'I think he wants to kill me.'

'I think you are unnecessarily getting flustered.' He sat down on a chair in front of me. 'Who is this Siddhartha that I do not know about in the neighbourhood?'

'Well, he is Siddhartha.'

'And how does he look like?'

'Just like me.' I replied.

'He looks like you?' Meshomoshai started laughing aloud, 'And he comes in from nowhere and vanishes into thin air?' He continued laughing. 'You have a great sense of humour. Now do you really want that salted coffee or should Urmila prepare you a good coffee with sugar and milk?'

I did not understand why nobody other than me liked salted coffee, particularly with an overdose of salt. Nobody seemed to have tasted it ever. Even Anjali was shocked in the beginning but nowadays she serves me salted coffee without questioning.

'I will take salted coffee.' I replied, 'You try it, you too will like it.'

'No, thanks. You try your experiments,' Meshomoshai said, 'I am fine with my milk and sugar coffee.'

I looked out from the door to the balcony. There was bright sunlight outside, seemed to be afternoon. 'Where did all the darkness disappear that I came in from?' I thought. I got up from the sofa and walked into their balcony.

Yes it was a bright sunny afternoon. Clothes gently swayed on the clothesline of the opposite apartment balcony across the road. I looked down on the road. There was a child playing with his rubber ball. I looked right, into the parking lot towards the end of the road. Yes my red car was parked there. I closed my eyes. Yes, here I am and this is reality. There I was, and that too, was reality. Both realities contradicted each other. There could not be two realities in the same span of time. So which was the real one?

'Siddhartha, your coffee is here.' Mashima called out.

I went in and sat down to have the coffee.

'Would you like to hear a new album?' Meshomoshai asked.

'Not now.' I was still trying to untie the entangled time and space.

'You must listen to this.' Meshomoshai was always adamant about music. 'Now that the copyright of Vishwa Bharati has ended on Tagore's works, many artists are experimenting with Rabindra Sangeet. This one is by Usha Uthhup. Tagore's songs sung in English with Celtic music accompaniment.'

He placed the CD in their home theatre system. The deep baritone voice of Usha Uthhup filled the room.

'This weariness, forgive me O My Lord . . .'

* * *

The entrance did not justify the enormous house, which was hidden by huge Neem trees. Behind the Iron

Gate, a small wooden door led to a flight of about ten stairs opening out into a gigantic drawing room. I had seen rooms with double height ceilings in residential apartments. But this had a three-floor high ceiling and a huge expanse. All the walls were adorned with huge, framed, paintings of a typical style. There were press-printing blocks with text in 'Devnagri' script, nuts, bolts, and other metallic objects stuck to the canvases in specific compositions, and painted over with oil paint. It was a revelation for me. I had never encountered paintings of the like before,—they were intriguing, mesmerizing. I realized this was the individual style of Shanti Varge, the renowned artist of the fag end of the 'Bombay Progessives' movement; the movement which highlighted the veterans like Souza, Hussain, and many others. Shanti Varge, a short robust Gujrati sat on a sofa at the far-end corner of the hall. The hall was well decorated in ethnic Gujrati style. There were a variety of artifacts from his home state all over. There was even a wooden 'Jhoola' at one corner. Every piece seemed to be part of a larger scheme, just like the metal pieces on his paintings.

Joydeep had briefed me about Varge beforehand. He had very few friends in the art world, quiet uncommon for somebody of his stature. It was not because of his outspokenness, but 'in your face' attitude. He had minted money and cared little about being lonely. A gallery owner once approached him to organize an exhibition of his paintings. He tabled his condition, 'If I am going to exhibit at this stage of life, you have to inaugurate the show with a sold out tag. Are you ready?'

On weighing the pros and cons, the gallery owner agreed. 'I will open the sold out show for fifty lakhs.' Which meant that Varge would receive fifty lakh rupees for the exhibition and it would be the gallery owner's liability to sell the paintings or acquire them himself.

'Fifty lakhs?' Varge exclaimed. 'Do not come to me with any offer less than two crore.'

And the deal fell through. It was a year later, the gallery owner re-approached Varge with Varge's demanded figure, two crores.

'That was a year back.' Varge retorted, 'I demand ten crores now. Do you have the guts to do it?' He did not need the money; he was filthy rich. He liked to play the game of cat and mouse. It was his pastime.

I felt like a tiny little creature as I walked with Joydeep and Kailash to pay our respect to this larger than life artist.

'Well Kailash, it has been a long time.' Varge spoke as we touched his feet.

'No, no,' Kailash felt embarrassed. 'No, once you called, I had to come.'

'Take your seat.' Varge directed us to the sofa next to him. 'What would you like to have?' And before any of us could react, he continued, 'My maid prepares 'Aam Panna' worth dying for.'

Aam Panna was a concoction of the pulp from roasted green mangoes, mint leaves and spices, taken chilled. It was a common antidote for the dry summer winds of Delhi. Driving sixteen kilometers in my non-airconditioned Marurti to Varge's house in the peak summer heat, I could not have asked for anything better. He called for his servant and asked to serve 'Aam Panna'. Joydeep, as a senior artist, was already known to Shanti Varge. In fact he was one of his favourite artists of that age group.

'Tell me Sir, why you call me.' Kailash asked after introducing me as his student. I was an artist in my own right, but I was always introduced by Kailash as his student, even though it was Joydeep who introduced me to this professional world of art. I was already used to everybody in this field marking out his pound of flesh and had started taking it into my stride.

'You know I have nobody here.' Varge said.

He had married off his son who had settled in the US, and his wife had passed away a few years earlier. He lived a sedentary life as old age would allow, all by himself but for a man Friday, in this enormous bungalow. He still enjoyed a peg of scotch whiskey every evening, but life was at poles apart from his vibrant public life of yore.

'I have an apartment in Vivek Vihar,' he continued. 'The builder had not used seasoned wood for the door and window frames. I visited it sometime back and found that termites had completely damaged the frames. I think the place is close to where you live.'

'Yes, it is not far away.' Kailash said.

'I want you to organize carpenters and get those renovated. By the way have you received the National Award from UP State Lalit Kala Akademi?'

'I have received the Akademi Award but not their National Award.' Kailash seemed to have got a hint. 'I have sent two paintings this time keeping that in mind.'

'I have been asked to chair the Jury Committee for this year. I will be going to Lucknow in August. You do not have to worry about the expenditure for the renovation. Obviously I will bear it.'

Two different conversations continued in one dialogue. Not related yet the relation slowly became obvious to me.

'Do not worry Sir. I will organize and have the renovation done.'

'So, congratulations on winning the National Award from UP State Lalit Kala Akademi.' 'The pound of flesh', I thought, and another award was added to Kailash's long list.

The drive back was a long one; not measured in kilometers or hours. Time rolled on as my white, non-airconditioned Maruti 800 hatchback metamorphosed into Teflon-coated red Skoda sedan. Everybody that I knew in the art world was running: running into an illusion, running into infinite time, as art fell by the wayside, disowned, abandoned, begging for resurrection.

Osmanbhai changed his residence thrice. He now lives in a duplex bungalow in Greater Noida. He has neatly wrapped away the beginning of his artistic career from a 'barsati' in Seemapuri in distant past. He has wiped out all the struggles out of his memory, but he could not wash away Robin Mondal, his mentor. Every time he had sex with his wife Reena, he felt the pain of penetration in his anus. Robin Mondal, the famous artist, fucking him as he squirmed in pain till the oozing sperms made it a little easier. He would bite into his lips till Robin Mondal thrusted hard, abused him loud, asked him to groan, and he would gurgle out groans. He was the dormant partner of homosexual Robin Mondal. There was nothing wrong in being a homosexual, but Osmanbhai was not one. He acted to be one, and he acted his way to success. Robin Mondal died in a car accident and a year later, Osmanbhai married Asma.

Usgaonkar taught painting to middle-aged divorcee Ms. Surjeet Randhawa in her sprawling Greater Kailash bungalow. It was a weekend engagement, and at times would stay the night over. He painted more with sweat, saliva, and sperm on her body than she would on canvas. He thus earned himself a pretty good superannuation financial security. He had never arrived in the big league of art, hence without Ms. Surjeet, he would have had a pretty poor retirement. But he survived and was proud to flash his Lalit Kala Akademi identity card to prove that he was an artist.

Ranadeep Dada became the Head of Departmentof College of Art. He was happy to vanish into the oblivion with a neat packet of pension and a lump sum provident fund. He no longer cared about the 'isms' and cared even less about awards. He never got one anyway, but was part of most exhibitions due to his networking capability. The exhibitions were like a day out for him from his college routine and family chores—an opportunity to be with the self-proclaimed artists, and feel to be an artist himself. Madhavan, Biplab, Bangash, all ran in this never-ending race. And for Kailash, he stopped getting awards as there were no more that he had not received. Joydeep got trapped in his style and experimented nothing new. I drove down the timeline as the world of art unfurled its true colours and my canvas started losing its lustre. As I reversed my car into the parking lot, the twilight set in. The world, my world, started transforming into a monochromatic maze.

As Anjali opened the door, I realized it was my sixty-second birthday. Anjali had organized a party for all my friends and acquaintances. They were all waiting for me, wearing masks. I do not know why. I did not recognize them. I had left them far behind in time.

'Happy Birthday, Sid' a chorus broke out. The two-bedroom apartment was packed up with no space to move. I jostled my way in. But it did not bother the guests as they wined and dined. I felt suffocated. I longed for the party to end and it did.

I sat at my table in my studio looking at the unfinished canvas on the wall. Whatever Siddhartha may say, I know my paintings were my creation. I wanted to take solace in them. But laughter rang out of the layers of paint. Slowly stark white teeth glistened out of the layers of black, grey and white paint.

'You are at my whim and fancy,' I cried out to the canvas, 'Look at you, you are not even complete.'

'Are you?' It retorted. I thought for a moment. 'What is completeness?' 'Am I complete?' 'Are human beings ever complete?' I was losing faith in my existence.

'You cannot do this to me,' I said it loud.

'Look at what you have done to me. Look at what you have done to art. It is all bogus and you believe you are an artist?' The canvas laughed on. I took out the kitchen knife from the buffet table drawer, and walked up to the canvas, raised the knife, and slashed through. Slashed again and again. The laughter vanished behind the screech of the knife against the wall, cutting through the canvas. Yes, the moment was under my control. I slashed on it again—again, and again, and again, till the canvas strips dangled dead from the wooden frame. The slashed canvas laughed no more. And I smiled.

The win calmed me and I sat with my wristwatch on the table in front of me. Anjali had long gone to sleep. The second's hand kept rotating and time kept ticking away. In my head. *Tick, tick, tick, tick.* It was monotonous and getting on my nerves, unbearable. I had to do something. I had to stop it.

I got up and fetched the small tweezer from the dressing table, took the watch in my left palm, and clamped the tweezer ends in the back cover slots, pressed hard, and turned counter-clockwise. The glass cover, case, and the back cover came apart. I took out the movement and held it between my left forefinger and thumb. There was a screw. I hooked one of the sharp ends of the tweezer into the screw slot, unscrewed it, and the crown came off. More screws and I kept unscrewing them all to disintegrate the movement completely. In no time the wheels, the bridges, the springs, and every small bit lay in front of me. Piece by piece I laid them away from each other. But Time ticked on. *Tick, tick, tick, tick.* The second's hand kept rotating; so did every other part independently. *Tick, tick, tick, tick.* I could not stop it. I picked up a large stainless steel bowl that was on the table and banged it on the watch parts. I banged on them again and again. Many broke into minute pieces but kept ticking. *Tick, tick, tick, tick.* Time moved on; I sat back as the pieces kept ridiculing me.

I could take no more. I walked into the bedroom, opened the cupboard, and pulled out the drawer. I gripped the revolver that I had stolen from Rohit. He had got it from the Army when he took the premature retirement. I felt the hard metal on the skin of my palm. It was a Taurus 85 .38 caliber five-shot revolver. I clicked open the magazine, took out the five live cartridges from the steel box they were kept, loaded the magazine, and then clicked it back. I looked at Anjali. She was deep asleep as I walked out of the bedroom.

Sitting on the chair for the last time, I looked at Time, still laughing at me. I closed my eyes and pressed the barrel on my temple. I could see them all looking at me: Esha, Anjali, Aitreyi, Jayant, Roy, Tirtha, Mankar, Pandey. Everybody I ever knew, even Lipika and Anwesha. Their eyes expressed sympathy, pity. I could take no more. I pulled the trigger lightly. Nobody believed me anymore. My world seemed only to be mine.

And I pulled the trigger harder.

A NEW BEGINNING

'THE BURST OF the revolver tore through the silent darkness of the night. Surprised, few crows cawed out harshly. The head lay in a pool of blood amidst a dismantled wristwatch. Darkness, silence, still'.

Siddhartha tapped the last words on the keypad, closed the 'Words' file and stretched back. It was a long night of typing the novel. Anjali was still sleeping. He got up and walked out to the balcony with the laptop. The first rays of a new dawn slowly peeped above the apartment roofs. He opened his Facebook account to check posts he had missed in the last few days of penning the novel. On the 'Friend Requests' icon, there was a request. A friend request from a distance of forty-one years. 'Lipika', and he confirmed. A new day was on its way.

GLOSSARY

'aaiye'	'come in'
adda	get together for chat and gossip
ashram	abode of saint and disciples
bapi	father
bhatura	pin-rolled, fried Indian bread
bondhu	friend
chapati	pin-rolled, roasted Indian bread
chhole	chickpeas
CISF	Central Industrial Security Force
CPI (ML)	Communist Party of India (Marxist Leninist)
CPM	Communist Party of India Marxist
dadu	grand father
dal	lentil
DDA	Delhi Development Authority
DGCA	Directorate General of Civil Aviation
didi	elder sister
ECL	Easter Coalfields Limited
GDA	Ghaziabad Development Authority
Gulmohur	Flamboyant (flower)
gupshup	chat
Gurudwara	Holy shrine of Sikhs
IMFL	Indian Made Foreign Liquor

jawan	soldier
jethu	uncle, elder to father
jhoola	swing (n)
kaku	uncle, younger to father
khalasi	crew/labour
kurta	long length Indian top wear
Lakh	One hundred thousand
LPs	Long Playing Records
LSD	Lysergic Acid Diethylamide (chemical intoxicant)
mashi	aunt
Mamoni/Ma	mother
MLA	Member of Legislative Assembly
muffasal	suburb
Naxal	extreme Leftist doctrine
paan	betel leaf
Paisa	Indian currency
pajama	loose Indian bottom wear
pallu	portion of sari used to place over shoulder
pandal	temporary fabricated structure for ceremonies
parantha	pin-rolled, fried Indian bread
'phut'	broke (slang)
piri	short height wooden stool
ponzy	dubious
puja	prayer
punjabi	long length Indian top wear
Rabindra Sangeet	songs of Tagore
RCC	Reinforced Cement Concrete
RCTC	Royal Calcutta Turf Club

RIMC	Rashtriya Indian Military College
rezala	a curry preparation of mutton/chicken
Sal	an Indian tree
sala	brother-in-law (used as abuse)
Shaptami	7th day of the fortnight of Durga Puja
SHO	Station House Officer (Police designation)
tabla	Indian drum
Tandoori chicken	chicken roasted Indian style in clay oven
UP State Lalit Kala Akademi	Uttar Pradesh State Lalit Kala Akademi
thali	plate
tilak/tika	a distinctive spot applied on forehead by Hindus
yaar	pal